FOR ALL ETERNITY

At a noise from outside, she spun around in time to see a tall dark figure step into the doorway.

"Go away!" she cried, her heart fluttering excitedly in her chest.

A rush of cool night air filled with the smell of the sea engulfed her and tugged heavily on her cape. Then a pair of strong arms encircled her.

She struggled, raising her fists to strike with all her strength, only to have her body crushed against a much larger, more powerful one while her mouth was captured in a burning, demanding kiss.

She surrendered to the feel of his lips on hers, kissing him back wildly.

He was here. He was real and he wanted her . . . whether for this moment or for all eternity, she didn't care.

ZEBRA ROMANCES FOR ALL SEASONS
From Bobbi Smith

ARIZONA TEMPTRESS   (1785, $3.95)

Rick Peralta found the freedom he craved only in his disguise as El Cazador. Then he saw the exquisitely alluring Jennie among his compadres and the hotblooded male swore she'd belong just to him.

CAPTIVE PRIDE   (2160, $3.95)

Committed to the Colonial cause, the gorgeous and independent Cecelia Demorest swore she'd divert Captain Noah Kincade's weapons to help out the American rebels. But the moment that the womanizing British privateer first touched her, her scheming thoughts gave way to burning need.

DESERT HEART   (2010, $3.95)

Rancher Rand McAllister was furious when he became the guardian of a scrawny girl from Arizona's mining country. But when he finds that the pig-tailed brat is really a voluptuous beauty, his resentment turns to intense interest; Laura Lee knew it would be the biggest mistake in her life to succumb to the cowboy—but she can't fight against giving him her wild DESERT HEART.

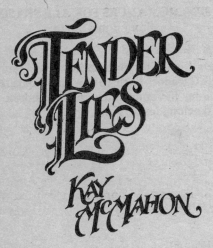

TENDER LIES

Kay McMahon

ZEBRA BOOKS
KENSINGTON PUBLISHING CORP.

ZEBRA BOOKS

are published by

Kensington Publishing Corp.
475 Park Avenue South
New York, NY 10016

First printing: May, 1990

Printed in the United States of America

Chapter One

Near Bray, Ireland
Fall of 1798

Night descended on the rocky countryside. The fiery sunset cast spider web shadows across the fields and roads, and splashed color against the faces of small, thatched-roofed cottages and huts nestled behind the endless stretch of stone walls. The sweet smell of newly-mowed hay and acrid smoke from the chimneys filled the cool, crisp air, and in the distance the diaphanous crashing of surf against shore made the ground tremble and sprayed a fine mist upward toward the heavens. Peace once again had spread across the land, but the bitter scars of defeat and rage still ran deep and festered with the promise that if those who had been imprisoned for speaking their mind were not released, a new battle would emerge.

Along the well-worn dirt road clattered a two-wheeled, donkey-drawn cart winding its way north-ward toward the town, whose faint lights sparkled against the ever-growing blackness in the vale. A dark-haired young man with brooding eyes and a hard set to his jaw held the reins. Beside him sat his brother, his auburn hair catching the last rays of light and glistening red-gold in the dying sun, his brow furrowed, his green eyes dark and intense. Neither of them spoke. There was no need.

Behind the pair and seated on a thick bed of straw in the cart rode a third brother, the look on his face equally expressive of the worry and rage the others felt. Yet his concern fell more on the young woman he watched sitting opposite him, rather than on the man whose fate was in their hands. News of their father's forthcoming execution had reached them three days ago, and even though it had been expected by the O'Rourke brothers, Bevan, their younger sister, had taken it quite hard.

"Why should he be hanged for speakin' the truth?" she had cried through a mixture of tears and anger. "And why not me as well? I've said the very same as me father and just as often. Am *I* not a threat ta their way of thinkin'?"

"'Twas not his words that got him in trouble, Bevan," Kelly, the oldest of the siblings, had explained. "'Twas the pitchfork he carried and the soldier he stabbed with it."

"But *you* carried a weapon!" she had shouted in defense. "And so did Shea and Ryan! Had father allowed me ta go, I would have had an ax or rake in me fist, too, and I would have swung it just as hard. If Father is guilty, then so are we. There isn't a one of us who thinks differently."

Shea, her twin, had tried to soothe her, but she had

6

slapped away his hands.

"Ah, don't go treatin' me like I'm a wee lass, Shea O'Rourke," she had raged. "We're the same age, ya know. Your bein' two minutes earlier than me comin' inta this world makes no difference, and I'll not let ya think it does." She whirled on the others. "I'm older than all of ya! In me head, I am. I can read and write and cipher better than any of ya!"

Ryan, second oldest and the only one who could ever talk sense into their sister, stepped forward. "Then act like it now, Bevan," he had scolded. "Your tantrum won't help our father."

"And who will?" She had spat the question and none of those in the room with her could ever remember seeing their sister as angry as she was at that moment.

"The Society of United Irishmen, that's who," Ryan had claimed.

"Ha!" she had exploded. "The Society is the reason our father has been sentenced ta hang, Ryan O'Rourke, and ya know damn well it is."

His own brows had lowered in an angry frown. "I also know I'll wash your mouth out with a strong bar of lye soap, if I hear ya swear one more time, Bevan Kathleen. Ya shame our dead mother talkin' like a trollop."

As he sat watching the solemn expression on his sister's beautiful face while she stared, unseeing, out across the rolling grassland toward the sea, he remembered how his reprimand had quieted her. Ryan always knew how to take some of the fight out Bevan Kathleen, and though some would say it wasn't fair of him to mention Kerry O'Rourke to make Bevan behave, Ryan was sure their mother wouldn't mind.

7

Kerry—all of them had loved the soft-spoken, gentle woman, Bevan more than the boys, and her death one year ago had had a dramatic influence on the youngest of her children. Bevan had gone from a quiet, well-mannered, obedient young lass to a spirited, hot-tempered, opinionated beauty in what seemed to Ryan to be overnight. Their father had tried to convince Ryan that it was merely a matter of Bevan's having grown up. Ryan thought otherwise. Without her mother's firm hand to guide her, Bevan had looked to her brothers for guidance. She had modeled herself after them simply because she hated being the youngest and she hated being excluded from manly things just because she was a woman. That was the reason why she had insisted on coming with them now. She had to be a part of any decision made concerning her father, and she had made it blatantly clear she would not be left behind.

"Are ya cold, Bevan?" Ryan asked when he thought he saw her shiver.

Emerald green eyes, outlined with thick lashes the color of an inky midnight sky, lifted to look at him, and for a moment he couldn't breathe. Bevan had their mother's subtle beauty, the kind of handsomeness that deepened the longer one studied her oval face, the slightly upturned nose, red lips, and luscious mane of chestnut hair with its reddish-gold tint, and he wondered for the very first time why there hadn't been hundreds of love-struck fools fighting for her attention. He wondered, and yet he knew the answer.

"No," she softly replied, then turned her face away.

Ryan doubted his sister had given any more thought to marriage than he or his brothers had. The strife that tore Ireland apart simply overshadowed everything else, and until there was a lasting peace where both sides could live happily and in harmony, Catholics and Protestants alike, marriage and all that went with it was a luxury no one could afford.

"I'd like ta tell ya not ta worry, Bevan," he said quietly. "I'd like ta tell ya everythin' will be all right, that Father will be home soon. But ya know I've never been one ta lie ta ya. I do know Kelly, Shea, and I will not stand quietly by and let Father be hanged. If it means violence, then—"

"Then what?" she cut in, her voice tight and her eyes moist with unshed tears. "Then I can bury me whole family?" Her lovely face hardened as she once again studied the scenery they passed by. "Father would be proud of ya for tryin', but he wouldn't approve, and ya know it. He'd never rest in peace knowin' his sons gave up their lives for him in a way that was hopeless from the start." She hugged her shawl around her shoulders and glanced up at the blackening sky overhead with its glittering specks of white light. "I was wrong ta accuse the Society, Ryan. I knew it when I said it. I was just angry and scared, is all. They're the ones ta help Father. They're provin' it already."

"Aye," her twin agreed, twisting in the seat of the cart where he and Kelly sat listening to the conversation. "'Tis just a shame we have ta rely on an Englishman ta get it done."

"We'll take whoever's help we can," Kelly said. "We don't have much of a choice."

"Aye, that's true," Shea reluctantly agreed. "But I hope ya don't mind me sayin' I don't like bein' in debt ta one."

"None of us do," Ryan claimed. "That's why we'll settle on a price *before* we give our consent."

The group fell quiet again while each of them considered how no price would be too steep. They would sell their souls to free their father.

The city of Bray lay on the eastern coast of Ireland about fifteen miles south of Dublin, and while most who lived there were Catholic, it was the Protestant families who owned the more prosperous businesses in town, held the seats in Parliament, and had control over their fellow Irishmen, backed by the wealthy English and King George. The war over religious equality had been going on for centuries and the only hope any of the Catholic Irish had was in the hands of one man, Prime Minister William Pitt the Younger of England. Yet the O'Rourkes, faced with the need for an immediate solution, knew they could not wait for a high authority to intervene. Something had to be done within the next two weeks or their father would die.

Through a network of friends belonging to the Society of United Irishmen, they had been put in touch with an English lord, who, for the right amount, would use his influence in changing the sentences handed down on the rebels involved in the uprising of a few weeks earlier. Since Patrick O'Rourke had not taken a life with his protest, he would be shown leniency and given a punishment fit the crime, a jail term perhaps but not execution. The length of his sentence all depended on what his children were willing and able to pay. The higher the amount, the shorter the sentence. The four, who rode in the cart as it entered the quiet, little town on the south road, knew the conditions before they were to meet Lord Douglas Rynearson. They

10

also knew they had very little with which to deal. The O'Rourkes were poor farmers with a few acres of land, fewer cattle and sheep and grain, and hardly any gold coins to give. They were on a mission to save their father from being executed, but their hidden fear was that they couldn't spare him any more than that. He would live, but he would spend the rest of his days locked up behind the cold, stone walls of a prison without a single window in his cell to let in the warm, bright cheerful rays of the sun.

Kyle Magee, a close friend of Patrick's, had arranged for Lord Rynearson to meet with the younger O'Rourkes in Magee's home, where the conference could be kept secret. The lord was putting his reputation at stake, and if word of their bargain ever slipped out, not only would he be held accountable, the O'Rourkes would be imprisoned as well. Reining the cart around in back of the cottage, Kelly guided the donkey inside the small stable before allowing any of his family to jump down.

"I want your word," Ryan announced, facing the two youngest of his siblings as they prepared to go into the house, "that ya'll let Kelly and me do all the talkin'."

Shea's green eyes, so very much like his twin's, flashed his indignation. "I can understand ya tellin' Bevan ta be quiet, Ryan. She's only a woman. But I've got as much say in this as the two of ya, and I resent the implication that I'm not smart enough ta make a deal." He started at the sharp contact he felt when the back of Bevan's fist hit his arm.

"Ya take offense at bein' called stupid, but think nothin' of it ta call me the same. A fine brother, ya are. Well, I agree with Ryan. We'd all be better off if ya

11

didn't say a word."

Insulted, Shea inhaled a sharp, angry breath, ready to add his thoughts on who was lacking wit, and caught sight of Ryan's warning glare. Frustrated that he couldn't at least put his twin in her place, he snapped his mouth shut and turned to tie off the donkey's reins.

"Your word, Shea," Ryan called after him.

A moment of tense silence passed before that one muttered over his shoulder, "Ya have it. But only for me father's sake and nothin' more."

Satisfied, Ryan turned on Bevan. Before he could ask for her pledge, she replied with her usual sarcasm.

"Ya'll have no trouble with me, dear brother. I know me place as the three of ya are so fond of tellin' me." She squinted her emerald eyes at him. "Would ya tell your mother ta be quiet, Ryan, if she were here? Or does the right of motherhood allow a woman ta speak her mind."

Kelly had an answer for that one. "'Twould have been a decision Ryan wouldn't have had ta make, Bevan. Mother would have stayed home and left this task ta us." His tall frame towered over her as he bent slightly and mimicked the face she made at him. "In that respect Mother would have been smarter than all of us." He roughly took her arm and squeezed when she tried to yank free. "And I suggest ya not give us anymore of your sass, Bevan O'Rourke, else ya find yourself waitin' here in the barn for us." He raised his dark brows at her and added, "Have I made meself perfectly clear?"

Seeing the smile Ryan tried to hide behind his hand as he rubbed the tip of his nose, then Shea's impudent look. Bevan quickly realized how close she was to

12

tending the mule. "Aye. Ya have," she replied with a respectful bob of her head, though each of the brothers suspected that if given the choice, she would rather repeat the honest thoughts going through her mind.

"Good," Kelly said, and nodded. "Then stay close ta me where I can remind ya of your pledge." He heard her sharp intake of breath, positive of the stinging reply she contemplated saying, and wisely chose not to allow her the opportunity as he firmly pushed her ahead of him toward the exit. The others followed, and the cold fingers of apprehension quickly closed around them all as they headed across the narrow stretch of yard for the back door of the cottage.

"Kelly, Miss Bevan," Kyle Magee greeted once he had opened the way for them and directed everyone in through the kitchen. "He's in the parlor." He nodded silently at the remaining brothers, then shut the door and hurried to lead the way.

Magee, like the O'Rourkes and most of their friends, was a farmer of small means. The tithing tax imposed on them for the support of the established church of Ireland left little with which to buy any extras, and the interior of the house showed the effects. Although the place was clean, there was a sparse assortment of furniture, threadbare rugs on the floors, and empty walls and cupboards. Magee, a widower whose children were grown and gone, existed from day to day and always allowed his pride to stand in the way whenever one of the O'Rourkes brought food. It was their kindness and generosity that had driven him to help find a way of freeing the eldest O'Rourke from prison. If no agreement could be reached this night, Magee and the Society would look for another method. They simply wouldn't let their friend hang.

The lean figure standing before the fireplace with his hands extended toward the heat of the flames straightened and turned to greet the new arrivals when Magee announced their presence. Dressed in fine silks and velvets, shiny black shoes with gold buckles, and a white ruffled shirt, Douglas Rynearson made it clear that he, unlike everyone else in the room, enjoyed the finer things only money could buy. He was the enemy, but for this night the O'Rourkes had to lay aside their hatred. They needed him, his wealth, his power.

"Lord Rynearson," Magee said quietly, "may I introduce ya ta the O'Rourkes? This is Kelly, the oldest. Then Ryan, Shea, and their sister, Bevan."

Rynearson's cold, brown eyes only briefly touched upon the brothers before they settled on the most beautiful young woman he had ever seen in his forty-seven years. Long, chestnut hair caught the firelight and gleamed a red-gold hue. Green eyes, the color of precious gems, stared back at him and stole his breath. She didn't have to speak for him to know that she had the dulcet voice of a songbird. Ivory cotton and plain brown wool covered her delicate form, and he could only guess what was hidden beneath, but he was sure that, too, was perfection. Nor could he make any comparison between this beauty and the sickly woman he called his wife. Bevan O'Rourke, a poor Irish girl looking to him for help, would be his next mistress and probably his best. She was young and healthy and would probably last longer than any of the others. He would enjoy her, the things he would do to her, her cries for mercy, the pain. He would promise her everything and give her nothing, while he used her time

14

and again to sate his lust. All he had to do was strike a bargain with her brothers and she would be his. He also realized from the protective way Kelly guided her to a chair, then stood behind her as if silently daring anyone to make a pass at her without his permission, that accomplishing his feat would take skill and cunning. Forcing himself to look away, he settled himself down in the rickety straight back chair Magee had brought in from the kitchen for him, while he made a mental note to thank his friend for telling him about her.

"Please excuse the bluntness of my query," he began, careful not to look at the lovely face he felt watching him, "but what has Patrick O'Rourke's family got to trade for the man's life?"

Ryan spoke up. "What will it take?"

Rynearson's gaze shifted to the middle brother and he quickly realized that of the three boys, this one was the one with whom he would have to deal, the one he'd have to persuade. There was an alertness in the man's green eyes, a spark of intelligence he hadn't expected to find in this band of Irish trash. He smiled in spite of himself. "Perhaps I should explain the risk I'm taking in just agreeing to meet with you, before I name a price." He noticed a glimmer of unbridled hatred darken Ryan's eyes and that the same emotion shone clearly on the face of the young man standing next to him, and Rynearson steeled his own feelings. Had the O'Rourkes not had a beautiful sister, he wouldn't have dawdled away a second of his time with them. He despised the Irish and thought King George had better things to do with his army than trying to prevent these fools from killing each other off. They were a waste of time and energy and money. The real threat was

15

France . . . and those damn Colonists.

"No offense, Lord Rynearson," Ryan interjected with a vague, meaningful smile, "but we're well aware of the risk ya're takin', as I'm sure ya're aware of ours. So I suggest we hurry this along and forget about bein' polite. All we have ta our name is a small farm, some cattle, sheep and a few crops, and very little money. But we're willin' ta give what it takes, whatever will satisfy ya."

Rynearson could hear the desperation in his voice. Masking the look of triumph he was sure had brightened his eyes, he rose and crossed the room to look out the window. "It won't be easy for me to have the charges dropped. Your father did try to kill a British soldier."

Even before she opened her mouth, Bevan's hot rebuttal was quickly squelched by the firm grip of Kelly's fingers pressing on her shoulder.

"And I'm not the kind of man to put a family out of their home. The size of your place isn't worth it and I truly have no need of a farm or its livestock."

"Then why have ya come, if we have nothin' of interest ta ya?" Shea blurted out, for which he received an angry glare from both his brothers.

Smiling to himself, Rynearson faced the group. He hadn't acquired his wealth by being honest, and these stupid fools were about to fall victim to his greatest talent. "I know you won't believe me—" He laughed as if doubting himself. "I know I wouldn't, if I were in your place. After all, I'm English. But I've never agreed with the treatment of you Irish. I think it's appalling as well as being unfair. I guess you could say I take a personal kind of pleasure in defying our king."

16

"Then ya should help for nothin'," Shea sneered, then grimaced when Ryan's elbow jabbed him in the ribs.

"Yes, I probably should," Rynearson conceded with a smile. "But I'm a businessman first, and I must admit I've never done anything for nothing. I'm no saint."

Ryan rammed his elbow in Shea's rib cage again, before the boy could offer his damaging opinion of Rynearson's comment, and stepped forward, placing his angry, hurting brother behind him. "Then what do ya suggest, Lord Rynearson? If ya're not wantin' our house or land, what can we give?"

As if contemplating his answer, Rynearson rubbed his chin while he casually strolled back to his chair and sat down. Hoodwinking this bunch of uneducated simpletons had been easier to accomplish than it had the Colonial sea captain a few months back, and nearly as enjoyable. The rewards, however, didn't compare. Adding to his charade, he pretended to change his mind about answering when he drew a breath, frowned, then shook his head.

"Just say it, Lord Rynearson," Ryan encouraged. "The decision will be ours ta make."

He glanced at Ryan, then Kelly, and left his chair again to pace the floor. A long while passed before he seemed to have made up his mind to say anything at all. "I should start by promising she'd be well cared for and that she'd live in a fine house with servants to look after her. She'd never want for anything and she'd always have plenty to eat and expensive clothes to wear."

"She?" Kelly parroted, his puzzled frown moving from the one who spoke to Ryan and back again. "What are ya sayin', Lord Rynearson? Have I missed somethin'? Who's this 'she' ya're talkin' about, and what has any of it ta do with our father?"

Ryan raised a hand to silence his brother's torrent of questions. "I believe I know," he revealed, his voice low and tinged with anger. "And the answer is no."

"No to what?" Kelly demanded. He always hated it when Ryan caught on to a conversation faster than he did. Ryan wasn't as tall or as strong as his older brother, but he always made up for it in common sense, and Kelly envied him that. "Would ya mind explainin', Ryan?"

That one's eyes stayed affixed to the Englishman. "The 'she' is Bevan, Kelly, and I doubt this viper wants ta make her his bride."

"You have it all wrong!" Rynearson shouted as he dashed behind a table, his hands raised in front of him to ward off the blows he was sure would momentarily descend on him, when Kelly's huge frame stiffened and he took a step forward. "Please! Let me explain. Hear it all before you decide. I swear I meant no disrespect." His nervous, frightened gaze darted back and forth between the two oldest brothers. "I—I have a nephew visiting me, a fine young man with more wealth than he knows how to handle. H-he's unmarried, in fact he refuses to wed because he claims he hasn't found the right woman. He's the last to carry on the Rynearson name, and since both of his parents are dead, I've taken on the responsibility of seeing him pass on his fortune to an heir. I must, since my estate will be his one day." Although the biggest of the pair seemed to be reconsidering his intention of smashing Rynearson's nose across his face, the Englishman could see he still had a lot of convincing to do, and that surprised him.

When a man was as poor as this lot, Rynearson never figured pride would even enter into the conversation. Gulping down the knot in his throat, he drew a labored breath. "It—it's only an idea," he claimed. "You're free to tell me to get on the first ship sailing back across the Channel, if you want, but in exchange for my help, I ask that your sister marry my nephew."

"Shall I take him outside so he doesn't get blood all over Mr. Magee's house, Ryan?" Kelly snarled, his chin lowered and his fists clenched as he eyed his trembling opponent.

"There's no need for violence, gentlemen," Rynearson proclaimed, eyes wide as they hurriedly searched the space around him for the nearest, safest form of retreat. It was clear to see he had misjudged this uncivilized gang of roughnecks, and if their father's life meant so little to them that they'd threaten an English lord, then Patrick O'Rourke could rot in his cell for all Rynearson cared. He was going home the second he was allowed to leave this disgusting hovel.

"We've been forced ta live in violence, Lord Rynearson, and we've done so because of people like ya," Ryan advised. "We've had ta fight just ta have enough food on our table, and ta be able ta hold our heads up high. We might be poor, but we're proud, and we won't sell our sister—"

"Ryan."

The soft, sweet voice that interrupted drew everyone's attention, most of all Rynearson's. Leaving her chair, Bevan crossed to the hearth to warm her hands, while she thought about the offer and how she planned to amend the details to her own benefit. Sensing all eyes were upon her, she turned and politely asked that Mr.

Magee fetch paper and quill. If Lord Rynearson agreed to her doctored proposal, she wanted it in writing.

"Bevan!" Ryan shouted angrily. "What are ya thinkin'? Ya can't be meanin' ya're givin' his offer some consideration. We can't allow it. Father would be furious if he knew."

"And how do ya think I'd feel if I let Father die knowin' there was a way ta stop it?" she rallied, her reddish-brown, finely arched brows slanting downward.

"We'll find another way," he barked. "I won't let ya do this!"

"What other way? Storm the prison and get all of ya killed?" She shook her head and took the parchment, quill, and bottle of ink from Magee. "'Twould be selfish of me ta even let ya think such a thin'." She laid her supplies on the small end table, then sat down in the chair beside it and turned her attention on the Englishman. "I have a deal of me own, sir. If ya find it fair ta your way of thinkin', I'll put it down on paper, and we'll both sign it." She waited for Rynearson's hesitant nod, then explained. "Ya say that in exchange for me promisin' ta marry your nephew—what did ya say his name was?"

"Ah . . . ah . . . Graham."

The answer seemed difficult for him to give, but Bevan excused the man's loss of memory on fear. Who wouldn't be nervous confronted by the likes of the O'Rourke brothers? "If I promise ta marry Graham, ya'll see that our father is freed," she easily continued.

Rynearson's face paled. "I—I never said—"

"Aye. 'Tisn't what ya said. 'Tis a part of me own deal. I agree ta marry Graham, me father is set free."

The Englishman hadn't counted on this beautiful, young woman being smart as well . . . *and* courageous enough to voice her opinion. That could mean trouble for him. Frowning, he sighed angrily, then allowed his gaze to study her face, while he imagined what it would be like to have her naked body moving beneath him. Yes, she was spirited and perhaps that wasn't so bad after all. She very well could prove to be quite passionate in bed.

"All right," he concurred. "Put it on paper and I'll sign it." When she didn't move to pick up the quill, but instead smiled somewhat victoriously at him, he squinted his eyes, silently questioning the delay.

"There are two more conditions before I sign." The confidence that uplifted her mouth never ebbed. "Ya stated that your nephew has refused ta marry because he has yet ta find the right woman."

Rynearson searched his memory, then nodded.

"Then here is me first condition. If your nephew chooses bachelorhood over me, ya will still see me father freed from prison anyway, as Graham's refusal will have nothin' ta do with our agreement."

Still not liking the proposal even with the condition, Ryan ground out his disapproval. "Bevan . . ."

She raised a hand to quiet his objection, her dark green eyes focused on the lord. "The second condition is much simpler. Since me brothers are obviously against this, ya'll have ta bring your nephew here ta meet me, so they can have a good look at him, too. Do ya agree?"

Rynearson's nervous gaze swept the hardened looks of the O'Rourke brothers, fearing his affirmative nod would unleash the hounds of hell to tear apart his flesh.

The Irish beauty, who offered an easy solution to his deceit, had also placed him in a very tricky situation. To turn down the offer meant he would lose her. To say yes raised the very distinct possibility that *if* they didn't kill him for it, he would be too crippled to strip himself of his clothes and climb into bed with her, once he got her alone in his house. Deciding that he might find another wench who was an only child, he looked at her with his denial on his lips and froze. If he searched the world far and wide, he would never uncover a treasure as rare as this precious stone. Suddenly his blood ran hot, his loins ached with wanting her, and without realizing it, he nodded his consent.

In a haze Rynearson watched Bevan's tiny, delicately boned hand pen the document for them to sign. At that moment he realized the corner in which he had backed himself. Since there was no Graham Rynearson, in fact no nephew at all, selecting an imposter might take a little doing. He smiled secretively, thinking that the right amount of coin and a new suit of clothes would convince even the town drunk to play the part. All he needed was the time to verse the man on the facts he should know about the Rynearson family should one of the O'Rourkes get personal.

"It's refreshing to see how much your welfare means to your brothers, Miss O'Rourke," he began as he took the quill she held out to him. "Not many families are that close." He paused long enough to read the agreement she had written, then signed his name below hers and laid the quill aside. "I'll bring Graham here to meet you . . . to meet your brothers. That way they can see for themselves what a wise decision you've made. Of course it must be done in utmost secrecy, you understand."

"And what if we don't like him?" Shea challenged. "If we don't approve, will ya still free our father *and* tear up the agreement?"

You'd love for me to say yes, wouldn't you, you little piece of worthless filth, Rynearson thought while he forced a pleasant smile to his lips. "I really don't expect such an outcome, Mr. O'Rourke. Graham is a very likable sort." He reached for his cape Magee had hung on the peg. "And your sister is quite beautiful." He smiled at her and extended his hand to lightly caress her cheek, but Bevan withdrew, fire flashing in her eyes. Yes, indeed the little twit had spirit, but he'd see it broken in no time at all. Bowing politely at her, he threw the dark cloak over his shoulders, tied the strings at his throat, and retrieved his tricorn from the table. "In one week. I'll bring Graham to the cove just south of town. You know the spot, don't you?"

Kelly and Ryan exchanged glances, their obvious disapproval glowing in their eyes, before Ryan sighed and nodded reluctantly. "We'll be waitin' there for ya. Just don't be late. Father's execution is scheduled soon after that."

"Late?" Rynearson mocked as he settled his tricorn on his head. "I wouldn't dream of it, good sir. I'm as anxious to welcome Bevan into my family as you are to welcome your father back to his."

"Just out of curiosity," Kelly called when Rynearson moved to exit the room. "What does your nephew look like?"

The question not only made Rynearson a little uncomfortable but limited his choice of possible candidates. Then he remembered Charles Alcott and

23

the money the young man still owed him. "He's around one score and ten, tall, rather good-looking, with dark hair and . . . blue eyes, I believe. I really don't pay that much attention to such details, I'm afraid. Why do you ask?"

The muscle in Kelly's cheek flexed. "Just makin' sure he isn't old enough ta be Bevan's grandfather or ugly enough ta scare her ta death."

Rynearson laughed. "I assure you, young man, Bevan will find him most handsome. Every single young lady in England does." Bowing slightly one last time, he turned and hurried from the room.

Green eyes, darkening with hatred and distrust, stared at the empty doorway long after the pompous Englishman had gone. "Then he must have two heads," Bevan muttered beneath her breath as she gave deep consideration to the foolishness of her promise.

The port of Liverpool, England, as usual, was already teaming with huge frigates, sailors, the local residents selling their wares out of wooden carts, and merchants overseeing the loading and unloading of their goods, when the *Lady Hawk*, an American vessel, glided toward the harbor, her main sails hoisted and her crew scurrying about as they prepared to dock. At the helm Captain Gordon Sanderson issued commands while he skillfully navigated the majestic merchant ship closer to shore. They had left the coast of North Carolina over a month ago, and aside from the short stay in Falmouth, a port in the southwestern part of England where they dropped anchor and replenished their supplies, their voyage had been long and hard and plagued with storms. The unrest between England and her neighbor to the south had awarded the newly formed United States with the perfect opportunity of trade with both countries, since the English had banned imports from France, and the French, in turn, refused to deal with England. Yet the mission of the *Lady Hawk* was not one of a neutral supplier. Reid Hamilton, owner of the *Lady Hawk* and a merchant, shipper, and planter from North Carolina, had been swindled out of a large shipment of tea, yarn, silk and wools, and other products, and he had decided to stand alongside his captain when they confronted the thief who had traded spoiled tea and water-stained fabrics for Reid's shipment of cotton, tobacco, and lumber. Not only did he plan on personally returning the worthless lot to one Lord Douglas Rynearson in exchange for the quality merchandise he should have received in the first place, it was his intent to be reimbursed in coin for the money he lost carrying a shipment of useless goods back across the Atlantic, as well as to inform the authorities of the deceit practiced by one of their merchants. After a visit from Reid Hamilton, Lord Rynearson would think twice about bilking his next partner.

The crew, anxious to set foot on solid ground again, hurried about their labors in record time, securing the mooring lines, tying off the sails, and lowering the gangplank on which they would disembark once the order was given. Every man on board had spent most of their adult life working on the *Lady Hawk* under Captain Sanderson's command and had grown to respect both the captain and the man who paid their wages. When the damaged goods had been discovered at the warehouse in North Carolina where they had been unpacked from the crates Rynearson's men had loaded onto the ship, no volunteers had to be enlisted. Each and every one of the men felt responsible to some degree and eagerly awaited the return trip to England. It would allow them to inflict a measure of retribution on the group who played them for fools.

"Shall I order the men to start unloading, sir?" Eric Dillion asked as he climbed the ladder to stand beside his captain at the helm.

"That decision is up to Mr. Hamilton," Gordon told his first mate. "But I rather doubt he wants it done right away. I think he prefers to have Lord Rynearson present at the time." He smiled, his green eyes sparkling merrily at the vision he conjured up. "He might even make the fool unload every crate by himself."

"Aye." Eric grinned, the lines at the corners of his mouth and eyes deepening. "I'll bet he would. It's what the bastard deserves . . . that and a whole lot more. I'd sure like to be around when Rynearson first realizes who Mr. Hamilton is."

"I don't think they'll have to be introduced. The minute he sees me, he'll know why I'm here again so soon and who the angry man at my side is," Gordon predicted. "The problem might be in finding him. If he cheats all his customers the way he did Mr. Hamilton, I would imagine he spends most of his time as far away from the warehouse office as possible."

"Oh, I don't know," Eric disagreed. "It might not be that difficult to locate him. Just find a rock and look under it."

That observation brought a hearty laugh from the captain. "You very well could be right, Eric," Gordon conceded as he threw an arm across the first mate's shoulders and guided him back to the ladder. "But I think Mr. Hamilton will want to try the warehouse first, then Rynearson's home. After that we'll look in more appropriate spots." Once they were standing on the quarterdeck, Gordon instructed, "Tell the men to prepare to go ashore, while I talk with Mr. Hamilton."

"Aye, aye, Cap'n," Eric responded with a nod before turning away.

Gordon lingered a moment to absently watch Eric Dillion issue the order and to once again wish this voyage hadn't been necessary. Reid Hamilton, his friend and employer for the past twelve years, had been very angry when he learned of the chicanery Rynearson had played on him, and even though Reid had tried to convince Gordon that he wasn't holding his captain responsible, Gordon still blamed himself for being so easily duped. He also understood Reid's desire to confront Rynearson face to face, rather than by proxy. Nevertheless Reid's presence made Gordon feel he wasn't trusted to handle the affair alone. This suspicion of his own inadequacy was the basis for his decision to resign his commission once they were back in North Carolina. He had a wife and two sons who needed him more than Reid Hamilton did. Inhaling and letting his breath out in a rush, he squared his shoulders and turned for the companionway leading to Reid's cabin.

"Come in," the deep voice called in response to Gordon's knock on the door.

Early afternoon sunshine filled the small cabin through the portholes in back of the desk where Reid Hamilton sat bent over the papers spread out before him. His gaze concentrated on what he wrote and a long moment passed before he returned the quill to the well and looked up, his gray eyes sparkling warmly at the man he called his friend.

"Seems like I'm never through with making notes, entering figures, and signing documents," he sighed good-naturedly. "I wish someone had warned me ahead of time what it takes to run a business. I might have been content with sailing as a way of life."

"And Laura would be engaged to your brother," Gordon pointed out, smiling.

"Yes," he thoughtfully replied, "she would. And both of us know she would probably be better off with Stephen. He's been ready for years to settle down and start a family to carry on the Hamilton name."

For a man who was betrothed to the most beautiful woman in all of North Carolina, Reid's response wasn't what one would expect. Only Gordon knew the reason and understood. "And so will you . . . one day," Gordon promised. "I think Laura knows that and that's why she hasn't pushed you to set a date. She's a fine woman. I'm sure you'll be happy."

The faint dimple at the corner of Reid's mouth appeared as a rakish grin stretched his lips. "Oh, you are, are you? Well, I wish I could agree with you."

"What makes you doubt it? Are you saying you don't love Laura?"

"No," Reid readily admitted. "I love her . . . like a sister."

Gordon couldn't help laughing. "A sister? You're engaged to one of the most alluring young women *I've* seen in a long while, and you look at her like she's your *sister?*" He shook his head. "Reid Hamilton, you have a serious problem."

Undaunted by the barb, Reid countered, *"You're* the one who'll have a serious problem if Sara ever finds out you're attracted to another woman."

"Sara knows better, my young friend," Gordon defended. "We've been married too long for her to believe anything you'd tell her. Besides, Laura's only a couple of years older than my oldest son. She's beautiful and charming and very gracious, but she's too young to suit me. You, on the other hand, are the right age for her. *And* you make a handsome couple. So why haven't you walked down the aisle with her?"

"You know why," Reid challenged as he pushed away from the desk and stood to collect his papers, stack them in neat order, then slide them into the top drawer. "The Bradburn and Hamilton families have been neighbors and friends for three generations. The day Laura was born our fathers decided she and I should wed and finally bring the two families *and* the estates together. I've known Laura her whole life. I watched her take her first step, heard her say her first word . . . for God's sake, I even took care of her when our parents went to Richmond one time. It's hard to fall in love with someone you've treated more like a sister all her life than a woman you want to make passionate love to."

"That's what mistresses are for," his friend offered sympathetically.

Cast in shadow with his back to the sunlight, Reid's raven black hair glistened in a warm contrast to his bronzed, suntanned face as he cocked a dark brow. "Perhaps you're right, Gordon.

Not wanting to discuss the issue any longer, he came to his feet and lifted his tricorn from the peg, then his cape. Heading to the door, he motioned for Gordon to step through ahead of him. "Come, good captain. Business awaits us. As does my fair Laura and your— Lord only knows why—faithful wife back home. Let us finish this transaction quickly and return to their opened arms before they both forget what we look like."

This wasn't the first time Reid Hamilton had cunningly changed the subject nor would it be the last. And that was the pity of it. Poor Laura, Gordon thought as he exited the cabin. And poor Reid. It wasn't that the two of them would be unhappy married to each other. Hardly that. They enjoyed one another's company, had the same interests, and loved the families into which they would marry. They just didn't love each other the way a man and a woman should. Reid knew it. Gordon knew it, and so did Lawrence Hamilton, the eldest of the clan. But a dream long envisioned was hard to forget just because those involved didn't love each other the way they should. That was Lawrence's reason for ignoring the obvious. It wasn't Reid's.

"I assume you want to talk to Rynearson first before the crew unloads the cargo, don't you?" Gordon asked once the two of them stood on the quarterdeck.

"Yes, I do," Reid answered. "Besides, the men deserve a little time to themselves. It was a rough voyage, and since we've waited this long, one more day won't matter."

Turning, Gordon motioned for his first mate to excuse the men, and amid hoots and hollers, the crew of the *Lady Hawk* rushed down the gangplank.

"Shall we find a place to stay, then look for

Rynearson?" Gordon suggested as the two men stepped onto the busy pier. "I would imagine you're ready for a good, hot meal and cold mug of ale, the same as me."

Now that they had dropped anchor in Liverpool and were close enough to walk right up to Douglas Rynearson, Reid's anger started to rekindle. He really preferred venting that anger on the man who had cheated him while it was at its peak, since it would be a very clear way of making his point. Yet he realized it wouldn't be very businesslike, and that Reid might wind up in jail as a result.

"A hot meal sounds good," Reid admitted as he pulled up his collar to fend against the cold draft of sea wind tickling his neck. "But first, I'd like to stop by the warehouse. I doubt he's there, but maybe someone can tell us where to look."

A short while later found Reid and Gordon finishing up their meal at Boor's Head Inn. As Reid had guessed, Rynearson wasn't at the warehouse, but then neither was anyone else, since the place closed up for an hour at noon. They had come to this particular inn under Gordon's reassurance that the rates were agreeable, the rooms clean, and the food good. Because it wasn't far from the wharf, they also hoped to find some of Rynearson's employees dining there, and that through casual conversation, one of them might divulge Rynearson's whereabouts.

"Well, was I wrong?" Gordon asked once the barmaid had cleared the table and brought them a fresh mug of ale.

"Can't really say," Reid teased while he signaled to the young boy who had just entered the pub to sell his newspapers. "I was so hungry I would have eaten just about anything without paying any attention to how it tasted." He plopped a coin in the boy's dirty palm, took the paper he held out, then smiled across the table at his friend. "The ale's good, though."

"I'm glad you approve," Gordon rallied with a touch of sarcasm.

Reid always enjoyed tormenting his friend and seldom let the chance slip by. "But it's rather hard to ruin ale," he added, hiding his devilish grin behind the newspaper he held up to read.

"And I suppose your room has cracks in the ceiling and lumps in the bed," Gordon finished. "If you'd been nicer to the young lady who showed you to your room, she might have given you the best in the place . . . the one at the end of the hall." He watched the newspaper lower slowly, confident that at last he had outwitted his partner.

"I was . . . and she did," Reid answered, then dropped his gaze on the bold print that headlined the day's edition, certain his friend would have no reply to that one. If he did, however, Reid wouldn't have heard it, for the feature story and gruesome depiction of the events described in it caught his full attention, and he frowned, displeased. "Gordon," he said, tossing down the newspaper for his companion to see, "have you heard about this? It says the constable is certain the young woman whose dead body was found two days ago is in some way connected to the other murders which have taken place here over the past two years. A total of ten altogether.

Gordon glanced only briefly at the article before

pushing it away and lifting his mug of ale to his lips, his contempt showing clearly on his face. "Yes, I've heard about it. It's the main topic of conversation around the pier every time we drop anchor. It's deplorable, and I had hoped that by now the bastard had been caught."

"The story's a little vague," Reid commented as he once again scanned the article. "Mind filling me in?"

"Are you sure you want to hear it?" Gordon tested. "It'll turn your stomach."

Reid shrugged. "Probably not, but my curiosity has gotten the better of me."

"I know what you mean," Gordon confessed. "It's the reason I listened the first time, too. Now I avoid discussing it, since there isn't anything I can do about it." Falling back in his chair, he stared off across the room for a minute as if he might be working up the courage to repeat the details he'd heard his last two times in Liverpool. "The first body was found two years ago, and everyone's opinion was that she had been beaten to death by a sailor she had refused. None of the *Lady Hawk*'s crew was questioned because we weren't around at the time. In fact, we've never been investigated because the murders always happened when we were midway across the Atlantic." He sighed, frowned, then began again. "A second body was found three months later and that's when the townspeople started worrying . . . because of the similarities between the two cases."

"What kind of similarities?"

"The doctor who examined the woman said they both died because someone beat them to death, but that there were other bruises and scars that indicated

33

the abuse had gone on for some time before they died."

Reid's dark brows came together. "I don't understand."

"No one else does either. One's first reaction would be that the women were beaten by their husbands, and that the similarities were just a coincidence. Then six months later another body showed up at the pier about three or four hundred yards from where the other two had been dumped. All three women died the same way, they had been only partially clothed, and none of them wore wedding rings."

"Which makes the constable think they were killed by the same man."

Gordon nodded.

"Interesting," Reid remarked as he quickly reread the newspaper article. "The fourth was found in August of last year, then two in November, one in March, May, and June of this year and the tenth last week." He glanced up at his friend. "And all ten died the same way, were half naked when they were dumped near or at the pier, and none of them have ever been identified."

"That's right," Gordon affirmed. "And because there were no blood stains, everyone believes the women were already dead when their bodies were left at the pier. And you know what else?" he asked. "All ten were young, beautiful women ranging in age from a score to a score and five, the kind of women you wouldn't find hanging around a wharf propositioning the tars."

"You're right, Gordon," Reid sighed. "It is deplorable."

"And there's nothing we can do about it," Gordon added. "I wish I could. I wish I'd have the luck to be around when this bastard tried to dispose of his next victim. It hits close to home," he confessed, his voice trembling. "I had an older sister whose husband was a violent bastard. At first it was only a few bruises and my father and I didn't do anything about it because Sis said she loved her husband and claimed he was drunk at the time. The beatings progressed and Sis managed to hide it from us for a while. By the time any of us realized just how bad it had become"—he paused, gritted his teeth, and growled into his mug of ale—"she was dead."

Any comment Reid might have made was interrupted when the barmaid returned to ask if they'd like another ale. Both men declined and each was silently thankful for the intrusion. It gave them the chance to abandon the subject, since Reid knew nothing he could say would ease his friend's agony, and Gordon preferred to leave the past behind him.

Pulling the gold watch from his pocket, Reid absently ran his thumb over the engraved initials on the cover when he was struck with a twinge of sorrow over never having met his grandfather. Although Garrison Rothwell had died before the birth of his first grandson, Reid's mother had talked at such length about her father that the thought of how Reid had been cheated out of knowing him personally often times had Reid cursing the accident that had taken his life. He wanted more of the man than just his watch . . . the same as Gordon wanted more of his sister than just painful memories.

Suddenly realizing where his thoughts had strayed and that Gordon was probably thinking along similar lines of regret, he shook off the melancholia, checked the time, and suggested they leave for the warehouse. Gordon, more than willing to be off on business, eagerly concurred. Together they left the inn and headed back toward the wharf, where they hoped to find Douglas Rynearson.

As before, the pier incorporated a host of people and if anything, appeared more crowded than it had earlier. The way was slow and filled with sailors, dock workers, an old woman selling flowers, street urchins begging for a coin, and harlots offering a pleasant afternoon in a nearby inn, the last three of which Reid and Gordon politely ignored. Up ahead they noticed, between the heads bobbing in and out of their way, an expensive landau wheeling toward the huge building on the left, and even before Gordon pointed out the gold emblem on the door signifying ownership, Reid suspected the rig belonged to Lord Rynearson. They hurried their step, dodging the bodies crushing in around them, and finally moved to walk the street instead and take their chances with the freight wagons, horses, and scores of buggies traveling the thoroughfare.

It became even more difficult for them to stay together the closer they got to the warehouse as the activity doubled around its opened doors and a string of workers carrying boxes pushed their way in between Reid and his companion. Delayed until he could wedge through the line, Reid found himself several yards behind Gordon once he was clear, as Gordon was determined to reach the man descending from the rig before he could get away. Gordon was nearly there when carriage and driver, an odd-looking little creature, pulled away from the curb, leaving its passenger, a man Reid guessed was Rynearson by the way Gordon rushed toward him, near the office door. The clatter of horses' hooves, rattling of wagon wheels, and chorus of chatter at the wharf prevented Reid from hearing Gordon's exact words to his foe, but from Rynearson's reaction once he turned and saw the one who had called out to him, it was quite clear to Reid that Rynearson feared Gordon Sanderson's retaliation. His eyes widened, the color drained from his face, and before Gordon could lay a hand on him, Rynearson spun on his heels and ran. Panic drove him, for he heartlessly knocked aside any and all who stood in his way. He raced down the busy street away from Gordon, who chased after him with coattails flying, and ducked to his left between two buildings. Always one to enjoy a good hunt whether it was man or beast and knowing the rewards of this particular pursuit were double-edged, Reid paused to calculate Rynearson's direction and where his choice would take him before he turned, backtracked several yards, and cut down an alleyway.

The back street, as well as the avenue it intersected, wasn't as crowded as the one Reid had left behind, but still posed enough of a problem for him that he wasn't able to catch more than a glimpse of Rynearson's well-dressed figure before he vanished within the throng of people dividing the two of them. Elbowing his way around a group of sailors, then half running, half sidestepping those on the sidewalk, Reid hurried toward the spot where Rynearson had disappeared, figuring to find Gordon at the same time. All he was awarded with was a sea of nameless strangers too busy to notice him or the man he chased. Annoyed but not defeated, he started off again in the direction he guessed Rynearson would take, and several minutes later he found himself standing at the edge of the pier absently watching a huge merchant ship drop her sails, hoist the gangplank, and weigh anchor. Deciding that perhaps Gordon had caught up to the scoundrel and was already hauling him back to the warehouse, Reid gave up his aimless quest and started back. Between the two of them, Rynearson was sure to have seen his luck evaporate.

Told where he could locate the manager of the warehouse, Reid went inside to the office and quickly realized that *if* Gordon had finally run Rynearson down, he had yet to return with him, when he spotted one man alone sitting behind the desk working diligently over the notes he entered in a ledger.

"Excuse me," he apologized when the man failed to look up and acknowledge his presence. "I'm looking for Lord Rynearson. Do you know where I can find him?"

Slow to respond, the man finished his listing before he dropped the quill in the inkwell and closed the book. "'Oo wants ta know?" he asked, his mouth twisting into a sneer as he crossed his beefy arms and laid them on the ledger.

Reid's temper flared but he managed to control it. "My name is Reid Hamilton, and—"

"A Colonial," the other spat with contempt. "'Ere ta bleed us dry, are ye?"

Breathing in a cool rush of air through flared nostrils, Reid glanced away as he ground his teeth and considered ending this short-lived conversation with a well-deserved fist to the man's pudgy face. He was in no mood to play diplomat to this bigoted half-wit, anymore than he was willing to listen to Rynearson's excuses. The fact he had fled from Gordon proved he knew about the damaged goods, and chances were this man was in on it, too.

"I'm here to collect," Reid answered, his gray eyes mirroring the threat behind his tone as they fell once again on the one behind the desk. "Now I suggest you answer my question before you become a party to your employer's deceit." He cocked a dark brow. "If you aren't already."

"Deceit?" the man challenged. "What deceit?" He puffed out his chest and stood as if highly offended. "We run a respectable business 'ere, and accusations like that will get ye a visit to the jail."

"Really?" Reid mocked as he casually strolled closer to the desk. "Would you like to find out? I'm more than willing to present my claim to your constable. In fact, once I'd dealt with your employer, that was exactly what I planned to do. Of course, if I'm unable to locate Lord Rynearson, I suppose I could hold you account-able." Reid could see some of the arrogance fade from the manager's pale brown eyes. "After all, it's your job to oversee the loading and unloading of goods, is it not?"

The man's Adam's apple bobbed up and down when he gulped back an obvious knot of worry. "I—I do what I'm told, gov'na."

"Do you?" Reid tested as he rounded to the side of the desk and boldly perched a hip on it while he reached for the ledger. Opening it, he thumbed through the pages for the date when Gordon had struck a deal with Rynearson. "Silks, velvets, tea . . . it's all listed prop-erly." He snapped the book shut and tossed it down, before he laid his crossed wrists on one thigh and lifted his gaze. "No proof in there of thievery. I'm sure the constable will see your side of it." He smiled with a touch of sarcasm marring the show of white teeth. "Maybe."

"W-wait a second, gov'na," the man argued, his trembling hands raised out in front of him, "I got a wife and five little ones ta care for. I—I don't want no trouble."

"Then tell me where to find Rynearson, and I'll make sure your name is never mentioned when I talk with the constable."

The manager was only too eager to comply. "I—I'm not real sure where 'e is right now—'e was supposed ta meet me 'ere twenty minutes ago—but . . ." He paused, glanced at the open door, and hurried to close it. "I can't tell ye the reason behind it 'cause I don't know what it is, but I overhead 'im telling a friend of 'is that 'e 'ad ta meet with some Irish rebels tonight."

"Where?"

The man shrugged. "Didn't say, and 'is friend didn't ask. But I'm willin' ta wager 'e's on 'is way there right now."

Via a detour, Reid thought. "Was he coming back here afterward?"

"'Ere?" the manager parroted. "Tonight? I don't see 'ow 'e could, gov'na. The trip across takes a good ten 'ours, it does."

"Across? To where?"

The question brought a skeptical look from Reid's companion as though he wondered how anyone could be as stupid as the Colonial he faced. "Ta Ireland," he answered. "Where else would a man meet with Irish rebels?"

40

The vision of the merchant ship and the knowledge that Reid had last seen Rynearson in the same vicinity ignited his temper. Growling an oath, he stormed toward the door.

The smiling face of Reid's younger brother flared up in his mind's eye as he stood at the railing of the clipper ship bound for the east shore of Ireland. Of those who waited his return back home, Reid always missed Stephen the most, and if it hadn't been for his handicap, Reid would have dragged his brother with him those four weeks back when the *Lady Hawk* set sail for England. The young man needed to get away from home now and then even if Stephen disagreed. Their mother knew it, Reid knew it, and even Stephen knew it deep down inside. He's simply resigned himself to living out his old age the same as he'd done so far; single and in the company of his family.

Glancing up at the turbulent black clouds racing in from the west, Reid found himself envying his younger brother. Stephen had always been the more sensible of the two of them, the more level-headed, and acutely more logical when it came to matters of the heart. For years Stephen had been in love with a woman who, as he put it, was out of his reach. She was engaged to someone else, and because he respected the young woman and her fiancé, Stephen had never made his feelings known to her. Nor had he ever revealed her identity . . . to anyone, and that included his own brother, since he knew Reid would try to do something to correct it.

"There's no sense in talking about it," he had told

41

Reid one day when the oldest had pressed him for information. "She's the same as married and I won't ruin it for her by complicating matters. Besides, who could ever love a cripple?"

Stephen's accident had happened when he and Reid were young boys. Reid had challenged his brother to do something daring, something forbidden to both of them, and he'd hounded Stephen about it until Stephen gave in. Being called a coward wasn't a name the young boy of ten wanted to be labeled, especially by Reid, since Stephen thought the sun rose and set on his older brother. So, he'd taken their father's favorite, high-spirited stallion from his stall, led the beast away from the house and stable where he wouldn't be seen, and used a huge rock to hoist himself onto the steed's back while Reid watched. To this day Reid could still remember every detail of that fateful afternoon as if it had happened only moments before, nor had he ever forgiven himself. There was only one person that beast allowed on his back and it wasn't young Stephen. The second that animal felt the boy's weight and knew it wasn't Lawrence who held the reins, the stallion reared, pawed the air, and bolted off with Reid chasing after them on foot. By the time he caught up to the pair again, it had been too late to do either of them any good. Somehow the stallion had fallen and broken its neck and in the process had thrown Stephen against a tree. His knee had been so badly smashed that the doctor had said the leg should be amputated. Reid had violently protested, saying that if anyone's leg should come off, it should be his, and out of worry for his oldest son's mental state, Lawrence had ordered the doctor to leave.

Stephen's recovery was long and slow, but Reid never left his brother's side. He read to him, fed him, helped change his clothes and the bed linens, and always told Stephen that he would walk again. Reid didn't know it at the time, but his faith had been all that pulled Stephen through. In less than a year, the boy was up on his feet and walking with the aid of a cane. Now at a score and eight, Stephen had learned to maneuver without the wooden stick, and aside from a knee that wouldn't bend, he was more of a man than any who could walk without a limp. Although Stephen saw himself as a cripple and had taken many such heartless attacks from both strangers and thoughtless acquaintances alike, his brother always berated him for letting the word slip into his vocabulary. To Reid's way of thinking, a man was only crippled if he let his disability get him down. Maybe Stephen couldn't sit astride a horse or run after some sweet young girl to steal a kiss, but his partial immobility was Stephen's only flaw. And someday the right woman would come to realize it.

"Excuse me, Mr. Hamilton," the first mate of the English clipper ship politely interrupted as he came to stand beside Reid at the bow of the vessel, "but the captain says perhaps you should go below." He nodded toward the blackening sky to their right. "He doesn't like the looks of that storm. It could be a bad one."

Distracted from his thoughts of the past, Reid glanced at the sky again. He understood the captain's worry. The ever-growing swirl of ebony clouds with its bright flashes of light splitting them in two promised they would be in for a rough voyage. "Tell him I appreciate his concern, but that I'm not new to this sort of thing. Before I became a planter, I captained my own ship for several years. If anything, maybe I can be of some help."

"I'll tell him, sir," the man replied. "But I'm sure he wouldn't expect it of you."

Reid nodded and absently watched the first mate walk away. His luck of late had left a lot to be desired, and judging from the chilling wind and cold droplets of mist he felt on his face, the situation wasn't improving. He had had to hire this vessel and crew after he had returned to the pier and learned that the ship which was already melting into the horizon had been the one on which Rynearson had booked passage for himself and a companion. The man with whom Reid had talked couldn't confirm that Rynearson had actually boarded the ship as he hadn't personally seen the English lord embark, but that in his opinion Reid could almost place a wager on it. Lord Rynearson had a reputation of being a very stingy man, and if he had changed his mind about sailing to Ireland, he would have demanded the price of his fare returned *before* the ship weighed anchor. It didn't explain where Gordon had gone, and although Reid would have preferred consulting with his friend before taking off on his own, he had been left with no alternative.

A sizable amount of gold coin had ensured the use of a fast-moving clipper, and while captain and crew prepared for the voyage, Reid had returned to the Boar's Head Inn to leave a message for Gordon. Time hadn't allowed him to go into too much detail in the note, only that he was following a lead that directed him to the southern shore of Ireland and a band of rebels with whom Rynearson obviously had some dealings. He further instructed his captain to seek out the warehouse manager and dispose of the damaged goods, replace them with either suitable merchandise or reimbursement in coin, then wait for him at the inn.

While he had penned the message, he hadn't forseen any real problem and had planned on simply forcing Rynearson to return to Liverpool with him—under threat of death, if need be, or at least the promise of a heartless thrashing. Now it appeared Reid, as well as the crew of the clipper, had more important things to consider. While he'd captained his own ship some four or five years ago, he'd ridden out many storms such as the one quickly moving in on them. Even the storms the *Lady Hawk* had faced during their voyage across the Atlantic these past four weeks had been dangerous. The difference, however, was the size of the vessel. Of lighter weight, fewer sails, and narrower dimensions, the clipper wasn't as apt to weather storms as well as her bigger sister, the merchant ship. It would be to their advantage to outrun the front.

He had just stepped onto the deck to go speak with the captain when the approaching squall exploded all around them and the black skies overhead seemed to open up with a violence bent on tossing him and every sailor on board into the churning waters of the St. George's Channel. Hit by a hearty gust of wind and a spray of biting, cold rain, he caught himself against the railing and made a halfhearted attempt to snatch his tricorn as it was torn from his head and hurled into the murky, green water. A crack of thunder and the howl of wind, which rapidly tripled in force, drowned out the shouts of the captain to his men and the warning to Reid that the water barrel had broken loose of its ropes. A second later the wooden cylinder came crashing toward him, and before anyone could grab him and yank him out of the way, he was struck from behind and hurled to the deck, his head striking the planks with such force that he lost consciousness almost instantly.

Time soon lost all perspective. Seconds seemed like hours, minutes like days, and somewhere in between the two, the unconscious man was rudely awakened by the wall of water that smashed against the ship and swept him across the deck. Frantic to save himself as the fury of the storm assailed its cripping blows against men and vessel, he reached out and caught his arm around one of the balusters to anchor his position and to wait out the eye of the tempest. Blinding glares of light lit up the seething sky. Torrents of rain and ice crystals pelted the decks. The angry howl of the wind harassed the white canvas sails and stretched them taut against their lanyards. Then a deafening moan, followed by a crack of splintering wood, riveted everyone's attention, and as he fought to raise his face skyward, the scream of one of the crewmen near him disclosed the source of the sound long before he was able to see it for himself. The unrelenting force of the gale winds had weakened the foremast midway up, and combined with the powerful tug on the sails, the abuse had become too much. Like a willow branch, the mast snapped in two, tore the riggings, sails, and guys free of their knots, then plummeted to the deck below, scattering debris and men alike in all directions as the latter rushed out of harm's way.

One of the tars, who hadn't been as fortunate as his mates, screamed in agony and fell to the wooden planks when a huge splinter of oak pierced his upper thigh. The lurching of the vessel, as it rode the waves then dropped rapidly to await the next, slid the man's half-conscious body toward the one secured to the railing. Before the ship heaved upward again, that one stretched out to grab the sailor's shirt and haul him close enough to wrap his legs around the man's midsection and hold him steady. His own body ached with exhaustion, but the stubborn will to survive refused to allow him to lessen his grip or to even entertain the thought that he might have a better chance of living through this if he were in the water than hanging on to a broken ship. At that moment, however, and amid the rush of sounds beating against his chest and ears, the clipper ship lunged upward, seemed to stand on end for an eternity, then fell at a dramatic speed and came to a bone-rattling, teeth-jarring halt as it crashed and broke apart against the rocky coast of Ireland. A wall of sea green water spewed forth and washed the deck clean, sweeping Reid, the sailor he still clung to, and everyone else into the black depths of a watery grave.

Chapter Two

Huddled beneath a rocky ledge, their coats pulled tightly around them to shield against the driving rain, three figures studied the shoreline of the cove and strained to see in the inky blackness between bright flashes of blinding light. Had their sister allowed it, the O'Rourke brothers would have returned to their small cottage to wait out the storm. But they stood shivering in the cold because of her insistence that they stay until they had Rynearson and his nephew in their company. Kelly had speculated that the pompous Englishman wouldn't travel in such a storm and that he was probably sitting by a warm fire in one of the inns in Bray at this very moment, and that the last thing on his mind was the O'Rourke brothers and how they would be waiting for him.

"I disagree," Shea retorted above the howling wind. "I'm thinkin' he's havin' a good laugh over it, and if I didn't know better, I'd say he had somethin' ta do with this weather."

A loud crack of thunder reverberated throughout

48

the cove as if a higher power wished to remind Shea of the one truly responsible. Grumbling to himself, he clutched the collar of his jacket tighter around his neck and scowled out into the darkness.

"Well, there's really no sense in all of us catchin' our death," Ryan observed. "Why don't the two of ya go back and get dried off. Then in a half hour, one of ya can relieve me. We'll take turns until we either hear from Rynearson or he shows up here."

"'Tis a grand idea," Shea easily concurred. "Me teeth are chatterin' so bad I can hardly hear meself think."

"Then go on with ya," Ryan urged. He watched his younger brother resettle his hat tighter on his head while he turned to climb the rock path out of the cove, but before he had gone two steps, Ryan added, "Just don't forget I'm out here. I'd enjoy a warm fire, too, ya know."

Shea waved a hand and continued to climb, unaware that his eldest brother wasn't following close behind, until he heard his shout. He turned back to see Kelly hurrying down the stony incline to the shore, with Ryan following. Shea forgot about his numb extremities and chased after his older siblings.

"What is it, Kelly?" Ryan called amid the thunderous wind and rain beating heavily against them.

"Down there," he yelled, pointing a finger at the muddy stretch of beach. "I saw him when the lightnin' flashed."

As if on cue, a bolt of bright light seared the black, turbulent sky and turned night into day for one brief second. But it was long enough for the brothers to spy the unmoving body of a man lying half in and half out of the water.

"Is he alive?" Shea inquired as he clung desperately to his hat and watched Kelly pull the man out of the water and roll him onto his back.

"Just barely," Kelly announced after pressing his fingertips to the pulse in the man's neck. "I don't recognize him. Do either of you?"

Shea shook his head, but Ryan was slower to respond. Apparently his brothers weren't thinking the same thing he was thinking and he hoped they were right as he briefly glanced up and down the shoreline.

"What is it, Ryan?" Kelly asked, once he saw the odd look on his brother's face.

"His clothes," Ryan shouted above the wind. "He can't be from around here. None of us can afford such fine garments."

"So why does that bother ya?"

When Ryan wouldn't answer, but instead dropped down and began to rifle through the unconscious man's pockets, Kelly pulled back, totally mystified. "What are ya lookin' for?"

"I don't know exactly," Ryan replied. But a second later, he held up a gold watch, and when a flash of lightning enabled him to clearly read the engraved initials on its lid, he loudly declared, "This!"

"A watch?" Shea hollered, wishing they could continue the discussion inside somewhere out of the storm.

"Not *just* a watch," Ryan answered. "This one belongs to Graham Rynearson!"

"What?" the other two echoed, and while they took turns studying it, Ryan turned back to the injured man.

A quick examination revealed no broken limbs, though it was hard to tell if his ribs had escaped harm.

50

The size of the lump on his brow, however, promised he more than likely would wake up with an awful headache, and if he wasn't taken in out of the chilling rain right away, he stood a good chance of succumbing to a fever.

"Kelly, you and Shea get him to the cart, while I have one last look around. I doubt I'll find anythin', but we can't leave until we're sure."

Together they hauled him up high enough for Kelly to drape the limp form over his shoulder. With Shea leading the way, and Ryan catching up after he had given the narrow shoreline a second inspection, the group slowly climbed the hillside to the spot where they had tied off the donkey and cart. After placing their ward in back, Kelly jumped in with him while Ryan took the reins and Shea sat on the seat beside him. The rain and wind, thunder, lightning, and biting chill continued their assault, but no one seemed to notice as much since the group had a more important matter to consider instead of their own discomfort. Although no one voiced his opinion, all three brothers were convinced that the man Kelly was tending was Graham Rynearson, one of the two men they were to meet in the cove. What plagued them more than the man's injured state was the fact that he was alone. Had something happened to his uncle? Was Rynearson dead? As this man nearly was? And if that worry proved to be reality, then what would become of their father? In silence and with troubled frowns, each of the brothers concentrated on getting Graham Rynearson home and nursed back to health. At this point he was the only one who knew the answers.

The distance from the cove to the thatch-roofed

house seemed to take longer to reach than ever before, and even though Kelly knew his brother was hurrying the donkey as best he could, Kelly had to fight the urge to tell him to go faster. The bruise on Graham's brow was enough cause for concern. The fact that he was soaked to the skin and that there seemed to be no immediate end to the cold, driving rain only added to his grave prognosis. Even Kelly was beginning to feel the effects of the cold, and he'd only been out in it for an hour. He had no idea how long Graham had been lying there before they found him.

Rather than steer the cart directly into the stable as usual, Ryan pulled the rig to a halt near the back door and jumped down to aid Kelly in lifting the unconscious man to Kelly's shoulder again. While Ryan hurried on ahead to open the way, Shea took the reins and headed toward the stable. But just as Ryan's hand touched the knob, the door was thrown open from inside and lantern light temporarily blinded him when Bevan thrust the yellow glow forward to see who had come to the house.

"Hurry, lass," Ryan advised as he took the lantern and held it high for his brother. "We've brought an injured man who needs your tendin'."

Bevan wondered who it was but did not take the time to ask. She spun round on her heels and flew to their father's bedroom, where she tossed down the covers before kneeling to start a fire in the hearth.

"He'll need ta be stripped of his wet clothes and put inta somethin' dry," Kelly said, and Ryan helped lower the unconscious man enough that he could get at the buttons on the man's shirt and breeches.

"We'll dress him later," Ryan counseled, slipping off

the man's shoes, stockings, and shirt before he ordered Bevan out of the room. "Right now we need ta get him warm."

"'Tisn't like to embarrass me, Ryan O'Rourke," she snapped as she begrudingly did as bade. "I was raised with three brothers, ya know."

"How well I do," he called after her, "but this man is not one of them. Go and fetch a towel ta dry his hair and anythin' else ya might need, and be quick about it. 'Tis up ta us ta see that he gets well, and arguin' won't help him."

Once the wet clothes were removed, Kelly and Ryan gently laid the man down on the bed and covered him with the thick, wool quilt. Satisfied that they had done all they could for him at the moment, they left the room and went to their own to change out of their damp things. Bevan had more of a talent for doctoring a person back to health than any of them, and unless she needed them, they planned to stay out of her way. More importantly, they needed the privacy her work would allow them to discuss their father's future. If what they had guessed was true and Lord Rynearson was dead, other measures had to be taken to free their father.

Bevan's temper was still simmering when she returned to her father's bedroom with a towel, bowl, and kettle of hot water. If seeing a man in the altogether didn't embarrass her, why should her brothers of a sudden take an interest in modesty? Especially since the one who was lying unconscious in her father's bed certainly wouldn't know the difference. Muttering to herself as she placed her supplies on the night stand, she glanced at the hearth to make sure the fire hadn't

53

gone out before she bent, retrieved the stranger's clothes from the floor, and hurriedly draped them over a chair to dry. It wasn't as if she was going to stare at him while they disrobed him, and it angered her to think they assumed she would. She had no curiosity about men and how they were built. In fact, she had no interest in men at all. Why should she? She'd lived under the same roof with four of them her whole life, and her future promised she would spend the rest of her days in the company of another, which meant she'd go from sharing a house with her father and brothers to sharing it with her husband. In her opinion, men weren't much different from each other. When it came right down to it, they all viewed women in the same light, and that was that women were only put on earth to feed and care for their men and to bear their offspring. A spark of rebelliousness darkened her emerald green eyes as she turned away from the chair she had slid closer to the hearth, that same defiant gleam her brothers had come to know so well. What they didn't know was the workings of her mind. She was more cunning and level-headed than the entire O'Rourke brood and certainly a whole lot more clever than Lord Rynearson. She'd proved that when she'd made him sign her agreement. Smiling complacently, she crossed to the night stand and picked up the towel.

Men, she thought with a short laugh. *They're all fools. If they only knew who really made all the decisions, they'd—*

The unfinished observation faded from her mind in an instant, once her gaze fell on the still face of the man who occupied her father's bed. Raven black hair, glistening with moisture, clung to a strong brow.

Ebony lashes lay thick against a coppery complexion. A perfect nose, wide cheekbones, a square jaw, and a full, sensuous mouth added to the rugged features of the most incredibly handsome man she had ever seen, and her heart fluttered in her chest as she fought to draw air into her lungs. A warmth started in the pit of her stomach and quickly spread upward to enflame her cheeks and lay heavy against her bosom. Every nerve fiber had come alive and tingled hotly over every inch of her body, and she suddenly felt the fool for ever thinking this man was even remotely similar to all those she had lumped together. Suddenly and uncustomarily timid, she slowly reached out to touch her fingertips to his cheek. The fever that had already begun to rage in his body scorched his face and the shock of it snapped Bevan to her senses. If she didn't start taking care of him at that very moment, he might not live long enough to open his eyes, let alone smile at her and verify how silly she had been in thinking a man like him never existed.

First she set about toweling dry his thick hair as gently as possible, and exchanging the damp pillowcase for a dry one. Next she sponged the ugly bruise and tiny gash in the center of it with warm water and lye soap. Since he seemed content to lie still, she dabbed on a little black salve and covered the area with a square of white gauze. Noticing a long, red scratch down the side of his neck, she lifted the quilt to examine the total length and the severity of the wound, deciding that a soapy cloth rubbed along the area, then a clean rinse, would suffice. She found another bruise on his left shoulder and rather than look for herself, she called out for Kelly and Ryan to join her.

"What is it?" the younger of the two inquired once they stood beside her at the bed.

"He's got several bruises and scratches on his neck and shoulders," she answered. "I was wonderin' if ya saw any others that needed lookin' after?"

"Just one that I saw," Kelly advised as he bent and pulled down the quilt to the man's lean waist. "Here."

He pointed to the stranger's thickly muscled rib cage, but Bevan hardly noticed the black and blue welt Kelly wanted to show her. The sight of a thick matting of dark curls covering a superb expanse of well-defined thews stole her breath away, and the heat that singed her fair face deepened the longer she stared.

"We have no way of knowin' if he broke a rib or two until he comes 'round," Kelly went on to say, "but it wouldn't surprise me any ta learn he had. 'Tis a nasty bruise. What do ya think, Bevan?"

The sound of her own name startled her. To cover up the fact that she hadn't been paying attention, Beven hastily dropped to her knees to examine the injury on the stranger's side. "He might have a broken rib or two, but we'll have no way of knowin' for sure until he wakes up and I can poke around ta see how much pain he's in," she declared as she nervously pulled the covers back up over his lean, sun-darkened chest with its rippling muscles and crisp, dark hair. She'd seen her brothers bare-chested plenty of times, but never remembered thinking how grand they looked.

"Bevan."

The lyrical impatience she heard in Kelly's voice turned her around. "What?"

Kelly paused, frowned, then sighed resignedly. Why bother to point out that she'd repeated what he'd just said? She would merely give her usual excuse of never listening to anything any of her brothers had to say. "Never mind, Bevan." Kelly shrugged and walked out of the room.

"There's nothin' any of us can do right now," Bevan said briskly, lifting the bowl of water from the night stand. "Except to keep him warm until the fever breaks." She unwittingly glanced at the stranger's quiet face and felt a warmth of her own course through her veins. Quickly masking her emotions, she turned to the door. "I need ta get fresh water and rags. Stay with him while I'm gone. I won't be but a minute." She didn't wait for an answer, but instead hurried out of the room.

Ryan's shoulders sagged as if a heavy burden had been placed on them, and he found himself blaming their father for the trouble they were in. Patrick O'Rourke had the worst temper of all of them, including Bevan. Their mother had been the only one who could calm the man's ire and only with a subtleness no one else could feel . . . except for Ryan. After she died, her husband's rages came more often and with more violence. Now their father was gone and Ryan felt keenly the responsibility of the family.

"How's he doin'?" a quiet voice asked. Ryan was startled to find Shea beside him; he hadn't heard him come into the room.

"Too soon ta tell, I'm afraid," Ryan answered, his dark brows wrinkled tightly over his eyes. "I'm more concerned about his uncle, however. If Lord Rynearson is dead . . ." He chose not to finish the statement.

"I was thinkin' the same thing meself," Shea said. "But I was also thinkin' his death wouldn't be the end of it."

Because of his youth and impulsive nature, Shea rarely said anything worth considering for more than a minute or two, but out of respect for his kin, Ryan always listened. "Oh?" he questioned. "And what makes ya say that?"

Shea pointed at the man lying quietly in the bed. "Don't ya remember what his uncle told us? He said that he wanted his nephew married because his estate would go to Graham when Rynearson dies."

As usual, Ryan thought, Shea wasn't making a whole lot of sense. "What has that ta do with us?"

"Well, if he inherits money, doesn't he inherit power, too? And if he took a real likin' ta Bevan, wouldn't he use that power ta make her happy? And what would make her happier than havin' her father sent home ta his family?"

Ryan hated to admit that for once Shea had come up with a logical theory. A half-smile worked Ryan's mouth as he shifted his gaze to Graham Rynearson. "Aye, Shea, I see your point. But ya're assumin' Graham's goin' ta like Bevan the instant he opens his eyes."

"And why not?" Shea exclaimed. "She's beautiful. She can cook and sew and handle herself both in words and with her fists." He automatically rubbed his arm where she had all too often proven one of her skills.

"That's true, Shea, but maybe he wants a meek and mild little mouse who'll jump whenever he calls her."

"Then Bevan will be meek and mild."

Ryan gave a short laugh. "Now ya've kissed the Blarney stone, Shea, me boy," he accused as he draped a long arm across his brother's shoulders. "Bevan could never be meek and mild, even if her life depended on it."

"Maybe," Shea objected. "But it isn't *her* life that'd depend on it now, would it?"

"Hmmm," Ryan murmured with a nod of his dark head. "You've got a point there. I still don't like the idea. The way I see it, she'd still be prostitutin' herself in exchange for Father's life. I'd feel much better if we came up with another method for freein' him."

"Would ya, now?"

The sharp question spun both brothers around. They hadn't meant to talk about their sister as if she had no mind to discuss such affairs, but they had, and now they would have to answer for it. And the fire they saw blazing in her eyes as she glared across the room at them from the doorway promised they'd be in for a good tongue-lashing if one of them didn't apologize and fast. Thinking it was his place to explain, Ryan stepped forward.

"I'll hear none of your sweet words, Ryan O'Rourke," Bevan cut in before he could open his mouth. "I'm well aware of how ya feel about me agreein' ta marry Graham Rynearson, but since it was me own decision ta make, 'tis how I think about meself that matters." Scowling angrily at Ryan then at her twin, as if daring them to argue, she moved farther into the room and crossed to the bed, where she placed the bowl of cool water and rags on the nightstand.

Ryan felt the bite of her words and knew he deserved them. Bevan had a right to be angry with him. She had unselfishly given up her hope for any future happiness in exchange for her father's life, and her brother accused her of being a whore. It wasn't what he had really meant to say and certainly not where she could hear him, but it was too late to take it back.

"And speakin' of me betrothed," Bevan went on, "shouldn't one of ya be out at the cove? Uncle Rynearson won't be too pleased with ya, if he's made ta wait."

"I don't think he'll be comin', Bevan," Ryan quietly confessed.

Bright green eyes full of panic turned to look at him. "Ever?"

Glancing first at Shea, Ryan drew in a deep breath and moved to stand next to his sister. "We can't be sure, of course, but we fear he was killed in the crossin'."

Bevan's face paled as she looked from Ryan to Shea, then at Kelly, who had heard their argument from the other room and had come to offer his advice.

"The storm is much worse at the cove, Bevan," he explained. "A ship of any size would have had trouble stayin' afloat. 'Tis where we found this lad, unconscious and lyin' in the water. There was debris washed up on the shore, boards and the like, and it appeared, ta me anyway, that the ship he was on broke apart when it hit the rocks."

"But that doesn't prove anythin'," she rallied, refusing to believe their only hope of saving their father had died along with Rynearson in the St. George's Channel. "If this man survived, then maybe Rynearson did too. Ya have ta go back ta the cove."

"We will, Bevan," Ryan promised. "But not now. As soon as the storm—"

"No!" she shouted. "Ya have ta go *now*. If he's injured—"

Ryan quickly grabbed her arms. "Graham was the only one there, Bevan. We looked. We wouldn't have left the cove without checkin' first. Ya know us better'n that."

The anger, the desperation, that had gleamed in her eyes changed suddenly. Surprise melted the lines in her brow and a strange calm relaxed the taut muscles in her slender body as she gently broke her brother's hold on her to look at the man who had ignited unexplainable stirrings deep inside her. *"He's* Graham Rynearson?" she asked in hardly more than a whisper. "How do ya know?"

Ryan and Kelly exchanged reluctant glances before the first offered an explanation. "Ya saw his clothes, ya touched them. Did they feel like somethin' a poor man would wear?" He looked at Kelly again, then continued, first quoting Rynearson's description. "He's tall, dark-haired, and rather good-lookin', and he was in the cove on the night we were ta meet him. But if that's not enough, then have a look at this." Unfolding his fingers, he held out the watch for Bevan to see. "I took it from his pocket."

A mixture of thoughts chased around in her head as she stared at the initials on the case, but one more than any of the rest made her ask, "Are ya sayin' he wouldn't have come alone? That he was supposed to have been with his uncle?"

"Aye," Ryan replied.

"But wouldn't they have gone ta the docks in Bray rather than anchor in the cove in such a storm?"

Ryan glanced at his older brother for help, since he really didn't have an answer.

"Knowin' what kind of man he is, I would have ta say he would," Kelly agreed. "He wouldn't have wanted ta get his fancy clothes ruined. But from the looks of the cove with all the debris, I'd say he ordered the ship ta drop anchor there and wait out the storm. Ya must remember, lass, he was riskin' a lot ta come here ta meet ya and he wanted ta keep it a secret."

"I suppose," Bevan relented, her gaze returning to her patient's handsome face.

"'Tis all we can do," Kelly stated, "until this lad regains his senses. He's the only one with the answers."

Tears began to burn Bevan's eyelids and she blinked as she turned away from the bed and crossed to the hearth to absently stoke the fire. "And if Rynearson is dead, than so is our father," she solemnly predicted.

"Not necessarily, lass." Ryan spoke up as he came to her side, touched her shoulder, and brought her around to face him. "'Twas what Shea and I were discussin' when ya overheard us. All of Rynearson's money *and* power will go ta his nephew as a result of his death. Just because the eldest is dead doesn't mean his kin won't be willin' ta help us. After all, we just saved his life." He bit his lower lip and dropped his gaze, wishing he didn't have to state the only other alternative they had. "And if he won't do it out of gratitude, then perhaps he'll do it for you."

Bevan's eyes lit up. "In exchange for me hand in marriage?"

"'Twas what we were thinkin'."

"Of course, ya were. After all, 'twas the reason he took this voyage . . . ta have a look at his potential bride. I'll have ta make him fall in love with me," she declared, more to herself than to anyone else in the room. "A man would do anythin' for the woman he loves." She tapped her chin with a fingertip and began to pace the floor, deep in thought. It seemed so easy to achieve when put so simply, but Rynearson had already told them that his nephew hadn't gotten married yet because he hadn't found the right woman. What made her think she could be the one he had been searching for all these years? Perhaps Rynearson had been wrong about his nephew. Maybe Graham *liked* not being married. Then what would they do?

Ryan had also been wondering what they would do if Graham refused to marry Bevan. "Well," he said, "I hope so. Because if it doesn't work, short of holdin' a gun ta his head, there's nothin' we can do. We can't force a man ta do somethin' he doesn't want ta do."

Suddenly an idea struck Bevan when the vision of her brother pointing a pistol at Graham's temple came to mind. Smiling gleefully, she asked, "Even if his life depended on it?"

The three brothers exchanged puzzled glances before returning their attention to their sister.

"England is holdin' our father prisoner, so why don't we hold one of her countrymen prisoner? If Graham wants ta be released, he'll have ta trade his freedom for Father's," she happily proposed. She could see the disapproval darken Ryan's eyes, but before he could open his mouth to object, she added, "Only as a last resort. We'll decide once we've had a chance ta talk with him. If he wants ta help because we saved his life, fine. If I have ta marry him ta get it done, that's all right, too. But whatever he decides, he's not leavin' here until he's helped us . . . with or without a gun pointed at his head."

"I think it's a grand idea," Shea announced with a grin that nearly matched his sister's.

"Ah, sure ya do," Kelly sneered as he gave his

younger sibling a slap on the shoulder. "Ya'd like nothin' better than starting a war between England and our homeland. Besides, it would never work."

"And why not?" Shea retorted, rubbing his bruised limb. "Do ya think the man would prefer livin' here with us for the rest of his life, when he could be livin' in a fine house with servants? Ya're crazy if ya do."

"I'm sayin' there isn't enough time. All he'd have ta do is outwait us. Father's execution is next week. Then we'd have no reason ta keep him."

That was an angle Shea hadn't considered. Neither had Bevan, but it didn't lessen her enthusiasm. "Maybe he doesn't know that," she countered. "And even if he did, we could change our threat. If Father dies, so does he."

"And who'll be his executioner, Bevan?" Kelly dared. "You? I certainly wouldn't do it, and I doubt Ryan would." He glared at the youngest brother. "This one might. He's foolish enough. But I suggest ya think of the repercussions, because ya very well could send your half-witted brother ta the gallows. Then where would we be? Further behind than ahead."

Bevan had a hot response for that one, but Ryan wouldn't let her singe her brother's ears with it.

"Enough!" he raged with one hand held out in front of him. "We're not even sure if his uncle is dead, so there's no use in callin' each other names. Besides . . ." He shifted his gaze to the man lying in the bed, then jabbed a thumb in that direction. "From the looks of him, we can't even be assured he'll live through the night. I can see from here that he's burnin' up with fever. So let's drop this conversation for now and take it one step at a time." He turned on his sister. "Bevan, you see that he gets well. The three of us will go back ta the cove as soon as the storm passes to look for clues that might tell us what happened to his uncle. Once that's done and we hear what our guest has ta say, *then* we'll figure out what ta do next. Understand?" His green eyes, so very much like Bevan's, glared at her while he waited for her nod. When he had it, he turned on Shea. More reluctant than his twin, Shea started to argue, cringed at the elbow Kelly jabbed in his ribs, and under duress, conceded.

With a jerk of his head, Ryan motioned for Kelly to escort Shea from the room. Once they had gone, he faced Bevan again. "I can't say your idea is totally without merit, lass, and if worse comes ta worse, maybe we will have ta threaten him. But rather than jump in before we see how deep it is, I'm goin' ta talk with Magee. Maybe the Society can think of somethin' else we can try." He studied her beautiful face for a moment, then impulsively reached up to touch her cheek. He honestly didn't believe they would have to resort to threats where Graham was concerned. One look at Bevan and any man would lay down his life for her. Dropping his hand away, he turned and left the room.

Pain wedged its way through his unconscious peace and brought him to the surface slowly, by degrees. Waves of burning heat seared his face and neck, his shoulders, chest and belly, and even his toes. His mouth was parched, his lips hurt to move them, and he felt as if he had sand under his eyelids. His ribs ached with every labored breath he took and the only excuse he could give for not assuming he was dead was that he doubted he'd be in as much agony if he were. Struggling to slip back into that quiet, black void where nothing could reach him, he turned his head away from the cool moisture touching his brow that only seemed to heighten his torment.

"Ryan!' he heard a sweet voice call out, and he fought to open his eyes. He'd been told there were angels in heaven, but since he'd already decided he wasn't dead, he wondered if he was merely waiting at the entrance gates, hearing some seraphic voice from within. If she looked anything close to the way she sounded, he would happily surrender to his destiny, even though he felt he was too young to depart this world just yet.

"What is it, Bevan?" a different voice asked, and he frowned. An angel named Bevan?

"I think he's comin' 'round," the celestial one replied.

And she certainly wouldn't be Irish! Not that the Irish didn't go to heaven, but he assumed everyone there would be one and the same, with nothing to set them apart. This was no angel he heard. Then who was she? And who was Ryan? The cool moisture touched his face again, and without even being aware of it, he moaned. The second he did, the thumping in his temples intensified to such a degree he thought his head would split in two and the fire that consumed his body raged higher. Blackness whirled about his tortured mind, and rather than fight the evils that pulled him down, he relaxed, half sleeping, half listening to the voices penetrating the murky fog around him and unaware that he had murmured the angelic name.

"Do ya still have any doubt?" Ryan asked as he stood

beside his sister's chair watching her bathe the man's fevered brow with a wet cloth. "He called your name. He has ta be Rynearson's nephew."

"I know," Bevan whispered, a slight frown wrinkling her brow. "I know." If she had had any doubt, it had vanished in that moment. It seemed more certain than ever that Graham's uncle had perished in the storm, and that their father's fate hung on their daring new plan. She felt Ryan's touch on her shoulder as a sign of encouragement, before he stepped into the next room where their brothers waited for news.

"Well?" Shea asked excitedly, rising from his chair. "Has he come to?"

"No." Ryan crossed to the hearth and the cup of tea he had set on the mantel. "But he called Bevan's name."

"He did?" Kelly said. "Then that must mean—"

"Aye," Ryan concurred. "Now all we have ta find out is what happened to his uncle."

"So what now?" Kelly finally asked when it seemed the silence among them outweighed the blast of the storm which continued its assault on the cottage.

Ryan had spent the last half hour contemplating that very question, and although he still wished there was some other way, he hadn't been able to think of one. Finishing off his tea, he set the cup back on the mantel. "Until someone comes up with somethin' better, somethin' that will work, we'll have ta concentrate our efforts on the nephew."

"What do ya mean . . . exactly?" Kelly posed.

"I'm not really sure," Ryan admitted, scowling. "I'd like to play on his sympathy—"

"I doubt he has any," Shea cut in. "He's probably just like his uncle. We'll have ta pay him ta help."

"Which means we'd be right back where we started," Kelly observed.

"Aye," Ryan nodded. "So we're left with no other choice. Once he comes 'round and we can see he isn't goin' ta willin'ly help us, then we'll have ta hold him prisoner and send a message to his family."

"His life for Father's," Kelly guessed.

"Aye," Ryan reluctantly admitted. "I'm not really fond of the idea, but I see no other way right now. I still plan ta speak with Magee as soon as I can ta let him know what's happened and ta ask if he can think of somethin' better, but until then . . ." He shrugged and let the statement go unfinished. "And remember, he's not ta leave the farm and no one's ta know he's here. Do ya agree?"

Both Kelly and Shea nodded.

"Good," he sighed. "Then I suggest we all get some rest."

Somewhere in the small hours of the morning, the worst of the gale passed and left in its wake a steady beating of rain against the small house. Its rhythmic sounds lulled everyone inside to sleep, including Bevan, though she had chosen the straight-back chair on which to rest rather than her bed. She would have preferred the comfort of a soft, feather mattress for an hour or so, but she knew she mustn't leave Graham's side until after the fever broke and he would sleep without thrashing around. He had stirred only once after calling her name and that was to murmur incoherently as he tried to push off the heavy quilt. His strength in such a vulnerable state amazed her, for it

68

had become a match of sheer determination between the two of them to see if he would lie with the quilt pulled up over his muscled frame or tossed on the floor. In the end, Bevan had won, but only because he gave up the struggle. He rested peacefully after that and had even allowed her to sponge his face and neck with cool water rather than turn away. Minutes stretched into an hour, the hour into several, while outside the tiny cottage another battle played out its fury, until all that was left was a soothing lullaby, and when she sat back to catch her breath, exhaustion had finally made its claim on her. Stiffling a yawn, she had closed her eyes and drifted off to sleep before she realized she had.

Sometime later, however, the sense that something was amiss jolted her awake, and she sat up with a start. Graham appeared to be sleeping comfortably, the house was quiet, and the thin rivulets of rain streaking the windowpane promised a calm sunrise. The fire in the hearth had nearly died out, and without giving her patient a second glance, she rose, crossed to the fireplace, and rekindled the flames.

A bright, yellow glow lay heavily against his closed eyelids. The sounds of someone moving about in the room teased his subconscious. The fire that had ravaged his body had lessened to a tolerable warmth, but the thumping in his head continued. He tried to concentrate on other things, and when he succeeded, the ache in his ribs brought back all the memories of how he had come to be in such a weakened, battered condition. He thought of the tempest and how the clipper ship had been caught in the storm. He remembered the sailor who had screamed in pain when the splinter of oak pierced his thigh and how he had tried so desperately to keep the young man from being washed overboard. He heard the howling wind, the crashing surf, and the thunderous moan of the vessel as it hit the rocks and exploded into hundreds of pieces. He could feel the wall of foamy water strike him, the agony he endured when it crushed him against the railing before the balusters broke and hurled him into the channel. The events after that were a jumbled kaleidoscope of images. He remembered fighting to pull himself to the surface for a gasp of air and how something in the water kept hitting him, his shoulders, back, and legs. The churning violence of the sea made it impossible for him to swim with any sense of direction, forcing him to ride the waves and pray they would carry him to shore, if indeed it was close enough to reach. Amid the blinding rain and salt water which stung his eyes, for a second he saw the rocky coast when a flash of light illuminated the black skies. The vision gave him hope and the strength to try. He remembered tearing his cloak from his shoulders, then his jacket to free his movements, and the cold, swirling water pulling him down. After that, his memory failed him except for the voices he had heard in his dreams. Someone had found him and had brought him in out of the storm. But what about the captain and his crew? Had they been spared? Struggling to clear his mind of the fog which threatened to plummet him back into a deep sleep, he opened his eyes and ignored the painful hammering in his temples while he focused on his surroundings.

The darkness beyond the window bore no hint of

morning, and for a moment he wondered how long he had been unconscious—a matter of hours, days, weeks? From the way he felt, it couldn't have been long at all. The heat of a warm fire drew his attention and he turned his head. The instant he saw the lithe form standing with her back to him at the hearth, he ceased caring. Flowing chestnut hair fell in a thick torrent down a slender back to a narrow waist and caught the golden highlights of the fire. Trim ankles and bare feet peeked out from beneath the hemline of a brown wool skirt, and even though he couldn't see her face, he imagined she was beautiful beyond his dreams.

Dreams, he thought, remembering the angel called Bevan and how much he had wanted to look at her. Could this be her? The one he had decided he would die for?

Wincing when he tried to rise up on one elbow, he closed his eyes until the wave of nausea passed and the pounding in his ears slowed its trip-hammer pace. The ache in his side made him dizzy, but he refused to give in to any of it as he pushed himself up. At that moment when the quilt slipped off his chest and puddled around his hips, he came to the shocking realization that he hadn't a stitch of clothing on. The idea of having been disrobed without his knowledge and by a woman he didn't even know discomfitted him. He grabbed the quilt and pulled it tight around his waist as he gingerly swung his feet to the floor and scanned the small room for his breeches. Failing that, he turned his frown on the woman.

"Would it be too much to ask what you've done with my clothes?"

The question brought a startled response from the

71

chestnut-haired beauty when the poker she held slipped from her fingers and clattered noisily to the floor before she could catch it. Wide, emerald green eyes with thick, black lashes shot around to gape at him, and the face he saw nearly took his breath away. Her beauty astonished him. The color of her creamy smooth skin was as delicate as a pearl. Softly arched brows complemented the shape of her eyes, the oval face, perfect little nose, and pink lips.

Firelight flickered in the hearth behind Bevan and alluringly caressed the strong features of the face looking back at her. Its golden glow touched his wide cheekbones, the full, sensuous mouth, the thick cords in his throat and the perfectly sculptured curve of his chest and shoulders. The smile, which parted his lips, revealed a flawless sparkle of white teeth, and when he moved to lean against the headboard, the ripple of iron thews down his belly drew more attention to the fact that he had nothing on under the quilt he let fall loosely around his hips than to the knowledge that she was studying every inch of that totally masculine body. His next comment, however, snapped her out of the paralyzing hold he had unknowingly inflicted upon her.

"You must be Bevan," he said as he ran long fingers through his black hair to sweep a defiant curl back off his brow. "I was beginning to wonder if I would ever get to meet you."

Shivering slightly at the deep resonance of his voice, she swallowed and managed to say, "Ya really shouldn't be sittin' up, Mr. Rynearson." She forced herself to bend and retrieve the poker from the floor. "Ya've taken a nasty blow ta your head and there's a chance ya broke a rib." Choosing not to look at him, she replaced the iron rod to its rack and added, "As for your clothes . . . they need a bit of mendin' and ta be washed before ya can wear them again. I'm sure Kelly won't mind loanin' ye a few of his things . . . if that's all right with you."

After she had left the room, he frowned. She had called him Mr. Rynearson, but for the life of him, he couldn't imagine why. His name was . . . A chill embraced him when it seemed a black void had invaded his memories. Closing his eyes, he swallowed hard and tried again. Nothing! All he could remember was the storm, the ship, and waking up here. His eyes came open and he quickly glanced around. But where was here? Unable to answer it for himself, he concentrated on the next question. Why had he been on the schooner? Again the answer evaded him. Then a thousand more. Sweet God in heaven, he didn't know who he was! Fighting the panic and helplessness that was closing in on him, he forced himself to think of his surroundings: the house, the girl, the things they'd said to each other. Then he remembered the faint voices he'd heard coming from the other room a while ago, bits and pieces of a conversation that hadn't included him, but that he feared was *about* him.

"If he won't help us . . . hold him prisoner."

"His life for Father's."

"No one's ta know he's here."

"He's not ta leave."

Good God, was it possible he'd been kidnapped and the girl's friends had been behind it? Was there something about him that made them think he could solve their problems? And what about Bevan? She didn't appear to be a threat, but how could he completely trust her when he didn't know the extent of their familiarity? Getting dressed and running off was out of the question. Where would he go? He'd be just as lost and just as ignorant as he was now, and in his weakened state, the others would catch up to him in no time at all. No, his only chance was to play along until he knew what they wanted. Then he'd have to concentrate on Bevan. Once he was sure he could trust her, he'd confide in her and ask her help. Until then, he'd keep quiet. He'd go along with whatever they asked of him . . . at least until he was strong enough to fight back.

Muffled voices from the other room lifted his gaze to the doorway and reminded him that earlier he'd heard Bevan call out to someone named Ryan. Her husband perhaps? A friend? He shrugged off the questions, knowing he'd have to let her tell him, since guessing would get him nowhere.

From the sound of it, Bevan and two or three others were about to join him. Wishing he had a pistol for protection, he shifted around on the bed for a more comfortable spot.

The room seemed to grow even smaller once Bevan and her three companions had filed in through the door, and the thought that he might not live out the night crossed his mind. The young man standing next to Bevan had the same hair coloring and green eyes as she and even the same bone structure and build, except that he was a few inches taller. He was probably her brother. To his left and standing a little ahead of the rest was a young man with dark hair and green eyes who gave off the impression that he was their spokesman. The third man was big and brawny; Reid would rather not take him on in a fight.

"Mr. Rynearson," Bevan began, unintentionally easing the strained silence, "I'd like ya ta meet me brothers. This is Shea." She nodded at the one closest to her. "And Ryan." She pointed to the one in the middle, then motioned at the tallest and biggest of the three. "And me oldest brother, Kelly."

Reid acknowledged the introduction with a nod. "I assume you are responsible for fishing me out of the channel?"

"Kelly spotted ya," Ryan confessed. "And lucky for you that he did. If ya had spent the night lyin' in that cold water, ya never would have lived ta meet Bevan." At Reid's puzzled expression, Ryan asked, "Didn't your uncle tell ya the reason for your trip?" He glanced at Kelly, then back at their guest. "He must have told ya. I heard ya call out for her while ya was thrashin' about. How else would ya have known her name?"

More confused than ever, but seeing an easy way for them to do the explaining, he decided to tell a half truth. "I heard *you* call her by name. And no, I was never told the necessity of this trip. Perhaps you'd fill me in, since my presence here seems to be of some importance." *It would be nice if you'd tell me who my uncle is, too,* he thought.

Ryan's brows dipped downward as he lowered his gaze in quiet consideration for a moment. Then, spying the garments his sister held in her arms, he took them from her and ordered her from the room with instructions to make some tea and a bowl of soup for their guest to eat. Once she had left them, he motioned for Kelly to shut the door behind her, while he approached the bed and laid the clothing on the mattress beside Graham.

"Are ya sure ya're strong enough ta get dressed?" Ryan inquired worriedly as he watched the man sort through the garments. "Ya still look a little flushed."

"I'm fine," he replied. "At least enough to be uncomfortable with only a quilt draped around me."

A spontaneous smile parted Ryan's lips, and out of respect for the man, Ryan turned away and went to the window to look outside, while the other donned the borrowed clothes and Kelly and Shea busied themselves with stoking the fire and lighting a candle.

Sliding the breeches up over his hips took more energy than he'd assumed it would, and the effort made him break out in a sweat. Light-headed, he eased back down on the bed and changed his mind about putting on a shirt for the time being. Although he couldn't remember ever having experienced a broken rib before, he was sure the pain couldn't have been much worse as he gingerly pressed his fingertips over the area. The throbbing in his head didn't bother him as much as his side, and he guessed that a good night's rest would work wonders. As for the fever that darkened his skin, he could already feel it beginning to lessen. In a day or two he'd be healthy enough to venture from his room and perhaps away from these brothers.

"Graham," he heard Ryan say. Was that his name? Graham Rynearson? And what else did they know about him?

"I'm sorry," Ryan quickly apologized. "I shouldn't be so bold—"

A raised hand stopped him from saying more. "Under the circumstances, you've a right to call me anything you'd like." He paused for a moment, wondering if he'd regret his next comment or if it might play to his advantage. "I believe I owe my life to you."

Ryan's green eyes glanced at his brothers, then lowered as he moved away from the window. "How much do ya know about us?" he asked solemnly as he sat down in the chair next to the bed.

Reid cocked a brow, cautious yet sensing these men weren't as evil as he'd first assumed. "Not even your last names, I'm afraid."

Surprise softened the lines in Ryan's face. "O'Rourke," he advised. "Our father's name is Patrick and he's the reason we asked your uncle's help."

"His help?" Reid repeated, puzzled. "To do what?"

"Get our father out of prison," Shea cut in as he and Kelly came to stand at the foot of the bed. "He's ta be executed next week."

"For what?"

"For takin' part in an uprisin' against the English Church and the rules set down upon us. They call us rebels, troublemakers, but we're not. We only want equality and a say in Parliament."

"And my uncle was willing to help?" he stated more than asked, since in his mind he couldn't understand why. Listening to himself talk, it was obvious he wasn't Irish, which meant his uncle wasn't either. So what interest could ol' Uncle Rynearson have in this family's problem? "He surely didn't offer out of kindness of his heart. What did he want in return?"

A tense silence fell over the brothers, and Graham could sense their reluctance to tell him.

"It concerns me," he provided. "That much is apparent. Well, I'm here . . . in your house . . . in debt to you. So tell me what my part is in all of this."

Even Ryan, the one who always spoke for the rest and never seemed to be at a loss for words, found it difficult to explain. Crossing to the hearth, he stared down at the glowing coals. A long moment passed before he turned back to look Reid in the eye. "Did anyone else stand a chance of survivin' the storm?"

Unaware of who Ryan meant specifically, Graham shook his head. "Why do you ask?"

"It means your uncle is probably dead."

Reid assumed the news should devastate him or at least be upsetting. But since he had no recollection of the man, he had no way of knowing how much his uncle had meant to him. More than that, however, he suddenly realized that Ryan had just told him an aspect of his arrival that Reid had failed to acknowledge. He had been traveling with his uncle, knew the ship sank, and never once asked where the man was. Feeling trapped, he struggled to push himself up from the bed and cross to the window Ryan had abandoned earlier. It would appear to those who watched that he was dealing with his grief, while in truth, he was figuring out an explanation to excuse his callousness.

It was apparent to Ryan that Graham hadn't come to their home looking for a potential bride. Even if he had, there was no way Ryan or his brothers or even Bevan could hold Graham to his uncle's part of the bargain, and they had been foolish to think that they could. And why should he help them? Who were they to him? Ashamed for having even considered it, he took a deep breath, willing to confess to everything, when Graham's question stopped him cold.

"How well did any of you know my uncle?"

"We only met him the one time," Ryan answered.

"And we didn't much like him," was Shea's added response, for which he received a thrust from the heel of Kelly's shoe against his shin.

Both replies were what Reid was hoping to hear. It meant that practically anything he said about his uncle would be taken as fact, since the O'Rourkes had no way of disproving it. Turning to face the three, he sighed, glanced at each man, and returned to sit down in bed again.

"You're not the only ones who didn't like him," he began, praying he'd never have to account for the story he was about to tell. "I didn't like him either, and I only came here with him out of respect to our family, since that's *all* he told me, that our trip concerned the family. To be quite honest, I didn't even think about him being on board the clipper with me and that he might have gone down with it. That's heartless, I know, but if you're not fond of someone, his welfare isn't exactly on the top of your list."

"We understand, Graham," Ryan assured him, mistaking the soft smile he received in return.

Curiosity drove Reid on. "However, the fact remains that my uncle made a deal and since he's no longer able to live up to it, suppose you tell me what it was. If I can, perhaps I'll take his place. After all, I do owe you my life."

A smile flashed across Shea's face and he started to say something when Kelly jabbed him in the side and cut short his chance. "Let Ryan tell it, Shea," the oldest warned. "He makes more sense than ya do." His comment awarded him a chilling look from his brother, but Kelly wasn't provoked by it. Shea was always making faces at him and had yet to back any of them up. He knew better.

"Yes, Ryan," Reid agreed. "Tell me. What did my uncle trade in exchange for his help? Money? Land? Servitude for the rest of your life?" He smiled crookedly and reached to don the shirt he'd been given. "It certainly had to be worth his while. He was always a businessman first, and seldom a humanitarian."

A soft rap on the door interrupted, and all eyes focused on the young woman who entered carrying a tray, but only one of the four men who watched her studied the gentle sway of her hips, the bare feet which tread noiselessly toward him, and the lush curves of her waist and bosom before his gaze lifted to the breathtakingly beautiful face haloed in thick, chestnut brown tresses with their coppery highlights. It was as if Reid were seeing her for the first time all over again, and he found himself hoping there wasn't a young lady waiting for him back home.

Chapter Three

The faint light of early dawn, its pinks, ambers, and aquas staining the dove gray of the sky outside the window, found Reid lying awake in his bed, his dark brows drawn tightly together and his mouth pressed in a hard line. The information that Lord Douglas Rynearson had agreed to help the O'Rourkes in exchange for Bevan's pledge to marry the man's nephew had taken Reid completely off guard and left him too numb to respond. It wasn't that the young woman wouldn't make a tempting choice—for any man—but her apparent lack of a dowery of any kind had confused Reid. Even Ryan's explanation about the lord's concern for his estate after he died and it was passed on to his nephew hadn't convinced him. He just couldn't imagine that a man of his uncle's apparent wealth and position would settle for just *anyone* to carry on the titled name. There had to be more to it than that, but until Reid's memory was restored, he'd have to go on wondering. And then there was Miss O'Rourke's willingness to wed a man she hadn't even met. Granted her father's life was at stake, but couldn't the O'Rourke family have found some other bargaining tool to use?

The sound of someone moving about in the kitchen intruded upon his thoughts, and believing it to be Miss O'Rourke as she prepared to make breakfast for her brothers and their guest, Reid pushed himself up and swung his legs off the bed. The moment his bare feet touched the floor, a chill darted through him and he shivered as he realized the fever which had owned him for the better part of the night had gone. Even the throbbing in his temples had vanished, which left him with a bruised side as the only reminder of his near fatal voyage across St. George's Channel. Straightening, he tested his sore ribs and winced at the sharp pain they caused him.

While lying in bed with his thoughts on the matter of Miss O'Rourke's foolish decision to wed, he had drawn his own conclusions on how his decision to keep quiet about his memory loss had put him in a difficult spot. If he set them straight now, they'd think he was playing some kind of cruel game with them or that he had changed his mind about helping them. Not so! He *wanted* to help. He just wasn't sure he had the power to free Patrick O'Rourke or how to go about it if he did. Yet aside from that, he had gotten the distinct impression from the brothers that in return for his help, they would abide by their part of the deal and he could have Bevan as his wife if he so decided. How could he decline without telling them the truth or hurting Bevan? Would they settle for the simple explanation he had given them earlier? That he owed them for saving his life? Would they let it go at that? These weren't imbeciles he was dealing with. They were smart, caring, desperate people, and to tell them suddenly that he's been lying all along and that he couldn't remember anything before the ship sank would come out sounding like an insult. Besides he still wasn't absolutely positive they wouldn't turn violent.

Disgruntled, he reached for the shirt he had left draped over the chair and spied the gold watch lying on the night stand next to it. Ryan had given him the piece of jewelry before he and the others had left him alone, saying that while Graham had lain unconscious on the beach, Ryan had found it in Graham's pocket after he'd searched his clothing for something with which to identify him. It no longer worked and the crystal was smashed, but Ryan had figured Graham would want it anyway since it probably meant something to him. It wasn't until that moment, when Reid held the timepiece in his hand and ran his thumb over the engraved letters, that he was struck with a flash of something from his past, a vague gnawing, an indistinct image. It eluded him before he had been able to fully grasp it, but the blur of recollection had raised a new and chilling thought. What if he wasn't Graham Rynearson? What if he'd been a thief on board the ship and had stolen the watch? Who was to say that wasn't what really had taken place?

The click of the doorlatch changed the course of his thoughts. Grabbing the shirt, he quickly donned it and haphazardly stuffed the tails into his breeches. He spun around to see the auburn-haired beauty enter. He noted the slight blush that rose in her cheeks under his gaze.

"I thought ta find ya sleepin'," her soft, mellifluous voice remarked. "You must be hungry. Shall I bring in a tray or would ya like ta eat in the kitchen?"

"The kitchen would be fine. I've caused enough inconvenience already, I'm afraid. Besides, I'd like to speak with your brothers."

"And they'll want ta talk ta you as soon as they get back," she replied. "They went down ta the cove ta see if . . ." She had obvious trouble in finishing her thought. "Ta see if anyone else survived the storm."

"There's no need to tiptoe around the possibility that my uncle is dead, Bevan. It's distressing news, of course, when one learns of the loss of a relative, but in my case, I wasn't that fond of him."

"No?" she said, surprised. "Why, then, did ya agree ta come ta Ireland with him? 'Twasn't ta meet me."

He smiled softly at her. "As I've already told your brothers, I came out of respect for my family. And now that we've met, I'm very glad I did." He stared long and hard into her eyes, those soft, alluring pools of emerald green. Then, wincing, he stood and reached for the jacket hanging on the chair finial, and donned the garment with a minimum of movement. "I hope I didn't give everyone the wrong impression last night after Ryan told me what my uncle had in mind for us. I didn't say anything right then because—to be quite honest—I was stunned . . . for several reasons." He fell silent for a moment to weigh his words. "First, I was surprised by how much my uncle had taken for granted. How could he have been so sure we would like each other? Then I got to thinking about the sacrifice *you'd* made and I . . ."

Suddenly the room in which they stood, the one with a bed in it, started to close in on him, and without a thought, he took Bevan's arm and guided her out through the door. "Please don't misunderstand," he continued as they entered the kitchen and he took a seat at the table while Bevan crossed to the hearth and the kettle of hot water hanging on the peg. "You're a very beautiful woman and any man would be honored to have you at his side, but there's more to marriage than that. Or there should be," he added as an afterthought when a vague feeling came over him that for some reason he should be paying close attention to what he said, that somewhere in his past he had offered the same piece of advise to someone else or that *he* had been the recipient.

The scent of freshly washed skin and hair, crisply starched clothes, and fragrant tea penetrated his thoughts and brought him out of his musings. Smiling at the young woman who stood at his elbow pouring him a cup of tea, he forced himself to concentrate on what he'd been saying. "Whatever my uncle was thinking or his reason behind it is something we'll probably never know now. But as Ryan said, the man wanted me wed and thought that my meeting you, I would change my mind about living alone." He frowned, straining his memory for the answer. When nothing stirred, he sighed. "I suppose it would have to do with a promise he made my father."

Bevan gave him a strange look. "I thought Lord Rynearson said your parents were dead."

A rush of total aloneness filled him. Wasn't there anyone left who could help him remember? A brother? A sister? He blinked away the desperation creeping over him, and focused on a suitable response to Bevan's statement. "They are. What I meant was that it was my father's wish I wed and my uncle simply took over hounding me."

The explanation seemed to satisfy her. "So ya're sayin' ya came not knowin' your uncle had dragged ya along with him because he'd already made a deal that involved your future," she stated as she filled a plate with a generous helping of scrambled eggs, crisp fried potatoes, and a thick slice of bread.

"That's right," he said aloud. "And in a way I'm glad he didn't. I might not have come if he had." He smiled warmly at her, at the blush he saw rise in her cheeks, and went on, "Hearing your brother tell it was a bit of a shock. I couldn't imagine a girl like you being unmarried in the first place. Then to hear you agreed to marry a stranger before you even laid eyes on him . . . well, that left me speechless." He thanked her for the food she set down in front of him and began to sample the mouth-watering fare, missing the odd way she looked at him.

"Where are ya from, Graham Rynearson?" she asked just as he popped the first forkful into his mouth.

He chewed, gulped, and frowned. "From?"

"'Tis obvious ya're no Englishman," she went on. "Ya sound like a Colonial. I noticed the first time ya spoke, but never thought ta ask until now."

Was this a trap? Had his uncle already given her the answer? A full account of his history? He smiled lopsidedly and took a drink of his tea. "Why do you ask? Did my uncle tell you I lived in England?" He watched her ease her slender frame into the chair opposite him and lean forward against her folded arms resting on the table's edge. It took every ounce of willpower he had to focus his attention on her face rather than on the rounded bosom straining to spill out over the low neckline of her ivory-colored blouse.

"He never said. I just assumed ya lived in England. Are ya sayin' ya don't?"

Without thinking, he said, "I own property in North Carolina."

"North Carolina?"

Where had that come from? Yet somehow Reid knew it to be true. "Yes. North Carolina is on the East Coast of the United States."

"Oh," Bevan murmured, then fell quiet for a moment while she watched him eat. "Does that mean ya're a farmer?"

"Sort of," he replied, more knowledge surfacing in his mind as he washed down his breakfast with a long sip of tea. "I'm a planter. There's a difference."

She raised a reddish-brown, finely arched brow. "Oh? How so?"

"Well," he sighed, frowning and falling back in his chair, "the only livestock one has on a plantation are a few horses, some chickens and geese, and an ox or two to pull the wagons. Tobacco, cotton, and the like are the chief crops and source of income, and the difference between a farmer and a planter is that a planter tells others what to do rather than do it himself."

"Ya mean ya don't like ta get your hands dirty," she observed, her head tilted accusingly to one side.

Had a man intimated he was lazy or worse a dandy, Reid was sure he would have been angered by the comment. He fashioned himself to be a hard worker even though he had no proof of it. He supposed a plantation required a lot of paperwork—most large businesses would—but he also felt he would never enjoy it, that if he were given a choice, he'd probably prefer working outside in the sun. Of course, he had no way of knowing for sure if that was a part of his character or not, and neither would Bevan O'Rourke . . . for several reasons.

Smiling softly, he leaned to wrap his hands around the teacup sitting on the table in front of him, his gaze absently studying the pale brown liquid inside as he decided to voice the logic he'd just gone over in his head. "I doubt I've ever been afraid of hard work, Bevan. It's just that a large plantation requires a great deal of book work. If I had a choice, I'm sure I'd rather strip to the waist and lend a hand planting crops or clearing a field or building a new barn." He paused a moment, envisioning the sight. "There's something about actually being able to *see* your accomplishments that gives you the kind of reward you can't get any other way. I'd guess your brothers would understand what I mean."

He glanced up then to find her fair face touched with a light blush, and he concluded that perhaps she was feeling ashamed of what she had implied. Unbeknownst to him, however, she was imagining him stripped to the waist, the broad back and rippling muscles gleaming a golden hue in the midday sun, the sweat dotting his brow, and those magnificent arms flexing with the labor he'd taken on. She had accused him of choosing the easy life, but she had known even before she voiced her opinion that it wasn't true. A man who sat around all day would be pale-complexioned and thin. Graham was hardly that. Suddenly aware that she had been staring at him, she quickly reached for his empty plate and rose to fix him a second cup of tea. As she watched him drink it, she silently vowed not to let her imagination run away with her again. Yet as he lifted the dark piece of clay pottery to his mouth, her eyes followed the movement, and she was suddenly struck with the desire to learn what it would feel like to have his lips pressed against hers. Blinking, she forced her gaze elsewhere while she asked, "Your uncle said you were in England to visit. Were you planning to stay long?"

Reid smiled warmly as he set the cup down and looked across the table at her. "I am now."

Bevan was hoping he'd say that he was, but his actual reply brought a stinging heat to her face again. She laughed nervously and rose to busy herself with cleaning the kitchen, while she inwardly prayed her brothers would return soon to distract her from her wayward thoughts. No other man, certainly not Aidan Galloway, whose farm ran adjacent to the O'Rourkes' and who had expressed his fondness for Bevan many times, had ever stirred such emotion in her, and she couldn't understand the difference. Aidan, though still a tall, willowy youth of a score and one, was quite sought after by all the other young, available lasses in the county. They saw him as a virile, handsome prospect for marriage. Bevan saw him as clumsy and shy, and not quite a man full grown—in the physical sense as well as in his thoughts and ideas. She liked him, but he never set her blood on fire. Why? What made him different from this Colonial?

She decided to go outside for a breath of fresh air to clear her head. Without comment, she grabbed the wicker basket from the floor and exited the house. She always seemed to do her best thinking while gathering eggs. Shivering in the cool, early morning air, she crossed the back yard to the chicken coop and shakily opened the door to step inside. The smell of hay and the cackling of hens greeted her. A stream of gray light filtered in through the single window and from the doorway behind her, and she quickly set about her task, ignoring the disgruntled noises from the feathered creatures who objected to being disturbed and the sharp peck on the back of her hand from a more active protester. It was silly of her to allow her feelings for Graham Rynearson to overpower her. He'd practically admitted that he'd been tricked into coming to their farm. He wasn't in the market for a bride and Bevan wasn't really looking for a husband. It had been a condition to the bargain she and Graham's uncle had made. Now it seemed apparent Lord Rynearson could never hold up his end of the deal, so marrying the man's nephew no longer mattered. And once Graham had fully recovered from his injuries, he would return to his home in the United States . . . to North Carolina, he had called it.

Seized by an overwhelming desire to cry, Bevan closed her eyes and hugged her basket to her as she leaned heavily against the wall, unaware of the shadow which filled the square shaft of light falling through the open doorway. Nor did she notice how the hens had started their angry protest all over again when a second unwanted visitor intruded into their domain. Only the sense that she wasn't alone pulled her out of her self-imposed misery, and with a start, she jerked upright and spun around to find him standing so very close.

Reid interpreted the droop of her shoulders, her silence, her need to be alone, as meaning she felt the despair of her situation, that without his uncle there was no hope of saving her father from execution. He had placed himself in her position and imagined the pain she endured, knowing that the feeling of hopelessness was almost too much for anyone to bear, and he had wanted to comfort her, to tell her he would do whatever he could to help.

Reaching out, he took the basket from her and set it aside, while his other hand gently brushed her cheek then slipped around to cradle the nape of her neck and pull her close. He intended only to hold her, to soothe her fear with comforting words and a promise that things weren't as bleak as they seemed. But in that same moment when her soft, green eyes, sparkling with unshed tears, lifted to look into his, his heart melted and his passion soared, and he wanted to do more than just act as a friend. Unable to hold back or to tell himself how wrong he was for taking the advantage, he started to lower his head, then paused and pulled his gaze from those tempting pink lips to look into a sea of emerald green trimmed in dark lashes. He saw no objection there, in fact a burning desire for him to continue, and the thought that perhaps he should hold back never entered his mind again as he kissed the young beauty who had hypnotized him.

It was an explosive kiss. He could smell the sweet scent of her—her skin, her hair, her clothes. He could feel her slender body molded against his own. The taste of her, the warmth of her lips on his, quickened his pulse, and he knew that this kiss was not enough, could never be enough. He wanted to draw her inside him, to be as one, to breathe the same breath, think the same thoughts, burn with the same emotions. He wanted to lay her down on the soft bed of straw at their feet and claim the sweet fury of her passion.

The tears she had felt burning her lids became tears of joy and slipped defiantly over the rim of her lashes to trail a moist path down her cheeks. Ryan had told her that her first kiss would be an experience to compare with nothing else in her life and he had been right. She felt hot and cold at the same time. She was scared and excited, safe and calm, giddy and self-assured all in the same moment. Yet what thrilled her more than the feel of Graham's hard, masculine body curved around her own was the knowledge that *his* desires matched hers. He had wanted this to happen. He had followed her from the house, sought her out, and caught her up in his arms without an ounce of regret. The feelings she'd guessed she had seen in his gray eyes had been real. He wanted her as much as she wanted him, and that glorious discovery took her breath away. Surely from now on, everything about her world would be filled with immeasurable happiness. Surely Graham Rynearson would see to that.

Cupping her tiny face in his hands, Reid kissed her with a driving eagerness to possess her. He slanted his head and parted her lips with his tongue while his hot breath fell against her cheek. He felt her hands slip beneath the jacket he wore and slide along his sides to his back, where her slim fingers clutched at the cotton cloth of his shirt as she hugged him to her. Her firm, round breasts teased the taut muscles across his chest and stirred a fire that all but consumed him. Ignorant of everything around them, he slid one hand down her spine to her buttocks and pulled her hips close against his aching loins while his kisses grew fierce and savage. He desired her more than any woman he had ever known and he wanted her right now . . . here on a bed of straw with feathered fowl observing.

Suddenly a sound disturbed his world, a rattling of steel and wood, of hooves against the muddied earth and the murmur of voices. Reluctantly he pulled his lips from hers. "We have company," he murmured, stepping back and allowing a frosty rush of morning air to brush his fevered face. He lifted Bevan's egg basket and handed it back to her, then he took her elbow and led her outside into the yard.

The warmth that had crowded every corner of Bevan's being quickly vanished with the rough entrapment of her arm. The look in his eyes, the coldness of his tone, and the stiff, angry manner in which he treated her chilled every wonderful thought she had about him. She wanted to believe he was merely abashed by the untimely interruption of her brothers, but embarrassment had nothing to do with his reaction. Their presence had simply brought him to his senses. He had had a change of heart once he had been forced to recognize what he was doing, and his near slip had enraged him. Well, if the kiss meant so little to him, then it would mean nothing to her. Yet as the bright cheerful rays of sunlight hit her face, she had to blink back the moisture brimming in her eyes.

Ryan, Kelly, and Shea climbed down from the two-wheeled cart. That could only mean there had been no other survivors from the clipper ship, a fact that Reid could not but regret, although it did make it easy to continue his charade.

"Graham?" he heard Ryan call out to him once the brothers had spotted him and Bevan near the hen-house. "So y'are well enough ta be up and about?"

93

"I'd say he's well enough for more than just that," Kelly quietly observed.

"What do ya mean?" Ryan turned a questioning glance his way as he motioned for Shea to tend the donkey and cart. He wasn't sure, but he suspected this wasn't something Shea should hear. Even though Shea fought continually with his twin, he was very protective of her reputation. They all were. It was just that Shea normally used his fists in her defense rather than reasoning and words, and he oftentimes reacted before knowing the whole story. Ryan could hardly be called passive, but at least he gave a man the benefit of the doubt before he responded, and he'd continue that practice right now as he asked Kelly to be a little more specific.

"Are ya sayin' ya never got caught kissin' a sweet, young lass, me sainted brother?" Kelly chaffed with a smile as he watched the couple walk toward them. "Or do ya think the basket was too heavy for Bevan to carry by herself?"

Ryan wanted to respond but the presence of the couple as they came near prevented it. Instead he turned to address the man who held his sister's arm, his gaze shifting from that one to Bevan and back again as he fought the desire to ask if Kelly's claim was true. Yet the more he studied the faces of the pair, the more certain he became of the answer, and he was plagued with conflicting thoughts. Graham had acted improperly, yet not a few hours ago it had been Ryan himself who had suggested he and his brothers give the couple as much time alone together as possible. Now that it had come about, he disapproved, and he didn't know why. He liked Graham and that had nothing to do with his being related to Lord Rynearson. Diverting his thoughts away from the subject for the moment, he concentrated on other, more important matters.

"We searched the cove, Graham," he said, "and we found nothin' other than debris from the ship. I'm sorry, but it looks like your uncle never made it. No one did."

"I had guessed as much once I saw that you were alone." After a moment of regret for the lost lives, Reid said, "It appears that we've been left to trust our own ingenuity, my friends, and we haven't much time to decide." He nodded toward the house, indicating they should all go inside, and he gently took Bevan's elbow again. Once they were seated around the kitchen table and Bevan had brought the quill and paper he requested, he slid the items across the smooth, wood surface toward Ryan and waited until Shea had joined them, too. "I need a diagram of the prison where your father is being held."

"What for?" Kelly asked, confused. "Ya're not thinkin' ta break him out, are ya?"

"Not unless you have a better idea," he challenged. "I know I said that perhaps I could take my uncle's place, but I spoke too soon . . . before I knew all the conditions. I'm sure you assume I have wealth and some influence in the States, but that won't do us any good here. Nor would I have enough money with me or a way of obtaining a sizable amount in time to stop the execution. I'm as helpless as all of you. What I can offer is a plan and my pledge to take part in it."

"Ya mean ya'd carry a gun and attack the prison with us?" Shea questioned.

Reid couldn't stop the chuckle Shea's assumption

provoked. "Figuratively speaking, yes. I do intend to go armed, but not in the way you described. If we know the exact cell in which your father is being held, as well as a layout of the prison, how many guards there are, and what time they are relieved, when meals are served, and if the prisoners are allowed visitors and at what time—"

"Ya can gain access without suspicion," Ryan cut in, a broad, approving smile on his face. "Ya can pretend ta be someone ya aren't and when the chance is ripe, ya'll walk out with him."

"Right under their noses!" Kelly joined in, laughing.

Reid wished he could share their enthusiasm. It sounded simple but it wasn't, and he told them so . . . at least the part about walking out with their father. He'd gotten quite good at pretending.

"I can draw a general outline of the prison," Ryan promised as he took the quill and began sketching a crude replica. "But we'll have ta rely on the Society ta supply the rest."

"The Society?" Reid repeated, thinking that the fewer who knew about the plan, the better. Its success would depend on surprise.

"Ya can trust the Society," Ryan explained as if he'd read his companion's thoughts. "It's made up of men like us. Not a one in this family wouldn't trust their lives with them."

"I hope you're right," Reid answered. "It just might come down to that." He frowned and added, "And that includes my own."

The excitement everyone felt ebbed with these words. They were willing to do anything for their father and the thought of dying didn't frighten them if it meant their father would be spared. Patrick O'Rourke wouldn't agree, of course. Nor would he approve of an outsider putting his life on the line for a cause that didn't concern him.

"Mr. Rynearson," Shea began, "Why are ya doin' this? Ya're under no obligation ta us."

"For two reasons, I guess," he admitted after a pause. "For one, I owe my life to all of you, and if I'm able to help give you back your father's, we'll be even." The second and more difficult to state came slowly. "I don't want you to think I'm judging you—I probably would have done the same thing had I been in your place—but I'm doing this for Bevan as well. She should have the right to choose who she wishes to marry and not because she's forced into it."

It may have sounded very noble to the others, but Reid knew he was being selfish. He wanted Bevan free of her obligation to marry him in return for his help. That way after he'd settled his uncle's estate in England and he'd learned the truth about himself, he'd be absolutely sure she loved him when he proposed later and she said yes.

Reid was instructed at the unyielding insistence of the O'Rourke boys to lie down for a part of the morning while they visited members of the Society to gather up the information he needed. He hadn't realized, until three hours later, how tired he truly was, and that a short nap would turn into a long one or how rested and alert he would feel once he awoke.

Afterward, in the kitchen, he and Bevan were once again alone together.

"Feel better?" she asked, turning back to the table where she had been rolling out the dough for her apple pie. "Ya have more color in your cheeks than ya did earlier."

"Yes, thank you, I do feel better," he replied, crossing to the hearth to make himself some tea. With cup in hand he went to the table where she worked and sat down on the tall wooden stool. Judging from the way the sunlight fell into the room through the open back door, he guessed it was close to noon, and Bevan still looked as fresh and appealing as she had at first light. More so, if that were possible. Noticing a spot of flour on the tip of her nose, he chuckled.

"What do ya find so amusin', Mr. Rynearson?" she asked without looking at him, her smooth, flawless brow furrowed and her tone sharp.

Reid didn't miss the icy edge to her question. He reached for a towel lying near his elbow and held it out to her. "You have flour on your nose."

A warm blush stung her cheeks, but rather than look at him or take the proffered piece of linen from his outstretched hand, she roughly brushed away the mark on her nose with her fingertips and resumed her task.

"Would you rather I wait outside for your brothers?"

"Ya can wait wherever ya want, Mr. Rynearson," she snapped. "It makes no difference ta me."

"Now what could I have done to annoy you? I don't like having you angry with me."

"Don't ya now?" she rallied, her spine ramrod straight, her arms akimbo, and her green eyes flashing sparks that seemed to bore fiery holes right through him. "And when did ya start carin' how I felt? Before or after ya kissed me?" She quickly raised a hand

and added, "Don't bother answerin'. I already know which it is. Ya're thinkin' I'm some trollop ya can have your way with while ya're here, then forget about with no trouble atall once ya're back home in North . . . North . . ." The name eluded her.

"Carolina," he supplied, fighting his smile.

"Aye." Her bright coppery curls bounced then shimmered red-gold in the sunlight. "In North Carolina. Well, I'm here ta say, Mr. Rynearson, ya've got me all wrong. I'll not bed down with a man unless he's me husband. And ya're right about sayin' *I* should get ta do the pickin'. I should. *I will.* And it won't be a man all grand and proper with rich clothes and too much land he can't farm himself. I'll marry a poor lad who'll think he's blessed ta have a hardworkin', strong-willed lass like meself standin' at his side."

She might not have realized her tirade had, in a roundabout way, revealed what was on her mind, but it had. She was having trouble justifying her earlier willingness to let him kiss her. She was even feeling guilty and embarrassed. More than that, she didn't want him to think she was free with her affections.

"Is there such a man in your life, Bevan?" he quietly asked.

"Aye." She smiled sarcastically at him. "There is. His name is Aidan Galloway, and he's talked ta me father about courtin' me several times."

"And yet he hasn't," Reid guessed. When she wouldn't respond, he asked, "Why not, Bevan?"

Thinking their conversation had gone on long enough, she turned to finish with her pie.

"May I tell you why?" he posed, then continued when she ignored him. "Because nothing about him

99

excites you. Yes, he can offer a secure sort of life with the comforts of food, a roof over your head, and a warm fire on a cold winter night. But nothing more. Before you realize it, your life will have slipped away and you'll be sitting in a rocker in front of the hearth wondering what it was you missed out on. You're really looking for a man who will keep you guessing, one who will chase you around the house even after your hair has turned gray, whose kiss will still spark a flame in you when you're too crippled to run anymore." He smiled softly as he leaned an elbow on the table and tilted his head to get a better view of her face. "And you know how I know that, Bevan?"

"I'm sure ya'll tell me," she scoffed as she lined the pie plate with the dough.

"Because it's the same way I feel about marriage." The amusement which had curled his mouth disappeared and he dropped his gaze. "I hadn't realized it until I met you."

"Oh, please," she moaned acidly as she dumped the bowl of sliced apples in the tin and sprinkled sugar and cinnamon over them. "Spare me your sweet words, Mr. Rynearson. Believe it or not, I've heard them all before."

The smile returned and he reached up to run his thumb along his lower lip. "No doubt you have," he said. "But were any of them serious when they said it?"

She cocked an auburn brow at him and lowered her chin challengingly. "And *you* are?"

Reid straightened. "Why do you find that so difficult to believe?"

"Oh, I don't know," she jeered as she laid the second crust over the pile of apples and fluted the edges with her thumb and finger. "Maybe because I've heard it so many times before, from so many different kinds of men, that I'm a little skeptical. Suppose ya tell me why I should believe you."

Reid shrugged then watched the gentle sway of her hips as she turned away and carried her pie to the oven. "When you put it like that, I guess there really is no reason why you should. We've only known each other for a few hours. Maybe I was thinking my kiss might have convinced you. You can tell a lot about a person by the way he kisses."

Bevan didn't bother to look at him. "I believe ya can tell more *after* he's kissed ya."

"Such as?"

She closed the oven door and straightened up while she wiped her hands on her apron. "Such as whether or not it was a true expression of one's feelin's. Take you, for example. Ya went from warm and gentle, demandin' I would say, ta cold and angry. Without sayin' a word, ya said more in your behavior than if ya'd recited half the Bible."

"Cold and angry?" The discovery that that was how she had viewed his reaction amazed him. "I wasn't angry, Bevan. We were interrupted and—"

"And ya're glad we were."

"No!" he rallied, leaving the stool to grab her elbow when she started to walk away. "If anything, I was embarrassed . . . for *you*. I was worried what your brothers would think or do if they caught us." He sighed heavily. "I was actually sort of thankful they had come home when they did because—"

"I'm sure ya were."

"*Because,*" he said again, tightening his grip when

101

she tried to pull away, "if they hadn't, I would have made love to you right there in the henhouse."

The declaration tickled her stomach and shortened her breath. Flustered, she forced herself not to look at him.

"And before you put words in my mouth again, let me say yes, I would have regretted it afterward. But not for selfish reasons or for whatever reason you might think. I would have felt guilty for taking advantage of you when I know there's no telling what the future will bring."

His last comment stabbed at her heart, and she blinked repeatedly to hold back the rush of tears that suddenly burned her throat. There was a hidden meaning to what he said and she feared what it might be. "No one knows that," she quietly replied. "If we did, we wouldn't take chances."

He seized her other arm and drew her around to face him, longing to speak the truth and knowing he couldn't. He didn't want to see the softness in her eyes turn hard when he told her that there was a chance his future didn't include her. "There are things about me that prevent me from making a commitment, aspects I must investigate before I can even consider spending the rest of my life with you. Once I'm sure nothing can stand in the way of our happiness, I'll be free to ask your brother's permission to court you."

Oddly, the mystery behind his confession sparked a spiteful vein in her. "Does insanity run in your family?" she asked, her tone icy yet filled with pain. "Or perhaps ya've already found the lass ta stir your blood and ya needed the time, a diversion ta help ya decide."

"Yes, I've found such a woman," he quickly

102

admitted. "In you. God, Bevan, if only my problem were as simple as insanity, I'd risk the chance of going crazy just to spend one night with you." He gave a short, derisive laugh. "The irony of it is that I'm sure I *will* go crazy if I'm denied the chance."

"Then what other reason could there be?" she demanded, her eyes filling with unshed tears. "A wife? Is that your secret?" She shook her head in answer to her own question. "Ya would have shared such news with your uncle." Her chin trembled but she raised it bravely to accuse, "A lass heavy with your child demandin' ya marry her and out of honor ya're obliged."

He started to deny it and couldn't. He'd walked into her life not knowing who he was or where he came from. How could he deny anything? Filled with pain, he slowly, absently shook his head, a gesture Bevan mistook for his answer.

"Then what, Graham Rynearson?" Sparkling tears fell hotly down her cheeks. "Am I not good enough for a man with wealth and fine clothes? Are ya afraid I'd shame ya?"

"Never!"

"Then what?"

The question hung in the air like an early morning mist waiting for a bright ray of sunshine to chase it away. But once again, the arrival of Bevan's brothers interrupted them.

"Did ya sleep well, Graham?" Ryan asked as he and Shea came into the house, their arms loaded down with papers, ledgers, and scrolls tied with ribbon.

"Yes, thank you," Reid replied with a lame smile. "From the looks of things, I'd say your trip was successful."

"Aye, that it was." Ryan grinned as he dumped the items on the kitchen table, tossed his hat aside, and took the scarf from around his neck. "I have all ya'll need, and the promise of any and all who can help. I'd not be tellin' ya a lie ta say our father is respected among the Society and that very same will do whatever ya ask of them, be it great or small, since the lot of them feel responsible for the man's plight." As he pulled out a chair on which to sit, he looked at his sister and asked, "Would ya be so kind as ta fix your poor brother a cup of tea with a touch of the spirits in it? I fear I've taken a chill." He glanced at Graham. "Would ya care for one yourself, Graham?"

Reid declined the offer then moved to the table, where he stood looking over the diagrams, notes, and charts Ryan had spread across the surface. When Graham had made his suggestion that they form some kind of scheme to get him inside the prison, he had known whatever they planned wouldn't be easy. But now that he saw the size of the building with its numerous corridors and cells and the tall stone fence surrounding it, he wondered if he'd raised the O'Rourkes' hopes when he shouldn't have. Absently lowering himself into a chair, he asked Shea for the list of guards and gave a low, disappointed whistle to learn how staggering the number was. His task grew even more complicated as he read that there was no set pattern to the serving of meals, visitors were allowed in at only one time during the day, and that day came once a week. Even then, if he were to get to Patrick O'Rourke, the cell door remained locked while prisoner and friend conversed through the barred window in the thick, metal barrier. One set of keys to

104

all the cells stayed with the warden in his office, and the man saw no one without an appointment and only then if requested by King George himself, a point Reid voiced aloud.

"That's really no problem," Shea encouraged as he searched through the stack of parchments in front of him, selecting one and handing it over. "Connie McFee can pen ol' George's signature without a flaw."

"That's fine, Shea," Reid replied, chuckling. "But what about the royal seal?"

"Ya mean like this?" Shea's smile had an impish twist to it as he dug in his pocket and withdrew a brass object.

Reid studied it a moment, then laughed. "Where did you get this?"

"Ya don't want ta know," the boy promised.

"Maybe not," Reid speculated, "but I would like to be assured it will pass for the real thing."

Shea's eyes took on a devilish glint as he guaranteed, "Oh, that it will."

"Because it is," Reid guessed, his dark brows raised as he looked at the young man with new respect . . . for him, his brothers, and their associates. "If ol' George had had the likes of you on his side, the United States would still be under British rule, friend."

Hearty laughter filled the kitchen. Reid appraised the King's seal a moment longer than handed it back to Shea. "I'm not sure if we'll need it or not, but just in case we do, keep it safe."

"I intend ta sleep with it," Shea announced.

"He might as well," Kelly added as he entered the kitchen after driving the donkey cart into the barn. He crossed to the hearth to warm his hands. "I doubt he'll ever have anythin' else ta share his bed."

"Oh, and ya're a fine one ta talk, Kelly O'Rourke!" his youngest brother countered. "Ya're past the marrin' age and I don't see ya settin' up a house of your own. But then what lass in her right mind would want ya?"

"I believe," Kelly bantered in defense, "it's because no woman in her right mind would want ta have *you* as an in-law."

Insulted, Shea started to respond, but Ryan cut him off. "'Tis good ta hear we all still have a sense of humor," he said, "but now is not the time or place. We've got work ta do and a short while ta do it." He leaned his arms against the table and looked across the cluttered surface at Graham. "So what do ya think? Have we a chance of gettin' ta our father?"

Reid shrugged circumspectly. "I'm sure there's a way to get to him," he replied. "That part should be easy. It's getting him out that may cause trouble." He picked up the list of guards' names and studied the tally for a moment, noting that the majority of those enrolled were of Irish background. "Is there some way of knowing if the warden or any of the guards have ever had any dealings with my uncle? Would they recognize him to see him?"

Ryan glanced at one brother then the other and said, "We can find out for sure, I suppose."

"Then do so," Reid instructed. "I also want you to find out if he had already been in contact with the warden in regard to freeing your father. I don't want to walk in there making an announcement that's already been made."

"Then ya have an idea," Ryan suggested hopefully.

Reid's brow furrowed as he slowly laid down the

paper. "Maybe. But I'll need time to think about it." He shifted his gaze on Shea. "How long before the prisoners are allowed visitors?"

"Four days."

Reid grimaced disappointedly. "Doesn't give me long to work out the details." He fell back in his chair with his arms folded over his chest and one hand stroking his chin. A moment passed, then, "Aside from the men who gave you this information, how many others know I'm here?"

"No one," Kelly advised as he came to the table, swung a chair around, and straddled the seat.

"Then let's keep it that way," he instructed. "And one more thing." He turned to Shea. "I want you to check with your neighbors and the people of Bray and perhaps the docks at Dublin. I know you've already said there isn't much hope that my uncle survived the storm, but we must be absolutely sure. If I lived through it, so might he have. There were other ships in the Channel that night. One of them might have fished him out of the water, and I can't have him making a sudden appearance that would contradict my story."

The others agreed and Shea hurriedly left to do as Reid asked of him. Ryan, deciding it was his place to talk with the Society members about any prior inquiries to the warden from Rynearson, asked his sister to pack him a meal he could take with him. He was hungry and didn't want to waste the time eating it there. While she prepared the basket, Kelly and he discussed what chores had to be done around the farm that day, and Reid lost himself in thought.

The success of whatever scheme he came up with would all depend on the accuracy of men he didn't even know. Instinct warned him of the foolishness of such a venture since by all rights he wasn't honestly sure he could trust the O'Rourkes. One slip, just one person who pretended loyalty, and Reid would wind up in jail right alongside Patrick O'Rourke. The vision of a very proud man with snow white hair, strong jaw, and intense green eyes came to mind as Reid pictured the eldest O'Rourke. For some unknown reason he guessed Patrick to be shorter than any of his sons, stocky, a lover of good Irish whiskey, and hot-tempered . . . determined to a fault when defending a cause in which he believed. No one had mentioned the man's wife and Reid had to assume she was dead. He also figured Mrs. O'Rourke had been the peacemaker in the family, the one who had held the silent strength among them.

The squeal of Ryan's chair as he slid it away from the table brought Reid around.

"Well, I'm off," that one announced. "I'll speak with Magee first, and if he can't give us an answer, I'll keep askin' until I get one." He squinted at Reid. "And *you,* me friend, had better go back ta bed. Some might say ya have a hard head for takin' on the kind of risk ya've cut out for yourself, but that has nothin' ta do with that lump ya're sportin'. Take it easy for the next day or two."

"I'm much better, thank you," Reid argued. "Besides, you said it yourself. There's a lot to do and little time to do it."

"Well, limit yourself," Ryan urged. "Ya won't be doin' any of us any good if ya make yourself so sick ya can't get out of bed." He reached for his hat and scarf, put them on, then headed out the door with the basket

Bevan had given him, calling back over his shoulder as he went, "I'll be home in time for supper."

Reid spent the rest of the afternoon seated at the kitchen table looking over the material the O'Rourkes had supplied. Kelly disappeared from the house after he'd eaten to tend the sheep, rethatch the roof on the chicken coop, and continue with the clearing of rocks from a field they planned to use for grazing. Bevan mended clothes, swept floors, which never took her very far from Reid. As the sun started to go down, she filled the kitchen with the rich aromas of supper, and as if Ryan and Shea knew exactly when the meal would be finished, they returned home in time to sit down with the others and share in a delicious helping of mutton stew and a thick slice of apple pie for dessert. Afterward, the men retired to the parlor to discuss Reid's plan and the news Shea and Ryan had brought him.

Later, as he lay awake on his bed fully clothed and staring out through the window at the black, starlit night, Reid realized Shea's report had truly disappointed him. Scores of people as far north as Dublin as well as several miles south of the farm had all given the young man the same answer: there were no strangers in the area nor had any of those Shea questioned known about the shipwreck. Reid was the only survivor. There was no one left who could aid him in the recovery of his memory. He'd have to do it on his own, and he could only hope what he learned about the man the O'Rourkes had pulled from the sea was someone he wanted to be.

Angry at his predicament, he shoved off the bed and crossed to the window to look outside. In the distance he could hear the roar of the surf crashing against the rocks. He could almost smell the salt air and feel the cold bite of mist against his face as the swells hit and sprayed a shower of tiny water droplets. The fury of nature touched his soul and seemed to mock him for his selfishness. He wasn't being fair . . . to Bevan or to himself. He was listening to his heart rather than thinking with his head. Or had he truly fallen in love? And did he have the right? He knew the answer without having to say it.

A dark, shapely figure moved across his line of vision and jolted him out of his thoughts. Blinking, he scrutinized the form as it hurried away from the house in the direction of the cove. Long, flowing skirts whipped about in the breeze, and from beneath the hood of her cape, Reid saw a lock of hair tumble free. Silvery moonlight caressed the coppery tress, and without a moment's thought, he spun around, stepped into his shoes, and grabbed his jacket from the chair. He had no idea of what he would say to her, only that he must say something. Their conversation earlier had been interrupted before he could explain and he knew how she must have drawn her own conclusions, the wrong ones.

The silence in the house, in fact *Graham's* silence toward her, had started to close in on Bevan. She had waited the entire afternoon while her brothers were away for him to say something to her, to finish the conversation they were having before her siblings came home and monopolized his time and attention. She had given him every opportunity by making sure she was within hearing range the entire while he sat at the kitchen table poring over the books and papers Ryan

110

had given him. His work was important; she knew that. It meant her father's life, and she was grateful for his devotion. Yet selfishly it seemed to her that he was deliberately avoiding her. After everyone had eaten and gone into the parlor, she waited again, hoping Graham would be the last to retire and thus give her the opportunity to bring up the topic they had been discussing earlier. Again she was disappointed when Graham excused himself from their presence and closed the bedroom door behind him. She soon followed suit, since there was nothing she wished to say to any of her kin and because the solitude of her own room promised the secrecy she needed in order to cry. But as the hours ticked away and the quietude of the house began to hammer in her ears, she fled the warmth of her room for a chance to cool the raging emotions within her in the crisp night air.

High on a ridge overlooking the cove and not far from her home stood the rotted remains of a two-room cottage the newly married Patrick and Kerry O'Rourke had lived in before Kelly was born. Although they had moved out long before Bevan and her twin joined the family, it was a place of sanctuary for Bevan whenever she was feeling sad and she refused to discuss her feelings with anyone. She had come here often during the past year as a way of being close to her mother without anyone guessing just how much she needed her parent's company, and it was the reason why she came here this night. She wanted to ask her mother to explain the pain she felt in her heart, to tell her why she had fallen so hard, so deeply, for a man she hardly knew, and to be told that in time it would all pass, that another young lad would enter her life as suddenly as

Graham had and that he would wash away all the memories of her first encounter with love. It was what she hoped her talk with her mother would guarantee, but as she went inside the cottage through the doorless front entrance and stood quietly in the moonlight shining down on her through the gaping hole in the roof, she knew the only peace she would have would come from her own strength to have it.

A noise from just outside spun her around in time to see a tall, dark figure step into the doorway and her heart fluttered excitedly in her chest. Even in the shadows she could recognize Graham's broad shoulders, the perfectly defined curve of his chest, the lean waist and hips, the muscular thighs, and the handsomeness of his face, those captivating gray eyes and that alluring smile that always took her breath away. But was he really here? Standing so close that all she had to do was reach out a hand and touch him? Or was he the vision she had conjured up in her mind? Had she wished for this moment so hard that her imagination had played a trick on her? Certain he was only a dream, she whirled away and buried her face in her hands.

"Go away," she sobbed.

A rush of cool night air filled with the smell of the sea engulfed her and tugged heavily on her cape. Then a pair of strong arms encircled her and she began to struggle. The grip tightened when she voiced her damnation and fought to free herself. She pushed back, raised her head and her fists, and prepared to strike with what strength she had, only to have her body crushed against a much larger, more powerful one while her mouth was captured in a burning, demanding kiss. The feel of his lips on hers was a staggering blow and for a moment she went limp in his arms, her mind whirling with cluttered thoughts of fact and fiction. The scent of him filled her senses then, while the feel of hardened muscles beneath her fingertips as she cautiously laid her hands on his arms soothed her nightmare and guaranteed reality, and in a flood of excitement she kissed him back with all the energy of one possessed. He was here. He was real and he wanted her . . . whether for this moment or for all eternity, she didn't care. She would love him, prove to him that she was worth loving, infect his mind and soul and haunt his memory for the rest of his days. He would come to learn the passion that burned within her and how difficult it would be for him to forget her . . . if he ever could.

His mouth moved hungrily over hers. His tongue parted her lips and tasted of the sweetness of their kiss while his hands slid the hood of her cape from her head. His breathing quickened as his fingers frantically worked the strings of her cloak then pulled the garment from her and let it drop to the floor. He breathed her name against her cheek, then lightly kissed her ear, the soft flesh beneath it, her temple, and the tip of her nose before capturing her mouth again, more fiercely, more savagely this time. Bevan could feel his heart pounding against her breast as she held him tightly to her. She sensed his growing passion, the consuming fire which burned within him, and she marveled at how it paled in comparison to her own. Driven by a blinding need to claim him, she pushed aside all thoughts of improprieties and the damning consequences should they be discovered, and tore her lips from his.

"Take me, Graham," she whispered hoarsely, passionately. "Here. Now."

He started to respond but she quickly pressed her

fingertips to his lips. She didn't want him to say anything that would change her mind or ruin the moment, since she had already decided this was what she wanted more than anything else in her young life. Emerald eyes, blazing with unbridled desire, locked and held his while her hands slipped the jacket from his shoulders then unhooked the buttons up the front of his shirt.

Silver moonlight caressed the bronze ripples of his chest once she had stripped away the garment, and she felt the need to trace soft kisses along the iron thews. With butterfly lightness she touched her lips to his throat, across his shoulder and upper arm, then moved to blaze a searing path with the tip of her tongue over the thick, sinewy expanse of his chest, delighted with the moan of pleasure she heard escape him. Warm fingers found the narrowness of her waist and leisurely slid upward to cup her breast, while his mouth swooped down to capture hers again. Through a delicious fog she felt him unfasten her blouse and the button on her skirt. Along with her shoes, she kicked the garments away and raised her chin as his hot, sultry kisses followed the slim contour of her throat. A bubbling excitement coursed through her and attacked her senses. She wanted this moment to last forever and yet she yearned to explore the full reaches of her desire.

The masculine scent of him, the warmth of his body, and the hypnotizing tranquillity of the embrace quickened her pulse and set her blood on fire. Her mind reeled, her limbs ached, and her flesh burned with his touch. Impatient to learn the joys his lovemaking could bring, she unhooked his breeches and, without shame, slowly traced the lean curve of his hips as she slid the garment down. He stepped away from her then only briefly to shed the rest of his things and hurriedly spread out her cape on the floor. Gently catching her hand, he pulled her down, curled her within his embrace, and lowered her onto their makeshift bed. Hovering close, he stared into her eyes while his hand followed the length of her waist and hip, then caught the edge of her stockings and slid first one then the other from her trembling limbs. That same hand tugged the ribbon of her camisole free and she closed her eyes when he lowered his head to sample the sweet treasure he had uncovered. A bolt of hot, searing electricity charged through her when his opened mouth captured the rosy peak of her breast and she moaned in sheer ecstasy as his tongue played lightly there. Every inch of her was on fire. She was breathless and eager, innocent and worldly, and she no longer wished for lesser things. She wanted all he could give her. She wanted him now!

He, too, must have sensed her urgency, for at that same moment he stripped away her camisole and rose above her, then parted her thighs with his knee and lowered his weight upon her. The touch of his manly hardness made her gasp then shiver, and when he eased the throbbing staff deep within her, her world exploded in a glorious rainbow of colors and images, all bright and beautiful and filled with boundless energy. Swept away on a tide of rapture she arched her hips to welcome each sleek and powerful movement he made, until a wildly soaring spasm of ecstasy burst upon them and sent them hurling back to earth in breathless wonder.

Chapter Four

Morning dawned with a brilliance that would lighten even the darkest of souls. For Reid it was a cold, stark reminder of the deception he played. With each minute that passed, he allowed this poor unsuspecting family, who had accepted him into their home and their lives with trust, to go on thinking he was a friend. Now he had done the inexcusable. He had stolen Bevan's purity without the benefit of wedlock . . . or even a promise that they would wed. He couldn't imagine why he had let it go that far when he knew in his heart it was wrong. Yes, he loved her and he hoped she would agree to be his wife, but he had to know the truth about himself first. How could he have been so stupid?

Pushing off the bed, he went to the washstand and splashed cool water over his face. He wanted to believe that she was the only woman in his life who had ever affected him the way she had, that he wasn't a rogue who moved from one love affair to the next without an ounce of remorse or guilt, or that back home on his plantation in North Carolina there weren't scores of servant girls eagerly awaiting his return.

"Damn it!" he raged, yanking the towel from its rack to wipe his face. The brothers would have done them all a favor if they'd just left him lying unconscious on the shore. He would have died and Bevan wouldn't have been hurt.

The flash of coppery tresses, green eyes, ivory skin, and a slightly upturned nose swirled around in his head and he smiled lamely, resignedly. He could never really wish not to have known Bevan. But what was he to do about her? The making of that decision was delayed a bit by the interruption of a soft knock on his bedroom door.

"Good mornin', Graham," Ryan greeted with a smile. "How are ya feelin' today?"

Pretty damn bad, Reid mused, reaching up to press his fingertips against the bruise on his forehead. The skin was still a purplish hue and it was tender to the touch, but other than that, it didn't bother him anymore. His side still ached a little and he guessed it would for a few more days, but his real pain came from deep inside him.

"Better," he finally answered.

"Are ya hungry? Bevan's got somethin' fixed if ya are," Ryan offered. "I thought maybe we could discuss your plan again while ya ate. Then afterward there'd be time for me brothers and me ta get some work done. We've ignored our chores and the farm too long already. Father won't be pleased when he sees it."

Frowning, Reid gently laid an arm across Ryan's shoulders and guided him back out through the door.

"Ryan, there's more to this plan than any of you were made aware. Are your brothers in the kitchen?"

Ryan could feel the muscles in his body tense. "Aye. Bevan too. I assume this concerns her as well?"

"Yes, it does," Graham replied.

As they entered the kitchen, Shea and Kelly greeted him from the table and Reid nodded his response. Ryan took a seat next to Shea. Bevan, meanwhile, had yet to turn away from the hearth, seemingly reluctant to look at him. Either she was regretting what they had done the previous night or for her brothers' sake she was pretending Reid's presence in the room didn't affect her. Reid sat down at the table. He thanked Bevan for the cup of hot tea she gave him and waited for her to sit down next to him before he began his explanation.

"I've been going over our plan in my head repeatedly and I believe it will work," he said, his hands cradling the teacup and his eyes focused on the brown liquid inside. "But getting your father out of prison is only half the battle."

"What do ya mean?" Kelly quickly asked, his dark brows drawn together.

"Have any of you considered what will happen after that?" He rushed on when he could see that none of the siblings understood. "Your father has been sentenced to hang by the Crown. Just because he's out of prison won't change that fact. He'll be hunted, and the first place they'll look is right here. He can't come home . . . not tomorrow or next week or ever. At least not until the charges have been dropped, if they ever are." These words met with silence.

"The four of you will be suspect simply because he's your father. One or all of you will be arrested, and there won't be any charges. They'll do it to set an example, and to force your father into surrendering so his children will be set free. Of course that won't happen. Once they have him in prison, they'll keep all of you there too. You'll all lose in the end."

"So what ya're tryin' ta tell us is that we'll have ta leave," Kelly guessed.

Reid nodded. "You'll have to leave Ireland."

"Leave Ireland!" Shea exploded. "And go where? To England? Ha!"

Reid could feel Bevan's eyes on him, and as much as he wanted to look at her, he wouldn't. "Of course not, Shea. I wasn't suggesting England. I was thinking of the United States. You'd be safe there."

"We don't know anyone in America," Shea vehemently argued. "How would we live? Better yet, how would we get there? And what would we do if we did manage it?"

Reid wanted to tell them that they knew *him,* that all of them could come to live on his plantation in North Carolina, if indeed there really was such a place, and that as soon as he'd talked to friends of his family and cleared up the mystery enshrouding his past, they'd leave the British Isles for good . . . *all* of them. That was what he would have liked to tell them, but he couldn't. He honestly couldn't promise them a thing.

"'Tis a grand idea, Graham," Ryan said. "But Ireland is our home. I, for one, don't want ta leave it. I'm sure our father wouldn't either. If he'd ever had the inclination, he would have left long before he took up a pitchfork ta fight. Thank ya, but no. We'll stay where we belong."

Reid's temper flared. "And do what?"

"The Society will take care of us," Ryan declared

119

matter-of-factly.

Reid snorted derisively. "The way they've taken care of your father so far?" He quickly raised both hands in the air as a silent apology for being so harsh, and left his chair to cross to the hearth. Once there, he laid a hand upon the stone mantel, rested a foot on the slab, and stared quietly down at the bubbling pot of water hanging from its hook. Several minutes passed with no one knowing what to say before Reid sucked in a deep breath, straightened, and turned back around. When he spoke, he directed his question to Ryan, since he had learned from the start that the others looked to him for guidance.

"What about your sister?"

Puzzled, Ryan glanced at Bevan for a second then back at Reid. "What about her?"

"Well, I assume the Society will hide you out until they can clear your father's name. That means you'll be constantly on the move. I'm sure that kind of life won't be too much to ask of the three of you." His gaze swept the brothers. "But what about Bevan? Are you willing to make her an outlaw right along with the rest of you?"

"Well, we can't leave her behind," Ryan scoffed.

"Of course you can't. So you'll drag her from one camp to another, from one town to the next. You'll make her sleep in a barn or someone's loft, in a field or cave. If she's lucky, she won't catch a chill and die of pneumonia." He tossed his hands in the air and walked to the back door, where he spun around and mocked, "But then I'm exaggerating. The most you'd have to live like that would be a month or two. She's young. She's strong. She'll make it." He glared challengingly at Ryan.

Shamed that he hadn't thought of his sister, Ryan lowered his gaze. "Then we'll have ta send her somewhere."

"Where?" Shea asked, unable to think of such a place.

"Yes, Ryan, where?" Kelly chorused. "She might have it easier not comin' with us, but she'd still have ta spend every day hidin' whenever someone knocked on the door. And ya know Father would never permit it either way." He shook hs head, frowned, and gripped the teacup sitting in front of him. "Graham's right. We'll have ta leave Ireland."

"Are ya deaf, man?" Shea exploded. "Ryan just said—" His remark was quieted by the hand that patted his arm and he turned to look at Ryan and silently question his subtle interruption. He frowned even more when he saw the odd smile on that one's face. "Are ya goin' ta share it with us or do we have ta guess what ya find amusin' about this mess?"

"Not amusin', Shea," Ryan corrected. "I'm pleased, 'tis all." His green eyes lifted to look at the man standing away from them. "Thanks ta Graham, he's given me an idea . . . one I'm sure our father would approve of, if we could ask him."

An uneasy feeling began to creep up the back of Reid's neck. Wondering if Bevan sensed trouble, too, he shifted his gaze on her and found her staring curiously at her brother. She had been quiet during the entire exchange as if whatever was decided would be all right with her, and that puzzled him. He'd already experienced one of her fiery tongue-lashings and knew she was as hot tempered as her twin. Her silence could be likened to a coiled snake ready to strike. Reid just

121

wasn't sure which of the men would get bitten first and how fatal it would be. If she was angered enough, she'd go for the neck, and all Reid could hope for was that he wasn't the one closest to her when she did.

"Well, Father *isn't* here ta ask, Ryan," Bevan said finally, "so why don't ya tell us . . . or rather me what ya've got in mind. After all, it's me ya're talkin' about like I'm not even in the room."

"That's because ya shouldn't be in the room," Shea jeered. "'Tis men talk we're discussin'."

Bevan's green eyes darkened. "Not when the subject is me. Graham wouldn't even be here if *I* hadn't made a deal with his uncle."

"Oh, and a fine deal it was, too," Shea rallied.

Bevan's tiny frame stiffened and she opened her mouth to bite back a hot reply when Ryan intervened.

"It *was* a fine deal, Shea," he declared. "Or it would have been if Lord Rynearson had lived to carry it out. Now we'll have ta make a new one."

"With who?" Shea barked.

Ryan's smile grew wider as he continued to stare at Reid. "With his nephew."

That uneasy feeling spread down Reid's spine.

"What kind of deal?" Kelly asked, totally confused. "And how does this have anythin' ta do with our leavin' Ireland?"

"It has everythin' ta do with it," Ryan admitted as he leaned back in his chair and folded his arms in front of him. "I've thought of a perfect way for us ta stay and for Bevan ta leave."

"What?" All three siblings voiced the question in unison.

Confidence sparkling in his green eyes, Ryan

announced, "She'll marry Graham and go home with him."

To hear his secret desire put into words by another struck Reid mute. It wasn't that he objected to the plan—hardly that. It was just that Ryan had the events in the wrong order. He couldn't marry Bevan and take her home until he knew where home was. All he wanted right now was for the brother to choose a place for her to hide where he could find her later without too much trouble.

"I'm honored," he finally managed to respond, "that you think enough of me to permit me to marry your sister. And I must admit that the thought had already crossed my mind. After all, that was the real reason why I was brought here in the first place . . . sort of." He smiled again and swallowed the lump in his throat. "However," he continued as he turned back around, "it isn't quite as simple as that. You see, I—"

"Oh, but it is," Ryan cut in. "Or have ya forgotten that we saved your life?"

"No," he replied coolly. "I haven't forgotten. It's the reason why I decided to help free your father. I'd call that a fair trade, wouldn't you?"

"It was," Ryan answered.

"But it isn't now," Reid finished, his anger rising. "You want more. You want me to risk my life again to save your father's *and* to marry Bevan. Is that it?"

"Ryan," Kelly warned, reaching to grab his brother's wrist. He sensed the anger their guest was feeling, and that if Graham was pushed too far, he might change his mind about helping. In Kelly's opinion, rescuing their father was far more important than whether or not Bevan had to chase around the countryside. Ryan was

123

asking too much.

"Aye. That's what I had in mind," Ryan admitted as he brushed off the hand touching his arm. "We're desperate, Graham. We'd do or say just about anythin' ta protect our family."

"Do or say?" Reid repeated. He'd recognized the shrewd promise in the man's statement. He just wasn't sure what he meant specifically.

Feeling in command, Ryan relaxed and lazily took a drink of his tea. "I don't suppose I have ta tell ya that your uncle was takin' a risk even talkin' ta us, now do I? He's a high-ranking official with a chance of havin' a seat in Parliament. If any one of his associates learned he was tryin' ta break a criminal out of prison, an Irish criminal, just so his nephew would have a wife, I'd guess Lord Rynearson would be stripped of his power and imprisoned himself."

"But he's dead," Shea pointed out, failing to understand what his brother was driving at. "What difference does any of that make?"

"I think I can tell you," Reid cut in, the muscle in his jaw flexing. "Just as I explained about this family being suspect if your father escapes prison, any of Lord Rynearson's relatives would be equally suspected of wrongdoing."

"But no one knows about your uncle's part in this," Shea argued.

"Not now, they don't," Graham replied. "And no one ever would unless someone let it slip." He glared at Ryan. "Am I right?"

Ryan didn't respond but took another slow drink of his tea instead.

"So in exchange for your saving my life, I'll help save

your father's. In exchange for your silence, I'm to marry Bevan and take her home with me."

"That's deplorable!" Kelly exclaimed.

"No," Reid corrected. "It's blackmail." The idea of it enraged him and he could feel every muscle in his body stiffen as he fought off the urge to strike the young man. What Ryan obviously didn't realize was how close he was to hanging his own father. All Reid had to do was turn around and walk out the door, and all the hard work, all the planning to free Patrick O'Rourke, would be wasted. Without *him,* without a foreigner to gain entrance into the prison, Ryan's father would be executed on schedule, and if it weren't for Bevan and how he felt about her, that's just what Reid would do— he'd walk and it wouldn't matter where he went. He could . . . he should . . . but he wouldn't. Trapped in a tangled meshwork of lies and hating it, he ground his teeth and turned away while he halfheartedly listened to Kelly argue with his brother.

"What ya're suggestin' makes us no different than the ones who put Father in prison," he declared. "Ya're usin' another for your own purposes."

"Aye," Ryan barked, "I am! But ya're forgettin' what that purpose is. *And* ya're forgettin' that ya found nothin' wrong with it when we talked about it earlier."

"It didn't include threatenin' a man's life!" Infuriated, Kelly slammed a huge fist down against the table top, rattling the dishes sitting there. "Ya've gone too far!"

"I could never go too far where me family is concerned," Ryan shot back. "Maybe *you* lack the courage, but—"

The explosive crash of Kelly's chair toppling to the floor as he bolted from it and kicked it aside spun Reid around in time to see the man lunge for his brother and Shea duck back out of the way. Reid hurled himself forward and caught Kelly around the chest before the man could reach his brother.

"No, Kelly!" Reid shouted, amazed by the man's strength and the depth of the rage he saw burning in his eyes. "This won't solve anything, and you'll only regret it later. He's speaking out of frustration. We all are." He held a steady, unyielding grip on the Irishman until he could feel Kelly's temper begin to cool. "Forget what was said . . . if not for me, then for Bevan."

The mention of his sister was all it took. Exhaling a long breath, Kelly nodded and tapped Reid's arm as a sign he agreed. Once he'd been freed, he righted his chair and sat down again. Shea also eased back into his seat, but Ryan chose to cross to the hearth and stare into it with his back to the group. Bevan, both shocked and angered by the outburst and the comments that had been made, sat silently glaring down at the table, her long chestnut hair falling softly about her face.

"So what do you suggest we do?" Kelly asked after a strained minute or two of silence. "Everyone's agreed we can't stay here, but no one knows where we should go."

"I guess I'd suggest you all split up for a while," Reid answered. "Ryan seems confident the Society will help you. Then when things have cooled off or when your father is cleared, you can come back here." He frowned and shook his head. "I just don't know. But I want you to remember my suggestion. It wouldn't have to be permanent, you know. You could live in the States for a while and then come home once you're sure you all will be safe."

126

The mantel clock ticked off a measure of time while everyone in the room thought about their future and what had been said. Kelly was the first to break the silence when he rose and headed for the back door with the announcement that he had work to do. Shea quickly followed his brother's lead, but once he had reached the exit, he paused to look back at Ryan.

"Are ya comin'?" he asked.

"In a minute," his brother promised. "I'd like ta talk ta Graham first. You go on ahead without me."

Uncertain, Shea glanced questioningly at Reid, then turned and departed the small cottage after Reid signaled with a nod of his head that he should leave the two of them alone together. The sound of his exit turned Ryan around, but several more long moments passed before Ryan was able to speak.

"I want ta apologize for what I tried ta do," he said. "To you and to Bevan." He shifted his gaze to his sister, who refused to look up from the table. "I had no right decidin' your future. But maybe ya'll understand why when I tell ya that Bevan's happiness, her safety, means everythin' ta me. When she first proposed the idea of marryin' a stranger ta free our father, I was outraged, and I knew Father would be too once he'd heard about it. I can't say right now if I'd have let her go through with it, but after meetin' ya and learnin' what kind of a man ya are, I realize her selflessness would have worked out all right." He lifted his eyes to stare directly at Reid. "Ya're a good man, Graham Rynearson, and I'd be proud ta have ya as a brother-in-law, but that decision has ta be your own ta make . . . yours and Bevan's. I was just tryin' ta help it along. I saw the way the two of ya looked comin' out of the henhouse. Ya like each other, and if there was time enough for ya ta do a proper courtin' . . ." He shrugged, lowered his eyes, and headed for the door, where he paused to add over his shoulder, "Think about it, will ya? That's all I ask."

Think about it? Reid mused ironically as he watched the door close behind Ryan on his way out. *That's all I've been doing. I just can't figure out a way . . . not until I'm sure.* Crossing to the table, he pulled out the chair next to Bevan and sat down. But when he reached over to touch her hand, she yanked away from him and stood.

"Bevan, please," he begged, quickly leaving his chair to grab her arm. "We need to talk."

"Ya've said enough already," she snapped, jerking loose of his hold and spinning away.

Reid hastened to follow her, surmising that her destination would be the privacy of her bedroom as she hurriedly left the kitchen and headed in that direction.

"You've heard only what you want to hear, Bevan," he argued, making a grab for her which she easily and agilely eluded as she cut through the parlor. The slamming of her bedroom door in his face ended the pursuit but in return flared his temper when he heard the bolt slide into place. Doubling up his fists, he banged them against the wooden planks. "Open the door, Bevan," he demanded.

"No," came the equally enraged reply.

"Bevan," he warned through clenched teeth. "Open the door. We have a matter to settle and we'll do it face to face."

"And if I say no, will ya kick in the door?" she challenged. "Try it and I'll scream loud enough for me brothers ta hear. Kelly and Ryan might not believe me when I tell them ya tried ta have your way with me the second their backs were turned, but Shea would. And he's foolish enough ta kill ya for it."

"He may try," Reid said. He waited for the threat to sink in, then added, "I don't think you'd sleep well after that knowing you were the cause of your brother's death. Now open the door, Bevan, or wishful thinking will become reality."

Several seconds passed before the metal rod scraped against its casing and the latch clicked free. But more than that she wouldn't oblige him. Pressing his hand against the door, he pushed it open and stepped into the room. She stood before the single window on the far wall looking out, her back to him and her arms crossed in front of her. Her head was cocked to one side and she was tapping her toe on the floor. By all appearances, she was angry enough with him that one wrong word on his part would send her flying at him with her fingers curled and ready to claw out his eyes.

"I'm sure you misunderstood my reaction to Ryan's attempt at blackmailing me," he began, moving farther into the room and closing the door behind him, since he didn't want to share his explanation with any of the other O'Rourkes. "I was angered because he *tried,* not because he was thinking to force you on me. I won't bow down to anyone. And I hope you'd have thought less of me if I had. You wouldn't want to marry me knowing I'd been trapped into it, would you?"

She didn't respond but continued to tap her toe, and his gaze dropped to the slippered foot that rhythmically moved up and down, its short, sharp sound grating on his nerves. He fought down the urge to cross to where she stood and deliberately rest his foot on hers. Instead he said, "Bevan, I love you."

The tapping stopped.

Strangely chilled by the declaration when he sensed it was the first time those three words had ever crossed his lips, he shook off the tingling and slowly lowered himself down into the nearby rocker. When he spoke again, he had a faraway look in his eye, for somewhere deep inside him a memory had stirred. "I've never said that to anyone in my life." He drew on the warmth he felt, amazed by the confidence that he spoke the truth. "I guess that's because no one has ever touched me the way you have." He leaned back and set the rocker in motion, his gaze absently centered on a distant spot somewhere in space, when the door to his past quietly closed again. "It's hard to believe a man could meet a girl one day and fall hopelessly in love with her in a matter of hours. Some would say it's only infatuation. But it isn't. I'd know the difference. What I feel is deep and lasting. And it's tearing me apart. I want to love you, to marry you, to run away with you to some far-off deserted isle where we could live out our lives chasing each other around on a sandy beach." A wicked grin parted his lips. "Naked," he added, then sighed and laid his head back to stare up at the ceiling. "And why shouldn't we? Why can't we just run away if we want to? I'll tell you why. It's called responsibilities, an invisible force that ties us to the past and determines our future." Frowning, he sat up and looked at her. "I have those responsibilities, Bevan, and until I can settle them or change them, I have no right to create new ones. You understand, don't you?"

Bevan wanted to say she did. She wanted to tell him

she loved him too, that once this whole ordeal was over, they could work out their problems together and then get married. She couldn't imagine her life unfolding without him by her side, to share her joys, her sorrows, her very existence. She wanted to say the words but she couldn't. His vagueness, his subtle refusal to tell her each and every detail about his life before they met, stabbed at her pride and raised suspicion. *If* he truly loved her, he would tell her *everything!* And he would do it without being prodded. There had to be a reason, a serious reason why he wouldn't, and Bevan could only assume it was because he truly had no intention of ever marrying her. He was using her . . . to sate his male needs and to pass the time away until he was ready to go home . . . to his secrets.

"Aye, Graham," she finally replied, her voice calm and edged with rancor. "I understand. I understand that last night should be forgotten. It was a mistake and that until ya've 'settled or changed' your responsibilities, we should make sure it never happens again." She stared at him for a moment while she strengthened her composure and fought the burning tears which threatened to crumble her conviction. Then, with a courageous lift of her chin, she pulled her gaze away from his handsome face and those hypnotizing gray eyes and moved toward the door. "If ya'll excuse me now, I have work ta do."

Reid's arms ached to hold her, to pull her close and kiss away her agony, for he had seen it in her eyes and heard it in her words. But as she walked past him, he realized that perhaps her way was best. He'd finish his work here, sail back home to confront what awaited him there, then return here, to Ireland and to Bevan.

He'd find her and court her as a man should . . . a man with no ties to anyone or anything. He'd proclaim his love and offer his life to her, because if last night meant as much to her as it had to him, he was sure she'd give him a second chance.

The stillness in the room turned him around to find that he was alone.

Reid busied himself for the rest of the day by working alongside Kelly, Ryan, and Shea as they cleared away the huge rocks from a section of their land and used the pieces of red sandstone to build a high wall to break the sea wind. While they worked, they talked about their scheme for getting the eldest O'Rourke out of prison. Reid had decided that he would act as himself, Lord Rynearson's nephew, and go to the prison with a letter signed and sealed by King George. The document would gain him an audience with the warden and further instruct the man to hand over one Patrick O'Rourke to the bearer of the message for transportation to England where he would meet with his accusers. Reid told the brothers that as a result of their heated debate earlier he had been prompted to alter the original idea in a way that would allow the family to continue to live on their farm free of worry, while he took their father to England. Shea's immediate reaction to such a notion was a violent refusal to allow his father to go. Kelly's frown showed his doubt in the wisdom of Graham's plan, while Ryan was only too eager to hear the purpose.

"It's quite simple really, and no one will be in any danger," he explained. "If my uncle had already thought of a plan to clear your father's name, then all I have to do is find it. Your father will be perfectly safe living with me in my uncle's house until that time, and who would ever think to look for him there if something went wrong? Which it won't."

The three men took several minutes to think it through, and although Shea still had doubts, his older siblings could see the logic in the proposal and yielded to Reid's wisdom on the matter. What Reid wasn't telling them was that once he had accomplished the feat and their father was free to go home, he planned to confide in Patrick and tell him the truth, that he had fallen into a trap not of his own making, rather one which had swallowed him up before he was able to recognize the signs of trouble, and that because of it, he had to find out who he was before he could make any commitments. He would tell Bevan's father how much he loved the man's daughter and that after Reid had straightened things out back home, he would return to Ireland to ask for Bevan's hand. Reid wished there was some other way to handle the affair, since the only drawback to the whole idea was that he wouldn't see Bevan for close to three months.

The tension among the brothers seemed to ebb after their discussion as everyone now experienced a strong glimmer of hope. What none of them voiced, however, was the danger in which they were sure their friend would place himself by going into the prison alone. Connie McFee had an exceptional talent when it came to copying someone else's handwriting and the King's seal would add the right touch of legitimacy, but that didn't guarantee something wouldn't go wrong, something they hadn't foreseen as trouble. For all their efforts, their father still might not escape the hangman's noose and the stranger who had risked his own life in an effort to prevent it would undoubtedly be executed right alongside him.

Tired and exhausted after a full day's work, the foursome headed back to the cottage and the delicious meal Kelly promised Bevan would have waiting for them. A bright, warm sun had shone all afternoon, and combined with the heat of their labor, each man was dirty, wet with perspiration, and yearning for the luxury of a long dip in a tub of refreshing bath water. Their mood light, they joked about who had done the hardest share of work and therefore deserved to be the first in line. Shea proclaimed he didn't care, since the idea of food was more appealing than taking a bath. That in turn provoked comments from his brothers that Shea considered *anything* more important than taking a bath and always had, and that the only time he enjoyed being wet was when he went for a swim at the cove. The youngest protested their claim, while the other two argued with him, and all three, therefore, missed the frown which had changed Reid's expression.

The vague image of two young boys swimming in a pond had assailed Reid without warning. Then a third person, a man, had appeared, and although the vision was weak and somewhat blurred, Reid sensed the man was angry. The thought faded and a new one emerged, one that left him feeling saddened and oddly full of guilt, for although he couldn't clearly understand the image, he could see a dead horse, a young boy writhing in pain, and a second lad standing over him crying. Fearing his companions would notice the agony registered on his face, Reid quickly shook off the vision and concentrated on the playful bantering between the brothers.

Once they had crossed the yard in back of the cottage and were headed toward the kitchen, Kelly was the first to notice the tub of fresh water sitting on the ground beside the well. Next to it was a bench with several neatly folded towels lying on top that Bevan had obviously supplied, and Kelly wasted very little time in stripping out of his shirt as he hurried over to it.

"Wait a minute," Ryan called out to him as he firmly grabbed Shea's shirt collar and yanked the boy around in front of him. "I thought we agreed that whoever worked the hardest would be the first in line."

Kelly started to announce that the right belonged to whoever got in the tub ahead of the rest, saw what his brother had in mind, and decided that tormenting Shea was worth giving up his claim on the bath. "Aye. That we did," he replied with a wide, delighted smile. "And who worked harder than you, me, and Graham?"

"Why, Shea did," Ryan answered.

"Then he should have the honor," Kelly joked as he made a sweeping bow and pointed at the wooden tub.

Before the boy could draw a breath, much less utter a protest, Kelly had joined Ryan in stripping Shea of his clothes. Amid the wail of outrage, hurled oaths of damnation fell upon the brothers' ears, but to no avail. Shoes, shirt, breeches, and stockings were tossed haphazardly in the air with little care as to where they landed or that their removal had angered their owner. Struggling uselessly in the iron grip of his two brothers, Shea was hauled unceremoniously to the tub, where without formalities he was deposited with a loud splash into the soapy water.

135

"Damn ya!" he howled, once he had surfaced spitting and spewing water from his nose and mouth. Eyes blazing, he glared at his older siblings, who were laughing uncontrollably a safe distance out of reach. "Damn ya both ta hell!"

In a rage and vowing to see that both men paid for their prank, he tried to pull himself up out of the tub, but the wet sides made him lose his grip and he plunged back in without anyone's help, which brought a second round of hearty guffaws from the pair and tested Reid's restraint to stay impartial. He, too, began to laugh, until a movement from the doorway of the kitchen caught his eye and he was forced to swallow his mirth. The fire he saw glowing in Bevan's green eyes clearly revealed her disapproval, and although he didn't understand it, he respected her right not to find the situation amusing. Kelly and Ryan as well must have had the same thought for once they spotted her glaring at them with her fists knotted on her hips, the desire to further torment their youngest brother faded. With eyes lowered, they stood as two troublesome youngsters caught in the act by a displeased parent.

"'Twas meant for the lot of ya ta bathe in," she scolded. "Now look." She flung out a hand to indicate their wastefulness. "Your tomfoolery has spilled most of it on the ground. Well, ya'll not have a second tub full, unless ya heat the water yourself. And I'll not wait supper a moment longer." She cast her brothers one last railing look, then turned and went back into the house.

"Bevan's much too serious these days," Kelly remarked as he headed to the tub. "There was a time when she would have laughed right along with us." He

136

glanced back at Ryan and winked with a nod of his head toward Reid. "Do ya suppose she's tryin' ta impress someone?"

Knowing what Kelly meant, Ryan played along. "Aye. Ever since we got company, she's been actin' all grown up. But *we* know the real Bevan." Removing his shirt, he joined Kelly at the tub, and began splashing water over his chest, neck, and arms as if Shea weren't still sitting in the middle of the wooden barrel. "What do ya suppose it means?"

"I'm not sure," Kelly joked as he, too, washed the dirt and sweat from his upper body and ignored Shea's demands for his clothes. "But I'm guessin' maybe she's in love."

"In love?" Ryan echoed, reaching for a pair of towels, one of which he gave to Kelly. "With who?" As if struck by a sudden dawning of the answer, he straightened and turned around to look at Reid. "Not with him. Ya've kissed the Blarney stone ta be thinkin' she could care for a Colonial."

"And why not?" the oldest argued as he wiped the moisture from his face and settled his gaze on the one who watched and listened in silent amusement. "He's not too bad ta look at. A little scrawny, maybe, but some of Bevan's cookin' will fix that."

"But he talks funny," Ryan continued with his objections.

Kelly shrugged. "Well, everyone has a flaw or two."

"Not the Irish," his sibling denied. "I've never known an Irishman ta have a flaw."

"Aye," Kelly agreed as he folded his arms over his bare chest and stepped away from the tub and Shea. "Maybe this one isn't the right choice for our sister."

His gaze swept Reid's tall build from head to toe. "But on the other hand we might be able ta make somethin' out of him. He seems intelligent and he's a hard worker." He tilted his head to one side, smiled, and nudged Ryan with his elbow. "And if I haven't been out in the sun too long, I'd say he's already smitten with her . . . which means we won't have much of a say in it either way."

"Aye," Ryan concurred with a mocking sigh and shake of his head. "I think ya're right on that account. Did ya see the look on his face when we caught them comin' out of the henhouse?" He gave his brother a stupid look. "What do ya suppose they were doin' in there? Collectin' eggs?"

"Collectin' somethin'," Kelly supposed with a devilish grin and his brown eyes sparkling.

Positive the pair would continue their game all night if he didn't do something to bring it to an end, Reid started for the tub, picking up Shea's clothes as he went and smiling softly. Then just as he was about to walk past the brothers, he paused, looked at them, mocked in a perfect Irish accent, "'Tisn't a matter of how a man speaks, me friend, that makes him worthy of a lass, but what he feels in his heart for her. Nor does it matter ta me that it's Bevan's misfortune ta have brothers like the two of ya. 'Tis a problem, I'm sure, but one we can overcome. We'll move away." He took a step, hesitated, and looked back at them again. "Am I speakin' plain enough for ya ta understand, laddies?"

Kelly and Ryan burst into laughter simultaneously.

"Aye! That ya are," Kelly chortled as he slapped Ryan on the back and pulled him off toward the cottage with him. "Plain as the nose on me brother's face. And an ugly nose it is," he teased, his elbow locked around Ryan's neck as he tapped a fingertip to the end of that one's snout.

"It's been a long time since I heard them laugh," Shea told his companion as he watched his brothers go into the house. "And I think we have you ta thank for it." He shifted his gaze on Reid. "We have a lot ta thank ya for, Graham."

"Not really," Reid corrected as he handed the boy a towel and laid his clothes on the bench. "All I've really done is give you hope. You should wait to thank me *after* your father's home safe again." He smiled at Shea then began unfastening the buttons on his shirt.

"Were they only playin' with ya, Graham, or do ya really like Bevan?" Shea asked as he stepped out of the tub to dry himself off and hurriedly slip into his breeches.

Yanking the shirttail free, Reid laid the garment aside and leaned to splash soapy water on his face and neck. "Would it make a difference?" he asked after a moment.

Shea thought about his answer. "Aye. It would. Bevan shouldn't have ta live the way we do. She's meant ta have fine things and a nice place ta live. She could have that with you."

"But shouldn't she love the man she marries, Shea?" Reid replied while he washed the dirt from his arms. "Having a nice house and richly tailored clothes won't guarantee happiness. I would think you'd want her to be happy more than anything else."

"I do," the young man admitted. "Are ya sayin' she wouldn't be happy with ya?"

"I'd like to think she would be," Reid confessed. "But

139

I've got problems to solve before I can even consider asking her."

"What kind of problems?" Shea couldn't see where a man like Graham Rynearson would have any. And if he did, Shea assumed the Englishman would just pay to get rid of them. "They can't be big enough ta stop ya from marryin' any woman ya'd want."

"Is that really how you see me?" Reid questioned in surprise, for he had guessed the underlying implication in the boy's statement. Toweling himself dry, he faced the young man. "Just because you think I have money doesn't mean I lack honor . . . or a conscience. A gold coin won't buy everything, Shea."

The boy shrugged. "It won't buy love," he agreed, "but it can buy just about anythin' else." Smiling with an air of certainty, he turned and went into the house.

Connie McFee, his brother-in-law Gannon Mac-Kinley, and Kyle Magee arrived at the house, just as the sun was beginning to slip over the horizon, armed with papers and ledgers and filled with ideas and hopeful expectations. Introductions were made, and while Bevan served their guests the whiskey Ryan had asked her to provide, the group of men gathered around the kitchen table to discuss Graham's plan. Tobacco smoke from Magee's pipe filled the air and hung suspended over everyone's head as the team of conspirators evaluated their scheme and the problems which might arise if something should go wrong.

Bevan stood back to listen to every word, but her gaze always centered on Graham. Until this very moment, she hadn't realized the depth of his vulnerability once he entered that prison. Just being caught with the forged papers signed by King George was enough to see him hanged, and she suddenly wished there was some other way to free her father. The announcement, however, that after he and Patrick walked out of that prison, they would sail for England to work on clearing her father's name, came as a surprise and filled her with a new anxiety. It meant that once he'd donned the clothes he'd been wearing when the boys found him in the cove and he left the cottage to execute their plan, she might never see him again. More upset than she wanted to be at the thought, she quietly left the kitchen without being noticed.

"I'm going to need a cape and hat," Reid told Gannon MacKinley when the man asked if there was anything else he required. "And a cane, if one's available. I must give the impression of a man with some authority and one who just stepped off the ship from England."

"I think I can fix ya up," MacKinley stated. "At least with the hat and cloak. I'm a tailor by trade and some of me customers are quite wealthy. If not, I'll steal what ya need. How soon do ya want them?"

Reid looked at Shea. "How many days before the visitors are allowed in the prison?"

"Three," the boy supplied.

Reid's brow furrowed. "I'd like to use their presence as a distraction," he murmured, "but I don't suppose your father has been treated well during his stay, and I need him as healthy as possible." He turned back to MacKinley. "As soon as you can have them for me."

"I'll bring them over tomorrow mornin'," Gannon promised. "Anythin' else?"

141

"Yes," Reid answered. "Once Patrick and I are clear of the prison, we'll need to leave Ireland as soon as we can. That means I should time this to coincide with the departure of a ship sailing for England."

"There's one tomorrow afternoon," Magee furnished. "'Tisn't a passenger ship, though. It holds cargo. Leaves once a week from Dublin at the same time . . . regular as the changin' of seasons."

"What time, exactly?" Reid questioned.

"Midafternoon. It varies."

"Depending on what?"

"On how quick it's loaded." Magee smiled with a devilish quirk to his mouth. "No need ta worry that it might leave without ya, if that's what's goin' through your mind. Several of the dock workers as well as their overseer are members of the Society. I'll tell them ta expect two important passengers and that they're not ta let the ship sail without them on board."

Reid remembered accusing the Society of negligence in regard to Patrick's imprisonment and how he had implied that same group wouldn't be able to protect Patrick's family once the man was free. He was sorry he had condemned them without knowing all the facts now that he had learned to what extent they would and *could* go to help out a friend.

"Then it's settled," Reid announced. "We do it tomorrow." He focused his gaze on Connie McFee. "That is, of course, if you can draft me a letter of introduction by then."

"That's why I'm here," the man replied as he patted the stack of papers sitting on the table next to him. "Tell me how ya want it worded and I'll write it up for ya right now."

A full moon shone overhead by the time Magee and

his companions left the house. The document had been prepared, sealed, and placed in a black leather pouch Connie had supplied, no doubt obtained in much the same way as everything else the men needed to achieve a certain effect. It was entrusted to Reid for safe-keeping which was how he wanted it, and after he and the brothers bid their guests farewell and he had gone to his room to place the pouch in the top drawer of the dresser, he realized for the first time that evening that this would be his last night to share with Bevan. He discovered, too, with much surprise, that sometime during the course of their meeting, she had decided to leave their company. Since all three of her brothers had guessed his fondness for her, he realized the foolishness in trying to pretend they were just friends, and he left his room to look for her, then to ask Ryan if he knew where she was since he hadn't been able to find her anywhere in the house. Told about the deserted cottage by the cove where their parents used to live and how Bevan went there quite often to be alone with her thoughts, Reid acted as though he had no prior knowledge of its existence while he listened to Ryan assure him that she was all right, that she probably would resent his intrusion if he chased after her, and that he, like his brothers, was going to bed.

"She'll come home when she's good and ready, Graham," Ryan added as he stifled a yawn and stretched the muscles in his back. "But if ya're worried, wait up for her." A sparkle suddenly glowed in his green eyes. "Which I'm sure ya planned ta do without me suggestin' it." After giving his friend a good-natured pat on the back, Ryan turned and headed for his bedroom.

Several minutes passed while Reid stood at the

kitchen door debating whether or not he should go after Bevan. He could remember with vivid clarity every detail of what had happened there the last time he found her alone in that deserted cottage, and although the idea of repeating it was far from objectionable, he didn't think it would be fair to Bevan. He certainly wasn't planning to get himself killed tomorrow, but there was always that chance, he supposed. So why leave her with a memory that would pain her rather than bring joy? He'd explain what he had in mind once he and her father reached England and how he hoped to clear up the mysteries around his past, then he'd promise her he'd come for her and that he'd court her the way he should have courted her from the start. Having reached a decision, he opened the door and stepped outside.

Moonlight flooded the yard with a soft, silver-white glow and darkened the already ebony shadows encircling the barn, henhouse and pair of trees growing near the cottage. At first he didn't see her, since his mind was filled with the words he wanted to say to her. Then a movement to his left brought his attention around to the shapely figure standing by the well, her long coppery hair shining in the ashen light, her green eyes watching him. A moment passed while neither of them moved or said a word. Then without comment Beven turned and went into the barn.

Reid followed her there. Platinum streams of light filtered into the darkened cavity and showed him the way once he had stepped through the open doors and pulled them shut behind him. There in the center of the room stood a chestnut-haired temptress haloed in moonlight, her shawl hanging loosely from her shoulders, her chin held high, her pink lips parted alluringly, and an unspoken invitation shining in the emerald depths of her eyes. Struck mute by the vision, his pledge—the words he had wanted to recite—vanished, and the burning lust the mere sight of her evoked rose again and darkened the shade of his gray eyes.

Wanton desires clouded Bevan's judgment. She had fled the house to escape the torturous thought that within a few days Graham would leave her and that she'd never see him again. She had forced herself not to think about it. She had gone for a long walk, visited the cove and the deserted cottage, and watched the sun melt into the horizon until all that remained was a brilliant red-gold sky. Finally, she had found peace. She had convinced herself that what she felt for this stranger—and indeed he was a stranger—that the feelings he stirred in her were only the imaginative yearnings of a young woman who had yet to experience love. She had assured herself that when she looked at him again, she would see him differently. Yet, once she neared the house, she couldn't go inside. *He* was in there. He would see the look in her eyes and know the truth, her every thought. She needed more time to build up her courage to face him. Then, just when she had decided to tempt fate and slip quietly through the house to her room, the back door had opened and his tall, majestic frame moved into the pale light. In that moment her will crumbled and her passion soared anew, even higher than it had before. In a trance she had gone into the barn, hoping he would follow, that his desire was as strong and shameful as hers. And now as they stood devouring the sight of each other, the need to feel his arms around her and his lips pressed warmly to hers betrayed her earlier pledge. If they were meant to go their separate ways, then so be it. But for tonight she would bask in the glow of his lovemaking.

From the stall beside her, the donkey snorted and pawed the straw-covered floor as if annoyed by his unwelcomed late-night visitors. Raising his head, he eyed the couple with seeming curiosity before he closed his eyes and swung away to settle himself comfortably once more in a restful pose, his tail swishing twice before it hung still. Mindful of the beast and oddly embarrassed by his presence, Bevan moved away and crossed to the mound of freshly cut hay on the opposite side of the barn, her gaze never leaving Reid's handsome face. Yet when he took a step toward her, she turned her back to him, suddenly afraid, though of what she wasn't sure.

The warmth of his lean, hard body standing close behind her made her heart flutter and her breath quicken. Lifting her chin, she closed her eyes and laid her head back against his shoulder just as his hand came around her waist and gently pulled her to him, the fingers fanned wide and burned the flesh of her belly through the cloth of her garments. His other hand felt the curve of her hip while his lips seared her throat. The heat of his kiss moved to scorch her ear and the delicate line of her jaw while one hand slid upward to cup her breast and the other traced the slimness of her inner thigh, his thumb extended to gently prob the valley where the treasure he sought lay hidden beneath the yards of her cotton skirt. His boldness ignited a sweet agony that left her weak and trembling and yearning for more. She could feel the hard expanse of his sinewy chest lining the curve of her back, the muscular thighs pressed against hers and his manly hardness touching her buttocks as he gently moved his hips from side to side. Her passion raged higher. Warm fingers agilely popped the buttons on her blouse free and pulled the cloth away while his teeth nibbled on her earlobe. She arched her back and moved with the sway of his body as she reached up to entwine her fingers in the thick mass of his dark hair and he pulled the strings of her camisole loose. His burning touch captured her breast, then gently pinched the hardened nipple as his tongue sought the curve of her ear. Liquid fire shot down her spine and unashamedly she laid her hand over his, silently encouraging his exploration of the sweet dampness between her thighs once he had lifted her skirts out of the way. Her other hand guided his over the full swell of her bosom then dropped to tug at her clothes, impatient to feel her naked flesh ravished by his kisses.

In a wild explosion of desire, they stripped away their restricting garments and tossed them into a discarded heap on the floor before coming together like the forging of steel with such fierceness and hunger that only the end of the earth could pull them apart. His mouth covered hers while his hands stroked the full crescent of her spine and buttocks; hers, the lean line of his thighs and hips. His kisses glided over her chin, down her neck to the taut peak of her breast, his tongue darting out to leave a moist trail of searing heat while she, now bold and driven by a powerful, unrelenting, insatiable lust, curved her hand around his hot, throbbing manhood and guided it homeward as she bent a knee and draped her leg across his hip to welcome his male hardness. Feeling clumsy and awkward, he caught her in his arms and lifted her up so that she could lock her legs around him. As his mouth descended upon hers again, he shifted her weight to

147

prod the hardened staff deep inside her and experience the enthralling rapture only this union would bring. Tiny shards of colored light filled his senses; his passion reached new heights; his breathing grew labored and a thin veil of perspiration glistened over his body. Groaning with the sheer bliss of it all and wanting to feel the thrust of her hips against his own, he half tumbled, half fell with her upon the bed of hay just as the broad summit of their release held them suspended for one long, breathless moment before hurling them both to the quiet tranquillity of fulfillment.

A long while passed before he lifted from her and rolled to her side, the glow of their lovemaking still warming his face and causing him to smile. Pulling her to him, he held her cradled in the crook of his arm while he tenderly brushed a lock of coppery hair back off her brow and kissed the tip of her nose. In the moonlight which covered their nakedness in a silky, ashen blanket, he could see the soft, contented look on her beautiful face, and he let the image burn itself into his memory. After tomorrow that would be all he would have of her to sustain him until his return. He prayed the task before him would go smoothly and without any delays, and that he and Patrick O'Rourke's difficult missions passed without incident. The sooner he learned the truth about himself, the sooner he could ask Bevan to marry him.

"Bevan," he whispered against her brow. "I have to tell you something."

"Shhh," she urged, not daring to look up at him. He would see the tears that had suddenly pooled in the corners of her eyes.

148

Chapter Five

Just as MacKinley had promised, he arrived early in the morning with a silk top hat, a black cape and even an ivory-handled cane for Reid. He had also included a gold pocket watch to replace Reid's broken one, along with a diamond stickpin and pinky ring, saying that since he hadn't noticed Reid wearing any jewelry, he though he should supply the items to complete Reid's attire and to add that certain air the warden was sure to be expecting. Connie McFee and Kyle had come along with him to check everything over once Reid was ready to go and to wish him good luck. They also guaranteed that the ship would be waiting for him and Patrick at the docks. As an added precaution, Magee had contacted one of the serving girls who took food to the prison and he'd paid her to tell Patrick that the Englishman who was about to pay him a visit was a friend and that he should cooperate fully with whatever the man asked of him.

"Ya don't need to be fightin' him as well as everyone else," Kyle declared as he reached up to brush a piece of lint off Reid's jacket.

Reid appreciated the forethought since he himself hadn't realized Patrick might object, and he thanked Magee for the effort.

"We also got ya a carriage to use," MacKinley added, smiling as if the idea had been his. "It's outside waitin' for ya. The driver is one of ours so ya won't have ta worry about him, and he'll see that Patrick and you make it to the docks in a hurry."

Reid expressed his gratitude a second time.

"And somethin' else," Magee went on. "Ya're to remember that the lot of us"—he swept his hand out to include the O'Rourke brothers, MacKinley, and McFee—"we'll all be somewhere close by should somethin' go wrong and ya need help. There's nothin' we can do while ya're inside, I'm afraid. Ya're on your own. But once ya leave the gate, ya'll be protected. We're plannin' a demonstration."

Reid's brow furrowed curiously.

"It's just a cover. We're doin' it ta help ya get away. It'll look peaceful, but most of us will be carryin' a weapon of some sort."

"You've thought of everything," Reid chuckled.

"We hope so," Magee replied. "Patrick's not only a neighbor of mine but he's a good friend. And he's in prison because of me."

"That's not true, Kyle," Ryan objected. "He's there because of the damn English Crown and their biased laws."

"And because he stabbed a British soldier with his pitchfork before the man could shoot me," Magee corrected. "He saved me life and traded with his own. I'll never forget that and I won't rest until I've seen your father freed."

"Then relax," Reid cut in. "By nightfall, you'll have your wish."

The group became quiet as they watched him don the borrowed cape and top hat, then pick up his cane and the black leather pouch from the table. Everyone in the room wanted to believe he was right in saying that in a short while Patrick O'Rourke would be on his way to England. They *prayed* he was right. Yet beneath all his confidence and their hard work, a small seed of worry took root in everyone's mind.

For Bevan it was a double-sided fear, and she doubted any of the men in the room felt it the way she did. She wanted her father home safe again, but she selfishly wanted Graham there too. Suddenly overcome with the closeness of the cottage and the need to be alone for a few minutes while she collected her wits, she secretively stole from the room and went outside.

Reid had been very aware of Bevan's presence while he talked with Magee and the others, and he was equally aware of her decision to make an exit. Last night while they had lain in each other's arms and quietly enjoyed the aftermath of their lovemaking, she had forbidden him to say a word, and he had obliged her. He'd sensed the mixture of joy and sorrow that consumed her and he understood it simply because he had been experiencing the same emotions. What he realized now was that he had let it end there . . . without a promise or explanation of any kind, something that needed to be resolved *before* he climbed in the carriage and rode away. He had to tell her he would be coming back. She had to know that. He had to be assured she believed him. Not caring if Kyle, McFee, and Gannon

151

MacKinley were added to the list of those who knew about his feelings for Bevan, he excused himself from their company and followed her outside.

"Graham, don't," she ordered the second she turned from the well and saw him walking toward her, his tall, well-dressed build looking grand in the early morning sunlight.

"Don't what?" he asked, slowing his step as he removed the top hat and held it at his side. "Don't tell you that I love you, and that as soon as this is over and I've had a chance to solve my problems, I'll come for you?"

Tears flooded her eyes, but rather than have him see her cry, she looked away. "Don't make promises ya can't keep," she told him.

Her answer surprised him. "I love you, Bevan. I want you to be my wife. Are you saying you don't believe me?" Anger flared up and he said the first thing that came to mind to explain her comment. "Or is this your subtle way of telling me not to bother?"

His remark cut deep but it gave her the excuse she needed to turn him from her. "Aye," she murmured, the pain in her heart contradicting her claim.

"I don't believe you." He reached out to grab her arm and pull her around to face him. "Look me in the eye and say it. Tell me last night meant nothing to you, that you were willing to make love to the first man who came along and showed an interest in you."

Shocked by the insult, her Irish temper flared and she drew back an opened hand to strike his face, only to have her wrist seized in an iron grip.

"You're not a harlot, Bevan O'Rourke, and if someone else had insulted you the way I did just now, your brothers would have to fight me for the right to cut out the bastard's heart." His gray eyes darkened in the flaxen light and the muscle in his cheek flexed as he ground his teeth. "I'm going to assume you're just hardheaded enough that you can't accept a man's word. I'm going to tell myself that I have to prove it to you. I'll even convince myself that once I return here—*and I will*—that I'll have to start at the beginning. I'll have to pretend to forget what we shared and make you fall in love with me all over again." He lowered his head and glared into her eyes. "And you are in love with me, Bevan O'Rourke, whether you care to admit it or not. Shall I show you how sure I am of that?"

A flash of worry glinted in Bevan's eyes as she imagined several ways he would go about achieving it. Then just when she had decided it would be wise to return to the house where her brothers could protect her, his hands caught both her arms at the elbows and roughly pulled her to him. His mouth swooped down hard to claim hers in a hot, passionate kiss, and while her mind cried out for her to fight him, to bring an end to this sweet torture, her heart thumped excitedly, her pulse quickened, and her knees went weak as she allowed her very soul to be consumed by the raging fires his touch ignited. Caught in the whirlwind of his passion, she began to kiss him back, mindless of her pledge and of the fact that they stood in plain sight of anyone who might happen upon them. She kissed him hungrily and desperately until, of a sudden, he released her and set her from him.

His own eyes dark with emotion, he stared at her, then said in a harsh whisper, "That was truth, Bevan." With that, he turned and strode back to the house, stiffly settling the hat on his head and angrily gripping the edge of his cape as a sudden gust of wind threatened to whip it off his shoulders.

Her lips still burned from the kiss. While she watched him through stinging tears, she involuntarily touched her fingertips to her mouth. "Aye, Graham," she whispered. "I do love ya. 'Tis the reason I have ta make ya doubt it." Overcome with sadness, she spun and fled the yard, knowing it would be too difficult for her to stand idly by while he boarded the carriage and rode off.

By the time horse and buggy rolled onto the road leading to the prison, it was nearly noon. Huge, white clouds drifted across the sky and covered the sun's bright face as if playing a child's game of hide and seek. A soft breeze wafted up the smell of freshly cut hay and mocked the danger in which Reid would soon find himself. The only evidence of turmoil in this quiet haven came with the sound of angry voices up ahead. Craning his neck as the carriage moved closer, Reid could barely make out the crowd of men surrounding the gate near the front entrance, but their presence neither surprised nor alarmed him as they were undoubtedly friends of Patrick O'Rourke and members of the Society. The size of the gathering and the knowledge that they were there to help in any way they could eased a little of Reid's tension. Clearly, Kyle Magee was a man of his word. Until now Reid had had no real proof that the Society of United Irishmen was involved, or that the Society even existed.

As he neared the throng of milling, chanting men, he

154

could see the wooden signs a few of them carried. FREE OUR BROTHERS! some of them read, while others proclaimed British rule was unjust. Behind the iron gate stood several red-coated soldiers with muskets in their hands and displeased, almost angry expressions on their faces. Just as Magee had promised, the demonstration held no threat of violence, and when the carriage neared the edge of the crowd, the way opened up for Reid without any oaths or insulting remarks pointed at him. Wondering if any in the group actually knew why he was there, he quickly scanned the sea of faces staring back at him and had to force down the smile that nearly caught him unawares, once he spotted Ryan, Kelly, and Shea among the protesters. Instead he gave them a slight nod of his head and turned his attention on the guard at the gate.

"I have a letter of introduction from King George and wish to speak with the warden," he called to the man who eyed him suspiciously from behind the metal bars.

"You'll have to leave the rig outside," the soldier instructed. "*And* you have to show me the King's seal before I let you in." His gaze traveled the length of Reid as he added, "Can't be too careful these days. You don't look like an Irishman, but a good set of clothes can hide a lot of faults."

Yes, from the eyes of stupid men like you, Reid thought sardonically while he climbed down and, for appearance's sake, instructed his driver to wait there.

"I'm sure you'll find everything in order," he advised once he stood before the gate and handed over the letter he had taken from the pouch.

"So you know the King personally, huh?" the guard

155

jeered as he studied the impression in the wax seal.

"No," Reid replied. "I'm only his agent. But if you'd like for me to give him a message . . ." He cocked a brow and silently challenged the man's arrogance.

An angry scowl settled over the man's brow and he roughly shoved the letter back at Reid through the bars before he turned to one of the men with him and ordered him to unlock the gate. The soldier's animosity, Reid guessed, came from the assignment he'd been given. Chances were he resented having to guard a prison full of Irish rebels on Irish soil and much preferred living in England. He probably would have liked giving Reid a message for the King, but knew his declaration wouldn't have been received with favor. Instead he was forced to hold his tongue and deal silently with yet another apparent nobleman who, by choice, would return to the soldier's homeland while he was left behind.

Reid's devilish nature got the better of him, turning back, he said in the manner of master to servant, "Keep an eye on the rig for me, will you? The Irish . . ." He shook his head and added in a hushed voice, "You can't trust them with anything, you know."

The soldier's neck reddened as he suppressed the sudden rage which assailed him, but before the crimson hue reached his face, Reid turned on his heels and walked away, feeling the heat of the man's regard burning holes in his back as he went. The jackass deserved to be treated disrespectfully and Reid only wished he could be somewhere close by when it was discovered that he, his men, and the warden had been tricked.

Another soldier met him at the huge iron door on the

face of the two-story building and asked from behind a barred portal for the same identification as his predecessor had. His reaction was strictly formal, and once he'd been satisfied that Reid and his letter were legitimate, he twisted the key in the lock and granted the visitor's request to enter.

"Down the hall and turn left. At the end of that corridor, turn right and you'll find the warden's office clearly marked," he advised as he swung the door shut again.

The sound of metal hitting metal, followed by the rattle of keys and the lock being secured, echoed throughout the cold, dimly lit stone cavity of the prison and tightened the muscles across Reid's belly. Getting inside had been easy. Now came the difficult part. He was on his own.

The sharp click of his heels as they struck the rock floor with each step reverberated off the walls and drummed in his ears. He hadn't given much thought to what the O'Rourkes would do to try and free him if something went wrong with his masquerade and he was arrested. But now that he was here—locked behind a thick metal door—it suddenly dawned on him that they wouldn't be any more successful in freeing him than they had their father.

You could plead insanity for me, he thought with a wry smile as his gaze traveled up the wall on his left to the ceiling overhead, then down the opposite side. *I certainly have to be insane to have gotten myself into this. Or terribly in love.* The vision of Bevan flashed to mind and he just as quickly blinked it away. He couldn't afford the luxury of crowding his thoughts with anything other than what he was about to do.

157

At the end of the hallway he turned left and continued on at a steady pace, taking note of the small, barred windows high above his head on the outer wall. Their purpose, it seemed, was to let in fresh air and light, for the deeper into the prison he walked, the darker it became, and the foul smell of the place grew stronger despite the wisps of cool, clean breezes. He turned again at the corner and before him he could see several closed doors on his right. Above the third one hung a sign that read WARDEN'S OFFICE. He paused beside it and removed his hat, while mentally bracing himself for the ruse he was about to play.

A moment passed before the latch clicked in answer to his knock and he came face to face with yet another guard who asked to see Reid's papers. Finding everything in order, the guard motioned Reid inside and told him to sit down in one of the chairs that lined the wall of the small outer room, while he went to inform the warden that someone wanted to see him. Only a matter of a minute or two passed while Reid waited, but to him it seemed like hours before the guard reappeared and gave the order to accompany him. Rising, Reid followed the guard into the adjoining room.

The elegance of the large office surprised Reid once he was inside and the guard had closed the door behind him on his way out. Bookshelves lined one whole wall on his left. To his right a huge fireplace filled the space and an oil painting of King George hung above it. A large, mahogany desk sat in the middle of the room, behind which tall, barred windows let in warm sunshine. Everything, including the floor, was spotless and the rank odor that had filled his nostrils while he walked the corridor failed to reach this isolated contradiction of how everyone else within the walls of the prison was forced to live.

Seated in the tall, leather chair behind the desk was a very rotund little man Reid guessed wouldn't stand tall enough to reach his chin. He had yet to look up from the paper he was studying, and although Reid always thought it was rude to stare, he found himself doing just that. The periwig the man wore sat lopsidedly on his head as if he had knocked it out of place when he reached up to scratch his temple and hadn't bothered to fix it. His gold, wire-rimmed spectacles rode the end of his broad nose, and Reid supposed the man was squinting because of the smoke drifting in his eyes from the cigar he had clamped between his teeth. Thick jowls hung in folds over his meaty neck and perspiration dotted his brow despite the coolness in the room and the fact that he had shed his jacket. Rolls of fat strained the seams of his white, ruffled shirt and damp circles of sweat stained the underarms. He was a pathetic sight, and Reid didn't know if he should blame the man for his own discomfort or pity him. Reid shifted his attention to scruntize the layout of the office once more and to figure out a safe escape route should his interview go poorly.

"Have a seat, young man," the voice behind the desk commanded, "but first give me your papers."

His tone was just as offensive as his looks. Reid came forward, handed over the sealed letter, then sat down in one of the chairs before the desk. Several moments ticked away while the warden read the forged paper, his face expressionless.

"I'm not one to question the King," he said finally as

he laid aside the letter and settled cold blue eyes on his guest, "but I fail to understand why he would want to personally talk with someone of O'Rourke's character. He's nothing but a wretched farmer. And a poor one at that."

"Perhaps," Reid coldly replied.

"Is the King aware that O'Rourke was part of a revolt and that he attacked a British soldier with a shovel?"

"I believe it was a pitchfork, and yes, the King's aware of it. He's also aware of O'Rourke's reason for being involved and that executing him will serve no purpose other than making more trouble. It's his desire to listen to O'Rourke's complaints and then try to solve them . . . peacefully. England, like the King, has had enough wars."

Squinting one eye, the warden asked through a haze of white, curling cigar smoke, "How did the King come to know about Patrick O'Rourke?"

"The Society of United Irishman contacted my uncle with their plea and he in turn spoke with the King."

"Your uncle?"

Reid nodded. "Lord Douglas Rynearson."

For the first time since Reid had stepped into the office, the warden took the foul-smelling cheroot from his mouth. "Lord Rynearson?" he questioned.

Reid hoped his apprehension didn't show in his face. "Yes," he replied as coolly as possible. "Do you know him?"

The warden jammed the cigar back between his teeth and stood as he answered. "You could say that. He's married to a childhood friend of my sister's. But I haven't seen him in years." He rounded the desk and crossed to the door, adding as he went, "From what my sister said, Douglas wasn't the sort to concern himself with someone else's problems." He turned the knob, pulled the door open, and motioned for the guard to come in. "Old age could change a man, I suppose." He smiled halfheartedly at Reid as he stepped aside to allow the armed soldier to join them. "But in his case, I doubt it. Douglas Rynearson was, is, and always will be a cold-hearted bastard. And you, sir, are *not* his nephew. That much I do know because Rynearson doesn't have one."

The shock of the announcement widened the gray-blue eyes of the man staring blankly back at the warden as the order was given and the muzzle of the long-barreled rifle raised to point at its victim's head.

The last contact Gordon Sanderson had had with Reid had been in the form of a letter left for him at the inn where they were staying. Reid had told him to unload the damaged goods at Rynearson's warehouse and exchange them for comparable merchandise, then he was to wait for him at the inn, while Reid explored a lead he'd been given. Gordon could only assume it had something to do with Rynearson and the idea didn't set well with him, since he didn't like the fact that Reid had gone alone. Rynearson couldn't be trusted and Gordon feared what might happen if Reid got him cornered. It worried him even more once Gordon had talked with the warehouse manager and had learned that he had told Reid about Rynearson's plans to meet with some Irish rebels. That apprehension had spurred him into going against Reid's orders.

Gordon knew Reid would be angry with him at first for deliberately ignoring his instructions, but at that point Gordon didn't care. He no longer even thought about it once he and Eric had talked with a man at the docks and they had learned that Reid had hired a schooner to take him to Ireland. In Gordon's opinion a shipload of damaged merchandise just wasn't worth the risk Reid was taking, and if nothing else, he and Eric would at least even up the odds a bit.

Once they had docked in Dublin, they asked around about the schooner Reid had hired and if anyone had seen a man of Reid's description. Of the few who were willing to talk, none of them reported seeing a stranger except for the two of them. The last man they questioned, however, gave them a chilling account of the rumor he'd heard about debris that had washed ashore after a recent storm and at just about the time Reid's schooner should have been sailing across the channel. As far as the man knew, there had been no survivors, since no bodies—dead or alive—had floated inland along with the wreckage, but Gordon couldn't accept that. He'd have to be shown Mr. Hamilton's remains before he gave in and returned home. Thus, he and his first mate had spent the next two days asking questions and looking around.

"Maybe we should visit the cove where we were told the wreckage was found," Eric suggested as he and his captain shared a table in the commons. "At least we'd be doing something instead of sitting around here all day."

"Perhaps," Gordon reluctantly agreed as he eyed the other patrons of the inn. "I was just hoping . . ." He let the comment trail off.

"Hoping what?" Eric replied. "That Mr. Hamilton would up and walk in? You're dreaming, cap'n. If we're going to find him, we're going to have to tear this countryside apart. Nobody here is gonna tell us anything."

"I know."

"Then let's try something different," Eric posed. "Let's go down to Bray and snoop around without letting anyone know we're not Irish. If these buffoons relax around us, one of them might say something worthwhile."

"We'll still be strangers," Gordon pointed out.

"Aye," Eric agreed. "But if we keep our mouths shut, we won't be nosy strangers."

Gordon studied the ale in his mug for a moment, then raised it to his lips and finished it off. "All right. Let's go."

Eric grinned as he shoved away from the table. "Now you're talkin'. Give me a couple of seconds to use the privy and we'll be off."

A disgruntled frown pursed Eric's thin features a moment later as he left the inn through the back door and spotted two men entering the double stall outhouse at the end of the dirt path. He was in a hurry—for two reasons—and the delay irritated him. Hoping they wouldn't take long, he quietly approached to stand at the side of the small wood structure, truly not intending to eavesdrop on the pair's conversation, but truly thankful he had once he heard the topic of their debate.

"I don't care what ya say, it's a stupid idea," the first remarked to his companion.

"Why? 'Cause you weren't the one ta think of it?"

"No," he rallied. "It's stupid 'cause it won't work. His

163

sons *and* the Society have been tryin' for days ta get him out of prison and nothin's worked. What makes Rynearson think he can? He'll wind up gettin' them all killed."

"Would ya care ta place a wager on it?" his friend challenged.

"A little late for that now, don't ya think?" the other barked. "Brady told me they were goin' ta the prison today. In fact, they're probably there right now." Hiking up his breeches, he kicked the door open and stepped away from him. "But if ya're willin' ta part with your money, I'm willin' ta take it," he boasted.

Standing among the crowd outside the prison, Gordon and Eric were just as anxious to push through the gate as any of the rest of the men chanting their protests, but for very different reasons. The argument Eric had overheard between the two men in the privy earlier had been the first solid evidence that Douglas Rynearson was in Ireland, and they had figured that wherever Rynearson was, Reid was sure to be close by. When they rode up, however, they *hadn't* expected to see their friend being escorted through the iron gate by armed guards, and if they hadn't feared for his safety, Gordon would have called out to Reid before that one disappeared inside the stone structure. Now all they could do was wait alongside everyone else crowded around the barred entrance, while they prayed Mr. Hamilton knew what he was doing. Gordon and Eric certainly didn't.

"What the hell is he up to?" Eric ground out as he and his captain moved back from the throng of angry men.

164

"I haven't the vaguest idea," Gordon admitted. "But whatever it is, he's taking an awful chance. If the rumors we heard about Rynearson dealing with rebels are true, I'd say these men are *his* friends and not Mr. Hamilton's. If something goes wrong—"

Just then, the sounds of a scuffle and angry shouts from behind the metal door of the prison stilled the crowd of men around him. In the next instance the heavy barrier was swung open and two figures stepped out into the yard.

"Mary, Mother of God," Eric softly exclaimed once he saw that one of the two men was Reid and that he was holding a pistol to the throat of the fat little man he held clutched by the shirt collar. "What the hell's going on?"

"I don't know," Gordon scowled. "But it's rather obvious Reid needs our help."

"But how? What can we do?" Eric nervously asked while he watched a crowd of armed soldiers follow Reid outside. "We're a little outnumbered."

Realizing that the locked gate stood between them and Reid, Gordon started to move toward it with the intention of pulling his gun and ordering the guard to hand over the key, when the crowd of Irishmen around him and Eric started pressing in ahead of him. What happened next was a jumble of visions and sounds for Gordon mixed with a horrible feeling of total helplessness. An explosion of gunfire rent the air, followed by enraged, hateful shouts from both the guards and the protestors, more shots, a rush of bodies which knocked Gordon and Eric aside, screams of agony when both sides opened fire on each other, and mass confusion everywhere. Gordon wasn't sure who

165

was to blame for the first shot nor did it matter now. Reid was in the middle of this melee and Gordon and Eric had to rescue him. Pulling their own weapons, they started to advance.

The chilling sounds of a battle raging and the smell of death in the air gripped Bevan's heart, and she broke into a run. She hadn't intended to come to the prison; in fact, Ryan had forbidden her to leave the farm. But once the silence in the house had closed in on her, she had grabbed a shawl and sprinted off across an open field to the road which wound its way through the hilly countryside. At the top of the next knoll she knew she would have a clear view of the prison, but once she stood on the crest, horror filled her as the scene below her turned ugly. Terror tore at her insides while her thoughts centered on her father locked in his cell, her brothers caught in the middle of the fight, and most of all Graham, whom she could see in the courtyard trapped behind the iron gate and tall, stone fence. His plan had failed—that was obvious—and now his life hung by a thin thread. Magee had promised to protect him, to do everything within his power to see that Graham got out unharmed. And maybe Magee had done just that, but it hadn't been enough. Heart-wrenching fear seized her entire body as she stood paralyzed and watching Graham's broad-shouldered frame fighting his way toward the gate which had somehow miraculously been opened up, yet was crowded with men struggling to get in and grab him. A volley of shots pierced the air and each one seemed to cut right through Bevan. Unknowingly, she held her breath as if the gesture would cloak Graham in an invisible suit of armor.

"Run, Graham!" she suddenly screamed when she saw the man he had used as a shield fall from a stray bullet. "Oh God, Graham, run!"

What followed passed in a blur. She saw Graham hesitate as if to help the stricken man, then raise his gun and fire at one of the soldiers. She saw him club another with the empty weapon, then turn for the gate. She saw him run with his head down and his cape fanning out behind him as if it were the wide-spread wings of a raven taking flight. She saw his step falter. She saw his head snap to one side. She saw the blood, the dark, crimson blood. She saw his body sag, then drop. She could almost feel his muscular frame hit the ground and hear the air knocked from his lungs when the earth came up cruelly to catch him. She felt his pain . . . then she felt nothing at all. Numb and drugged with shock and disbelief, she stood motionless as she watched two strangers hurry to him and lift his limp, lifeless form in their arms to carry him away. She wanted to scream out to stop them, to tell them that he wasn't dead. Then from somewhere in the crowd Magee appeared beside them. He touched the arm of the one closest to him as he mouthed a question Bevan couldn't hear, and she saw the stranger shake his head in sullen remorse. Suddenly, the collage of images melted and blended into a swirling mass that turned from bright pastels of happiness to the grays and blacks of grief. Its jagged edge cut deep. Ebony shadows whirled before her eyes. Her breath seemed to leave her as she staggered, then fell to her knees.

"Oh, Graham," she sobbed forlornly. "Me dear,

sweet Graham. How will I ever go on without ya?"

Giving way to her agony, she folded her tiny frame forward, cupped her face in her hands, and wept, deep and hard.

Bevan had no idea how long she had sat beneath the huge oak tree after order had been restored at the prison and everyone had been sent home. Nor did she honestly care. Her life had ended the moment she witnessed Graham's death. Nothing else mattered to her now. She would never love again. Her days would pass slowly; her nights in torment. Yet, the closer she walked toward the cottage she shared with her family, the more she realized how selfish she was being. She would grieve for her lost love as she had a right to do, but she mustn't force her family to suffer along with her. Graham had died trying to help them, to help their father escape execution, and his death should not be in vain. It was up to her now to finish what he had started. She would meet with Magee and other members of the Society and between them all they would think of another way to free her father . . . even if it meant she would die trying . . . just as Graham had done.

A new strength suddenly surged within her and she straightened her small frame, squared her shoulders, and raised her chin in the air. Everything she did from this point on, she would do because of Graham. She would honor his memory, his courage, his love. From the heavens above he would smile down on her and have reason to be proud. Graham Rynearson would live forever in her heart and mind, and as soon as her father was home again, she'd tell him all about the man with whom his daughter had fallen in love, and Patrick O'Rourke would come to love him too.

As she left the road that wound its way past her home and cut across the field instead, a determined smile softened the sad line of her mouth as she hurried her step. As soon as she reached the cottage, she'd send Shea to fetch Magee and as many of the Society members as he could find and bring them back to the house. The sooner they started plotting out a new scheme for freeing her father, the better. His execution was scheduled for early the following week, which didn't give them much time, and they'd need every second they could get.

The long shadows of sunset stretched out across the field before her. Caught up in the beauty of its golden light painted across the green grasses and mixed with splotches of gray-black, Bevan failed to notice the elegant carriage drawn up beside the front door of the cottage until she was nearly upon it. Stumbling to a halt, she frowned as she studied it, knowing it wasn't the one the Society had supplied for Graham's ill-fated journey. Her first reaction was that perhaps it belonged to someone of authority and that they had come to arrest her brothers for their part in the attack against the prison. But the more she considered it, the less likely it seemed. First of all, they would send soldiers on horseback . . . several of them. And the boys *wouldn't* invite them in for tea! Besides, the moment shots had been fired, she had seen Magee, George Connery, and Thomas Flanagan shove her brothers away, and she had guessed they were told to go home before someone recognized them and decided *they* were the reason for the riot. No, whoever was paying them a visit more than likely had come for another reason entirely. Bracing herself for whatever lay ahead, she took a deep breath and opened the front door.

The second her eyes met those of Douglas Rynearson as he sat in a chair near the hearth, Bevan's heart tumbled in her chest. He was alive! He hadn't drowned as everyone had thought . . . as Graham had thought. He had survived the shipwreck! Her elation turned suddenly to a mixture of confusion, anger, and suspicion. This man might be Graham's uncle, but she still didn't like him. If he'd been on that schooner with Graham when it went down, where had he been all this time? Why hadn't he tried to find his nephew or to contact the O'Rourkes? Why hadn't her brothers found him the way they had Graham? But worst of all, his being alive meant Graham's death had been senseless! If they had known he was all right, they wouldn't have gone to the prison. They would have let *him* take care of it just as they had agreed he would earlier. Graham wouldn't have been killed!

Ryan could read the thoughts going through her head, perhaps because he had asked himself the same questions, and before she could voice them and demand an explanation, he left his place next to Kelly and crossed the parlor to take her hand in his.

"Bevan," he said softly, "I . . . I . . ." He frowned, lowered his gaze, and sighed, deeply troubled. "I don't know where ta begin."

"Start by explainin' what *he's* doin' here," she snapped, her green eyes focused hatefully on the man who had risen from his chair. "Explain why he let his own nephew die when he didn't have ta."

Surprised to learn that she already knew about the

170

tragedy at the prison, Ryan glanced up at her, chin sagging.

"I saw it all," she supplied, her gaze never wavering from Douglas Rynearson's face. "I was there. I saw Graham get shot. I saw him fall. I saw two men carry him off." She shifted her angry scowl on Ryan. "I saw him die when he didn't have ta die."

"Miss O'Rourke," Rynearson started to respond, but Ryan raised a hand to stop him.

"If ya don't mind," Ryan said, "'tis my place ta tell her."

Bevan's eyes narrowed. "Tell me what, Ryan?"

He drew her farther into the room, swung the door shut behind her, then guided her to the chair Rynearson had vacated. Puzzled, yet sensing she wouldn't like what she was about to hear, she quickly scanned the faces of the men in the room for a clue—Kelly's, Shea's, Kyle Magee's, and finally that of a stranger's she hadn't noticed when she first opened the door.

"Don't baby me, Ryan!" she exploded when he tried to push her down in the chair. "Tell me what ya have ta say and be quick about it." Jerking free of his grasp, she stepped away and stood with her back to the hearth, where she could watch everyone in the room with her.

Ryan knew this wouldn't be easy. Even he'd had trouble believing what Rynearson had told him, and he doubted Bevan would accept it any easier than he had. But she had to be told. There was no sense in putting it off. "It concerns Graham," he began, pausing a moment to steel his nerve and ready himself for his sister's rage. "Or the man we thought was Graham."

Auburn brows crimped and green eyes shot sparks

171

at him.

"Bevan, I'm not goin' ta try and explain what happened or who that man was we fished out of the cove, why he lied ta us and then gave up his life for our father. I'll never understand it meself and now that he's . . . dead, I guess we'll never know for certain. What's fact is that *this* man"— he motioned at the stranger who stood quietly watching Bevan—*"he's* Graham Rynearson."

A flood of thoughts raced through her head while she eyed the man claiming to be Rynearson's nephew. Although he wasn't nearly as handsome as . . . Graham, *her* Graham, he was as tall with dark hair and blue eyes. His clothes fit him well and he carried himself with a certain kind of dignity and pride. The suggestion that he was related to Lord Rynearson made her see a few vague similarities, or at least she thought the man had Douglas's chin and the same-shaped nose. Her gaze fell on the elder Rynearson while she considered the possibility he could be lying. But why? What would he gain? Why would he have brought this man to her house claiming he was his nephew if he really wasn't? And if that was true, then who . . . ? She shook her head, lowered her gaze, and sank down in the chair. It was all just too horrible to think about right now.

"Bevan," she heard Ryan softly call out to her, "would ya like ta lie down for a while? Ya've had a terrible shock."

Shock? she thought bitterly. *Me life has been torn apart and I feel as if there's a heavy rock lyin' on me chest so I can scarcely breathe, and ya're askin' if I want ta lie down, like it will make a difference? No. I*

172

don't want ta lie down. I want Graham. The Graham who loved me and promised ta marry me!

"I'm sorry, Lord Rynearson," Ryan went on when he could see Bevan wasn't up for any more disturbing news, "but I think maybe you and your nephew had better come back tomorrow . . . after Bevan's had a little time—"

"Come back?" Emerald eyes glared at Rynearson. "For what? Why did ya come here in the first place? Ta gloat? Are ya enjoyin' our pain? Our embarrassment?"

"No, Bevan, not at all," Rynearson hurriedly denied. "I wasn't aware of this man pretending to be my nephew or your attempts to free your father. I'd *never* gloat over someone's misfortune. I'm here to help, to fulfill my part of our agreement. I brought Graham with me so the two of you could meet. Tomorrow I had planned to use my influence in court to free your father . . . the way we had discussed."

A chill embraced Bevan's slender form and she hugged her arms around her. The bargain. She had forgotten all about the deal they had made with this man—the deal *she* had made. By agreeing to marry his nephew, Lord Rynearson would see to it that her father's life was spared.

"There's no need ta come back tomorrow," she finally replied, her voice flat. "There isn't time." Rising, she forced herself to look at the stranger. "I assume ya're aware of why your uncle brought ya here?"

The dark-haired man nodded.

"Well, I don't mean ta rush ya, but me father's goin' ta hang in a few days and I need ta know if I should pack up me things or see ya ta the door."

"Bevan, no!" Ryan shouted.

173

"Hush," she rallied, her eyes the shade of a dark, precious stone. "'Twas me own decision ta make and it still is. I'm doin' it for me father. Ya don't really expect me ta sit by and let him hang, when there's somethin' I can do ta stop it, now do ya?"

"Of course not," Ryan barked. "But I'm sure we can find another way other than havin' ya marry a stranger."

"Aye. We probably could," she agreed. "But can anyone guarantee it won't turn out the way it did this mornin'? How would our father feel if he knew one or all his sons were killed in exchange for his freedom? There's no danger in what I'm doin'. No one will get killed. And father will be home with ya again." She turned stormy eyes on the young man who had listened to the siblings' heated discussion. "So, Mr. Rynearson, have ya made up your mind."

His blue eyes blinked, glanced at his companion, then Ryan, and back to Bevan. "Yes, Miss O'Rourke, I have. I'd be honored to take you for my bride."

"And I'd be honored if you and your uncle left our house before I—"

"Kelly!" Bevan exclaimed.

"Kelly what?" he snarled. "Stand back and let your sister make a foolish mistake without openin' your mouth? Well, I won't. I can't. Ryan's right. We'll find another way."

"Oh?" she challenged. "Name one. Tell me a way that's simpler and any less dangerous." She waited only a few seconds for him to answer. "I'm sorry, Kelly, but even *if* ya could come up with somethin', Father can't wait." She brushed past Ryan and headed for her bedroom. "Now, if ya'll excuse me, I have ta pack a few of me things."

Silence followed her from the parlor.

Silver moonlight struggled to peek through the thick clouds skimming across the sky in an effort to reveal the passage of a lone figure hurrying down the wooden walkway near the wharf. At the corner he turned, paused, and looked back in the direction he had come as if making sure he wasn't being followed. Satisfied that no one had an interest in his late-night activities, he rushed on. At the end of the street he stopped at the front door of an inn, looked back a second time, then went inside. Only two customers remained in the commons, both of whom he ignored as he headed for the stairs. A moment later he entered one of the rooms near the end of the hall, closed and locked the door behind him, then turned to look at the man lying unconscious in bed.

"He still hasn't come around?" Eric Dillion asked.

"No." Gordon sighed with a worried frown as he leaned down to gently lay his hand across Reid's brow. "Maybe it's for the better anyway. When he wakes up, he's going to have a hellava headache." Straightening up, he looked at his companion. "So what did you find out?"

"Two things," Eric told him. "There's a ship leaving in the morning for Liverpool. If we're there at sunup, the first mate said he'd smuggle us on board."

"Good," Gordon replied. "The sooner we leave Ireland, the better I'll like it. What else?"

"Apparently the warden was killed by one of his own men, and to cover it up, they're holding Mr. Hamilton responsible, even though there were plenty of witnesses to the contrary. And our stealing him off the way we did has created another problem. They're not convinced Mr. Hamilton is dead since they don't have a body to verify it."

"I was afraid of that," Gordon scowled as he crossed to the dresser and the bottle of whiskey sitting there.

"Well, the good news is that no one seems to know his name or anything about him, except that he told the guard he'd been sent to the prison by King George."

Gordon's head snapped around. "What?"

Eric shrugged. "I can't figure it out either, Cap'n. According to the rumors flying about, Mr. Hamilton had a sealed letter of introduction and asked to speak with the warden. No one else seems to know why or what happened specifically once he got inside. You and I saw as much as everybody else after that."

"What about Rynearson?"

"His name was never mentioned."

"Curious," Gordon replied after a moment of thought.

"To say the least," Eric agreed. "I guess if we're to learn what this was all about, we'll have to wait until Mr. Hamilton comes around."

Gordon poured them both a drink, handed one over to his first mate, then crossed to stand beside the bed. "It sure looks that way. But right now knowing what brought it all on isn't really that important. Getting him on that ship is."

"Which could prove to be a little tricky," Eric advised. "There's British soldiers wandering all around the harbor, asking questions and stopping anybody they think looks suspicious. To tell you the truth, I think we'd be wiser sending Mr. Hamilton on back to North Carolina ahead of us, rather than taking him to Liverpool to wait while we're unloading and loading the ship. We can't be too sure someone didn't get a good look at us there at the prison, enough to identify us anyway, which means there's a good chance we're being hunted too. If we're spotted, the ship will be boarded and searched, and they'll find Mr. Hamilton." He could tell by the thoughtful look on his captain's face that Gordon was considering his suggestion. "There's just such a ship at the pier right now. It's American and they're sailing for Virginia in the morning. I'm sure for the right price they'd gladly take on an extra passenger."

"Go talk to the captain and see how much he wants to take on an extra passenger."

"Aye, aye, sir," Eric said, turning for the door. "And while I'm at it, I'll see if I can't pick up a change of clothes for him. They're looking for a man of wealth, not a sailor, and if we're stopped, we'll pretend he's passed out from too much whiskey."

"Good idea," Gordon concurred as he reached for the gold watch, diamond stickpin, and ring he'd laid on the night stand. "Trade these for whatever they're worth." Rising, he met Eric in the middle of the room and handed him the jewelry. "I know they don't belong to Mr. Hamilton, so I don't imagine he'll be too upset to learn we gave them away."

"All right," Eric consented as he briefly analyzed their value. "It might even be enough to pay for his passage." Stuffing them in his jacket pocket, he turned and unlocked the door. "I'll be back as soon as possible," he added before making a quiet, hurried exit.

"Sooner, if you can," Gordon murmured as he closed the door behind his friend and turned the key in the lock. "This whole mess makes me nervous."

Deciding he could use another drink, he did an about-face and started back toward the night stand where he'd set his glass. At that moment Reid stirred, and Gordon forgot about the whiskey he thought he needed as he anxiously approached the bed and hovered close. A second or two elapsed before he saw Reid's eyelids flutter, then open, and the thought crossed Gordon's mind that perhaps while he had the chance he should bind Reid's wrists and ankles. If he'd been right about Reid wanting to finish what he started, restraining the man would be the only way Gordon and Eric would get him on a ship bound for home.

"Reid," he called softly. "How are you feeling?"

His world had opened up slowly and for Reid the first sensation was a sharp, throbbing pain behind his eyes and in both temples. Even the pale light from the hurricane lamp on the night stand seemed to blind him, and he quickly blocked out the glare by laying his arm across his face.

"Horrible," he managed to whisper. "How'd you find me?"

"It wasn't easy," Gordon told him. "I guess you could say luck had a lot to do with it. Next time you decide to run off like that, would you at least tell me in person instead of leaving a cryptic note? *And* would you mind explaining what you were doing in that prison?"

One gray eye peeked out from above the crook in his arm. "Prison?"

178

"Yes," Gordon mocked impatiently. Now that he was sure Reid was going to be all right again, given time, he had no room for being polite. "It's a stone building with high fences and bars on the windows. I realize it's not the kind of place you're accustomed to visiting, but you surely knew that's what it was *before* you went in."

"What are you talking about?"

Gordon gritted his teeth. This was no time for playing games. Or for keeping secrets. "Reid, if Eric and I hadn't come along when we had, you'd be dead right now. I'm not asking for your gratitude, but I feel I, at least, deserve to know what the hell you were doing."

"I was following Rynearson," he quietly answered as he covered his eyes again. "Would you mind moving the lamp? The light's too bright."

Half rising out of his chair, Gordon cupped his hand around the top of the glass cylinder and blew into it, plummeting the room into darkness, save the silver streams of light falling in through the window.

"That much we figured out by ourselves," he jeered as he sat back down and squinted in the shadows to see his companion's face. "What we couldn't understand was what possessed you to go inside after him."

"Inside what?" Reid grumbled while fighting to focus his eyes on the shadowed expression of his friend. "You're the one not making any sense. Or have I missed something?"

An icy shiver tickled the hair on the backs of Gordon's arms. Rising, he crossed to the wash stand, dipped a cloth in the cool water, wrung it out, then returned to fold it over Reid's brow. "What's the last

179

thing you remember, Reid," he asked.

Closing his eyes again, Reid wrinkled up his face and jeered, "Waking up to your fool questions."

"I mean before that," Gordon instructed.

His head hurt just lying still. Thinking made it throb. "I remember holding on to the railing and praying I wasn't going to die." He gently touched his left temple. "I'm wondering now if I might not have been better off."

"Railing? What railing?"

"On the schooner. We encountered a storm just off the coast. It was too much for the vessel, I'm afraid. I'm sure it sank."

Gordon collapsed in the chair. "It did. We'd been told there were no survivors."

Reid forced a weak smile. "Lucky for me you didn't believe it." He winced at the pain he caused when he tried to sit up. "I must have hit my head on some of the debris, though I don't really remember anything else except how violent that storm was." He shifted the rag on his forehead and slowly tried to push himself up again.

"Just lie still," Gordon ordered, touching his friend's shoulder and gently pushing him back down. "There's no need to rush off."

"I was thinking maybe we might still be able to catch up with Rynearson," Reid admitted, curiously eyeing the man staring back at him. "Unless there's something you're not telling me."

"There is," Gordon confessed. "But it has nothing to do with Rynearson." He frowned, reached for the glass on the night stand, and went to refill it as he added, "Not directly, anyway."

Reid ignored the pounding in his head and swung his legs off the bed. Dizzy, he leaned forward with his hands braced on his knees and waited a moment for the sensation to pass. "I get the feeling we're dancing around a subject you'd rather we not discuss, Gordon. If it concerns me, I think I have a right to know what it is."

Handing his friend the glass of whiskey, Gordon told him to drink it, and while Reid did as instructed, Gordon pulled the chair away from the bed, swung it around, and straddled the seat with his arms folded along the top back rail. "You're in serious trouble, Reid," he began. "It's even worse now that it seems you can't remember getting into it."

The whiskey burned going down but Reid hardly felt it. Even the hammering in his head didn't bother him quite as much as before. "I think you'd better explain," he ordered as he laid aside the damp cloth and empty glass.

"There's not much *to* explain," Gordon replied. "Eric and I got in on the tail end of it, I'm afraid, but I'll tell you all we've managed to find out." His story lacked details as he repeated the events which had happened after he and Reid split up at the warehouse, and by the time he was finished, Reid was as confused as Gordon. "I never mentioned this to Eric, but I got the distinct impression those men outside the prison, the Irishmen, were trying to get to you as hard as Eric and I were. I'd like to think it was because they were trying to help you, but I'm not really sure." He frowned and asked hopefully, "Does any of what I've said mean anything to you?"

The only memory it stirred was the conversation

Reid had had with Rynearson's warehouse manager and that he'd been told Rynearson was going to Ireland to meet with a band of rebels. Beyond that he couldn't remember a thing.

"Well, don't let it worry you, Reid," Gordon encouraged once he realized the frustration Reid was feeling. "It'll come back. It might take time, but it will. Meanwhile, we've got to get you out of here. Eric's at the pier right now booking passage for you on a ship sailing to Virginia in the morning. Once we've seen you off, he and I will go back to Liverpool and . . ."

Reid stopped listening as other matters clouded his thoughts instead of Gordon's plans. Stretching out on the bed again, he gently laid his head on the pillow and stared up at the misshapen shadows on the ceiling above him. A piece of his life was missing, days which held all the answers to why he was in that prison, how he had gotten ahold of a letter written and sealed by King George and where he had spent his time after the schooner went down. All of that troubled him. But what disturbed him more than anything was the haunting sweet smell of freshly mowed hay.

Chapter Six

Saying good-bye to her brothers at the harbor in Dublin had been one of the hardest things Bevan had ever had to do in her life. She hadn't wanted to leave Ireland until she was sure her father had been released from jail, but Lord Rynearson's claim that it would take a day or two before the papers authorizing his release were validated *and* his insistence that neither he nor his nephew could afford to be away from their business matters that long had forced her into relenting. It had all been compounded by the sailor she saw from a distance as he worked on one of the huge ships anchored at the end of the long pier, for he bore a striking resemblance to the stranger with whom she had fallen in love. Dark hair curled from beneath the edge of the red bandanna he wore on his head. A broad shoulder and thickly muscled arm cradled the large crate he had hoisted up to carry on board the American frigate. His back was straight, his frame long and lean, and although he never once turned to face her, she envisioned rugged good looks and soft gray eyes. The second she had seen him, her heart had done a flip-flop, and she had had to force herself to look away. There was no use in torturing herself when she knew there was no hope in changing what had already happened. The man she had grown to love was dead, and it was time she got on with her life.

Ryan had seen where her attention had drifted and he had known what thoughts had crossed her mind. His own heart ached with the realization that this was one time he couldn't protect his little sister. He could, however, promise her peace of mind.

"Shea, Kelly, and I are goin' to ask around," he had told her as they stood at the bottom of the gangplank awaiting permission for her to board the English Capitol ship with Lord Rynearson and his nephew. "None of us can rest until we know who that man was and why he lied, why he gave up his life for somethin' that didn't concern him." Noticing the tears which had suddenly pooled in the corners of her eyes before she had turned her head away, he had gently pulled her into his embrace. "I know ya felt somethin' for him, Bevan, and I'm willin' ta believe he helped us because of you, because he loved ya. He must have had a good reason for keepin' the truth from us, and with some luck, we'll find out what that was."

"I'm not sure I want ta know," Bevan had confessed. "I get the feelin' it's somethin' horrible."

"Like what?" Ryan had asked.

Glancing back to look at the sailor and finding that his ship's gangplank had already been raised, the sails unfurled, and that he was nowhere in sight, she had sighed forlornly and admitted, "That he was married and had wee ones tuggin' on their mother's skirts. I'd rather just go on wonderin' than knowing he played me for a fool."

Ryan had wanted to argue the point, but at that moment the other passengers standing near them had started for the ship, and they had been forced to abandon their discussion. She had hugged and kissed each of her brothers, including her twin, who normally never appreciated a physical show of affection but who had clung unnaturally hard to his sister when she pulled him close. Kelly promised to send word to her the instant their father was home with them again, and just when she was about to break down in tears, the gentle touch of someone's hand on her arm gave her the courage to be strong, if not for her brothers' sake, then to hide how truly frightened she really was. Forcing a smile, she had turned and ascended the gangplank with Lord Rynearson leading the way and the man she would soon call her husband at her side, and while the ship weighed anchor and drifted slowly out into the channel, Bevan took up a vigil at the railing of the ship, where she remained until the distance between her and her brothers made them disappear from sight.

The journey across the St. George's Channel that morning had passed smoothly and without incident. The day had blossomed with bright, warm sunshine, clear skys, and gentle breezes. To all the others on board, it was a perfectly beautiful passage. For Bevan its quietude had been traumatic, for it gave her nothing to use as a distraction while the peacefulness of the voyage mocked her very soul. She was leaving a comfortable, loving existence behind her in trade for an uncertainty in her future, and the longer she thought about it, the more puzzling it became.

Rynearson and his nephew had left her alone on the quarterdeck, where she had stood gazing out across the waters at the coast of Ireland she could no longer see, while they mingled with a few of the other passengers, whispering and laughing as though this day was no different from the one that had passed before it or the promise of the one that had yet to come. The sounds of their merriment had drawn her attention to them and, unnoticed, she had stared openly at the man who would soon be her husband, a man she had difficulty referring to as Graham. His features were well chiseled and impressive. His dark hair, pulled back at the nape by a black satin ribbon, shone in the sunlight, and his richly tailored clothes fit him in a complimentary fashion. Generalizing his appearance, Bevan had to admit he was handsome, and that was what confused her. Perhaps it *was* true that he hadn't married because he hadn't found the right woman. That was not to say it was because there had been a lack of hopeful, young girls all bidding for him—Bevan was sure there had been many—but why he had never found any of them suitable was a question on which she could only speculate unless she was able to find the courage simply to ask him. What truly bewildered her, now that she had had time to consider it, was how, after a moment's glance and a few words, he had so easily decided that *she* would be the one with whom he'd settle down, and that of all the choices she was certain had been presented to him, he had picked not only a young woman of no means, but an Irish one besides. The English hated the Irish, yet he was eagerly willing to take one as his bride. She simply couldn't justify his reason, and because of it, instinct hinted that something just wasn't quite right.

The sun had already begun to set by the time the rooftops of Liverpool popped up over the horizon, and Bevan viewed the scene with mixed emotions. Ireland was full of troublemakers as far as the English were concerned and she was Irish. She hadn't come here by choice—not really—and while she was fighting the homesickness that had already begun to settle in, she knew she'd have to be fighting prejudice as well. She didn't have to be well educated to know that just being married to an Englishman wouldn't guarantee her that the elite would accept her. She was an outsider, and she would always be looked upon that way for as long as she lived. A large house with servants, fine clothes, and expensive jewelry, and introductions to all the right people, would never change the fact that she was an Irish lass living in England. And before long, the pressures her husband would experience from his friends and colleagues would turn him against her as well. The only solace she could afford came from the knowledge that she had done this for her father, and that in itself was what turned the corners of her mouth upward when Graham came to take her arm and escort her down the gangplank to the busy pier.

"You must be tired," he said, drawing her to a less-crowded spot on the wharf while his uncle excused himself for a moment to find the carriage and driver that were supposed to be waiting for them. "You never left the deck during the entire voyage."

"A little," she replied, suddenly conscious of the fancy gowns the other women around her were wearing. Her clothes alone set her apart.

"Did you eat anything?" he continued, his tone soft

and polite. "I saw the cabin boy offer you a plate."

That had been around noon, and although she hadn't been hungry at the time, she was absolutely famished now. Smiling uncomfortably, she shook her head.

"Well, maybe my uncle won't mind if we stop at one of the inns," he remarked. "I must say I'm hungry too. There's something about the fresh sea wind that builds one's appetite." He smiled down at her before his mood turned serious. "How well do you know Lord Rynearson?"

The question surprised her. "Hardly at all," she responded. "We met the night he came ta make a deal. Why do ya ask?"

He shrugged his wide shoulders and looked away, but not before she saw the frown settle over his brow. His reaction made her curious and a little uneasy, but not enough to question him about it, and once Rynearson joined them again, other matters took precedence.

"I'm afraid there's some trouble at my warehouse," he announced, the expression on his face clearly showed his irritation.

"Would you like for me to see Miss O'Rourke home, while you—"

"No!" Rynearson barked heatedly, startling both Bevan and the man at her side. "I told Faber to do it. Besides, you and I have business to finish. Remember?" He roughly took Bevan's arm and practically pulled her off balance when he yanked her forward toward the carriage waiting at the end of the pier.

From the first moment he'd been told about the beautiful Irish girl living near Bray, Rynearson had experienced one problem after another in his quest to have her. Tricking her into coming to England had been the hardest. Once that had been settled, he had difficulty in locating Charles Alcott. The man had been away on business when Rynearson first tried to contact him, and when he had finally returned and had heard what Rynearson wanted from him, Alcott had flatly refused. All that changed his mind was Rynearson's threat to confiscate the man's property in exchange for the money he owed him, and even then he'd been very reluctant. But Rynearson's worst turn of bad luck had come on the night he and Alcott were to meet the O'Rourke brothers in the cove. He'd already booked their passage on the frigate, and if he hadn't decided to stop by the warehouse first, he wouldn't have missed the boarding time *and* his appointment with the O'Rourkes. As it was, he'd run into the captain of the American vessel he'd swindled sometime back, and fearing for his life, he had gone into hiding until he'd learned that Captain Sanderson and his first mate had sailed for Dublin. Only then did he chance hiring a private vessel to take him and his conspirator to Bray, a town far south enough of Dublin that he wouldn't accidentally meet up with Sanderson again. Now it seemed more trouble awaited him at the warehouse, and his temper was dangerously raw.

Bevan could understand a man's ill-humor when his livelihood was threatened, but in her opinion it didn't give him the right to be rude. She tried to pull free of him and winced when his grip tightened. Puzzled and a little irked at Graham for allowing his uncle to treat her in such a fashion, she cast him an angry scowl only to find that her future husband had seemed not to

189

notice . . . or to care. Deciding to take it upon herself to bring an end to the manhandling, she grit her teeth and stopped dead-center in the middle of the crowded walkway, pulling hard against the restraint despite the burning sensation it caused.

"I'm quite capable of walkin' on me own, Lord Rynearson," she hotly advised, her emerald eyes glaring back at his raging expression.

He appeared to be angry enough to strike her right there in front of witnesses, and Bevan could only guess it was because he'd very seldom come up against a person's open defiance, and especially a woman's and *never* in public. The look on his face frightened her, but she managed to hide her feelings, since this would, after all, be the last time she'd have to deal with the man if she had anything to say about it . . . which didn't seem to pose much of a problem. Graham obviously had no backbone, since he hadn't bothered to step between them or to say a word in protest. Several seconds passed while they silently challenged each other, and to everyone's surprise, Rynearson was the first to back down. Bevan wasn't sure if it was because he had realized she meant what she'd said or if it had suddenly dawned on him that they were drawing curious stares. Whatever the cause, he released her arm, bowed from the waist, and smiled as he held out a hand for her to lead the way . . . without an escort. Feeling only a small victory since the gleam in his eye was far from pleasant, she raised her chin, glanced at Graham to find him reluctant even to acknowledge what had just transpired, and started off again on her own. Her opinion of Graham was changing rapidly.

At the end of the long wharf, Bevan spied a finely

crafted coach and four, the likes of which she had never seen, and she slowed her step to appraise its worth. The shiny lacquered body of it glistened blue-black in the dying sunlight. Brass handles, passenger steps, lamps, and footrest sparkled a gold hue. Leather shades hung down from the windows, and four identically marked French coach horses stood ready, their rich coats shimmering in the faint light. The vision pleased her and aroused a feeling she had never before experienced: a pretentious air that riding in such a fine coach would somehow change how people viewed her. Then her gaze drifted to the man who sat rigidly holding the reins, the one she assumed was Faber.

Delicate in stature, the man had milky white flesh that seemed to be stretched tight over his tiny frame and barely disguised a fragile skeleton. Small brown eyes, closely set, peered out over the end of his long, birdlike nose. Thin, pale lips were pursed in a stiff manner as if he'd just tasted a tart apple, and the aura that enveloped him was one of cold, silent aloofness. Upon further examination, Bevan noticed that his left hand was webbed and the sole of one shoe was thicker than the other. The suit of clothes he wore hugged his narrow-shouldered build, and although the garments were made of rich cloth, they fell short of flattering anything about him, and Bevan shamefully wondered if others would look at her and think the same as she thought of this man, that in spite of one's attempts to mask one's faults, a person's true identity would still shine through.

She forced her attention away from him when she suddenly realized that the topic of where she would spend the night and how soon her marriage to Graham would take place had never been discussed. Turning with the intention of asking, a cold rush of nerves washed over her once she discovered that while her back was to him, Graham had left without a word *and* that he had left her alone with his uncle. The smile that failed to reflect in Lord Rynearson's eyes heightened her fear and she unconsciously stretched up on her toes in an effort to see past the people crowding around her for Graham's tall build.

"If you're looking for my nephew," Rynearson surmised with a half-smile, half-leer distorting his mouth, "I should tell you that I sent him on ahead to the warehouse. It's time he learned the business since one day it will be his." He stepped forward, opened the carriage door, and held out a hand to assist her. "Faber will see you home."

"Home?" she repeated, not moving. "And where is that, Lord Rynearson? Where are ya plannin' I stay until the weddin'?"

"Why, you'll be our guest until all the arrangements have been made," he answered, reaching for her elbow.

Bevan shied away from the thick fingers adorned with large stones. "Your guest?"

"Yes. My wife and I have a lovely place on the edge of town. You'll like it. I've had a special room made up for you with your own servant, and it overlooks the gardens in back. It's quiet and restful, and if you'd like, you can sleep until noon."

Bevan appreciated the fact that Rynearson's wife would be there. She couldn't quite explain it, but now that she didn't have her brothers close by to protect her, she didn't trust this man. "For how long?"

Laughter rumbled in his wide chest. "Just as long as

it takes, my dear," he replied. "To get you and Graham married, I mean." He wiggled his fingers at her. "Please, Bevan, get in the coach. I can't even begin to think about a wedding until I've taken care of my business at the warehouse. Faber will see to it that no one bothers you. Now come . . ."

If Bevan had had any choice in the matter, she wouldn't have allowed Lord Rynearson to assist her into the carriage. She would have declined, stated that this was a mistake, and then looked for the first ship sailing back to Ireland. But she couldn't. Her father's life was at stake. Envisioning the stocky, white-haired man with green eyes, hot temper, and soft, loving smile, she settled herself stiffly on the plush leather seat and jumped at the sound of the carriage door clicking shut behind her. She gritted her teeth when the driver called out a command and the rig lurched forward, then swung around and rattled off down the cobblestone street. Tears threatened to spill from her eyes and she blinked them away as she reached for the window flap and drew up the shade. Had it been another time, another place, someone else's coach, she might have enjoyed the ride. Instead she studied the scenery passing by with subdued hostility. This city, *England,* was her home now. She could never go back to what had been. It would never be the same for her, and for one brief second, she wondered if she had done the right thing.

The journey to Lord Rynearson's estate took close to an hour and seemed to wind and turn down every avenue in Liverpool before the way stretched out ahead of them. Bevan viewed the panorama with reluctant curiosity. The shops, inns, and houses along the way bore a similarity to her beloved homeland, and once they had traveled past the edge of town, she noticed the countryside lacked trees and that the rolling fields were divided by stone fences . . . the sort of description one might apply to Ireland. Yet in Bevan's mind the area lacked more than just trees. It lacked warmth and friendliness, and she doubted she would ever come to call this land her home. Struck with melancholy and missing her father, her brothers, and the cottage they shared, a tightness formed in her chest and the tears she had fought so hard to control broke free. Her despair heightened when the vision of dark hair, gray eyes, broad shoulders, and sparkling warm smile edged into her thoughts. The happiness she had dreamed would be hers one day had slipped between the cracks of reality, and the thought of ending her dismal life once her father was freed flitted around in her head and offered the sweet promise of release. Then and only then would she find peace.

The swaying of the coach as it rounded a bend and headed up the long drive roused Bevan from her morbid thoughts. Leaning, she peered out the window at the huge, stone manor up ahead. Thick green ivy clung to its face, around the front door, and over each window. The two-story mansion, nestled among giant pines and bathed in the golden light of the dying sun, took on an air of foreboding despite the artistically scupltured lawn, the abundance of flowers, and the gentle breeze which stirred up the fragrance of rose blossoms and pine, for not a single person walked about the place or appeared in the doorway to greet their visitors. Bevan's disquiet intensified when Faber guided the carriage away from the main entrance into the house and took them around back. Perhaps she was unaccustomed to the rituals of the wealthy, but she couldn't understand why even they would require a guest to enter the premises from the rear . . . unless of course her status was such that it wouldn't be proper.

Proper, she mused bitterly. *A person's rank has nothin' ta do with good manners. It's almost as if ya're smugglin' me inta the house. Well, that will change, Lord Rynearson. When I'm the mistress of me own home, I'll teach ya how ta treat people no matter what their rank.* A sarcastic, somewhat devious grin curled her mouth. *And I'll start by makin' ya use the back door. Or maybe I won't let ya in me house at all!*

Faber's whining voice called out for the horses to halt and Bevan's attention once again centered on the scene beyond the window of the coach. Thickly leafed vines of ivy continued to hug the walls of the manor, yet more densely than on those out front. The air was damp, the shadows deep, and the sense of doom heightened when even the last rays of daylight failed to reach this spot. The rig rocked as Faber climbed down and a second later his thin face appeared in the open carriage door. A bony hand reached out to offer assistance and Bevan hesitated, though she didn't know why. She truly felt no safer inside the coach than she was sure she would feel free of its leathered interior. Perhaps descending the rig marked the end of her life as Bevan O'Rourke and the beginning of Lady Graham Rynearson. She cringed at the irony of it, swallowed hard, squared her tiny frame, and unwillingly allowed Faber to help her down.

"I'll show you to your room," he said flatly as he turned from her and hobbled toward the door that was

195

all but concealed from view within the leafy overhang.

"But what about Lady Rynearson?" she asked, frowning and quickly glancing at each of the windows for the face of someone she guessed would surely be watching. "I'd like ta thank—"

"Time enough for that later," he threw back over his shoulder. "Besides, Lady Rynearson hasn't been feeling well. She's probably retired." Twisting the brass handle, he swung open the door and looked back. "I was told to see you to your room first, and then have a tray brought up."

Up? Bevan thought uneasily and without realizing it, her gaze followed the tangled web of vines climbing the side of the manor. High above her a dormer peeked out through the bed of dark green as if it were the head of a snake and she its prey, and the doom which had assailed her earlier grew twofold as she recalled the hearthside stories her father had delighted in telling his wide-eyed children long ago. They dealt with dragons and dungeons and knights in shining armor who came to rescue the fair princess locked in the tower. Even though his tales ended happily, the chill of the adventure had always frightened his young daughter of six and many times awakened her in the middle of the night when the stories turned into ghoulish, bad dreams. *This* was no nightmare—Bevan had her eyes wide open—but just the same, it felt dangerously close, and it magnified once Faber motioned for her to follow his uneven, lumbersome gait.

The musty, dank smell of the place truly didn't surprise Bevan once she had stepped inside. Nor did its dark interior, narrow hallway, and winding, spiral staircase that turned sharply to the right and disappeared behind the limestone wall. Flickering lamp-light from the sconces just above her head cast eerie shadows all around them and lent an air of demonic ghostliness to the crypt. The echo of their footfalls bounced off each tread as they made their ascent, and the higher they climbed, the more nervous she became. At the top, a winded Faber withdrew a key from his pocket and placed it in the lock, and the sound of cold steel and squealing hinges hammered in her ears.

"Faber," she began, her voice reverberating in the stairwell, "are ya sure—"

The little man ignored her to go inside the darkened room. A moment later, warm candlelight fell against her face, but it failed to chase away the chill that played havoc with her nerves. Not wishing to be rude and hoping that perhaps he hadn't heard her speak, she opened her mouth to repeat her words and gasped when the odd little man suddenly stepped back into the doorway, his webbed hand waving her inside. Hesitant, yet strangely curious—what else had she to do with her time?—she did as he bade.

Her trepidation and worry that Faber had misunderstood his employer and had taken her to the wrong room faded the instant she walked across the threshold. To her right stood a huge four-poster brass bed covered with a pink and white floral quilt. Beside it were a rocker and a night stand, the latter of which held a brass hurricane lamp and a book of poetry. A trifold dressing screen filled the far corner, its cloth inserts done in the same fabric as the quilt. A red brick fireplace greeted her from across the room and before it sat two matching wing chairs upholstered in crimson velvet. To her left was the same dormer she had seen from outside in the yard, but this time it provoked a feeling of cozy seclusion with its white, eyelet lace curtains tied back by pink bows to show off its diamond-shaped panes of leaded glass. A tall, beautifully crafted armoire flanked one side, an ornate dresser on the other, and Bevan couldn't hold back her moan of approval for the pearl-handled comb, brush, and mirror set she saw lying there. Drawn like a magnet, she slowly approached the treasures and stood running her fingertips along the satiny smooth surface of each piece.

"If you'd like, I could have a bath brought up for you before you eat," she vaguely heard Faber offer.

"Aye," she murmured as she lightly touched the bottles of fragrances she found sitting there and imagined their sweet scent filling her nostrils while she bathed. "That would be nice." A black lacquered jewelry box caught her eye, and while she stared in awe at the fine necklaces, earrings, and bracelets she found inside, she vaguely heard the door shut behind the servant on his way out.

Below in the kitchen, Uriah Faber instructed one of the staff to heat water and see that a tub was taken upstairs to their guest, before he turned and headed for his own room. Shutting himself in, he limped to the small writing desk in the far corner and sat down. Pulling open the drawer, he emptied its contents, reached for the letter opener, and easily pried loose the false bottom to reveal a tattered, leather-bound book which he carefully withdrew and placed on the desk top. A strange look came over his face as he leafed through the pages for the last notations, and once he'd found them, he reached for a quill, dabbed it in the ink well, and leaned forward to jot down his latest entry, his disfigured hand holding the book still.

She's Irish, this one, he wrote. *A pretty, young thing with hair the color of a golden sunset. Her eyes are an emerald green like I've never seen before. Her skin is smooth and the shade of pure ivory. We haven't spoken much, but I sense she has a fiery temper, and I believe he'll have his hands full with this one. He likes them that way, but this sweet girl is different. She'll fight him. She may even try to kill him.* He paused and glanced up at the last light of day struggling to shine in through the window. A half, vindictive smile twitched one corner of his mouth, and with new zeal, he began to write again. *I hope she does try to kill him. And I hope, no, I pray she succeeds. Then everyone will know what kind of a man he really is, and we'll be free of him.* The quill shook in his hand, and he missed his first attempt at dabbing it in the well. *If only I had the courage, I'd do it myself. But I don't. I'm a coward—except when it comes to picking out a new girl for him. How can I lure someone into this house when I know what will happen to her? Where do I find the strength to dispose of her after he's finished with her? Some would say I have no feelings, but that's not true. I feel fear, disgust, and hatred. And love.*

His entire body began to tremble as it always did while he wrote in his journal. Deciding to complete his entry later, he put away the quill, closed the book, and slid it back inside the secret panel of the drawer. If his intuition about the Irish girl was correct, perhaps he could think of a way to help her without her knowing he had. But it had to be done discreetly, of course. If she failed and he was found out . . . He shuddered at the thought of the consequences he'd pay. Awkwardly he rose and turned for the door. It wasn't that he feared for his own life as much as he feared for Lady Rynearson's. Without him there to protect her, her husband would surely abuse her . . . again. And this time he'd more than likely kill her.

Pushing his thoughts aside, Uriah braced himself for the events of the evening yet to come and opened the door. He felt sorry for the poor Irish girl, but it wasn't his fault she had allowed herself to get into this predicament. As always, he'd block out the sounds of her screams during the night, then tend her wounds in the morning and pretend not to hear her pleas for his help. It was the only way he could deal with the demented games his employer played . . . that and the knowledge he had traded a stranger for Lady Rynearson. If he distanced himself from the girls he brought to that upstairs bedroom, he wouldn't feel their pain. He had enough of his own to contend with. Pulling the door shut behind him, he started to turn for the kitchen when a movement from out of the corner of his eye made him jump.

"Damn it, Margaret," he hissed, once he recognized the woman standing in the shadows of the hallway. "Must you sneak around like that? One of these days I'll drop dead of apoplexy and it will be your fault."

"Won't be too soon if you ask me," she rallied with a sneer, her thin arms folded over her small bosom and her brown eyes snapping with hatred. She glared at him a moment longer, then jerked her gray head in the direction of the spiral staircase. "I suppose you've brought another one into the house."

"Ain't none of your business," he countered, attempting to brush past her, but the maid quickly blocked his path with her tall, willowy frame.

"It is when it concerns Mistress Lillian," she told him. "Do you think she doesn't know? Just because she's bedridden doesn't mean her mind is weak." She squinted her eyes at him and added jeeringly, "Like some people I know."

Nettled by the woman's insult, Uriah snarled, "Would you rather he share Mistress Lillian's bed?"

The ultimatum set the woman back on her heels. The color in her face quickly paled, and it took her a moment or two to draw a breath to speak. "Of course not," she spat through clenched teeth. "But you'd think he'd have the decency to take his mistresses elsewhere, rather than bring them in this house right under everyone's noses. If he's thinking to spare his reputation, let me assure you that he hasn't. The entire staff knows about his infidelity, and there isn't a one of them who can keep quiet about it. Everyone in Liverpool is probably gossiping about how he has the audacity to shame his wife right in her own house. And *you,* you little guttersnipe, are helping him to do it. The two of you should be horsewhipped."

Uriah had never liked the sassy woman who looked after his beloved Lillian. She, obviously, had never liked him. If there was a reason to have her on his side, he would have explained why he did what he was doing. Her hatred, however, worked in his behalf and he wasn't going to jeopardize that. Let her hate him. Let her think the worst of him. As long as she did, it meant she had no idea what was really going on upstairs . . . the awful, ugly truth, the twisted, deplorable acts of a sick mind, and the horrid results.

"Maybe you're just upset because he never picked you, Margaret," he scoffed. He knew if he made her angry enough, she'd stomp off in an indignant rage. And that was what he wanted. He had to get back to the girl. He had to keep her upstairs, and he couldn't afford to lock the door just yet. His employer said that he wanted her fed and bathed first, and if he locked her in, she'd demand to know why and that would lead to trouble. She'd get scared and refuse to eat or to take a bath. She'd start screaming, and then the kitchen help might hear. And if they heard the screaming . . .

"You're the most detestable little man I know," Margaret was saying. "You're almost as disgusting as Lord Rynearson." She grabbed both hands full of her skirts, raised her nose in the air, and added, "And you can tell him I said so . . . if you have the nerve." With that, she turned and walked away.

I'd do a lot of things, if I had the nerve, Uriah mused as he watched the woman's tall, slender shape disappear within the shadows of the hallway. *And the first thing I'd do is take Lillian away from here. But only after I cut out her husband's heart.* Knowing that neither of his well-hidden desires would ever become fact, he sighed dejectedly and headed for the kitchen.

Bevan had hardly been able to believe her eyes once she had opened the armoire and found a complete wardrobe of exquisite gowns, petticoats, lacy under-things, satin robes and nightclothes, shoes, stockings, capes, muffs, and frilly hats. The lavish raiment was suited for a queen or at least a princess, and Bevan knew she hardly fit either category. What surprised her

202

even more was Faber's insistence that Lord Rynearson had had the garments made up especially for her even before he knew his nephew would agree to marry her. The hot bath had done wonders for her sagging spirit, but the silk nightgown and matching robe made her forget all about her troubles while she sat on the Oriental rug before the hearth brushing out the dampness in her hair and enjoying the warmth of the fire. Outside her room she could hear distant thunder, and for the first time since her arrival, she thought of her father and the cold, stone cell in which he had been forced to live. Could he hear the thunder, too, she wondered. Was it already raining there? Was he shivering in the darkness? Were his thoughts centered only on his discomfort or was he thinking of her and his other offspring? Did he know how much he was loved, and that she and her brothers had never given up trying to free him? Would he understand her sacrifice and forgive her?

Suddenly the cheery fire, the soft feel of satin against her skin, and the pleasure of her bath made her feel horribly sanctimonious. Why should she have such luxuries when her father had none? What right had she to be happy when nothing about his existence could bring a smile to his face? Angry with herself for having forgotten why she'd come to this place, she jerked up to her feet, crossed to the dresser, and laid the brush down beside its matching mirror and comb. There was only one reason why she was marrying Rynearson's nephew and that was in exchange for having all charges against her father dropped. It didn't mean she could forget about her family and how they lived, how they would continue to live while she enjoyed her husband's wealth. Ashamed, she turned toward the rocker, where she had laid the plain brown skirt, white blouse, and shawl she had worn there, only to find them gone. Frowning, she glanced at the closed door. She couldn't remember seeing one of the servants pick them up when they'd come for the tub a short while earlier, but apparently someone had. Deciding to ask Faber about it, she tied the sash around her waist and took a step toward the door just as a soft rap and Faber's meek voice called out for permission to enter.

"I have your dinner, Miss O'Rourke," he told her.

Hurrying forward, she opened the door and motioned him inside, then asked while he set the tray on the edge of the bed, "Did someone take my clothes?"

"Your clothes, miss?" he repeated, careful not to let his gaze drift any lower than her exquisite face. His heart might belong to another and many might surmise that his disability affected his male needs, but he was still a man and being alone with a young woman of Miss O'Rourke's beauty, and she clothed only in a thin, silky nightgown, tested his moral fiber as a gentleman. "I'm afraid I don't understand."

Bevan waved a hand in frustration at the empty rocker. "The clothes I had on when I arrived . . . the ones I laid there. Where are they?"

Uriah's eyes followed the direction in which she pointed, then looked back upon the lovely face again. "I would imagine they've been burned."

"Burned?" Bevan gasped. "Why?"

Uriah couldn't comprehend her surprise. "Because they were nothing more than rags, Miss O'Rourke, and because you had no further use of them, I suppose." His pale brows dipped downward. "Aren't you pleased with the things Lord Rynearson has given you?"

"I'm not pleased at bein' taken for granted," she shot back. "I have a mind of me own, and I'm quite capable of makin' decisions. I should have been asked before someone took it upon themselves to dispose of me things."

"Yes, miss," Uriah yielded. "It won't happen again."

Flustered and feeling a little panicky, she whirled away from him as she frantically looked around the room for the bag she had brought from home, knowing before he even confirmed it that it, too, had been tossed out with the rest of the household rubbish. Near tears, she grit her teeth and demanded, "Where is it?"

"*It,* miss?"

"Me bag . . . the one I brought with me. I saw Mr. Rynearson carry it on board the ship. Did he give it ta you?" She shook her head. "No, he couldn't have. He never took it off the ship." As if she really expected him to be honest with her, she asked beseechingly, "Why, Faber? Why didn't he give it ta you?"

This was the part of the whole sordid affair he hated most, having to witness the slow dawning by Lord Rynearson's newest mistress that she hadn't actually been hired as governess to children he didn't have or as personal maid to his wife when she already had a trusted servant, or in Miss O'Rourke's case, that she would not marry the man's nephew when he didn't have one. Lord Rynearson used whatever lie he could think of to lure a young woman into his house. It came easy for him. Uriah could almost see the smile on his employer's face while he fabricated some story to win the poor girl's pity, her trust, and he wondered if Rynearson had used the same plot on Lillian. But of course he had. Why else would she have married the bastard?

Feeling sick inside, he turned without answering and left the room.

Terror shot through Bevan's heart the instant she heard the key hit the lock. Too numb to move, she just stood there staring at the closed door. Surely she wasn't being punished for speaking her piece. Good lord, she had a right to complain about someone stealing her clothes. Then why had Faber locked her in? Was he afraid she'd get angry enough to run off? How foolish of him. That was the farthest thing from her mind. She had given her word she would marry Rynearson's nephew, and she would never go back on her word . . . she *couldn't!* It would mean her father would die. Surely Rynearson realized that. So what had provoked such measures? Had Faber been instructed to lock her in? Or had he taken it upon himself to see that she stayed in her room until Lord Rynearson came home? As hard as she tried to reason it out, she couldn't guess what harm there would be in her wandering through the house. Nor could she fathom a need to imprison her. Anger rolling up inside her, she stormed the door.

"Faber!" she shouted at the fading thump of footsteps she could hear descending the staircase. "Faber, come back here and unlock this door! Do ya hear me?" Tilting her head, she listened for a second or two, realized he wasn't paying any attention to her, and grabbed the ivory knob with one hand while she beat upon the door with the other. "Damn ya, Faber!" she howled. "Perhaps ya're doin' what Lord Rynearson has told ya ta do, but I'm sure his nephew won't be

206

pleased when I tell him. And ya can wager your next month's salary that I will!" Hot tears burned her cheeks. "Ya hear me, Faber? I'll tell Graham ya locked me in here for no good reason!"

"I hear you," the little man sighed in hardly more than a whisper as he rounded the last bend in the staircase and slowed his awkward gait to pause on the last tread. "I wish I hadn't, but I did. And there's nothing you nor I can do about it." Fighting down the bile that had suddenly begun to rise in his throat, he hurriedly covered his mouth with his webbed hand and fled for the privacy of his room, unaware that Margaret stood in the shadows only a few feet away.

Exhaustion had been the only reason Bevan fell asleep that night. She had tried to stay awake. She had paced the floor until her feet were bruised and aching. She had sat up in the rocker and forced herself to think about her father. She might be feeling like a prisoner, too, but she was a lot better off than he was. She'd been given a bath and a hot meal, for which she'd lost her appetite and hadn't eaten, while her father was probably forced to lie on the cold floor with only a thin layer of dirty straw for his bed. His supper had, in all likelihood, consisted of day-old porridge and a tin of water. Chances were he'd had to endure unwarranted beatings as well as the callous taunts of the English guards about how soon he'd be marched to the gibbet. Bevan knew she had no right feeling sorry for herself when her father was the one who was suffering. Yet, she did. And she was scared.

She'd left the rocker to stoke the fire, then stand

beside the window seat in the narrow dormer and watch the lightning chase across the sky. A soft rain had begun to fall and before long its icy droplets hit against the leaded glass in a mixed cadence that drew in volume until its fevered pitch hurt her ears. Driven away from the window out of fear the storm would shatter the panes, she had gone to the bed to sit propped up against the headboard with the pillows at her back. How long she sat there before sleep dulled her thoughts and comforted her worry, she didn't know. If she had guessed her mind and body would give in, she would have resumed her pacing or at least she would have sat on the window seat and watched the storm. Only Lord Rynearson had the answers to her many questions and she had wanted to be awake when he came home.

The tapping of the raindrops against the roof came fast and furious. The fire crackled in the hearth. Bevan stirred at the sound of a key in the lock. Hinges squeaked. A rush of cool air fell into the room. A shadow touched her face when a tall figure moved in front of the fire. The sense someone watched her chipped away at her slumber until her eyelids fluttered and a cold shaft of consciousness bolted her upright in bed.

"Lord Rynearson," she breathed, the quilt clutched tightly under her chin as she scrambled to her knees and edged herself to the opposite side of the bed. "I didn't hear ya come in." She glanced nervously at the door. "I didn't hear ya knock either." Her worried gaze fell on the mantel clock she could see over his shoulder. "'Tis late. What are ya doin' here at this hour? And why was I locked in this room?"

A strange smile came over his face. "So many questions," he mocked. "Aren't you pleased with your room?" His hand swept out to indicate the armoire. "Or the clothes you've been given? The roof over your head that doesn't leak? The warm fire? Your bath and a meal you didn't have to prepare yourself?" He spotted the mentioned tray of untouched delicacies sitting on the dresser and he frowned. "You didn't eat. Is something wrong with—"

"Wrong?" she echoed, the question shrill with anger. "Aye. There's somethin' wrong, but it has nothin' ta do with the food your toady brought me." She noticed for the first time that Rynearson was dressed in a silk floor length lounging robe and slippers, and for a second she wondered if he had anything on underneath. Instinct screamed at her to get off the bed and put it between them, which she wasted no time in doing. "I realize, Lord Rynearson, that I come from a family who has very little in comparison to you, but I had always assumed good manners and proper behavior was somethin' rich and poor alike had in common. I think ya should leave before your staff gets the wrong idea."

Deep laughter rumbled throughout the room and blended with the heavy thunder which bounced off the walls and rattled the windowpanes. "I've never been one to care what the hired help thinks of me. They're paid to work, not form opinions." He eased his stalwart frame into the rocker, crossed his legs, and rested an elbow on the arm. "There's been a change in plan."

Fear knotted the muscles in her stomach. "What kind of change? And why couldn't it wait until mornin' ta be told?"

He smiled again, the firelight reflecting the gleam

in his eyes. "I believe in settling problems as they arise . . . before they get out of hand. In your case, I feel you should be told the truth right away so that we can come to an understanding."

The man's pomposity, his arrogance, riled Bevan's temper. "Then get on with it," she ordered acidly. "Pretendin' ya care about me feelin's won't change what I think of ya. I didn't like ya the minute I met ya, and I doubt anythin' ya say or do will make a difference."

One corner of his mouth twitched in a half-smile. "You've got grit, Bevan O'Rourke. I like that in a woman. Just don't let it get in the way."

"Of what?"

"Of doing what is necessary."

Her green eyes narrowed. "Necessary?" she repeated.

He inclined his head in a slow, meaningful gesture that left no doubt in her mind which of them held the upper hand. "Graham has decided not to marry you."

Bevan wasn't sure if she should be relieved or worried. Their original deal stated that Rynearson would see her father freed whether she married the man's nephew or not. His presence in her room right now and the cunning, evil look on his face hinted that the change to which he referred meant the entire arrangement. "And ya're here ta strike a new deal."

He shrugged and pushed himself up from the chair. "I suppose you could call it that," he relented as he rounded the end of the bed and slowly approached her. "The truth of it is simply that there is very little choice where you're concerned. Either you do as I say or your father is executed." He chuckled at the horrified look on her face. "Come now, Bevan. You're an intelligent girl. Surely you've figured it out by now. If I have the power to free your father, then I certainly have the power to speed things up." He grinned sardonically and added, "Say, tomorrow afternoon?"

Bevan's slender body began to shake. "What is it ya want from me?" she asked in a whisper.

He raised a brow and reached out to curl a lock of her chestnut hair around his finger. "Isn't it obvious, my dear? I want you."

The announcement made every inch of her flesh crawl. She wanted to cry, to scream, and to laugh all at the same moment. Instead, she stealed her nerves and pulled back to free his claim on her hair. "I would think your wife might object."

"My wife," he snorted derisively. "She's a sickly old hag who lost her beauty and charm years ago. If it weren't for the inheritance she'll receive once her father dies, I'd throw her out of my house."

Bevan's stomach churned. "So what ya're proposin' is that I become your mistress right here under the same roof as your wife?"

"Very astute, Bevan," he mocked.

"And that if I say no, ya'll have me father hanged," she finished.

He nodded, quite sure of himself.

Bevan drew confidence from the man's cocky air. Displaying a bittersweet smile, she walked past him and went to the window to stare out at the raging tempest assailing the countryside. A moment passed before she turned back around to glare at him. "I'm afraid ya went ta a lot of trouble for nothin', Lord Rynearson. Before I'd give meself ta ya in exchange for me father's life, I'd throw meself out that window." She

211

jerked her head in the direction of the mentioned aperture. "And don't go thinkin' ya can scare me inta changin' me mind. Me father would rather die than have his daughter lay down with the likes of you."

Her insult had very little affect on him, since he'd heard it countless times before. "And that's supposed to make me turn you loose?" He shook his head. "I went to a great deal of expense and inconvenience to get you here, Bevan. As I said before, you really have no choice. You'll stay here for as long as I wish it. If you cooperate, your father will live. If not . . ."

Bevan could feel the trap closing in around her and she hated herself for having walked blindly into it. Knowing that all she had left was her dignity and the slim hope of escape, she also realized she'd need time to figure out a plan and that she'd need someone's help if she was to escape this place untouched and with enough time to get word to her brothers and the Society. *Someone* had to make a second attempt at getting to her father before Rynearson could order his immediate execution.

"How do I know ya'll keep your word?" she asked, wondering if her idea would work . . . for now. "So far ya've proven ta me that ya're nothin' more than a lyin', deceitful old man who mocks his weddin' vows. If ya'd lie ta your wife and ta God, what's ta stop ya from lyin' ta me? In fact, how do I know ya're tellin' the truth about Graham? If ya want me ta surrender, then here's the condition." When he continued simply to stare at her, Bevan took it to mean she had a chance. If she could convince him into bringing Graham to see her and be allowed to talk with him alone, Graham might be the one to help her. After all, he'd shown a caring side earlier there at the pier, *and* she'd play upon his guilt for being the reason she had come here in the first place. "I want ta hear Graham tell me in person that he's changed his mind about marryin' me."

Rynearson could hardly believe his good luck. He'd always liked his women to have a little spirit, but he never enjoyed their whining. This young lady had offered a way to eliminate the latter, while still promising excitement. All he had to do was bring Charles Alcott here, have him tell her that he wished to remain unwed, and Bevan would be his for as long as he desired her.

"All right," he easily relented. "I'll have Graham pay you a visit in the morning." He took a step toward her. "Meanwhile—"

"Tonight," she corrected. "Right now."

Rynearson's temper flared, and he drew in a breath to tell her that any decision making was his alone to do, when he realized such a declaration would be defeating his own purpose. Exhaling an angry breath, he pulled himself up and cooled the raging desires which threatened to ruin what promised to be an exquisite night of passion.

"So be it," he calmly replied as he looked past her to the bright flashes of light outside the window and the runnels of rain streaking the panes. "I would prefer waiting at least until the storm has passed, but I can see this is important to you." His hungry gaze fell upon the translucent fabric of her night shift and boldly feasted upon the shapely curves it outlined as he silently told himself the ride to Alcott's home would be worth it. With the vision of her creamy white skin, supple body, and luscious chestnut hair firmly implanted in his brain, he reluctantly turned for the door. Once he'd unlocked it, he stood with a hand resting on the knob while he glanced back and added, "You'll never regret your decision, my dear. I can give you everything. All you'll have to do is please me." He smiled an evil smile, nodded his head, and left the room, making sure to lock the door after him. This was one treasure he wanted to make sure never escaped him.

At the bottom of the steps, he paused to glance back up the winding staircase. He hoped Bevan O'Rourke would last longer than the rest, that her spirit was harder to break, and yes, he even hoped she would like what he did to her. It would make it all that much more pleasurable if she did. Inhaling a deep breath and letting it out slowly, he tossed the key in the air, caught it in his fist, and headed to his chambers. He'd get dressed, then rouse Faber from his bed and be on his way. There was still plenty of time to sample the young woman's charms before the sun came up.

The moment his shadow left the foot of the stairs, another took its place, quietly, secretively. It lingered, then ascended the spiraling treads on slippered feet.

Lillian Rynearson hardly looked young enough to be a mere score and thirteen. Her black hair had lost its luster and the gray at her temples seemed to accentuate the lines at the corners of her eyes. Her skin was pale, her face drawn, and even her voice lacked the sparkle it once had. She was sickly, suffered from bouts of deep depression, and was too weak to leave her bed. She had been that way ever since the accident.

Although her marriage to Douglas had been

arranged by her father, Lillian had fallen in love with the wealthy lord the second she met him and had looked forward to a wonderful life with him. Their first year together had been exactly the way she had dreamed it would be. He showered her with affection and expensive gifts, and devoted all of his time to her. He took her to all the stylish, important functions in Liverpool to show her off to his friends, and entertained guests in their home at least once a week. They laughed, stayed up late drinking wine and sitting cuddled up in each other's arms before a roaring fire, and made love every night until early dawn. They were the ideal example of a happily married couple.

The first time Douglas struck her, Lillian had blamed herself. She had made him angry and he had retaliated without thinking. His attack had seemed to shock him just as much as it had her, and near tears, he had begged her forgiveness. They spent the night in bed making love and for both Lillian and Douglas it had been the most wonderful time they had ever shared.

Only a few weeks passed before it happened again, but this time Lillian could not fault herself for the assault. Nor did Douglas beg forgiveness. He merely stripped her of her clothes and forced himself on her until he left her bruised and hurting. It worsened after that, and before long, Lillian's love for him turned to fear. He complained about everything she did . . . or didn't do. He began to drink heavily and often times stayed away all night. She suspected he had taken a mistress, but she didn't care . . . especially after she learned she was carrying his child. Douglas took the news of her pregnancy with polite surprise. He even seemed to mellow. But on the night he approached her with lust burning in his eyes and she courageously denied him, telling him that it wouldn't be safe for the baby she had carried to its seventh month, he became enraged and hit her. And he kept hitting her until she had lost consciousness. The next morning it had been Margaret's painful duty to inform her mistress that the baby had come early and had died.

Lillian's condition never improved after that. Margaret, her valued servant, cared for her day and night, and Douglas went about his business as if none of it had been his fault. From that day on, he seemed to behave as if his wife had died as well.

The entire staff knew the truth about the accident despite Douglas's claim that Lillian had fallen down the stairs when her heel caught in the hem of her gown. Those who feared Rynearson quit his employ; those who loved Lillian stayed on, and that included Uriah Faber, a shy, crippled little man Lillian had begged Douglas to hire when Faber knocked on their door asking for food.

More than ten years had passed since the awful night, and every time Lillian learned of the newest mistress her husband had the nerve to bring into their house, her fear of him lessened and hatred grew in its place. She longed for the day she could make him pay for what he'd done to her and repeatedly entrusted that fact with her maid. Thus, every chance Margaret got, she watched and listened and made mental notes. Finally, after all the waiting, Margaret had what her mistress needed.

Shadows engulfed Lady Rynearson's bedchambers as heavy velvet draperies were drawn to keep out the night. The thin light of a candle penetrated the ebony darkness with a flutter, then grew once its flame touched the long white tapers in the candelabrum on the night stand. A warmth seemed to brighten the room and the presence of someone standing next to her bed slowly awakened the mistress of the manor.

"Margaret?" Lillian called from within the curtained interior of her canopied bed. "Is that you?"

"Yes, mum," the maid quickly responded, her voice in a whisper. "I'm sorry to disturb you at this hour but it's important."

A delicately boned hand and long fingers parted the draperies and swung them aside. "What is it, Margaret? You sound upset."

The woman glanced at the door, checking to make sure it was closed, even though she had shut and locked it herself after coming into the room. Lord Rynearson and his lacky were up and about, and despite the fact that she had waited until the pair drove off, Margaret feared their return. Sitting on the edge of the bed at her mistress's insistence, she could feel her body tremble when Lillian reached out to hold her hand.

"Has my husband threatened you?"

The question crackled with anger and a vitality Margaret hadn't heard in a long while. "No, mum," she quickly assured her. "But I've learned something I think you should know."

"About my husband?"

"About his latest mistress," Margaret corrected before she realized how it would bother Lillian. It always did whenever she heard that her husband had brought a new woman into the house. "She hasn't come here of her own free will. In fact she'd been lied to. I heard her talking to Uriah about telling your husband's nephew that she'd been locked in her room. She was angry and frightened. I could hear it in her voice."

"Margaret," Lillian cut in, "he doesn't have a nephew."

"I know, mum," Margaret replied. "That's why I decided to wait up for him. I wanted to see if I could get close enough to her room to hear what he had to say to her."

"And?" Lillian pressed excitedly.

"Apparently the girl was told she would marry the nephew. That's why she's here. But when he told her that Graham—the nephew—had decided not to marry her after all, the girl said something about a new deal."

"What kind of deal?"

"I don't know. I heard m'lord moving about the room and I was scared he'd find me eavesdropping outside the door. I hid at the bottom of the stairs until after he left, then tiptoed back up. The door was locked, but I could hear the girl crying."

"Where's Douglas now?"

"He and Uriah left."

"Left? For where?"

Margaret shook her head.

Flipping off the covers, Lillian swung her bare feet to the floor and asked Margaret to fetch her robe. "I want you to bring the girl to me," she ordered as she drew the silky fabric up over her shoulders. "Search Uriah's room for the key. If you can't find it, then wake David and have him break the door down. But hurry. We don't know how long it will be before Douglas returns."

"Yes, mum," Margaret nodded, helping her mistress

218

rise when it appeared the lady wished to greet her visitor from the rocking chair before the hearth. "Are you sure you have the strength . . ."

"I've never felt better," Lillian assured her, enthusiasm bubbling in her words. "After all these years, I believe we've found a way to pay Douglas back for all the heartache he's caused. Now hurry! We mustn't let it slip through our fingers."

Lillian Rynearson could never have asked for a more devoted and loving servant than she had in Margaret. The woman would lay down her life for her mistress and it was that friendship which turned Margaret for the door without the slightest thought as to what would happen to her when Lord Rynearson learned of her part in the conspiracy. With skirts held up well past her ankles, she raced down the long corridor to the staircase, practically flew down the steps, and rushed on toward the back of the house. At the kitchen, she turned and darted through the narrow hallway to Uriah's room, where she paused, breathless, and tried the knob. Darkness spilled out to welcome her in a chilling reminder of the evil that dwelled within the walls of the manor, but she was undaunted in her quest to find the key, to free the young girl, to punish Lord Rynearson. Stumbling in the defused light of the storm which hailed its fury against the windowpanes and the bleak glow of embers in the hearth, she made her way to the fireplace, took a long taper from the mantel, and touched its wick to the hot coals. A spark of fluttering light caught, then grew, and with her hand shielding the tiny flame, she crossed to the first likely place she'd find the key: the ornate writing desk.

The usual things cluttered its surface, and after she

had shuffled through the blank pieces of parchment and moved the letter opener, paperweight, quill, and inkwell, she decided to try the drawer. Lighting the candle which sat in its own brass holder on the desk, she blew out her taper and laid it down, then pushed aside the chair to get at the drawer. A frustrated growl escaped her lips when her first attempt to pull it open failed. Since it had no keyhole, Margaret knew something inside the drawer was caught. Bracing one hand on the front of the desk, she tightened her grip on the brass handle and yanked again. Her third try had irritating results when whatever obstructed the way broke clear and the entire drawer bolted out and clattered to the floor at her feet.

"Damn," she muttered, staring down at the mess of papers and other supplies that had scattered in all directions. She couldn't afford the time to search every inch of the floor in case the key had scooted to a far corner, nor did she have the time to be curious. Yet, she was. *Terribly* curious.

"What's this?" she questioned aloud as she knelt to examine the broken drawer and the leather book she found partly concealed beneath its splintered bottom. "It appears ol' Uriah is keeping secrets."

She knew she hadn't the time to sit down and read every word or even a line or two, but the temptation as well as a strange intuition wouldn't allow her to do anything else. Laying it down on the desk close to the candlelight, she carefully opened the volume to the first page and briefly scanned what was written there. It appeared to be a diary of sorts, and she would have dismissed reading any further if she hadn't noticed her mistress's name . . . not the formal usage befitting a servant, but her given name—*Lillian, my beloved.*

An icy chill shot across Margaret's shoulders and down her spine. Scooping up the book, she fled the room.

Bevan knew she had to get ahold of herself before Rynearson returned. *She* had to be the one in control, the one making all the conditions. She had to make him believe she would really let her father die before she'd give in to him. If she failed, however, and if she couldn't convince his nephew to help her, it would take sheer force of will on her part to voluntarily allow Lord Rynearson to touch her. If it came down to that, then that was what she'd have to do. As she had repeatedly told her brothers, she couldn't let their father hang when there was something she could do to stop it.

Angrily brushing at her tear-streaked face, she pushed herself off the bed and went to the armoire. She wouldn't greet the men dressed in a robe and gown. She had to be presentable and that meant a nice dress with a high collar, her hair pulled back off her face, and no tears. Rynearson must never know how truly frightened she was.

While she stood staring at the array of beautiful dresses the armoire had to offer, an image of smiling gray eyes and a warm smile flashed through her mind. Determined not to let *him* interfere with her task, she blinked and forced herself to concentrate on finding the simplest, least revealing dress in the collection. A green satin seemed the best choice, and she quickly took it down and carried it to the bed. A few minutes later she was examining the results in the mirror, not totally pleased with what she saw since the low décolletage of the dress strained to cover the swell of her bosom, but knowing it would have to do.

She had just decided to sit down in the rocker to wait when she heard the sound of hurried footsteps climbing the stairs. She couldn't imagine how Rynearson had managed to return so quickly when he'd been gone less than half an hour, but apparently his nephew's home was closer than she had guessed it was. Bracing herself for the confrontation, she moved to the middle of the room and waited for the click of the lock. Instead she heard muffled voices, then a heavy thud against the door. Confused and startled, she jerked back. The thick oak door rattled a second time, and Bevan frantically looked about the place for a weapon she could use to defend herself. Whoever was trying to break in certainly hadn't come to discuss the weather or to ask her what she wanted for breakfast.

Bevan screamed at the splintering of the wood door frame and the sight of the huge, broad-shouldered man who stumbled in as the door swung inward. But before she could ask what he wanted or even who he was, another figure stepped past the broken entryway, and a glimmer of hope stirred inside her.

"Lady Rynearson?" she asked, her voice and her body trembling.

"No, miss," the woman replied as she came forward to reach for Bevan's hand. "But I'll take you to her. Don't be frightened. We're here to help."

The first vision Bevan had of Lillian Rynearson shattered her brave facade. Warmth and friendliness radiated from the woman's blue eyes and a hint of compassion softened the lines at the corners of her mouth.

"Come in, child," she urged, holding out a hand.

Bevan eagerly obliged. Fighting back tears of relief, she fell to her knees before Lillian's chair.

"We haven't got a lot of time," Lillian told her, "since we have no idea where Douglas has gone, so I want you to listen very carefully, and don't interrupt. Margaret tells me you were brought here under false pretenses, that my husband had arranged for you to marry his nephew. I can guess why he told you such a story, to lure you here of your own free will. Well, it was a lie. I don't believe he's ever been truthful in his life." She lowered her gaze and took a second to compose herself. "My husband is an evil man," she continued, a mixture of pain and hatred spicing her words, "as this journal can prove." She ran her hand over the leather surface of the book she held in her lap. "I want you to take this and swear to me that you'll give it to the authorities. What's written in here will warrant his arrest and subsequent execution. It will guarantee he'll never harm you or me or anyone else ever again." She lifted the book and handed it to Bevan. "It's your way out of here, my dear, and all I ask in return is your oath to give it to someone who can see that Douglas is punished."

The well-worn leather covering seemed to catch fire and burn Bevan's fingers. Its contents mocked her. It played games with her. If it had had a voice, she imagined it would laugh at her, *dare* her to do as Lady Rynearson asked. Closing her eyes, Bevan clutched the book to her bosom and rested back on her heels.

"I can't," she whispered. "'Twould mean me father's

death as well."

Lillian frowned over at her maid, who stood just inside the doorway next to David. When Margaret shrugged her failure to understand what the young girl was saying, Lillian leaned forward and cupped Bevan's chin in her hand, drawing Bevan's attention. "Tell me why," she softly urged.

Bevan had no misgivings about reciting every detail. She knew she could trust this woman and Bevan owed her an explanation just for wanting to help. "So ya see," she pleaded once she had finished relating the events which had brought her into the woman's home, "I need your husband's influence ta spare me father."

"No, you don't, my dear," Lady Rynearson objected with a smile that glowed in her eyes. "As a matter of fact, I don't know why I didn't think of it in the first place." She cast her attention on the man at the door. "David, I want you to take this young lady to see my father."

"Your father?" Bevan questioned.

"Yes, my dear. He lives on an estate along the coast just a few miles north of here. He has money, power . . . everything it takes to make someone listen to what he has to say and to obey him. Tell him what you've told me, show him that journal, and he'll see that your father is cleared and that my husband is arrested." She waved a hand toward the exit. "Now go," she strongly advised. "Before Douglas returns. You're our only hope."

Bevan absently came to her feet. "But what about you? What will he do ta ya when he finds me room empty? He'll know 'twas you who helped me escape."

"He can't do anything more to me than he's already

224

done, child. Besides, I'm sure David won't mind if I tell Douglas that *he* took off with you." She smiled at the young man. "Would you, David?"

"No, madam, of course not," he solemnly returned. "There isn't a person in this house who would. We've all been praying for something like this to come along."

"Thank you," she softly replied, choking back a sob.

Bevan recognized the respect David had for Lady Rynearson, but she couldn't understand why she and her maid didn't just come with them, and she voiced her confusion.

"I'm too weak to travel," Lillian confessed. "And with the storm . . ." She shook her head and motioned them out of the room. "I'll be all right. Margaret will see to it. Now go. Please, before Douglas comes home again."

Impulse made Bevan lean down and place a light kiss on the woman's cheek. Their eyes met for a brief moment, then Bevan turned and hurried from the room, Uriah's journal hugged tightly against her bosom.

Chapter Seven

Lightning flashed. The thunder cracked and echoed all around. Rain fell in icy sheets and beat upon the ground. Pools of water gathered on the cobblestone streets and ran in rivulets along the curb until, bold and reckless, it spilled out to cross to the other side. The storm and its fury had long since chased the last brave soul inside by a warm fire and the comfort of his bed.

This dismal night cloaked the passage of a carriage within a chilling embrace and hampered its swift exodus through the dimly lit avenues of Liverpool. Horses' hooves clattered against the stones. High wheels cut through the murky puddles and splattered crystal droplets in their wake. A hulk of a man held the reins and shouted a command to his steeds that was hardly audible above the roar of the tempest which assailed him from all sides. Inside the coach, a frightened young woman clung desperately to the seat as she was jostled and bumped around, the hammering of her heart nearly as loud as the thunder booming overhead. Several times the book Bevan had laid on the seat beside her slid off and dropped to the floor, and she had risked letting go to retrieve it. But as the journey seemed to grow more perilous, her need to see the journal in a safe place became less important. Then just as she was about to holler up at David and beg him to slow down, the carriage wheel hit the curb as the rig rounded the corner. The impact made the coach jump, lurch, then hit the cobblestones with such force that the axle shattered under the abuse. The scream of the horses rent the air and blended with the cry of terror from inside the carriage when the rig scraped, jerked, became airborne, and was hurled onto its side.

Cold raindrops fell against Bevan's face and stirred her from her unconscious state. An aching pain in her left shoulder and hip and the lump on her head soon roused the last memory she had before she was thrown against the side of the carriage, and she sat upright trying to focus on her surroundings. The storm had lessened its noisy blast but a heavy mist continued to blanket everything. Lamplight fell down at her through the door of the carriage, which was now above her. Rising, she pulled herself up, freed the latch, and tossed the door open, then bent to retrieve Uriah's journal. With great effort, she climbed out of the broken remains and awkwardly slid to the ground.

Her first thought, once she had seen the extent of the damage to the rig, was of the horses and whether they had escaped unharmed. But after she had moved around in front and saw that they had broken loose of their hobbles and had run off, her concern suddenly changed to David. Combing her fingers through her damp hair and raking it back off her brow, she called out his name as she circled the rig. When he didn't answer, she worried that he, too, had been knocked unconscious and was lying facedown in one of the many puddles in the street, and she hurried her efforts to find him. Yet once she had moved to the back of the rig and found him crushed beneath the frame, his eyes open and staring blankly up at the dark sky above him, every muscle in her body froze. Tears burned her throat. She felt sick to her stomach, and an immense guilt gripped her heart.

"Oh, David," she whispered, dropping to her knees with the book hugged to her chest. "Oh, David, why did ya have ta die? There's been too many already who have sacrificed their lives for somethin' they believe in. When will it all stop?"

The image of another man who had laid down his life because of her materialized in her mind's eye. She could see his face, the bright smile, his handsomeness, could feel his gentle touch and hear his pledge that he loved her. He had tried to help her the way David had and now both men were dead. Was it an omen? Was someone trying to tell her something? Was this an indication that no matter how hard a person tried, he couldn't change the future? Did it mean her father was destined to be executed and there was nothing she could do to alter that fact? Well, she refused to believe it. Her father shouldn't have to die for fighting against the evils imposed on his people, and it was up to her to see that he didn't.

Brushing angrily at her tears, she jerked back up on her feet and quickly looked all around her. The buildings on both sides of the street were dark, which explained why no one had come to offer help. From the design of the wood-framed structures, she guessed them to be warehouses, and because of the late hour, the men who worked them were at home . . . in bed. That conclusion reminded her of Lady Rynearson and the reason why she was standing there in the middle of the street, why David had driven so recklessly and so fast, and why he had taken this route. Lady Rynearson's father lived on an estate north of town . . . along the coast, she had said. Apparently the quickest way there was through the dock area, and for one brief instant, Bevan considered continuing on foot, until she realized she had no idea where she was going exactly. More than that, she knew she couldn't afford the time to wander aimlessly up and down the coast road looking for a man whose name she hadn't been given, since Rynearson was probably already on his way home. The minute he learned of her escape, he'd be searching every inch of Liverpool for her, and if he caught her, if he found her with Uriah's journal, he'd know the truth, he'd know everything, and that meant Lady Rynearson would be in danger, too. It also meant he'd send word to have her father executed immediately, and that was a risk she couldn't take. She had to get away, she had to leave England, and she had to do it quickly. Glancing down at David's still form once more, she silently promised him that his death would be avenged. She'd return home, give the journal to Kyle Magee, and let the Society decide just how to deal with Douglas Rynearson. Having made up her mind, Bevan started off in the direction of the tall masts she could see faintly outlined in the stormy sky above the warehouses' rooftops.

Another worry beset Bevan once she had turned the last corner and stood facing the pier. Three ships were anchored there and because of the misty darkness which enshrouded them *and* because of her lack of knowledge concerning sailing vessels, she had no way of knowing which of the three, if any, was preparing to make the voyage across the channel to Ireland. She couldn't venture asking anyone for the simple reason that the minute she opened her mouth, they would know she was Irish. And she could only guess what kind of treatment she'd receive. Yet despite that frightening thought, she had no money to pay for her passage, which left her with no other alternative but to smuggle herself on board, and if she was courageous enough to inquire as to which ship would take her home, the one she questioned would undoubtedly keep a close eye on her. However, there was no point in worrying about the dangers of talking with someone, since no one was around. Apparently, anyone with any sense had gotten in out of the rain, and that was exactly what she planned to do as she eyed the ship nearest her with its canvas-covered longboat moored on deck.

"Cap'n?" Eric Dillion gently called from the doorway of Gordon's room. "The storm's passed and it won't be long before the sun is up. Shall I give the order for the crew to board the *Lady Hawk?*"

Rubbing the sleep from his eyes, Gordon awkwardly sat up in the middle of his bed and glanced at the window. The faint pinks and yellows of predawn had already splashed color in the dark sky and hinted at a clear sunrise, the kind of morning needed to swing a ship the size of the *Lady Hawk* safely out of port. "Aye," he agreed. "We've wasted enough time here already, and I don't mind telling you that if we *never* come back to Liverpool again, my feelings wouldn't be hurt at all."

"I know what you mean," Eric concurred. "We're lucky to have gotten Mr. Hamilton out when we did. Do you plan to have breakfast first?"

Gordon shook his head as he tossed off the covers and swung his feet to the floor. "I really don't want to waste another minute. I don't trust Rynearson even though I personally supervised the exchange of goods. I wouldn't put it past him to try and make a switch or call the authorities in on it with some phony charge. No, as soon as I'm dressed and I've thrown my things in a bag, I'm getting out of this inn and out of Liverpool as quickly as the *Lady Hawk* will take me."

"Shall I see if I can hire a rig to get us to the dock? We'll save time."

"Aye," Gordon instructed. "And tell the men that whoever isn't on board when we're ready to sail will be left behind."

"Aye, aye, Cap'n," Eric replied with a quick salute before he closed the door behind him on his way out.

A short while later found the two men riding comfortably inside their rented carriage. The sweet smell after a cleansing rain filled their nostrils and the humid air gave Gordon a chill, since the sun was just beginning to break over the horizon and had yet to warm the earth. The harbor was coming to life with the sounds of men at work, horses pulling carts, and the usual street urchins chasing about asking for a shilling or crust of bread. Neither Gordon nor his first mate spoke, though each knew what the other was thinking. They both longed to put this town far behind them and to return to North Carolina without any further problems. The voyage had been rough, their dealings with Rynearson even more complex, and the mystery behind Reid's disappearance had left everyone on edge. The storm last night had delayed their departure and forced them to wait until morning, which no one had wanted to do. Reid had been safely shipped off on the huge brigantine heading for Virginia, but as long as the *Lady Hawk* remained anchored in port, tension ran high. Now in less than a half hour, she too would be trudging the waters for home, and the danger would be past.

The excited voices of a crowd up ahead drew Gordon and Eric's attention, and before either of them could ask the driver what the problem was, the carriage jerked then slowly rolled to a stop. A second later someone shouted for them to move on, and as the rig took up its pace again, the two men peered out the window, grimacing at the sight they saw. A team of dock workers had gathered on one side of an overturned carriage and were lifting it up, while a second group was pulling the stiff and broken body of a young man from beneath it.

"Anybody know who he is?" Gordon and Eric heard someone ask.

"No, but I recognize the coach," came the reply. "It belongs to Lord Rynearson."

"Do you suppose this man had stolen it and was trying to get away before it was discovered?" a third person guessed.

"Hard to say," the first answered. "But it's possible,

since he wasn't carrying a passenger. Has anyone gone to tell Rynearson?"

Eric chuckled at the sneer he saw twisting Gordon's face. "I take that look to mean you and I were thinking the same thing."

"That it's a shame Rynearson wasn't inside and that those men were trying to haul his body out of the wreckage?" Gordon finished. "That's what I was thinking. But since we weren't that lucky, I'll just have to hope the young man *did* steal the rig. It would serve Rynearson right to have someone treat him the way he treats everyone else, even if it is on a smaller scale." Sighing disgustedly, Gordon fell back against the seat and added, "I guess what makes me the angriest in a situation like this is knowing that a man like Rynearson, a man who has wealth, can buy his way out of trouble. And he'll keep doing what he's doing until the day he dies without any repercussions simply because no one has the courage to stand up to him."

"Mr. Hamilton did."

"Aye, and look what happened."

Eric frowned. "Are you saying you believe Mr. Hamilton's problems might have something to do with Rynearson?"

"I have no proof, but my instincts keep saying so." Gordon shifted in the seat to look his companion straight in the eye. "There was only one reason why he hired a schooner to take him to Ireland. Rynearson is a thief and a liar, and he knew Mr. Hamilton and I were chasing after him. Who's to say he didn't fix it so Mr. Hamilton was arrested and that we didn't stumble onto the plan just in time to spoil it?"

Eric shrugged. "I suppose. But there's one flaw in

your thinking."

"What's that?"

"No one there at the prison knew Mr. Hamilton's name. I never once heard anyone in the crowd say they knew who he was."

"I'll wager the warden did."

"And he's dead."

Gordon nodded.

"And Mr. Hamilton is on his way home, and as far as everyone who saw him get shot is concerned, the man at the prison is dead too. So why don't we just forget about it? You're working yourself up over something you can't correct."

"And that's the very reason why I'm upset. Rynearson has gotten away with something again, and I resent being chased out of town with my tail between my legs like some mangy dog who's been smacked with a broom."

"That's not how *he* sees it. You forced his warehouse manager to take back the damaged goods he gave us."

"That doesn't erase the fact that I was cheated in the first place, that I was made to look like a fool," Gordon snarled. "I'd love seeing that man put out of business, that's all, so that nobody else is humiliated the way I was." A devilish, playful smile moved his mouth. "Maybe I'll set his warehouse on fire just before we weigh anchor."

Amused by the idea that Gordon Sanderson, an honest man who had lived his life according to God's law, would even *think* such a thought much less say it, Eric laughed outloud. "You worry me, Cap'n," he chuckled. "There's a dark side to you that's beginning to make itself known." He was quiet for a moment, then added, "If you want, I'll help."

Rumbling laughter spilled out of the carriage which rolled to a stop at the end of the pier, then followed the two men as they made their way toward the huge frigate anchored on the opposite end. Perhaps they could never live with the knowledge of having done such a vengeful act, but it certainly made them both feel better just considering it.

The gentle rolling of the ship, the clap of sails as they flapped in the strong breeze then billowed full, and the splash of water against the hull caressed Bevan's sleep-starved brain and guaranteed her that she was safe for the time being. The voyage across the St. George's Channel would take the better part of the day to complete, and although she was terribly hungry, she knew she mustn't dare lift her head out from under the canvas awning of her hiding place. She wasn't even sure she could. She had been lucky enough not to encounter a single person while boarding the ship and climbing into the longboat, but what hadn't gone in her favor was the chill she had taken when she was forced to keep on her wet things and had no way of drying her hair. She had spent most of the night shivering, and now that the sun had come up, it beat down on the canvas and turned her retreat into a damp, sultry cubicle that wouldn't allow her the space to sit up. She wasn't sure if her fevered flesh was due to the sun's warming rays or because she'd caught cold, but in either case, she felt miserable. Thinking that the best way to pass the time would be in sleep, she closed her eyes and rolled over on her side, her arm tucked beneath her head as a pillow.

A few moments later she fell into a deep, undisturbed slumber.

Bevan's world opened up to her in a slow, distorted fashion. She could see her father's smiling face, hear his voice, and even smell the lingering scent of tobacco from his pipe. Ryan, Kelly, and Shea were there, and everyone was laughing. Then suddenly their father disappeared. The day turned dark and ominous. They no longer sat around the kitchen table sharing the meal she had prepared; rather they stood beneath a hug oak tree in the yard outside the prison. Her father's voice called out to her and begged her not to worry, but when she looked up, she could see his troubled expression from between the bars in his cell window. In the distance an expensive carriage approached, and when it had reached the gate of the prison, it came to a halt and its passenger climbed down. He was tall, broad-shouldered, and well dressed. He carried himself with pronounced self-confidence, and when he turned her way, Bevan could see his handsome face and smiling gray eyes. She raised a hand and waved to him, but he seemed not to notice her, and when she called out his name, he frowned as if confused, shook his dark head, and turned away. She shouted at him not to go inside the gate and she tried to run after him, but Ryan caught her arm and held her back. A shot pierced the air, and she saw a flood of crimson, heard a man scream, then found herself locked inside a tall, cold, stone tower.

"I don't want to marry you," a voice kept repeating.

"I want you," another declared.

"I love you, but I've lied to you," confessed a third.

Then the leering face of Douglas Rynearson loomed close and she struck out at him only to have someone seize her wrist. Bright sunshine and stifling heat closed in on her. Her body was soaked with sweat. Her mouth parched, her lips dry, and her soul on fire.

Muffled voices and a coolness on her brow chased away her dreams. A soft pillow cushioned her head and a bed of feathers cradled her aching limbs. A rocking motion lulled her back to sleep, and without knowing she had called her mother's name, Bevan slipped back into unconsciousness.

The O'Rourke brothers had just gathered around the kitchen table to eat their last meal of the day when the explosive thunder of hooves and the rattling of a cart shook the tiny cottage. A second later, the back door of the abode burst open and Kyle Magee staggered breathlessly into the room.

"Kyle?" Ryan asked, bolting from his chair. "What is it?"

Winded and his side hurting, the man bent at the waist and pressed his fingertips in his side, while he motioned for the boys to give him a second to catch his breath. "Somethin's gone wrong," he was finally able to reply. "Ya've got . . . ta get away before they come."

"Who?" Kelly demanded, leaving his place next to Shea and coming to stand beside Ryan.

"English troups," Magee answered. "There's been a warrant issued for your arrest." His gaze swept the brothers. "All of ya."

"On what charge?" Ryan petitioned, his eyes flashing fire.

"Does it matter?" Magee challenged. "We know ya haven't done anythin' against the law, and if ya stood before a jury of your own peers, ya'd be found innocent. But these are *English* men who want ta see ya thrown in prison. Now don't stand here arguin' with me!" He waved them all outside. "We'll talk on the way."

"On the way where?" Shea questioned as he hurriedly followed his brothers from the cottage.

"I've arranged ta get ya on a ship bound for England. Ya can't stay here anymore . . . not now."

"England?" Kelly echoed as he climbed into the back of Magee's cart. "That's the last place we should go."

"Aye," Magee agreed. "That's why they'll never think ta look for ya there."

At the wheel, Gordon watched his first mate cross the quarterdeck then climb the ladder toward the helm. Before he had both feet off the rungs, Gordon asked, "How is she?"

"Sleeping, I guess," Eric admitted. "Kind of hard to tell."

"Has she said anything?"

"She mumbled a name. Sounded like she said Kerry."

"Was that all?"

Eric nodded as he stretched the muscles in his back and glanced up at the clear, blue sky. "All that I could understand. She seemed to be fighting something or someone." He wrinkled up his face. "I would suppose whatever or whoever that might be is the reason she hid herself in the longboat."

Glancing up at the mainsail, Gordon noticed that the wind had shifted slightly and he spun the wheel port a turn to correct it. "I just wish we would have found her sooner. If we had, I don't think she'd be this sick."

Eric's eyebrows raised and lowered. "And we'd have been able to put her ashore. I don't think Mr. Hamilton will be too pleased learning we had a stowaway."

Gordon started to agree and changed his mind. The young woman he'd ordered taken to his first mate's cabin was probably one of the most beautiful ladies he'd ever seen, and if she had gone to the extent of smuggling herself on board the *Lady Hawk* without knowing its destination, then it had to mean she was in serious trouble. The combination was something that would surely raise Reid's interest, since he'd never been one to ignore a beautiful woman and because he always seemed to enjoy helping out someone in trouble.

"What are you thinking?" Eric asked when he saw the smile on his captain's face.

Checking the binnacle, Gordon gave the wheel another half-turn. "That for a man who should live a very uneventful life, Mr. Hamilton has a way of winding up in the thick of things."

Gordon had figured out long ago that underneath Reid's seemingly contented nature burned the spirit of an adventurer. It was part of the reason why he'd had to go to Liverpool. He wasn't satisfied with the slow, tedious routine of running a plantation and looked for every opportunity to do something about it.

"Cap'n?" Eric asked, when he saw Gordon smile. He always liked a good joke and obviously Gordon Sanderson had found something amusing about this situation.

"Oh, I was just thinking about Miss Bradburn," he finally replied, the corners of his mouth twitching.

"Mr. Hamilton's fiancée? What about her?"

"Do you suppose she'll be upset when she sees the new houseguest?"

"Miss Bradburn?" Eric mocked. "I doubt it. She's never gotten upset about much of anything. Of all the people I know, she's probably the most level-headed, understanding, and sympathetic person God ever put on this earth. Why, she'll more than likely take this young lady under wing—" The devilish gleam he saw shining in Gordon's eyes cut short his string of compliments. Frowning, he folded his arms over his chest, cocked his head to one side, and demanded, "All right. Tell me why you think I'm wrong."

"I'm not saying you are," Gordon grinned. "I'm just *hoping* you are."

Eric rolled his eyes. "You know, my father always told me I was a little slow-witted, and up until now I took great offense to it. But apparently I shouldn't have because I haven't the vaguest idea what you're talking about."

Glancing at the brass arrow housed behind glass to make certain the *Lady Hawk* was still on course, Gordon asked, "How long have you known Mr. Hamilton?"

Eric shrugged. "Four, maybe five years."

"Have he and Miss Bradburn been engaged all that time?"

"Aye. But it's my understanding their fathers decided their future for them while they were just little tykes."

"True. So why do you suppose they're still unwed?"

240

Gordon shook his head before Eric could answer. "Don't bother guessing. I'll tell you why. Or least what I think." He spun the wheel starboard a turn, then back several degrees. "I'm sure they have feelings for each other. Mr. Hamilton has told me as much. And I'm sure one day he'll give in and marry her, if someone doesn't come along and change his mind. Don't get me wrong. I like Miss Bradburn and she'll make him a good wife, but she's taken him for granted. There's never been any competition for her because no other woman has dared. The result has been disinterest on Mr. Hamilton's part. Nothing about her stirs his *desire* to get married."

"And you're saying there's a chance Miss Bradburn will get jealous of this girl we've been forced into bringing with us?" Eric shook his head in firm disagreement. "Won't happen. And I doubt the Hamiltons will make her a houseguest. If anything, they'll treat her as an indentured servant. Or have her arrested. She didn't pay for her passage, you know. This isn't a passenger ship."

"I only said I was *hoping*," Gordon remarked defensively. "And you're probably right . . . to some degree. But I can't see any of the Hamiltons turning her over to the authorities . . . at least not until they've heard her story."

Eric's upper lip curled. "What story is that? How she ran away to escape being thrown in debtor's prison?"

"Debtor's prison? Are you blind, Eric?" Gordon hotly posed. "Was she dressed like someone who was bound for debtor's prison?"

"Maybe she stole her clothes," Eric argued.

A sudden gust of wind caught the sails and rocked

241

the ship, drawing Gordon's attention back to the helm. Overhead the white canvas flapped noisily and brought an end to their discussion as Gordon took up the task of changing course to utilize the full extent of the strong breeze. Pivoting the wheel a hard port, then waiting for the bite of water on the rudder, Gordon set her heel into the sea and swung the prow of the ship around. The sails billowed full almost immediately, and once he had her under control again, he yielded the helm to his first mate and headed for the ladder without another word on the subject of the young woman in Eric's cabin.

That same coolness she'd felt before on her brow stirred Bevan from her deep sleep. But when she opened her eyes, a strange light fluttered behind the menacing dark shadow of a man hovering over her. Before she could focus her eyes and recognize that he wasn't Lord Rynearson, she threw up a hand to thwart off the stranglehold she was sure would descend upon her at any second.

"Easy, miss," an unfamiliar voice commanded. "I'm not going to hurt you. If I meant you any harm, I'd have ordered you locked in the hold rather than brought here to my first mate's cabin. However, if I don't get some answers out of you, you still might spend the rest of the voyage in the hold. And I guarantee you won't like it. There's rats down there bigger than you."

Although his words held a threat, his manner, tone, and the gentle touch of the cool cloth he pressed to her brow contradicted his promise, and she relaxed, closing her eyes again.

"Here," he said, slipping his hand beneath her head as he held a tin cup to her lips. "Drink a little water. I'm sure you must be parched."

She did as he instructed and drank until he warned her not to overdo it. Too weak to thank him, she hoped he understood her gratitude as she lay back on the pillow and closed her eyes once more.

"I'm Gordon Sanderson," he said softly. "I'm captain of this vessel we call *Lady Hawk*. Might I know your name?"

Bevan ran her tongue over her lips and started to respond when she suddenly realized what the consequences might be. Her family had enough problems already, and until she knew what this man wanted from her as payment for smuggling herself on board, she'd protect her family's name by keeping quiet. She closed her eyes and turned her head away.

Gordon had expected as much. The young woman had risked her life to get on his ship. She wasn't about to jeopardize that reason by telling him anything about herself. However, she had to be made to understand that she had, in turn, put the *Lady Hawk*, its crew, and her captain in the same sort of danger by inadvertently seeking their protection.

"I had the cook make you up some broth," he told her. "Do you think you can sit up long enough to eat it?"

Her skin still burned with fever. She was weak, scared, and horribly nervous, since she had no way of knowing what was going to happen to her once they reached the coast of Ireland. But despite all that, she was still hungry. Without answering, she clumsily pushed herself up.

The first spoonful tasted good but cramped her empty stomach. The second eased the discomfort, and by the time she had finished the entire bowl, with the captain's help, a little of the ache left her bones and she wasn't dizzy anymore. She was even able to smile her appreciation.

"Well, now," Gordon remarked, grinning. "You're looking better already. I'll have to be sure to tell Mr. Welch that at least one person on this ship likes his cooking." He set aside the dish and dipped the cloth in the cool water again. "Here," he said, handing it to her. "Lay this on your forehead. It'll help bring down the fever and it might even dull the pounding in your temples." He watched her for a moment, noticing the dirt smudges on her neck and arms and how her hair matted in long, tangled strands. "We don't have a tub on board, but I can have Mr. Welch heat up a bucket of water, if you'd like to bathe and wash your hair later. I might even be able to find a brush or comb somewhere." His gaze dipped to her torn and soiled dress. "As for something to wear . . . well, that will be a problem."

"I won't need ta change," she answered softly, her eyes closed, "but I would enjoy cleanin' up a bit. How much longer will it be before we dock?"

Her question both surprised and confused him. She talked as if she thought their arrival would only take a matter of days. Frowning, he wondered how upset she would be to learn that the *Lady Hawk* was sailing for America, and had been for the past week while she lay fighting for her life.

The man's silence triggered an alarm in Bevan's

244

brain. "How long have I been lyin' in this bunk?" she asked.

"Almost a week," Gordon reluctantly admitted. "One of the crew heard you moan as he walked by the longboat. But that wasn't until our first night out. It was too far to turn back, and even if it hadn't been, I wouldn't have given the order. Like you, we needed to get away from England as quickly as possible. That *is* why you were hiding, isn't it?"

A week! Bevan could feel her lower lip quiver. Gritting her teeth, she swallowed hard and courageously held back the flood of tears she could feel raging up inside her. A week meant her father had probably already been executed, unless her brothers and Kyle Magee had somehow been warned ahead of time that Rynearson wasn't going to follow through with his part of the deal. God, how she prayed that was true.

"Miss?"

Clinging to that hope, Bevan was able to present a brave front for the captain as she opened her eyes and looked questioningly at him.

"I won't ask what you were fleeing," he said. "That's your business. But I do have to know if your crime was such that someone would come after you. I want the crew ready if we run into trouble. Will we?"

The only reason Bevan felt Rynearson might send someone after her was to retrieve the journal. Yet he wouldn't know she had it unless his wife had told him, and Bevan doubted she would have simply because it would have been too dangerous. *If,* for some reason, he *had* learned about it—perhaps from Uriah Faber or Margaret—Rynearson would have expected Bevan to

245

go to the estate of Lady Rynearson's father. Once he had figured out she never made it there, he would conclude she had left England and gone home. And since *Bevan* hadn't expected to be where she was, how could Rynearson have deduced where she had gone?

"No," she mumbled. "No one will come after me. No one knows where I've gone." She lowered her eyes and added ruefully, "Not even me, I'm afraid."

Gordon could hear the sadness in her tone and he wished he could say something of comfort to her. But how could he ease her pain by telling her that it would be another five weeks before they reached North Carolina, that many more to sail back to England, and only then if she had the money to pay for her passage . . . which he truly doubted she had? And it wasn't as if a ship left every hour for England. Sometimes days, weeks, even months passed between voyages. The best Gordon could tell her was that if she never lost hope, she would return home one day. The question was, how long?

Deciding he had already overburdened the poor girl, he rose from his chair and picked up the empty dishes from the floor.

"I think you should rest now, Irish," he suggested with a sympathetic smile. "We'll talk more when you're feeling better." He started for the door, then paused to look back and add, "My cabin's above this one if you need anything. But I'll have my first mate check in on you every so often. His name is Eric Dillion." He tried to smile again, couldn't muster the will to pretend he felt even remotely cheerful, and left the cabin without another word.

Bevan listened to the latch click shut behind Gordon

Sanderson while she tried to convince herself that things could be worse. She realized that she hadn't asked him where the *Lady Hawk* was destined. If it wasn't Ireland, it hardly seemed to matter. Wherever they landed, it wouldn't be close enough for her to swim home and she didn't have any money to buy her way there. The only good that had come out of her predicament was that she had luckily chosen a ship captained by a kind man. He'd seen to it that she'd been cared for and fed, and he'd offered her the use of his first mate's cabin for privacy. All of that should have made her want to be honest with him, to confide in him, to tell him the whole sordid mess. But it didn't. She just couldn't admit to how stupid she had been, how her stubbornness, her blind determination, and her foolish decision in thinking only *she* could save her father had gotten her in so deep she couldn't even imagine getting out.

Tired of lying down, she rolled onto her hip and slowly rose up with her legs dangling over the edge of the bunk. All she had to show for her efforts was a diary written by an odd little man the existence of which Lady Rynearson had said would destroy her husband. Maybe it could, she reasoned as she leaned back and rested against the wall. But what good would that do her now? She couldn't use it to blackmail Rynearson into releasing her father from prison. The date of his execution had past, and all she had ever wanted from the stuffy, old English lord was his help in preventing it. He was of no use to her now.

Her head began to throb again and she reluctantly decided that perhaps she should lie down. With her knees drawn up and the pillow tucked beneath her

247

head, she closed her eyes and was listening to the water lapping against the sides of the ship when it suddenly came to her that she wouldn't be here right now if it hadn't been for Rynearson. They had made a deal which in Bevan's mind had guaranteed her father would be spared no matter what. But then Rynearson changed the conditions after his nephew had decided he didn't want to marry her after all—*if* that was true. Yet the longer she thought about it, the more she wondered if Graham had *ever* wanted to marry her. What if the whole thing had been arranged between the two of them beforehand just to lure her into Rynearson's home? It certainly made more sense than an Englishman marrying an Irish girl, a decision he had made after having talked with her for only a few minutes. She hadn't given it much thought at the time simply because her mind had been on much more important matters. But now . . . now it truly bothered her. And there was Graham's odd behavior at the docks when he asked her how long she had known his uncle. Had he asked such a question as a subtle way of trying to warn her? If he had, it hadn't worked. She'd walked right into the trap with her eyes wide open . . . well, almost. She hadn't actually had her mind set solely on her future. She'd been thinking about her father locked up in a cold, dark cell, about her brothers and how she'd had to leave them behind and whether or not she'd ever see them again, and of course she'd been dealing with the anguish of losing the only man she had ever come to love . . . the mystery man, the one with the gray eyes.

Her lashes grew moist as she tried not to cry. What good would it do her except to make her head hurt all the more? Crying wouldn't bring him back. It wouldn't answer all her questions or erase the lies he'd told her. It wouldn't tell her his name or ease her pain, the emptiness she suffered, and even the bitterness at having been cheated by his death.

A new thought struck her, a wild, crazy idea that dried her tears, brought a vague smile to her lips, and stirred hope in her heart. Pushing up, she drew the blanket around her shoulders and sat cross-legged on the bunk with a faraway look in her eyes. Maybe it *was* preplanned as she had guessed, only Rynearson's *real* nephew, the man she had fallen in love with, hadn't approved, and he had come to Ireland to tell her of his uncle's deception. But when they met, he fell in love with her just as he had vowed and wanted her for himself. Knowing how his uncle would react, Graham had taken it upon himself to rescue her father before Rynearson could stop it. Meanwhile, however, Rynearson had hired a man to play the part of his nephew not knowing that Graham had already introduced himself. Then he got killed before he could explain and the unanswered questions made her think she'd been lied to.

"And I was," she murmured hatefully. "But not by me beloved Graham. 'Twas his uncle who lied, and I'll see the bastard pays for lettin' his nephew die. As soon as I return home ta Ireland, I'll give the journal—"

A bolt of lightning striking just outside the window of her cabin couldn't have shocked her with a more stinging sensation than the realization that she didn't know where the journal was. The last she remembered of it was when she had curled her arms around it and fell asleep in the longboat. Springing off the bunk, she frantically eyed every corner, every niche, even the small closet and the drawers beneath the bunk for the leather-bound book, only to come up empty-handed. Could it mean the tar who had lifted her from under the canvas hadn't noticed it lying there beside her? Or had he given it to the captain? She wanted to believe she'd find it on the floor of the longboat, since Gordon Sanderson hadn't mentioned a word about the book. In fact he'd had to ask her if she was running away from something, which could only mean he hadn't read what was written in Uriah's diary or he'd have known the answer to that one.

A queasiness washed over her and she had to sit back down. When it had passed, she glanced up at the window and whispered a word of thanks for the starry black sky she saw just beyond the glass. Although she knew very little about ships and how they were managed, she assumed most of the crew were in their bunks for the night. If she was quiet and if she moved slowly and without causing a disturbance, she might be able to reach the longboat without anyone seeing her. She'd retrieve the book, return here to the cabin, and find a safe place to hide it.

Bevan's knees were shaking so badly by the time she was able to sit down on the bunk again, she wasn't sure if it was from exhaustion, fear, or both. The journal had been just where she had prayed she'd find it, and once she had it locked securely in her grip, she had raced back for the cabin as quickly and quietly as she could manage. The only two men she saw were at the helm, one steering and the other checking the map he held up to a lantern. They were arguing about something, which had to account for the reason neither of them noticed her. Twice she had to pass beneath them, once when she left the corridor leading to her cabin, and then when she returned. Her success, however, was still nerve-racking and had taken nearly every ounce of strength she'd had. Too tired to read even the first page of Uriah's diary—something she still hadn't done—she slid the volume under the covers all the way to the foot of the bunk, extinguished the candle, and climbed in bed. Maybe tomorrow she'd feel up to it.

Chapter Eight

Kelly O'Rourke had announced that *he* would make the decision for the group based solely on the point that of the three brothers, he was the biggest, brawniest, and most thick-headed. If he met up with someone who took offense to his questions, his size, the clothes he wore, or even his Irish accent, Kelly explained that that person could hit him over the head with a flat-bed wagon and do no damage, where in Ryan's case and certainly Shea's the result would be fatal. The other two resented the implication that they weren't the brawlers Kelly was, even though they knew most of what he said was true. Yet that wasn't what truly upset them. They didn't like the idea of him going alone to the wharf and they told him so. Safety meant numbers. But Kelly wouldn't hear of it. It was bad enough that their father was dead and Bevan was missing. He didn't want something to happen to one of them, too, if he could prevent it. Thus he had left them behind to go to the wharf where he intended to snoop around and listen to the gossip he guessed would be the topic of conversation that morning.

All Kyle Magee had been able to tell them the night he whisked them off to safety had been the horrifying news that their father had been executed ahead of schedule. There had been no announcement, no fanfare, no public speech warning his friends that they could expect the same punishment for defying the Crown. They had simply taken him out in the yard at sundown, marched him up the steps to the gallows, put the rope around his neck, and dropped the trap door. Then he had been placed in a wooden box and set outside the gate for whoever wanted to claim his body. One of the members of the Society and a good friend of Patrick O'Rourke had been assigned to stay close to the prison that day and had seen the proceedings, and he had been the one who, while loading the coffin into his cart, had heard the guards talking about the warrant that had been issued for the O'Rourke brothers. There hadn't been time for any of them to contact their informers in England or even inside the prison to find out why Patrick O'Rourke had been executed when Rynearson was to have prevented it, and that failure had, therefore, sent Kelly, Ryan, and Shea off on their own to learn what they could.

Friends of the Society had taken them in once their ship had docked in Liverpool, and they had spent the next two days hiding out in the attic above a cobbler's shop waiting for information concerning their sister. Tension grew among the brothers when they were told of the strange happenings at Lord Rynearson's home on the night Bevan arrived in Liverpool, and that aside from the reports that she had been seen climbing into Rynearson's carriage at the docks, no one knew where she had gone after that. It was assumed she would take up residence at Rynearson's estate until her marriage to Graham . . . that was until it was learned Rynearson didn't have a nephew. That bit of knowledge was startling enough in itself. Then the brothers were told of a series of events concerning the Rynearson household and their concern for their sister's welfare turned to outright fear.

The following morning word had begun to circulate around town that Rynearson's sickly wife had died in her sleep. Since she had been ill for years, no one thought much about it. The mysterious aspect, the part which raised a few questioning eyebrows, was the sudden, unexplained disappearance of Lady Rynearson's devoted maid, Margaret. The puzzle grew more complex when one of Rynearson's servants, a stocky young man named David, was found crushed beneath one of the lord's carriages and that he appeared to have died in the accident sometime that same night. Speculation hinted he'd been running from something and many wondered if it concerned Lady Rynearson's death and Margaret's curious departure. Rynearson was quick to explain that he had sent David after the surgeon when his wife's condition became grave, but few believed him. For one thing, the doctor didn't live near the docks. More than that, it was a well-known fact he hated his wife, had many mistresses, and looked forward to the day he no longer had to care for her. He wouldn't have been *that* eager to get help.

What really surprised everyone was Rynearson's announcement that he had fired his longtime servant, Uriah Faber, on the grounds that he'd been caught stealing, and that he, too, had seemed to disappear. As for the rest of the staff . . . most weren't talking. Of those few who found the courage, they reluctantly had to admit they couldn't contradict anything their employer had claimed nor did any of them know anything about a young girl called Bevan O'Rourke.

The only vital clue they were given didn't surface until two days later. The man, they were told, who had accompanied Rynearson and Bevan off the ship that day was Charles Alcott. When asked to describe him, his physical characteristics matched those of the nephew Rynearson had introduced to them, and it seemed then that the brothers were close to finding their sister. However, when Kelly demanded to be taken to see Alcott, he was told that the man had left for the Continent three days earlier and that no one knew if or when he'd return.

"Me guess is that he'll *never* be back," Ryan had snarled. "He's a part of this whole arrangement, and I'd say he's been paid ta live somewhere else."

"What will we do now?" Shea had asked, his tone clearly marking his fear and worry. "We can't go home. We can't chase after Alcott, and we really shouldn't leave England until we're sure Bevan isn't here."

"I say we should catch Rynearson alone and beat the truth from him," Kelly had proposed, his tall, broad frame stiff with rage. "And I'll start by waitin' at the warehouse for him."

"No!" Ryan had ordered, jumping from his chair to grab Kelly's arm. "The minute he sees ya, he'll send for the authorities. He'll deny even knowin' us. Or Bevan. We'll all wind up dead."

"Then what do ya suggest we do? Hide out here for the rest of our lives?" Kelly had demanded. "I can't!

255

Bevan's alive. I feel it in me bones, and I won't rest until I find her."

"How, Kelly? How will ya find her if ya're locked up in prison or dancin' at the end of a rope?"

As Kelly neared the wharf, he remembered telling his brother how laying down his life in search of their sister was better than doing nothing at all, and how Ryan had appeared about to disagree before changing his mind. He knew each of them had spoken out of frustration, anger, and fear, and he had forgiven Ryan's outburst as he hoped Ryan had forgiven him. He hadn't really lied to his brother when he said he wanted to go alone. Only his reason hadn't been completely honest. He needed the time by himself to clear his head and do some thinking without anyone crowding him.

Since Rynearson was the only one left who knew the whole story *and* where Bevan could be found, Kelly turned the corner and headed for the spot where he'd been told he could find Rynearson's warehouse. It had rained earlier that morning, but now that the sun was peeking through the last of the clouds, the air had grown hot and sticky. Stepping around one of the puddles in the street, Kelly moved onto the wooden walkway as he wiped the sweat from his brow with the back of his hand. He knew he couldn't talk with Rynearson or even let the man see him, but he hoped to get close enough to where he worked in the hope of overhearing something he had to say, a possible clue or slip of the tongue. And if Kelly was really lucky, he might even run into someone who disliked the man as much as he did and who wouldn't flinch at repeating every bit of gossip he'd heard in the last few days . . . even to a total stranger.

The area in and around the front doors of the warehouse bustled with activity, making it easy for Kelly to wander about without being noticed. A ship had just docked a short while earlier, and while one string of workers unloaded the vessel and took the merchandise into the warehouse, a second group was loading the frigate with goods taken from storage. Electing to stand near the doorway, where he might have a better chance of hearing something, Kelly leaned a shoulder against the wall of the building and carefully listened to and scrutinized everything around him.

Several minutes passed in which nothing of any real interest happened or was said, until a young boy dressed in dirty, tattered clothes deliberately stepped in one man's way to draw his attention. Begging for a coin, the urchin wailed his loudest when his victim gave him a kick instead and sent him flying. For a second, Kelly thought about defending the youngster, since in his opinion no one, especially a child, deserved to be treated so roughly. Then he heard the recital of oaths the boy flung at his attacker, and he realized the little beggar was probably used to getting knocked on his backside and that he'd more than likely resent Kelly's help . . . except, of course, if it came with a handout.

Kelly tried to focus his attention back on the men and their various conversations simply because the lad's problems were unimportant compared to Bevan's *and* because he hadn't come to the docks to be someone's hero. But only a minute passed before the child was tossed to the ground again, and this time, besides the profanity, he heard real pain in the boy's voice.

257

"Ye bloody cur," he yelped, a single tear cleaning a path down his dirt-smudged face. "Ye wouldn't knock me around if I was a man! I'm only asking 'cause I 'ave a baby sister ta feed."

Whether it was true or not, Kelly ignored his impulse to stay impartial. He knew what it was like to be hungry and not have the necessary coin to remedy the problem. Leaving his post by the warehouse door, he approached the lad, grabbed him by the shirt collar, and hauled him to his feet.

"Ya'll not help your baby sister this way," he scolded, dragging the youngster to a safer spot where no one would notice them.

"Oh, yeah?" the boy retorted as he struggled to free himself from Kelly's firm hold. "And what am I supposed to do?"

"Stay out of the way while the men are workin'. Ya've only succeeded in makin' them angry. If ya want somethin' from someone, ya have ta wait until they're in the givin' mood."

"And when's that?" He took a swing at the fist claiming his shirt and received a bone rattling shake in return.

"After they've eaten and had a fair share of ale," Kelly advised. "Ya'll still get turned down most of the time, but ya'd have fewer bruises ta show for it."

"And I won't 'ave no bully pushin' me around, either," the boy fired back.

Kelly let go so abruptly the urchin stumbled to the ground. "Ya could try gettin' work and earnin' the money ya need. 'Tis far more honorable and it'll guarantee food for your table." He glared at the dirty face for a moment, thinking with an attitude like that

258

the boy deserved what he got, before he turned away and went back to stand near the warehouse again.

Half an hour passed in which Kelly heard nothing of importance. The work on the ship was completed and most of the men went inside to stack and mark crates, make an inventory, and fill the orders of local merchants who wanted to buy the newly arrived goods. Sometime around noon he saw a fancy black carriage coming down the street toward him and instinct warned him to move far enough away so the passenger wouldn't see him when he stepped to the sidewalk. The instant he recognized Rynearson's bulky shape descending the carriage, it took every ounce of strength Kelly had to stay put. His face reddened, his body turned to granite, and his clenched fists shook with rage. It had become painfully obvious over the past several days that the only person with any knowledge of Bevan's whereabouts was Rynearson, and seeing him now strained Kelly's good judgment. He wanted nothing more than to beat the man to death with his own bare hands, slowly, methodically, callously. No one had to tell him that Rynearson was the one behind his father's hurried execution and the resulting warrant for his and his brother's arrest. The man was a liar who used his wealth to have his own way. Well, no more. Kelly would see to it.

He had just moved to take a step forward when a tug on his shirt sleeve startled him and spun him away with his fist raised and ready. It took a second or two for the red haze to clear around the image he saw, and once he recognized the sharp-tongued street urchin staring questioningly back at him, he muttered an oath beneath his breath and dropped his hands to his sides.

"Ya sure are determined ta get yourself hurt," Kelly barked as he looked back at the warehouse in time to see Rynearson go inside. "Damn!"

Unscathed by the Irishman's ill-temper, the boy casually walked past him to climb up on an empty crate, where he settled himself down and boldly declared, "Ye don't like 'im too much, do ye, gov'na?"

"Who?" Kelly snarled, his dark brows twisted tightly together as he continued to glare at the vacant doorway.

"I ain't blind," the youngster sneered. "I saw 'ow ye looked at 'im. What did 'e do ta ye to make ye so angry? Steal from ye?"

"That's between him and me, laddie," Kelly growled.

"Well, ye'll 'ave to stand in line," the boy announced. "There ain't many Rynearson 'asn't cheated."

Some of Kelly's anger disappeared. "Ya know him?" he asked, turning to face the sassy-mouthed imp.

"Sort of," the boy replied with a shrug. "I work the docks a lot. So I 'ear things."

A knot formed in Kelly's stomach. "Like what?" he asked, moving closer.

Recognizing an easy way to earn a coin or two, a devious grin parted the boy's lips. "Oh, I don't know. What is it ye'd like to 'ear me say?"

Kelly's eyes narrowed. He knew what the boy was really after. "The truth," he told him as he leaned and placed a hand on the crate on either side of the youth's legs, trapping him between Kelly's outstretched arms. "Do ya suppose ya know how ta tell the truth?"

The subtle threat had little affect on the boy. "Sometimes I 'ave to 'ave me memory jogged."

"Do ya now?" Kelly challenged. "When I was a wee

lad and had a case of the forgetfulness, me father used ta jog me memory with a slap ta me ear. But I don't suppose that would work with someone as smart as you, now would it?"

The boy fearlessly shook his head.

"Then maybe ya should tell me what it takes . . . if I haven't guessed already."

Green eyes trimmed with dark lashes looked Kelly up and down. "I'm not sure ye 'ave what it takes."

Kelly knew he didn't. He and his brothers had left home so quickly they hadn't taken anything with them, including money. But he mustn't let this beggar know that. "And I'm not sure ya have anythin' worth buyin'. I guess we're at a standstill then, aren't we?"

The pickings had been slim that day, and since this stranger had been the first in a very long while to show him a little kindness, the boy decided to trust him. "Ask."

"I'm lookin' for me sister. She came here with Rynearson five days ago and hasn't been seen since. She's got fiery chestnut hair and green eyes. If ya've seen her, I'm sure ya'd remember her. She's a pretty young lass, and from the clothes she was wearin', she'd have looked out of place with Rynearson."

The expression on the youngster's face changed several times. "I never saw 'er with Rynearson."

Kelly's hopes plummeted. Disappointed, then angry, he shoved away and out of frustration smashed his fist into his left palm.

"I didn't say I never saw 'er," the boy corrected with a touch of sarcasm. "I said not with Rynearson."

Kelly spun back, his face twisted with hope and anguish.

"Now don't get all silly on me, gov'na," the urchin demanded. "I can't be sure it was yer sister I saw. But she did 'ave red hair."

"Where? Where did ya see her?"

A dirty finger raised to point at the end of the pier. "I saw her sneakin' on board one o' the ships anchored there the same night ye said yer sister arrived. It was the *Lady Hawk*, an American vessel. It sailed the next morning."

"With her on it?"

"Guess so. It was raining that night so I didn't 'ang around 'ere long." Squinting curiously at his companion, the boy asked, "Was she in trouble?"

"Isn't everyone who deals with the likes of Rynearson?"

The boy shrugged.

"Why do ya ask?"

"'Cause Rynearson's lacky, Uriah Faber, was asking the same questions ye're asking."

A cold dread closed in around Kelly's heart.

Standing at the helm, Gordon watched the spry movements of the young woman on the quarterdeck below him with a broad, easy smile on his face. Irish, as everyone called her, had taken to the ways of the sea as quickly as any of the men on board had done their first time out . . . perhaps better. She had never complained, got sick only once that had been during a frightful storm that had even made Gordon's stomach a little squeamish, and she had insisted that she be given her share of the work to do in exchange for the meals she ate. Her presence in the confined living space of the ship

262

never caused trouble among the men simply because she wouldn't let it. She never flirted or compromised herself by letting any of them see more than her bare feet even on the hottest of days. She had hidden her long, luscious red-gold hair beneath a bandanna, her shapely curves within a baggy shirt Eric had loaned her, and the long length of willowy legs inside cotton breeches which were large enough to fit someone half again the size of her.

When Mr. Welch came down with chills, Irish had volunteered not only to see to his care but to cook for the captain and crew as well. Gordon planned not to tell his galley chief that during the man's illness, the meals Gordon had been served were the best he'd ever eaten on board the *Lady Hawk*. He was sure the crew would agree, although no one ever said, for the simple reason that it wouldn't change things for them. Once their ship docked in North Carolina, Irish would go ashore and that would be the end of it. The best they could hope for was that once she was ready to return home, she would choose to sail with them.

In the past five weeks Gordon hadn't been able to get the young woman to talk about herself. All she had allowed him to learn was that her mother had died the year before, that she had three brothers, one of them her twin, and that as soon as she had earned enough money, she planned to go home to Ireland. She never mentioned her father, which conjured up all sorts of reasons in Gordon's mind, the worst being that perhaps the man had deserted his family when the children were young and Irish had merely refused to acknowledge he even existed. She had let it slip one time that she had met a young man who wanted to marry her, but that he

263

had been killed during some kind of revolt against the English authorities in Ireland. He had seen by the expression on her pretty face just how much she had loved the young man, but when Gordon asked what his name was, she had gotten a funny look in her eyes, abruptly excused herself, and walked away.

Gordon had never had the courage to ask her where she had gotten the expensive gown she was wearing the night they found her hiding in the long boat, but Gordon had his own theory on that. From the easy way she had taken over the job of cook and because of her thoroughness in keeping the galley, her cabin, and anything else she touched as clean as possible, he knew she was accustomed to such menial labor, which indicated to him that her family was too poor to hire servants to do the work. Therefore, the gown she was wearing had to have been a gift—from her lover or . . . He hadn't liked the idea that Irish was someone's mistress, but it certainly offered a possible explanation for her having wanted to flee England. She must have decided that whoever gave her the dress represented a life-style she didn't want to be a part of, and when she had voiced her opinion, she had met resistance and had had to run away. It was what Gordon wanted to believe, anyway, since the young woman had not only won his friendship over the past weeks they had spent together, but had won his heart as well.

Irish hadn't bothered asking the destination of *Lady Hawk*, which truly didn't surprise Gordon. It obviously didn't matter to her and he could only guess it was because she knew she couldn't do a thing to alter their journey's end. Yet she had shown a hint of apprehension about her future once Gordon had announced his prediction that the *Lady Hawk* would reach the coast of America in a day or two.

"If you're worried about what will happen to you once we've docked," he had guessed as they sat sharing a meal in his cabin, "don't be."

Bright green eyes sparkling with a vague touch of humor had glanced up at him from across the table. "Oh?" she had challenged. "And why do ya say that, Gordon Sanderson? Are ya plannin' ta take me in?"

Gordon's face had reddened, but not because he was afraid she had misunderstood his intentions. It embarrassed him to think she might have read his mind when she suggested something he had already considered and had decided against. He knew his Sara would approve, since she had always wanted a daughter, but Irish needed a job that would pay in gold coin, not merely a roof over her head and food to eat. He couldn't afford to hire a servant and he hoped she knew that.

"I'd like to say yes," he finally managed to reply, "but you know the reason why it wouldn't be practical, don't you?"

"Aye," she answered with a smile. "Just as you know I'd have had ta decline your generous offer. Ya're a nice man, Captain Gordon Sanderson, and I owe ya a lot. But if fate hadn't played a trick on me, I'd be home with me family right now. I need ta find me a job that will earn me the money I need ta go back ta Ireland."

He smiled as he pushed his empty plate to the center of the table. "And selfishly speaking, I wish there wasn't a family waiting for you, that you'd decide you like it here and stay because you want to stay. I know my wife would feel the same way about you as I do." He grinned devilishly. "My boys would too."

"Your boys?" she repeated, genuinely surprised. "Ya never told me ya had sons."

"Two," he answered proudly. "Thomas and James. They're a little older than you, and unless something drastic happened while I was away, they're both still unmarried."

"Captain," Bevan mocked playfully. "Are ya tryin' ta pick a wife for your sons? Shame on ya."

"And what father doesn't?" he challenged. "I want them to marry someone worthy of them, someone who will love them, care for them, and bear them strong sons the way Sara has for me."

Beven could hear the love in his voice and wasn't offended by his boldness. "Ya honor me," she said in all seriousness. "Ya know nothin' about me, but ya're willin' ta introduce me ta your boys."

"I know enough," he contradicted. "I know you're a hard worker, you're a woman of principle and morals with a strong will and one who doesn't burden others with her problems. I won't judge someone because they choose to keep secrets. I respect their right to consider their business is none of mine." He waved off the topic and reached to pour hot water over the tea leaves in his cup. "But that's not why I brought it up," he continued. "I wanted to let you know that I'm reasonably sure the Hamilton family will take care of you."

"Hamilton?" Bevan repeated.

Gordon nodded. "They own the *Lady Hawk* and several other ships." He chuckled. "They own a lot of things, actually. They're probably one of the wealthiest families in the area. They come from good stock, and everything they have, they worked for. It wasn't inherited. And they're the nicest, most sympathetic bunch of people I've ever known when it comes to someone else's problems. Except for Lawrence, maybe."

Bevan raised a questioning brow.

"He's the father of the clan. But he doesn't take an active part in any of the decision making anymore . . . not since his stroke a while back. His oldest son, Reid, is in charge. Now there's a mistake," Gordon confessed, a smile twinkling in his eyes as he stroked his chin and leaned back in his chair. "Stephen, Reid's younger brother, is the one who should have been born first." He laughed at the confused look on his companion's face. "When Reid was just a boy, his father decided who Reid would marry and how he would live his adult life. I guess because Lawrence thought a father should hand over his business to his eldest son. But Stephen is the one with the business kind of mind, and *he's* ready to settle down with a wife and children. Reid isn't. He's restless, and I suspect that's why he and Laura haven't set a wedding date yet. Reid told me not long ago that once he got married, he'd never stray from his vows. Which is as it should be," Gordon admitted. "I know he loves Laura, but I guess there's just something about being a husband that makes him nervous." He sighed, took another sip of his tea, and settled his gaze on his companion again.

"Anyway, I'm sure once we tell Reid what happened to you—I mean, that you boarded the *Lady Hawk* accidentally and wish to return home, he'll find a job for you there on the plantation. It's such a big place, they're always looking for help." He smiled at her, then straightened with a frown at the worried look he saw. "What is it?"

267

"I'm sure ya know the Hamiltons well enough," Bevan replied, "but can ya be so sure they won't have me arrested?"

"Positive," Gordon assured her. "Just as long as we talk to Reid first. One of his biggest faults, according to his father, is being softhearted when he knows someone is in trouble."

"Then he should really like me," Bevan remarked sarcastically as she left her chair to stack the dirty dishes on a tray. "Trouble seems ta follow me around."

Gordon would have liked asking her to explain, and he nearly had until he realized that if she wanted him to know something about her personal life, she would have told him long before then.

They had gone on talking about Reid and his brother, Stephen's accident as a boy that had left him crippled, and how devoted Reid was to the young man. They talked about Lyndsy Marie, a married sister; Laura, Reid's fiancée; and finally Charlotte, the matriarch of the Hamilton clan. A petite lady with black hair and gray eyes, a soft smile, a pale complexion, and loving gentleness, she, like her oldest son, thought very little of being wealthy. All that mattered to her was her family, their happiness, their safety, and their health. She always hated when Reid announced he would be sailing across the Atlantic. Sudden storms had a way of popping up unexpectantly and with such violence they would sink a ship and drown everyone on board. The entire voyage to England and back took close to three months and during that whole time she would worry about her son's safe return, even though Reid preferred sailing over his role as businessman. She had a special kind of love for her firstborn son, and Gordon concluded it was because the two of them were so much alike in their thoughts and feelings. And that was why Gordon knew that Reid, and especially his mother, would welcome Irish with open arms once they heard her story.

She had sat there quietly listening to his recital, and once he'd finished, she had remarked about how wonderful a family they seemed to be and that Laura surely realized how fortunate she was to be asked to help carry on the Hamilton name. It hadn't been until Gordon noticed the tears in her eyes that he deduced talking about such happiness had reminded Irish of her own family and, because of a twist of fate, *her* happiness had been taken from her. He had apologized for making her sad, which she had laughingly refused to blame on him, and had changed the subject anyway.

They parted company after he told her that they would have a lot of work to do once the ship docked the next day and that they'd both need a good night's sleep. She had agreed, but about an hour later, he had found her standing at the bow of the ship staring up at the black sky, its bright array of stars and full moon, and he could only conclude she was preparing herself for the new adventure which lay ahead.

He had meant to seek her out the next morning and reassure her that everything would turn out all right. But the sighting of land came sooner than he had expected, and everyone on board, including Irish, had lost themselves in their work. Now that the ship was nearly ready to drop anchor, Gordon knew there wouldn't be time to comfort his ward as his other duties were more pressing at the moment. However, once he had seen to it that the crew had begun to unload the cargo, he planned to personally escort Irish to the main house, where he prayed he would find Reid before Lawrence learned the ship had sailed into port.

Bevan hadn't meant to neglect her job—slight as it was—once the rest of the crew began the preparations of seeing the *Lady Hawk* safely through the barrier reef that stretched endlessly port and starboard off the huge vessel. But her first sight of America numbed her and held her captive as she absently moved toward the bow of the ship where she would have an unrestricted view. Crystal blue water lapped against the shoreline. A soft breeze rustled the tree tops. The wide expanse of the ocean narrowed to the mouth of an estuary which seemed to be luring the frigate home. Warm sunshine overhead bathed the green grasses, and seagulls squawked their welcome as they circled high above the ship. The flap of the sails as some were dropped, others taken in, added to Bevan's uneasiness, for the sound marked the coming of an end to their voyage and the uncertainty of another which was about to begin. Yet despite that chilling promise, for a brief moment while she listened to Captain Sanderson's sharp commands to his men and watched the *Lady Hawk* swing closer to shore, she wished above all else that Kelly, Ryan, Shea, and her father were standing at the railing beside her.

A shout from someone in the crow's nest pulled Bevan's attention upward. Shading her eyes with one hand, she saw him point at something on shore and out of curiosity she turned to look in that direction. At first nothing was visible through the dense growth of trees and shrubs lining the bank. Then as the ship skimmed closer, she caught a glimpse of white among the thick green foliage. Ever so slowly it seemed to magically grow and take shape behind a leafy curtain of fern, pine, and oak, until the vision burst forth with such splendor it took Bevan's breath away. Set back and nestled snugly amid a forest of cypress, white mulberry, moss, and vines stood the majestic brilliance of a huge, two-story, multicolumned mansion, the only semblance of civilization in this foreign land she had seen thus far. A wide, spacious front lawn spread out before it, and was divided in half by a cobblestone drive which wound its way toward the jetty and the pier where the *Lady Hawk* would dock. Numerous buildings crowded the perimeter and a score of people hurried about the place as word of their arrival had obviously been heralded.

A fluttering of nerves tickled Bevan's stomach as she watched the crew secure the sails, tie off the mooring lines, and ease the gangplank to the pier. In a matter of minutes she would have to plead her case to a stranger and hope he would understand the vagueness of her story. The man had every right to shun her, as well he might once he got a good look at her. Instinctively she glanced down at what she was wearing and cringed at the image she would present dressed in baggy clothes and bare feet. Reaching up, she pulled the bandanna from her head and shook out her hair. He might be more sympathetic if she met him dressed as she was, but Kelly had told her one time that a woman's best advantage over a man was just that—being a woman. Men enjoyed protecting helpless females, and although she couldn't really say she was all that helpless, she guessed it would work in her favor if she pretended to be. With a disapproving sigh, she turned for her cabin, where she would change into the dress she had taken from the armoire in Rynearson's house, hating the idea but knowing she must.

"You look beautiful, Irish," Gordon complimented her a short while later, his gaze sweeping the length of her as he took her hand and walked her down the gangplank. "You hardly look like the seaman I had dinner with last night."

She tried to smile but couldn't. She didn't feel beautiful. She felt cheap and used, violated even though she had escaped Rynearson untouched. And now she had to put herself on display again to win her freedom. But in the end it would be worth it, she kept repeating to herself as she tightened her grip on the cloth bag she carried.

A carriage awaited them at the end of the pier, and once Gordon had issued his final instructions to his first mate, he helped Bevan board the rig.

"I was told Miss Laura is here visiting," he said with a soft, encouraging smile. "You'll like her. She's a very nice young lady." He could see the doubt in her green eyes as she stared out the window at the manor and decided to use another approach. "Did I mention Mrs. Hamilton . . . Charlotte? She's an exceptional woman. She—"

"Cap'n," Bevan interrupted. "Ya don't have ta sell me on the Hamiltons. If ya say they're fine people, then I believe ya. They have ta be, if *you* like them." She smiled warmly at him. "I know what ya're tryin' ta do, and I'm grateful. But no matter what ya say, it won't stop me from worryin'." She looked back outside. "What happens ta me is up ta them now."

They rode the rest of the way in silence while Bevan studied everything about the estate. She'd heard the planters in America were wealthy but she had never imagined anything like this. To the right of the elegant mansion were three small buildings she guessed might be the kitchen, ham house, and cook's quarters. Beyond that was the stable, a long, brick building with an exercising paddock enclosed by a three-rail, whitewashed fence. On the left of the manor and set back a good distance was a blacksmith's shop and a huge building she assumed was the warehouse that would hold the goods the *Lady Hawk* had delivered. As the carriage rounded the circular drive leading to the front door, she caught a glimpse of an endless row of log cabins behind the trees shading the warehouse and a field of tobacco plants the servants were harvesting. The vast, complex plantation with its scores of workers was a far cry from the farm where she had grown up, and for a second she envied anyone who had had the opportunity to call it home. Then she remembered the laughter, the good times, and the love her family had shared despite being poor and she reminded herself that a person could be wealthy in other ways besides money.

A young lad of less than a score came to greet the carriage and open the door for them. Once Gordon had stepped down, he turned to assist Bevan, and a frown creased his brow when he felt how cold her fingers were. Rather than letting go of her hand, he curled it in the crook of his arm, smiled at her, then escorted her across the wide veranda to the front door.

"Good morning, Jeremy," he greeted, once the butler had responded to Gordon's summons. "We'd like to speak with Mr. Reid. Is he here?"

"Yes, Captain Sanderson. He arrived home just this

273

morning," the man replied, his gaze briefly evaluating the woman before him. He stepped aside to allow the visitors to enter and motioned toward the back of the house. "He and Miss Laura are in the gardens. Shall I announce you?"

"That won't be necessary," Gordon declined. "I would imagine he's expecting me since I'm sure he's been told the *Lady Hawk* has docked."

"Yes, sir," Jeremy answered with a polite bow.

The size of the foyer was larger than Bevan's entire house back home in Ireland and she couldn't help staring in awe. The black and white tiled floor spread out before her to the base of a grand staircase which graciously ascended to a long balcony above her. To her right just beyond the opened, double sliding doors, she could see the parlor, which seemed to stretch on for miles. To her left was the study, its walls lined with books from floor to ceiling. Ahead of them was a triple set of French doors with diamond-shaped, leaded glass panes covered with white lace curtains. The late morning sunlight poured through them and warmed the entire foyer with a bright, cheery glow that eased some of Bevan's nervousness. Then she felt Gordon give her a gentle tug and her mouth went suddenly dry as she allowed him to lead her across the tiled floor.

"Wait here," he instructed as he opened the middle pair of doors to the gardens beyond. "I'll speak with him first."

Nodding, she watched Gordon step out into the bright sunshine and across the flagstone patio. From there he skipped down a trio of steps to a rock path that wound its way through neatly trimmed, knee-high hedges. A short distance farther on she could see a gazebo bedecked with the colorful brilliance of rose blossoms climbing the latticework to its Oriental-style roof line. A couple stood inside, unaware they were being watched or that Gordon was about to join them. The man had his back to Bevan, but *his* presence hadn't aroused her curiosity as much as the woman who had turned slightly to him and was fidgeting with the lapel on his jacket. Even in the defused light of the summer house, the woman's hair shone a pale yellow-gold and her complexion was as smooth and creamy as fresh butter. Her exquisite silk gown hugged her slender body in all the right places, and when she bobbed her head at something her companion said, diamond earrings twinkled beneath a soft platinum ringlet.

So this is Laura, Bevan mused with a quiet sigh. *I can see why the captain is smitten with her. She's beautiful.*

Her attention was drawn back to Gordon when he crossed into her line of vision, and her heart started its trip-hammer beating again when she realized he was about to lay her future in the hands of his friend. Anxious to know what Mr. Hamilton would decide, yet dreading his answer at the same time, Bevan hugged the cloth bag to her chest while her gaze repeatedly shifted between Gordon Sanderson and the back of Mr. Hamilton's head. To Bevan it seemed as if hours passed while the two men talked back and forth, and if she hadn't been so frightened, she might have paid more attention to how tall Mr. Hamilton was compared to the captain or how wide his shoulders were, the way his richly tailored clothes molded his physique, his black hair, his confident manner, his stance . . . But her worry, exhaustion, and all the horrifying events she had encountered over the past few months had dulled her perception and left her vulnerable, and when she saw Gordon nod his head her way, she straightened and readied herself with a smile as she watched the gentleman beside him turn around.

A buzzing started in her ears the instant she saw those warm gray eyes. She blinked, certain she was dreaming or that the shadows of the gazebo were playing a terrible trick on her. Then he stepped into the sunlight, and she could feel the blood drain from her face.

Dear God, Graham! Her lips moved but no sound escaped them.

Her head began to spin, she couldn't breathe, her knees shook, and her whole body shivered with an electrifying chill that charged through every nerve. Her world and everything around her grew fuzzy. She staggered sideways, reached out to grab something to steady herself, and lost her balance. Long before the cold, hard tiles at her feet came up to catch her, the sweet void of oblivion cushioned any pain she might have felt when her legs gave out from under her and she dropped to the floor.

Suspended somewhere between the real and imaginary spheres of her existence, Bevan could feel herself being lifted up. Strong arms encircled her. She could smell the masculine scent which clouded her reasoning, feel the beat of someone's heart which wasn't her own. She sensed someone's worry and the speed with which he hastened to see to her care. Faint voices began to spin around inside her head, indistinct messages that hinted of a greater shock yet to come. Fighting to bring herself to the surface of awareness, she focused on the words she heard as those same strong arms gently laid her back down.

"Don't know much . . . been sick . . . scared . . . needs your help . . ."

The soft fragrance of perfume invaded her senses, followed by a feminine voice. "Pretty little thing . . . poor girl . . . her name?"

"Irish," came the reply, and it seemed to ricochet inside her brain.

"Why did she faint?" the woman asked.

"I have no idea," a man admitted with a troubled sigh.

The swirling gray fog began to lift, and with every ounce of strength she had left, Bevan forced her eyes open in time to see the beautiful woman from the gazebo rise and walk away. It took Bevan a second or two to realize that she had been carried into the parlor and laid on the settee and that the voices she had heard belonged to Laura and Gordon Sanderson. Too weak yet to sit up, she moved only her head to look about the room for the man she had seen in the summer house with Laura.

"Curious thing, the way she took one look at you and fainted, Reid," she heard Gordon remark. The back of the settee prevented her from seeing either man, and if she'd had the courage, she would have pushed herself up. "It was almost as if she knew you."

"Sorry, Gordon," his companion announced, and Bevan's heart felt as if it were breaking in a hundred pieces. "I've never seen her before today."

There was no mistaking it . . . that voice, those eyes, even the male scent of him and the feel of his arms around her as he carried her to the parlor. This man, this Reid Hamilton, was the stranger she had cared for while he was hurt, the one she had fallen in love with, the one who had said he had wanted to marry her, the one she believed was Graham! She didn't know how, but he hadn't really died that day. She had seen him get shot, had seen the blood, and the two men who had carried him off. Everyone who had been there at the prison had assumed he was dead, even her brothers. Yet obviously he hadn't been fatally wounded. Then why the charade? Pained by the answer she didn't want to admit, she closed her eyes and held back the flood of tears which knotted her throat. It had all been a game to him. Hadn't Gordon told her that this man's weakness was helping out others in trouble? He had certainly gone to the extreme in risking his own life in the hope of rescuing her father, but that, she concluded, was a part of what made it all worth doing . . . the risk, the excitement, the danger. She'd have to hear it from his own lips, but she was sure he'd confess that his plans had been to free her father and then simply to disappear. He had to, for God's sake. He was engaged to be married. He had an entirely different life waiting for him. His feelings for her had been only a pleasant distraction, and he had lied to her to bring her panting at his heels. The pain in her heart deepened as she remembered how easily, how *willingly,* she had obliged him, and she wondered how he had ever managed not to laugh out loud. Well, he wasn't laughing now. Her sudden appearance had to be twisting his stomach into knots! He'd been caught in his own little web of deceit, and *she* had the power to see to his destruction.

"Oh, Gordon," she heard Laura laughingly tease. "Haven't you seen the affect Reid has on every woman he meets? This young girl wouldn't be the first to swoon at the sight of him. Isn't that so, darling?"

"You're exaggerating a bit, Laura," he answered, his

tone heavy and edged with concern. "I really don't think *I* had anything to do with her fainting. Neither does Gordon."

"No, of course not," he said, though his tone seemed a little uneasy. "Miss Laura, weren't you going to get some smelling salts and a glass of water for the young lady?"

"Oh. Yes," she answered. "Has she eaten lately? I could have Cleo make her up a tray. After all, an empty stomach could have been the reason she swooned."

"That's a very kind gesture, Miss Laura. Yes, why don't you ask Cleo to fix a tray?" Gordon encouraged, though he knew she'd had a large breakfast only a short while earlier.

"Are you sure you don't know her?" Gordon asked a moment later once the sound of Laura's footsteps had faded down the hall.

"Of course I'm sure!" His boot heels struck the floor as he moved away from the door in short, angry strides toward the settee. "Sweet Mother of God, Gordon, look at her. I could never forget a face like that!"

A moment of silence followed in which Bevan willed herself not to move, not to let the tears slip from between her lashes.

"I know that," Gordon finally replied with a wearisome sigh. "I suppose I'm letting my imagination get the better of me. But there's something strange going on."

"Like what? Just because this girl fainted from hunger?"

"After that big breakfast she ate only a couple of hours ago? No, she fainted because of you—almost as if she recognized you!"

"Recognized me? What do you mean?"

"Maybe she had something to do with the mess you'd gotten yourself into there in Ireland. She's Irish, you know. That's about all I know about her. She's been totally close-mouthed about her personal life, right down to not telling me her name or why she smuggled herself on board my ship. She claims she wanted to go home. I hope this doesn't have something to do with Rynearson."

"Rynearson," Reid snarled. "Somehow I knew his name would come up. Every time I think of him, I feel I should scrape something off the bottom of my shoe. Damn," he growled. "I thought we were through with him."

"Apparently not," Gordon said. "At least not until we see this little lady on a ship bound for home."

"And what do we do in the meantime?"

"Have a talk with the girl when she comes to. Warn her off. Give her a job to do away from the house, and the first ship we hear of that's sailing for England, we'll see that she's on it. After that, she'll be on her own." He gave the little redhead one long, last look and murmured, "Too bad it had to turn out this way. I'd grown to really like her." Spotting Laura coming through the doorway, he turned with a smile, his hand extended as he walked toward her with an offer to carry the items she'd brought along.

"I hope it's as easy as you make it sound," Reid whispered, his gaze still locked on the face of the young woman with flowing chestnut hair. "I really do."

Suddenly, green eyes, the color of which took his breath away, were glaring heatedly back up at him, and the vision of another time, another place stabbed at the dark recesses of his memory.

Chapter Nine

Reid had had to stand by and helplessly watch without saying a word while Laura took charge of the young girl Gordon had delivered to his doorstep. Until he had the opportunity of confronting the little minx, he was left wondering just how much, if any, of their conversation she had heard while he and Gordon assumed she was still unconscious. The look she had given him was full of hatred. The question was why? What had he done to her to warrant such a powerful emotion? And was she looking for revenge?

Laura had insisted the young Irish girl be taken to one of the many guest bedrooms upstairs and that Reid carry her rather than let her walk for fear she might faint again. As he stood alone in the study now recalling the event, he remembered the sensation which had come over him once he held her cradled reluctantly in his arms. He never once looked at her while he climbed the stairs, but the heat of her glare seemed to scorch the side of his face. There was a pure, unbridled loathing for him which seemed to seep out of every pore in her body as she hung stiff in his grasp.

For the past month and a half he had done nothing but search his memory for those lost days between the time he and Gordon had gotten separated at the pier in Liverpool and when he woke up in Gordon's room at the inn with the most dreadful headache he'd ever had in his life. Something mysterious had happened to him during that span of time, something he didn't want to remember or simply couldn't.

Leaving his place by the window where he had stood absently watching the crew unload the *Lady Hawk*, he moved the tall, brown leather chair away from the desk and eased himself down onto the seat with his elbows resting on the arms. He sat there for only a moment before he jerked upright, crossed his wrists, and laid them on the desk with his chin resting on top. He knew there was no use in trying to force himself into remembering. The doctor he had visited in Richmond had told him he couldn't.

"It takes time," the man had promised. "You'll get your memory back, but only when you're completely healed. You received a serious blow to the head and it's God's way of telling you to take it easy."

"It's God's way of telling me I did something I shouldn't have," he grumbled as he pushed himself up and went back to stare out the window again.

A little later, Reid stopped outside the bedroom in which their mysterious guest was resting, and listened to Laura's pleasant voice as she tried to make conversation.

"I've never been to Ireland or England . . . or *any-*

where in Europe, for that matter," she was saying, laughter trickling from her words. "Once you're up to it, maybe you'd tell me all about where you live. I imagine it's quite beautiful there. Is Irish your real name?

Reid leaned a little closer to hear the girl's response. Laura had a gift for making friends and putting anyone at ease, and if the girl trusted her, she might say something that would help him remember.

"No?" Laura continued, and Reid assumed the girl had merely shaken her head rather than speak. "Well, I think it's a sweet nickname."

He could hear Laura moving about the room and he was tempted to peek in at them.

"Would you like a nice hot bath? I don't suppose you had such a luxury being on a ship all that time. Men never think of such things, and even if they had, you wouldn't have found much privacy to enjoy yourself." She laughed merrily. "Nor do I imagine they had any soaps or perfume for the water. Do you like jasmine? It's my favorite, and I'm sure Charlotte has some we can borrow."

The rustle of skirts came close to the door and Reid backed away a step.

"And we'll have to do something about your clothes. You certainly can't wear the same dress every day. Oh," she added as though she'd just remembered something important, "I put the bag with your belongings there on the night stand beside you. See it? I didn't snoop, I promise. But I could tell there isn't much in it. Why don't I go and see about a bath, and while you're soaking, I'll have Vesta wash that dress? You can borrow something of mine in the meantime. All right?"

Dainty heels clicked across the wood floor, and before Reid could make up his mind whether or not to find himself a hiding place, Laura had stepped into the hallway and spotted him. The scowl he saw dip her pale eyebrows together told him she didn't approve of his eavesdropping. He smiled lamely and pulled her away from the door she had left open behind her.

"Talkative sort, isn't she?" he mocked as he led her to the staircase.

"How long were you standing there?" she demanded, unnaturally cross with him.

"Long enough to know a little of me is rubbing off on you," he smirked. "And if my father hears how hospitable you've been to a stowaway, he'll burn your ears the same as he'll burn mine."

Halting abruptly at the top of the stairs, she turned and flashed him an irritable glower. "What are you talking about?"

He jerked his dark head in the direction of the bedroom. "Irish. I'm talking about Irish, the mystery girl. Didn't you hear Gordon tell me where he found her? You're treating her like she was the Queen of England."

"And how should she be treated?" Laura challenged. "Would you have me rant and rave at her as I'm sure you're wanting to do? She's frightened, Reid. She's a long way from home without family or friends. She doesn't know a single person here or if she can trust any of us. How can she? Gordon said she was running away from something so terrifying that she risked her life just to be free. If they hadn't found her when they had, she probably would have died of pneumonia!"

Laura's show of temper surprised him. Taken aback,

he could do nothing more than stare at her a moment. "Yes," he finally admitted. "But—"

"Then don't tell me what I'm doing for her is wrong!" Seizing her skirts in both hands, she started down the steps without him. "I'm sure your mother wouldn't have acted any differently, so I suggest you go about your business and leave Irish to me."

She had nearly reached the bottom of the staircase before the shock of her outburst faded and he was able to speak again. "I'd like nothing better," he called after her as he hurriedly followed her descent. "But that's not possible." He caught her arm and ushered her toward the back of the house. "We need to talk."

"Reid!" she exclaimed testily as he dragged her through the French doors and out into the gardens. "What has gotten into you?"

"That's just it," he admitted, glancing all around them to make sure they were alone. "I'm not sure."

Confused, she shook her head, pale curls shimmering in the sunlight. "You're not making any sense. You haven't, ever since Gordon showed up with Irish and she—" Of a sudden her pretty face whitened, her chin sagged, and her blue eyes got a horrified look in them. "Are you trying to tell me something?" She glanced back at the house, then up at the second-story window before she jerked her head around and settled her gaze on him once more. "Gordon wasn't teasing when he asked if you knew the girl, was he? You *do* know her. Reid, did you and she . . . ? Are the two of you . . . ? My God, she isn't . . . ?" Slender hands came up to cover her mouth, and when she blinked, a tear ran down her cheek. "Oh Reid, how could you?"

"Laura, no!" he proclaimed, grabbing her arms and

pulling her close. "That wasn't at all what I meant. Please, just listen while I try to explain."

He'd only just arrived home shortly before the *Lady Hawk* had docked that morning, and therefore hadn't been allowed much time alone with Laura before Gordon intruded. From there everything had become chaotic, and more disturbing matters had crowded his thoughts. Until now he hadn't realized how it would all seem to Laura or that he'd never taken her aside to give her a detailed account of everything that had happened to him after setting sail for England almost three months earlier. Or to explain that a part of his life was missing, a measure of time in which anything could have happened.

"And you don't even remember being in Ireland?" Laura asked once he had finished his story.

"No. I have to take Gordon's word for it. I do know I was damn lucky the bullet only grazed me," he confessed, "and that Gordon and Eric found me before someone else could finish the job."

"And you think Irish might be involved in some way?" Her blue eyes had grown into wide, attentive circles.

He recited Gordon's speculation and added his own opinion as well as his observation on how Irish had reacted to him.

"Oh Reid, that's too much to believe," she argued. "Do you honestly think she'd come all the way to North Carolina just for the sake of revenge? That she'd start by causing trouble between you and me?"

He crimped one side of his mouth. "It does sound a little farfetched, and maybe Gordon and I are putting too much into this. But the girl seems not only to know

286

me but to hate me.

"Why don't you try talking to her? Ask her what she's doing here and what she hopes to gain."

He knew Laura's suggestion was the only way to settle the matter, but for some reason he was reluctant. "Yes, perhaps I should," he admitted with a smile. "But I want you to promise me something."

"What Reid?"

He pulled her against his chest, wrapped both arms around her, and kissed the top of her head. "That you'll wait to pass judgment on me until after I can remember what happened. If she tries to tell you something, listen but don't believe . . . at least not until I can defend my actions. I'm worried she'll try to set you against me. Remember that I care a great deal for you, Laura. I always have and I always will. Nothing anyone can say or do will change that."

"I know," she murmured, hugging him tight. What she couldn't tell him was how his physical show of affection surprised her. In all the years she had known him, he had never held her in his arms. He had played the loving protector but that was as far as it went. He never seemed to care when a man flirted openly with her, and only rarely did he hold her hand for any length of time other than when he helped her down from the carriage. And he had never kissed her except on the cheek or brow or the top of her head as he had just now. When he said he cared a great deal for her, she knew he meant it. But it wasn't the kind of love she wanted from him. His feelings for her were nothing more than brotherly. Hardly the sort of emotions on which to build a long and lasting married life. Yet even so, all of that wasn't what frightened Laura. She had seen a change in him—a small one, one she couldn't quite describe—but a change nonetheless. And whatever it was, it had to do with the time he'd spent in Ireland, the days he couldn't recall.

"Go and talk with her," she finally managed to tell him as she gently, unwillingly pushed away from him. "It might even help you to remember." She laughed softly at the frown which marred his handsome face. "She's Irish, isn't she? Perhaps just listening to her will spark a memory of sorts. You'll never rest until you know what happened while you were away."

His scowl deepened. "Maybe it's better I never remember."

"Are you afraid you might have done something horrible?" She laughed at the expression her proposal evoked. "Oh, don't worry," she scolded playfully. "You and I both know you would never do anything reprehensible. At least not deliberately."

That idea made him groan.

"Oh, go on," she giggled, taking his arm and turning him around. "Go talk to her. Settle this affair so we can go back to being our boring selves."

"Boring?" he questioned. "Is that how you see us?"

Laura hadn't meant to say it . . . not out loud anyway. But yes, their lives were boring. From the time she was old enough to walk, she'd been groomed to act like a lady, a genteel lady, and she longed for a little excitement to liven up her days. "Not really," she lied. "I meant calm."

Reid raised a dark brow at her. "You're not the same sweet girl I left behind, Laura Bradburn. Has someone come along while I was away? Tell me the truth. I can handle it."

Knowing he only teased, she played along as she slipped her hand into the bend of his arm and directed them back to the house. "Well, if you must know, I've spent a great deal of time with a young man who seems to care about me even more than you."

Reid pretended to be alarmed. He stopped, puffed out his chest, and scowled, "Who is this man? I fear I shall have to call him out for taking liberties with my fiancée."

Laura laughed at his buffoonery. "You'd challenge your own brother?"

"Oh," Reid replied with a faint, lopsided grin as he started them off again. "Stephen's who you meant. Well, I guess there's no danger there."

The smile on his lips faded as he thought about his brother. Laura truly deserved someone like Stephen. He was sensible and good-natured, and he'd already decided what he wanted to do with his life. Reid hadn't. He wasn't even sure he wanted Laura or his father's plantation. The vision of a small farm, a thatch-roofed cottage, a barn, and a lop-eared donkey pulling a cart came to mind, and he frowned, wondering what the image meant and if he'd really seen such a place. Suddenly drawn to look up at a second-story window, an odd warmth tingled every nerve in his body when he spied the young Irish girl staring back at him.

"Ya bastard," Bevan seethed through clenched teeth, her green eyes snapping fire and her slender body rigid with anger. "Ya lyin', good-for-nothin', deceitful piece of—" The last was lost in a throaty growl as she watched the couple disappear from view beneath her window. "Are ya tellin' her the same things ya told me? Are ya tellin' her ya have some problems ta clear up before the two of ya can get married?" She whirled away from the window, hot tears of rage shining in her eyes. "Well, ya have more than a few, Reid Hamilton." She spat the name disdainfully. "Ya may convince your fiancée that ya've never seen me before, ya might even trick her inta thinkin' I'm here because Rynearson sent me, but you and I will always know the truth." In short, jerky strides she crossed the room to the door. "Ya even have the captain believin'," she quietly hissed as she glared out into the hallway and listened to the sounds of someone's footsteps in the foyer below her. "Ya've made it so no one will give me the chance ta tell me side of it. They'll all think *I'm* the liar, *I'm* the one who can't be trusted. And what will happen ta me if I dare ta make a stand? Ya'll have me thrown in prison, that's what ya'll do. Well, I won't give ya the satisfaction."

Realizing whoever was starting up the steps would soon come into view and see her standing there, she moved away from the door and went back to look out the window again. She certainly didn't want to talk to *him,* and she wasn't up to Laura's sweet politeness. She wanted to hate the woman, but she was finding it rather difficult to achieve. It wasn't Laura's fault her fiancée was a blackhearted rogue. The shame of it was that Bevan couldn't tell her. And she needed to know *before* she married him. Recalling the sight of the couple locked in an embrace a moment ago and how he had lovingly kissed Laura tore at Bevan's heart. She closed her eyes, praying she wouldn't cry, and unknowingly crossed her arms over her bosom as if *she* were the one he had held.

"Ah, Graham," she murmured, her lower lip quivering. "I loved ya so."

The instant Reid stepped into the doorway and saw the young beauty standing at the window, her thick, chestnut hair falling in luscious curls down her back, her profile bathed in golden sunshine, and her slim body covered in expensive cloth, his heart thumped in his chest and the sweet aroma of freshly mowed hay was stirred up within his memory. He saw the indistinct outline of a small cottage set upon a knoll and the figure of someone walking toward it. Then the image faded and Reid frowned, trying to bring it back. Both Laura and Gordon had suggested that the presence of this Irish girl might help stimulate the memory of those lost days and apparently it had, but only in bits and pieces, and that frustrated and worried Reid. He had gotten himself into some sort of trouble back there in Ireland, and until he knew exactly what it was, he feared the uncertainty of knowing how, when, or even *if* someone was coming for him. He guessed this girl knew. He also assumed she'd never tell him, not unless he forced her. And how would he manage something like that? he mused. He didn't even know her name. But he *had* seen the hatred blazing in her eyes, and short of threatening her life, he doubted anything else would make her talk. Unless . . .

A shrewd smile parted his lips as he stepped farther into the room where the chances of their being overheard weren't as likely. "I assume," he began, his voice low, "that we should both admit we know why you're here, and therefore avoid any verbal games we might have played otherwise. I should probably also tell you that as soon as it can be arranged, I'll be shipping you back to Ireland." He paused a moment, expecting her to respond. When she didn't, he wondered if perhaps his idea hadn't been as brilliant as he had first thought. "I think you should also know that Laura and I had a long talk. I told her everything, so you can forget about getting even with me through her. The feelings we had for each other are still just as strong as they've ever been." He cocked a brow, waited, then inwardly sighed when she continued to stare out the window without saying a word or looking his way. "My family is away right now, but they're expected home this evening. They, too, will be informed about the reason you're here. So you can dismiss any notion you have about befriending one of them. Blood is thicker than water." He frowned, wondering what it would take to provoke her, since nothing had worked so far. "You'll be given a job to do and you'll be treated as a servant, nothing more, until we can send you home. Have I made myself perfectly clear?"

Another long minute passed. Finally she turned suddenly and settled a cold, malevolent glower on him.

"Aye, Mr. Hamilton," she replied in a rancorous tone. "Ya've made yourself perfectly clear. Ya want me out of your life as quickly and as quietly as possible. I'm not ta talk with any of your family, and I'm not ta tell your fiancée anythin' about us. It wouldn't do any good anyway, since ya've already guaranteed her anythin' I might say would be a lie. Besides, the two of ya love each other. Ya always have and ya always will. 'Tis a shame, though," she went on, her voice having lost a little of its bitterness, "that she isn't given a chance ta know the real you before it's too late. She's a nice lass and she deserves better. But then, on the other hand, she'll be doin' the rest of womankind a favor by marryin' ya. Or won't your vows mean anythin' ta ya?"

292

She shook her head and the long length of coppery curls glistened in the sunlight streaming in through the window behind her. "No, I don't think they will. Lyin' comes easy ta ya, and it's hard for a man who gets his way dishonestly ta change overnight . . . if ever." Without waiting for him to deny her accusations, she turned her back on him to gaze out the window again. "So, Mr. Hamilton, I'm sorry ta have ta tell ya that your threats were wasted, for ya see, me bein' here is purely accidental. When I sneaked on board the *Lady Hawk*, I thought I was goin' home ta Ireland. If I'd known where she was sailin' and who'd be there when we docked, I would have thrown meself overboard rather than have ta suffer such humiliation." A trembling sigh shook her whole body. "I want nothin' more than you want, Mr. Hamilton. I want ta leave this place, and the sooner that happens, the better it will be for all of us."

There was a sadness, a pain twisting the edges of her confession, and although her pledge wasn't exactly what Reid had expected to hear her say, he sensed an honesty in her words. He also, much to his surprise, discovered that a hint of sympathy had creeped into his feelings for her, despite his initial reaction to the cruel, unfounded insults she had thrown at him. He still didn't know what it was she had planned to do or how she had decided to go about achieving her goal, but the fact that she had given up without too much coercion on his part made him think she might have recognized the uselessness in trying. He truly didn't believe her claim that she had gotten on the wrong ship simply because it was too coincidental, just as Gordon had pointed out. And the fact that she was Irish, that she'd appeared suddenly from out of the blue with obvious hatred for him, that he'd just returned home from Ireland where he'd gotten himself into the thick of things, and that Rynearson's name kept floating around in his head, instinct begged him to consider the strong chance they were all connected in some bizarre way. But how? Could it be Rynearson was using the girl to get back at Reid? Might *he* have deliberately sent Irish once he'd stumbled across her hatred for the Colonial?

Reid shook his head. *You're getting carried away, ol' boy,* he mused. *Rynearson's a coldhearted, devious scoundrel, and I wouldn't put it past him to use women for whatever purpose suits his need. But this?* He shook his head again. *Yet, if I thought for one minute that that was exactly what had happened, I'd—*

The realization that he was about to say he'd pack up this girl, put her back on the *Lady Hawk*, and sail with her to confront Rynearson caught him so off guard that a half-smile lifted the edge of his mouth and he nearly laughed out loud. Would he *ever* stop fighting other people's fights? Hadn't he learned by now that it usually only caused *him* trouble? Hadn't his big-brotherly nature been the lure that had sent him to meet Rynearson himself rather than let Gordon take care of it? Of course, it had. But it hadn't been because he hadn't trusted his good friend to see that the damaged goods were replaced. Hardly that. No, Reid had wanted to make sure Rynearson couldn't cheat anyone else the way he had Gordon.

Always thinking of everyone else rather than yourself, he inwardly sighed with a drop of his shoulders. *And knowing that, you continue right on.*

What will it take to make you stop?

His gaze absently shifted to the young woman in the room with him. She hadn't moved, and for a second he wondered if she was even aware he was still there. If he hadn't had the need to save the world from Rynearson, this young lady wouldn't be here now. But he had. In truth he'd spent his whole life chasing around solving other people's problems and he'd never stopped long enough to settle his own. Maybe that was the root of his restlessness—he simply avoided making any decisions that would affect his life by keeping preoccupied with someone else's.

Maybe, he thought. *Maybe not.* If all he had to do was set a weding date and his problems would vanish, why hadn't he? *Because you're looking for something,* he told himself. *Damn. If only I knew what it was.*

An emptiness tugged at his heart, a strange kind of pull he couldn't explain, and while his gaze openly admired the slim figure of the woman dressed in green satin, a warmth curled his insides and slowly spread through every limb. He had an undeniable urge to go to her, to take her in his arms and kiss her. What startled him was the feeling that he'd done it before, that somewhere buried deep in his brain was the knowledge that she wouldn't object, that she *wanted* him to hold her. Suddenly, a blast of icy wind swirled around the sensation and lifted it beyond his reach, and before he could raise a hand to bring it back, a black void engulfed the pale light in his memory.

Frustrated and angry, he turned on his heels and left the room.

*   *   *

295

Just as Bevan had expected, she never saw Laura again after Reid's silent departure. Nor had she expected the bath Laura had promised. In a way, she'd been grateful for the solitude she'd been given. She had used that time to cry, to burn Reid's rejection of her into her heart so that she'd never let herself think for one moment there might be some hope of winning him back. He had never been hers to lose and she had had to convince herself of it.

She had just managed to pull herself together when a young black girl Bevan guessed was no more than sixteen came to the room and shyly directed her down a back flight of stairs, past the servants' quarters, and out through a side door. From there, they headed across the yard toward the building Bevan had earlier surmised was the warehouse and on to a well-worn dirt path which led to the row of identically designed cabins, twenty in all. At the fourth one, they stopped, and while the girl lifted the latch and pushed the door open, Bevan paused a moment to look around and decide how good her chances were of finding a ship bound for home on her own, or whether she should resign herself to staying on and letting Reid do it for her. Just being on the same continent with him was almost more than she could bear; four hundred feet from the house where he entertained his fiancée tested her limits.

"Ah should warn yo', missy," the young girl began as if she had read Bevan's thoughts. "Massuh Connors knows yo' is here. He'll be keepin' an eye on yo', so don't go thinkin' yo' can run away."

Bevan's long, coppery curls bounced erratically

when she jerked her head around to question the girl. "What?"

"He's de overseer, missy. It's his job ta keep us here."

Fire flashed in Bevan's eyes. "His job?" Her nostrils flared as she gritted her teeth and took a second look around. "Ya mean we're prisoners?"

"Oh no, missy," the girl quickly denied. "We is slaves." She frowned when she realized her companion didn't really fit that description. "Ah mean some of us is. Yo' is different. But he'll keep yo' here anyway 'cause yo' owes Massah Reid."

"I'll say I do," Bevan hissed beneath her breath. "More than anyone can imagine." Knowing the girl wouldn't understand her comment and because she had no desire to explain, she waved the girl inside the cabin and followed after her.

Although the sparsely furnished living quarters consisted of only one room, Bevan was impressed with how clean it was. A narrow, straw cot wide enough for one person stretched out along the wall. A chair and table sat in the middle of the floor and in front of a stone fireplace. A stack of wood was piled neatly beside the hearth and a hurricane lamp sat on the mantel. She frowned disapprovingly when she noticed that the single window had no curtain and the door had no lock. Privacy was obviously something not enjoyed by the others, but if she had anything to say about it, there would be some adjustments made.

"Ah's sorry dere is no bed fo' yo' ta sleep in," the girl announced, "but Ah's willin' ta take turns."

A hot rush of embarrassment scorched Bevan's cheeks—she had boldly assumed the place was hers

297

alone. "I don't think that will be necessary," she replied, her eyes lowered as she turned for the door. "I'll find somewhere else ta stay."

"Dere is no other place, missy. All dem cabins is full, and Massah Reid, he says yo' is to stay wid me."

Anger turned Bevan around. "Well, at least we'll be given an extra bed, won't we?" She jerked her hand at the dirt floor. "He can't be expectin' us ta sleep there, can he?"

"A lot of us do. It ain't so bad. At least we is dry and cool. De days and nights here gets awful hot."

The girl smiled brightly at Bevan and Bevan noticed for the first time how pretty she was. What she couldn't understand was how she found anything to smile about. *She* was doomed to live here the rest of her life with no hope of ever being free. Bevan, at least, had that to comfort her. Shifting the cloth bag to her left arm, she held out her hand to the young girl.

"Me name is . . . Irish," she told her, thinking that perhaps later, once they were friends and Bevan knew she could trust her, she'd tell the girl her real name.

Big brown eyes danced with a friendliness that came all the way from her soul. "Ah's Bess," she said, happily shaking Bevan's hand.

"Pleased ta meet ya, Bess," Bevan replied. "As for takin' turns, I wouldn't think of it. I'm the one who's intrudin'."

"Oh, Ah don't mind sleepin' on de floor," Bess told her. "Ah done it a lot 'fore Massuh Connors got me dis here cabin. Ah used to share one wid five other women and two babies."

Bevan's gaze reevaluated the size of floor space. "I

certainly hope it was bigger than this one." When the girl didn't answer, Bevan glanced up and saw the sheepish look on her young face. "I'm sorry, Bess," she apologized once she realized how insensitive that had sounded. "I've got a lot ta learn about how a plantation works. It's me first time in America."

"Ah know," she answered excitedly. "Yo' is from Ireland. Ah's never know'd nobody from dere 'fore. So Ah guess yo' and me gots a lot to learn 'bout each other."

"We sure do." Bevan smiled, infected by the girl's vivacious spirit. "And the first thin' ya can teach me is me job."

"Sho' nuff," Bess replied turning to lead the way, but Bevan caught her arm and stopped her before her second step. Surprised by her new roommate's odd behavior, Bess frowned and asked, "Somethin' wrong?"

Bevan hesitated a moment, debating whether or not her first impression of Bess was accurate. She wanted to trust her . . . she needed to trust her. Looking past the girl and outside into the yard to make sure no one was wandering close by, she pulled Bess back toward her, then moved to close the door.

"This is all I have in the world, Bess," she told her, patting the cloth bag she held against her chest. " 'Tis important no one takes it away from me. Is there someplace I can hide it, a place that will be our secret?"

Bess's brown eyes widened and a spark of worry, possibly fear, then mischief glowed in their depths. She raised a finger to her lips as a sign for Bevan not to say another word and crossed to the window. Glancing outside, she then turned for the hearth and waved

Bevan near as she knelt by the stack of wood and began moving the logs aside.

"Ain't no place real safe," Bess whispered. "But dis is de best Ah knows of . . . fo' now anyways. We can figger somethin' else out later."

Bevan crouched down beside the young girl, eager to help. Once the pile was cleared, Bevan spied a tin box partly covered with dirt, and she frowned curious. Before she could ask, Bess swept it clean and picked it up. She removed the lid and held it out for Bevan to see.

"It's all Ah got of my mama's," Bess explained, fingering the bright red bow. "She used ta wear it in her hair. Ah have ta hide it 'cause some of de women here, dey'd steal it if'n dey knew." She popped the lid back on the box, returned her keepsake to its hiding place, and started to reach for her companion's bag when she saw the distressed look on Bevan's face. "Is yo' all right, missy?"

She'd been thinking of her own mother and how she didn't even have a ribbon to hold, when Bess's sweet voice intruded upon her thoughts. "I'm fine. I was just thinkin' about me own mother," she revealed.

"Is yo' mama dead?" Bess asked as she hurriedly widened the hole to accommodate Bevan's cloth bag, then covered both articles with dirt.

"Aye," Bevan quietly replied. "A year ago."

"Mine, too, Ah think."

Puzzled by the girl's remark, Bevan straightened and asked, "Ya mean ya don't know for sure?"

Bess continued her work of replacing the pile of wood into a neat stack. "Ain't got no way a' knowin'. Ah was bought by Massuh Reid when Ah was younger. Ain't never seen her no more, but Ah hear'd she is."

Bevan's head began to spin. A knot formed in her stomach and for a second she thought she might get sick.

"Miss Irish?"

"I'm all right," she promised, pushing up shakily on her feet. The conversation around the O'Rourke dinner table while she was growing up was usually meant to be a joyous time, a sharing of pleasant thoughts. Only once had it turned to the way of life in the Colonies and Bevan couldn't remember what had provoked it. Her father had talked about the size of the plantations compared to their small farm and one of the boys had asked how one man could handle so much. They were told about the slaves brought over from Africa, how the rich planters bought them . . . like cattle and sheep. Bevan recalled how shocked she had been to hear of it and how her father must have sensed it upset her, for he quickly changed the subject. She wished now that he hadn't. He would have prepared her for Bess's confession.

"Oh," the young girl was saying, "Ah almost forgot. Ah was told ta give yo' one of my dresses ta wear 'til Claramae gots some made fo' yo' own." Crossing to a small three-drawer chest at the foot of the cot, Bess retrieved a cotton dress from inside, flipped out the folds, and held it up in front of her, a proud smile on her young face. "Dis here's my favorite. Ah want yo' ta wear it."

Bevan's heart ached and tears rushed to her eyes. Amid the despair, this beautiful young black girl was able to find happiness in the simplest form and she unselfishly wanted to share it with someone she had only just met. Bevan realized the idea was useless even to consider, but if there was a way, she'd offer Bess the chance to go with her when she went back home to Ireland.

The arrival of Lawrence and Charlotte Hamilton was met by the staff of their plantation with the kind of fanfare awarded President Adams and his wife. Work stopped the instant their fancy coach was spotted coming down the drive, and everyone filed out onto the lawn to wave and cheer the eldest Hamilton's good health and to welcome him home. Bevan joined the crowd only at Bess's insistence. They had just started for the manor, after Bevan had changed and tied back her long hair with a piece of string, when the call went up that a carriage had been sighted. Bevan truly couldn't understand all the fuss, especially since her opinion of the entire Hamilton family had dropped considerably and she said so to Bess.

"I think the way they treat their slaves is deplorable," Bevan snarled as she eyed the coach rounding the drive.

"Ah don't know whad dat mean . . . de-deplor—"

"Deplorable," Bevan finished. "It means I don't approve. How could someone *buy* another human bein'? And on top of that, they separate a mother from her child. They shouldn't be cheered. They should be shot."

"Shhh!" Bess quickly warned, grabbing Bevan's arm and pulling her back away from the others. "Don't talk like dat, Miss Irish. If'n Massuh Connors hear'd yo', why yo'd be beat fo' sho'."

"Beat me?" Bevan gasped. "For speakin' me piece? Ya can't be serious."

Bess's dark head bobbed up and down. "We's here ta work, not complain. And it ain't so bad. We's fed and kept warm and give nice clothes ta wear."

Bevan's gaze fell to the cotton dress Bess wore, then down to the girl's bare feet. "And shoes in the winter?"

"Yes'm. But it don't get so cold here like it does up north a ways."

Bevan started to ask the girl if she really thought being forced to sleep on a dirt floor was her description of being treated fairly, realized it was probably the only way she'd ever been treated and therefore wouldn't know the difference, and decided against saying anything at all. Instead she turned to watch as the occupants of the coach descended the rig and a string of servants, some black and some white and all dressed in crisply starched uniforms, rushed forward to personally greet them.

The first man Bevan saw piqued her interest right away, and it took her a second to realize he must be Stephen. He was relatively tall but very slender, and she noticed how difficult it was for him to step down onto the walk when one knee refused to bend. Captain Sanderson had told her about Stephen's riding accident, and that he walked with a limp. A bit of an understatement, Bevan silently observed, for the man hobbled rather than limped. His clothes fit him well, and when he turned, she could see the strong, chiseled features of his profile.

"Ain't he de most handsomest man yo' ever did see?" Bess bubbled, an appreciative smile on her face.

Bevan stared at her for a moment without responding as she wondered how a girl like Bess, a slave to a man who thought of her as property, could find *anything* appealing about him. She looked at Stephen again. Aye, he was handsome, she supposed.

"He weren't born dat way, yo' know," Bess continued, her eyes locked on the well-dressed man helping an older woman from the carriage. "He done fell off his papa's horse, a devil horse. Massuh Reid dared him."

"What?" Bevan asked, looking at her again.

"Dey was boys, Ah hear'd. Massuh Hamilton, he fo'bid dem boys to ride de horse but dey did anyways. Massuh Stephen, he fell when de horse run away wid him. Smashed his knee up good. Massuh Reid, he blamed hisself 'cause he dared his brother ta ride and he did. Cleo, she's de cook, she says de doctor took one look at dat boy's leg and said it have-ta come off, but Massuh Reid put up such a fuss, Massuh Hamilton says no. After dat, Massuh Reid took care of his brother and wouldn't let nobody else touch him. *He's* whad made Massuh Stephen walk again . . . anyways dat's de way Cleo tells it."

The Reid Hamilton that Bevan had known at her farm would have done something like that. He cared about other people, even strangers . . . like her father. But *this* Reid Hamilton . . . She shifted her gaze back to the young man and the woman with him who Bevan surmised was Charlotte, the soft-spoken, gentle lady of the manor whom Captain Sanderson had described. She wasn't very tall, and her dark brown hair had a few strands of silver in it. The peach-colored gown she wore covered her ample, but pleasing curves, and there was a youthful bounce to her movements which reminded Bevan of her own mother.

Behind Charlotte came another lady Stephen assisted from the coach. It took Bevan only an instant to notice that she looked to be expecting her child any day. Her pretty face was drawn and tired as if the journey had almost been too much for her, and once both feet were on the ground, she shoved a fist in the small of her back and stretched, the blue satin of her gown shimmering in the early afternoon sun. Stephen, obviously sensing her discomfort, wrapped his arm around her and helped lead her to the front door.

"Dat's Miss Lyndsy Marie," Bess whispered. "Massuh Stephen and Massuh Reid's little sister. Her husband's gone ta West Point and won't be home fo' de baby's birthin'. Dat's why she come home. She wants her mama 'round when de time comes."

A flurry of servants buzzed around brother and sister, and in a flash of color, they seemed to disappear inside the house before Bevan had had her fill of looking at them.

"And dat's Massuh Hamilton hisself," Bess announced, drawing Bevan's gaze on the last to descend the coach. "Ain't he grand? On de outside he seem to be all mean, like everybody got to do as he says, but underneath all his caterwaulin', he gots a pretty big heart." She laughed at what she said, then added, "Ah don't su'pose Massuh Reid think so. He and his papa is always fightin' and feudin'."

"Oh?" Bevan asked, trying to sound as if she didn't really care to know. "What about?"

"Lawsy, just 'bout *everything*," Bess exclaimed. "But mostly 'bout Massuh Reid not marryin' Miss Laura."

Bevan forced herself to study the eldest Hamilton rather than ask Bess to explain any further. She noticed that Lawrence Hamilton was as tall as his younger son, that he was still in fine physical shape for a man his age, and that his silver-white hair was neatly combed. He had the same profile as Reid and he probably didn't need the walking cane he held in his left hand while he politely took his wife's arm and led her into the house. Bevan guessed from the stern look on his face that he wasn't someone to tangle with, talk back to, or make a fool of. And apparently, from what Bess claimed, it enraged him when someone openly defied his orders.

"Do ya mean Mr. Reid doesn't *want* ta marry his fiancée?" Bevan asked of a sudden, then inwardly cringed when she realized she had. She mustn't let anyone think she cared one bit what Reid Hamilton did. If everyone else believed it, then so would she . . . sooner or later. Now Bess might suspect she had asked for other reasons besides mild interest.

"Ah ain't sho'," Bess replied offhandedly as she touched her companion's elbow and nodded toward the side of the house. "Cleo says he ain't interested in gettin' hitched."

"Then why—?" She caught herself before she had finished the question, but not soon enough for Bess not to interpret what she meant.

"Oh, he didn't ask her to marry him, if'n dat's whad yo's askin'. Dey was promised to each other when dey was youngin's. Miss Laura, she lives on Cotton Hollow, de plantation next to dis one, wid her folks and a little brother. Mistah Bradburn, Miss Laura's papa, he and Massuh Hamilton's been friends fo' years, so's it's only natural dey want deir chil'ens ta marry. But Massuh Reid, he ain't real sho' he wants to." As they approached the servants entrance into the house, Bess lowered her voice and paused outside while she added, "Everybody says he loves her, but Ah don't

306

think so. Not de way he should, anyhow. He loves her like she was his sister."

Bevan thought about what Bess had told her, remembered Reid's claim that he had some problems at home to settle before he could marry Bevan, and she wondered if that had been what he meant.

Aye, Bevan, she bitterly mused. *That's exactly what he meant. So why did he pretend he didn't even know ya when ya showed up here this mornin'? Because Cleo is right. He isn't interested in marriage . . . not when he can have his pick of love-struck lasses fallin' for his sweet words. The bastard. I curse the day I met ya, Reid Hamilton, and I curse the fate that put me on the* Lady Hawk. Lowering her eyes so that Bess wouldn't see the rage burning in them, she concluded, *And before I leave this place, ya'll be cursin' the day ya ever thought ta woo me with your lies.*

Chapter Ten

Since everything else in her life of late had been one unpleasant experience after another, Bevan hadn't really expected her assigned duties to be any different. She had always hated doing laundry even when her mother was around to help and make a game of it. But this wasn't home and she doubted anyone in the entire household had a sense of humor. So, when Bess instructed her to strip the beds of their linens and replace them with fresh ones, it hadn't surprised Bevan. It didn't please her, but it didn't surprise her either.

Told that the Hamiltons were on the veranda having a late lunch, Bess took Bevan to Lawrence and Charlotte's room first. Once Bevan had finished there, she was to do Master Stephen's and Master Reid's bedchambers next, then start on all of the guest bedrooms. Bevan had questioned the need to wash bedclothes that hadn't been used, but before Bess could answer, Bevan withdrew the query. From what she had seen so far, she deduced that the Hamiltons intentionally kept the servants too busy to complain about their disgraceful living conditions.

Bevan's dislike for the entire Hamilton family and the injustices she had witnessed in the short while she'd been there blinded her to the furnishings of the room where she worked. She'd already decided they had more than their share and had gotten it at the expense of others, so how could she even acknowledge the things their money had bought? Within minutes she had replaced the soiled sheets with clean ones, spread out the thick quilt and tucked the pillows beneath it, straightened the edges, and smoothed away any wrinkles that had stubbornly fought to remain. Her plan was to take the white linens to the washtub out back to soak in the hot sudsy water, while she changed the sheets in Master Stephen's room. Reid's bed she would leave until last . . . *if* she did it at all, since sabotaging his comfort any way she could had become her main goal for the duration of her stay. He might not ever recognize the source, which would have greatly pleased her, but just knowing he suffered because of her would be enough.

Gathering up the awkward bundle of linen, she left the room and started down the hall toward the back stairs, absently glancing off to her right each time she passed an opened bedroom door. Bright sunshine had filled each one and the quick look she gave them had been enough to satisfy her mild, subconscious curiosity . . . until the last. Her forward momentum carried her right on by, and instinct warned her to keep going, but the sight of the dark-haired young woman lying in bed and struggling to reach the glass of water beside her on the night stand chiseled away at Bevan's usually generous nature. Coming to a slow, hesitant stop in the middle of the hallway, she gritted her teeth and silently scolded herself for caring in the least. But then Lyndsy Marie wasn't responsible for her brother's actions. The truth of the matter was she probably didn't even know about Reid's adventures. The shattering of glass, the tearful moan, and the absence of anyone else nearby turned Bevan around, and before she could argue just cause for *not* going to the woman's aid, she retraced her steps and entered the room.

The pain and frustration Bevan saw on Lyndsy Marie's face struck a tender nerve. The young woman was trying to get up, but her large belly was making a normally simple feat quite difficult.

"Stay where ya are," Bevan ordered, tossing her linens on the floor. "I'll clean it up and get ye another glass."

"Thank you," the young woman replied, trying very hard not to let her emotions get the better of her.

Lying back in the bed as comfortably as she could manage, Lyndsy Marie watched the pretty redhead gingerly pick up the broken pieces of glass and discard them, then blot up the puddle of water from the rug with a towel she had taken from the wash stand. She left the room for a moment, and when she returned, she carried a fresh glass to the night table and filled it with water from the pitcher sitting there.

"I would have rung for someone," Lyndsy Marie explained, "but I thought I could do it myself." She frowned irritably into the glass she'd been given, took a sip, and tried to set it on the night stand when she was finished, only to discover the same difficulty she had had before. "I really hate being so big," she mumbled, allowing her companion to do the task for her. "And I really hate having to let someone wait on me just because I'm too fat to do it myself."

"Ya're not fat, Miss Lyndsy Marie," Bevan told her. "Ya're goin' ta have a wee one. There's a difference, ya know."

A soft smile brightened Lyndsy Marie's dark brown eyes. "My Henry was always trying to convince me of that."

"And apparently he never succeeded," Bevan observed, a twinkle showing in her eyes.

"Up until he had to leave," Lyndsy Marie sighed. "I miss him so and he's only been gone a few days." She winced at the sudden pain which shot through her lower back. "I'm so miserable," she moaned. "If someone had told me how awful it was going to be, I think Henry and I would have had separate beds."

Without thinking, Bevan replied, "'Tis the price ya have ta pay for a few moments of bliss." She'd meant it to cheer Lyndsy Marie and to get her mind off her agony. It worked, for the young woman laughed, but for Bevan it brought back memories of her own. *Bliss* was the right word, but in Bevan's case the resulting pain had come from emptiness and betrayal. The deceit Reid had used with her had turned those wonderful moments into shame. The only redeeming grace she had been awarded for her weakness was that she hadn't grown heavy with his child. Angry of a sudden, she turned to leave.

"I've got ta get back ta work," she announced, wondering if Reid's sister had heard the bitterness she felt seep into her words.

"Will you tell me your name first?" Lyndsy Marie asked as she awkwardly shifted her weight and tried to

311

rearrange the pillows at her back. "You're new here."

There was a kindness in the woman's voice Bevan wished wasn't there. She didn't want to like anything or any*one* connected to Reid, and his sister was making it difficult for her.

"I'm called Irish," she reluctantly told her. "I arrived this mornin'."

"This morning?" Lyndsy Marie echoed, obvious disapproval sharpening her tone. "From Ireland? And they put you to work right away?"

"I have ta earn me keep, Miss Lyndsy Marie. The sooner I save enough money, the sooner I'll go home." She missed the frown which came over the young woman's face when she turned her back to pick up the dirty linen or she might have regretted her statement. Most indentured servants came to America to stay. She had so much as told her she wasn't here by choice.

"Do you have a last name, Irish?"

Feeling closed in, Bevan entertained the idea of walking out without responding. That would be rude and she honestly didn't have it in her. Yet she couldn't lie either, and she didn't want to tell the woman any more about herself than she already had. Glancing over her shoulder at her, she saw how Lyndsy Marie was struggling to find a comfortable position on the bed, and she hurried over to her without answering the question.

"Here," she said, helping with the pillows and setting one aside. That one she placed beneath the pregnant woman's knees. "Sometimes it helps ta raise your legs. At least that's what me mother always said."

Lyndsy Marie felt better almost immediately, and she smiled her gratitude. But before she could ask her

312

question again, Bevan excused herself and hurried from the room.

Doing the laundry kept Bevan busy for the rest of the afternoon, for which in a way she was glad. It gave her very little time to think, except for a short spell when Bess appeared with a glass of lemonade. She took her refreshment to the shade of a huge willow and sat down beneath its wide spread limbs to enjoy it at her leisure. Bending over a tub of hot water in the bright sunshine had tired her out. Her back ached and her feet hurt, and the thought of sleeping on the floor that night made her cringe. She'd be just as tired, if not more so, when she woke up the next day, and she considered telling "Massuh Reid" that if he wanted a full day's work out of a person, she had to have a restful sleep the night before. But he wouldn't care, and she knew it. The only happiness which concerned him was his own. She could drop dead from exhaustion and he'd applaud.

Infuriated that she had let *him* slip into her thoughts, she forced herself to think on other matters—such as a way to send a letter home without any of the Hamiltons finding out. But that would be difficult, she was sure. Yet she must get a message to her brothers. She had to let them know where she was and that she was safe, and that as soon as she could manage it, she'd come home.

The idea of writing a letter sustained her during the last of her work. It gave her new hope and something immediate to consider. Even the task of finding someone she could trust to see it delivered added a spark to her lagging step. At one point she even found herself humming a merry tune while she draped the last of the bed linens over the rope strung up between two sturdy oaks. The smell of something delicious being

313

prepared for dinner drifted out from the kitchen and she decided that if she had to spend the night on the floor, she would at least do so with a full stomach. And going to bed hungry was a lot harder on a person than a lumpy cot . . . or no cot at all.

The sound of children's laughter coming from the side yard drew her attention to them, and she paused a moment to watch their antics and to wish she were their age again. Life was so simple for youngsters. They had their chores to do but once that was out of the way, they had the rest of the day to do whatever they wanted. Not so for adults. They had laundry to do. Curling her upper lip at the washtub she had yet to empty of its dirty water, she started for it when the prancing of hoofbeats against the ground distracted her. Lifting her eyes, she spied two figures on horseback approaching the manor from the rear of the estate, and she thought it odd that the visitors hadn't used the main road. Then she noticed that one of them was a woman, and before full recognition had developed *and* she had had time to retreat out of sight once it had, Reid and Laura were riding close enough to see her. Her immediate reaction was to resort to her childhood behavior whenever one of her brothers made her angry and stick out her tongue at them. Then Laura smiled at her, a soft, sympathetic, nervous sort of smile, and all Bevan could bring herself to do was nod back at the woman. *He* was the one she hated, not Laura. So there was no need to make Laura an innocent victim when it was Reid she wished would see her disdain.

Her gaze shifted to that one, and the second their eyes met, the ache in her heart returned. He sat tall and proud astride the black stallion, his back ramrod straight, his dark hair combed neatly off his handsome face and tied with a blue ribbon a shade lighter than the jacket and breeches he wore. It painfully reminded her of the last time she had seen him dressed that way and what the end result had been. Near tears, she quickly pulled her gaze away from him and forced herself to see to the emptying of the washtub, unaware of the troubled frown which followed her movements until the corner of the house took her out of view.

The snapping of the sheets as they were tossed in the breeze, a sharp, staccato noise of uneven tempo, helped divert Bevan's distress over having seen Reid just then. She hadn't changed the linens on his bed, and hearing the freshly laundered sheets flapping in the wind reminded her of that and made her smile. Mild as it was, she had still enjoyed a subtle form of vengeance, and she hoped the bedclothes were graying by the time she left for home so that he would know it too. However, part of her plan was for him not to suspect until it was too late, until after she was gone. Now if he noticed, it wouldn't take him a second to discover the culprit since he had seen her there by the washtub. Bess had told her earlier that Master Reid and Miss Laura had gone to visit her parents at Cotton Hollow shortly before his family arrived home and how upset he'd be when he realized he had missed their return by only a few minutes, but Bevan had never given much thought to the possibility that she'd have to meet him face to face sheerly because of unfortunate timing. If she had, she would have finished her work much sooner or at least she'd have had a hiding place picked out where she could disappear while he passed by.

"And there's no sense in thinkin' about it," she

muttered, sidestepping the rush of water which spilled out on the ground as she turned the tub upside down. "What's done is done."

"Irish!"

Bess's urgent call startled Bevan. She wasn't sure if she'd done something wrong or if Bess was in serious trouble. The first she could handle. The second she wasn't so sure about, but before she could decide what action to take, she figured she better hear what Bess had to say first. Turning around, she watched the girl run toward her.

"Ah think yo' and me should go to de cabin," Bess cried as she grabbed Bevan's arm and started pulling her along.

"Why?" Bevan asked. "What's happened?"

"Nothin' yet," Bess replied, nervously glancing over her shoulder at the house. "But it could. Ah mean it probably will."

"What, Bess? What will happen? Does it concern us?"

"It concern yo'."

"Me?" Bevan echoed. "What about me?" She jerked Bess to a halt and grabbed her by the arms. "I have a right ta know, Bess. If I'm in trouble, I need ta know what I've done."

"Yo' ain't done nothin' really," Bess confessed, her dark eyes round and filled with worry as she again looked back at the house. "Least ways Ah don't think yo' have. But Massuh Hamilton and Massuh Reid, dey's screamin' and hollerin' at each other, and Ah hear'd dem say yo' name."

Bevan, too, settled her gaze on the house while she strained to hear a single word. From that distance it

316

was impossible. Without realizing it, she started for the house. Maybe if she got closer . . .

"Irish!" Bess shouted in a high-pitched voice. "Ah don't know whad yo' done but yo' better stay here! If'n dey sees yo', why yo' could gets in mo' trouble'n yo' already is."

"I'm not in any trouble, Bess," Bevan promised with a grin. "I think if ya'd stuck around long enough ta hear what was said, ya'd find out that Master Reid is the one who's payin' his due."

"Ah don't understand," Bess admitted, her pretty face wrinkled with confusion.

"I know ya don't," Bevan replied as she locked her arm in Bess's and started them off toward their cabin again. *Only Master Reid and I know,* she thought, grinning impishly. *And it's me guess that his father is hearin' the truth from him right now.* The image of Laura came to mind, and she sighed, truly regretting that part of it. *I wish there was a way to avoid hurtin' her,* she silently confessed. *Laura's a nice lass who doesn't deserve what he's done ta her.* A devilish half-smile dimpled one cheek. *But he deserves what she'll do to him as well as the humiliation of havin' ta explain to his friends why he and Laura are no longer engaged ta be wed. Wouldn't it be grand if the pompous jackanapes decided that maybe I'd take him back and he came crawlin' ta me on his hands and knees? Oh, how I'd enjoy spittin' in his eye.* The silent declaration of her feelings toward him warmed her face. But it wasn't long before it cooled. She had good reason to hate him, even to want him dead. Yet deep in her heart, she could feel the ache that stirred whenever she was caught off guard, and she knew it wasn't hatred that

317

burned there.

The two girls ate their meal alone in the cabin a little while later. The fare they had been given wasn't what Bevan had expected, for the aroma of baked ham, cornbread, sweet potatoes, and hot apple turnover had been the smells she'd enjoyed earlier while finishing her work in the back yard. They had been served a stew of some sort, although it looked more like mush. It had been overcooked and even so it had begun to cool by the time Bess filled their bowls from a huge pot which hung over an open fire in the yard outside the slaves' quarters and returned with it to the cabin. The first taste of it had wrinkled Bevan's nose, but rather than have Bess see her reaction, she turned her head away and cautiously studied the ingredients. As hard as she tried, Bevan found only one or two pieces of meat among the salty white potatoes, lima beans, and juice, and even then she wasn't sure what kind of animal had been butchered for the meager offering. It wasn't that she was being ungrateful, but from all she had observed about the Hamiltons and how they treated their servants, she was afraid to ask the name of the creature that had been sacrificed for their meal, thinking that perhaps it was better left a mystery.

The sampling settled like a rock in her stomach once she was finished and the milk she'd been given to wash it down had an odd flavor. Again she elected not to ask why, but apparently her companion had seen the tentative look on her face.

"Cow's milk," Bess explained. "Cleo told me yo' might not like it 'cause yo' is used to goat's milk."

318

"Well, 'tisn't that I don't like it," Bevan replied. "It's just different, that's all. I'll get use ta it." She scowled at her half-empty bowl. "I'm not so sure about the rest."

Bess had never had the courage to complain about the food she was given and it delighted her to hear that someone else felt the same way she did. "On Sunday we gets chicken and sometimes a piece of pie. It don't make up fo' dis, but it helps."

Bevan's jaw sagged. "Ya're not sayin' we're fed this every night except Sunday, are ya?" She groaned at the sheepish look Bess gave her. "Good Lord, this isn't fit ta throw out, let alone eat. Who decides what we're given? 'Massuh Hamilton'?" She mimicked Bess's use of the name and instantly wished she hadn't. She didn't want Bess to think she was ridiculing the way she talked. All she was really doing was mocking the title. In her opinion no man on earth was another man's master!

"Ah don't really know," Bess softly replied. "It just ain't never changed since Ah got here. Ah knows it don't taste good, but it sho' is better'n starvin'."

Bevan doubted that was really true. The knot in her stomach had seemed to grow, and unless she forced her mind elsewhere, she wasn't too sure she'd be able to keep her food down. "I'd wager the Hamiltons wouldn't eat it," she grumbled as she left her chair to collect the dirty dishes.

The vision of Reid, Laura, Stephen, Lawrence, and Charlotte sitting around a huge table with its white linen tablecloth, crystal goblets, silver, and china dishes and being served such a meal flared up in her brain. A smile tugged at her lips and she had to fight to control her glee when an idea struck her, a mean,

319

coldhearted, *perfect* idea. Holding back her laughter, she casually turned to Bess.

"Have the Hamiltons been served their dinner yet?" she asked, hoping to sound as if she were making polite conversation and that the answer truly meant nothing to her.

"Ah don't know. Dey eats de same time we does, but with Massuh Hamilton and Massuh Reid arguin' dat way dey was, maybe nobody have no appetite no mo'." Curious, Bess asked, "Why yo' want to know?"

"Just wonderin'," Bevan lied as she turned for the door. "I have ta see if the laundry's dry, so I'll take the dishes to the wash kettle, if that's all right with ya."

Bess realized she didn't know Irish all that well, but there was a funny edge to her words that bothered Bess . . . as if her friend was up to no good. "If'n yo' want to," she answered guardedly. "Ah's gots to get mo' firewood anyhow. Could get chilly tonight."

"All right," Bevan smiled. "Then I'll see ya back here in a little while."

The silence around the dinner table that night had a heaviness that seemed to be pouring its entire weight down on Reid's shoulders. The conversation he'd had earlier with his family had gone just as he had predicted it would. Stephen saw only humor in what had happened to his brother, and he was still having trouble keeping the smile from his lips as he sat across from Reid waiting to be served. And each minute that passed without anyone saying a word only heightened Stephen's delight. No one spoke because of Reid, and Stephen liked it when his big brother did something to provoke their father . . . which it seemed he did quite often.

Charlotte, as Reid had guessed, had been horrified to learn how close to death her son had been. She had nearly broken down in tears until she heard the rest of his story. Then her distress had turned to motherly encouragement once she had seen how upset he was, and she had been quick to assure him that whatever Reid had done there in Ireland couldn't have been all that bad. That was when his father exploded in a fit of rage.

"You had no business going over there in the first place," he had shouted. "Gordon could have handled it. Now Lord only knows what sort of mess we're exposed to. Our livelihood depends on our trade with England and you so much as slapped her in the face by consorting with her enemies. England has had problems with Ireland for years and the French have been begging for the chance to step in between them and in turn isolate her from her allies. They're nearly at war as it is, and because of your arrogance, you very well might have helped bring it to a head."

"I rather doubt that, Father," Reid had calmly disagreed. "One man can't start a war. You're making it sound like I shot King George."

"How do you know you didn't? You can't remember anything," Lawrence had mocked.

Normally Reid knew how to handle his father. He also knew just how much of his tirades were valid and when to bring an end to the man's rantings. But this time was different. Reid couldn't defend himself because he didn't know what needed to be defended. The girl knew. He was sure of that, and perhaps after he'd eaten he'd have a talk with her. Right now all he wanted to do was get through the meal without any further confrontation with his father.

Their dispute had delayed dinner for nearly an hour, and because of it each of them was served an individual plate covered with a silver lid to keep it hot. Reid wasn't very hungry and he would have liked to excuse himself from the table, since he couldn't get his mind off Irish and the puzzle she could solve by talking to him. But his father was angry enough as it was, and leaving the table before dinner was over would only set him off again. Thus when Pearl set his dish down in front of him and removed the lid, he hardly noticed the movement since his gaze and his thoughts were elsewhere. However, only a couple of seconds passed before an unpleasant odor drifted up and filled his nostrils, and he jerked with a start when he realized the smell came from his plate.

"Good God, what's this?" he exclaimed crossly, staring down at the concoction of lima beans, lumps of potatoes, and questionable chunks of meat swimming in a milky white sauce. The sight of it as well as the salty, sour aroma of it turned his stomach. "Pearl, what is this?"

The black maid, her eyes filled with horror, rushed back to him and quickly reached for the plate, gasping when Reid seized her wrist before she had accomplished her mission. "Ah . . . Ah's sorry, Massuh Reid. Ah . . . Ah don't know how—"

"I don't care how, Pearl," he interrupted, trying very hard to remain calm. "I just want to know *what.*"

"It's . . . it's . . . it's whad de slaves eats, Massuh Reid."

The knowledge stunned him and he slowly released his grip on the woman's arm. "Take it away," he ordered quietly. "But *don't* throw it out. When I'm through here, I'll be speaking with Cleo about it. Do you understand me?"

"Yassuh," Pearl replied nervously with a quick bob of her dark head and bend of one knee. "Ah'll tell her yo' wants to see her."

The offending plate of food was removed in haste and Reid was given a share of the meal the rest of his family had been served. Warm, rich aromas of ham and sweet potatoes wafted up from the dish, but the foul smell of the stew he'd originally been served continued to sting his nostrils, and he could not rouse any interest in eating. Pushing the helping toward the middle of the table, he reached for his wineglass and took a long swallow, his dark brows twisted in an angry, disapproving scowl.

"You really should eat something, dear," he heard his mother say, and he looked up to find a worried expression wrinkling her face.

"I'm afraid I've lost what little appetite I had, Mother," he replied. "I can't imagine *anyone* having to eat that slop or why our people were given it in the first place." He glanced at Stephen, then at his father sitting at the head of the table. "None of us is responsible, are we?"

"That's Connors's job," Stephen answered while their father acted as though he hadn't heard or seen anything going on around him. "But I would suggest someone check into it. I'm sure he was never told to skimp when it came to feeding the field hands."

"That's exactly what I intend to do," Reid guaranteed

him. "But I'll start by asking Cleo. Connors has a way of skirting around the truth if it comes too close to making him look bad."

"I really don't know why you keep him on, Reid," his mother remarked as she dabbed the corner of her mouth with a napkin. "He's such an evil-looking man."

"Now, Mother," Stephen chided playfully. "How many times have you told me a person shouldn't judge someone by their appearance?"

"Ordinarily that's true," Charlotte countered. "But there's something about Emmett Connors that gives me a chill."

"I have to agree with Charlotte," Laura cut in. "He has such a lewd expression on his face every time I catch him staring at me. He has a way of undressing you with his eyes and it always makes my skin crawl. I don't mind saying I hope I never get caught alone with him."

"Laura, my sweet," Stephen joked, "I doubt there's a man alive who doesn't look at you that way. He's just been careless in letting you see it."

Laura could feel her cheeks pinken. "Coming from you, Stephen Hamilton, I'm not sure if that was meant as a compliment or not. I'll take it as flattery then tell you I disagree. I've never seen anyone else look at me the way he does."

Stephen's devilish nature rose to the occasion. "That's because you don't pay any attention. If you did, you'd be telling Mother how afraid you'd be to get caught alone with me."

"Oh, Stephen," she rebuked. "You're such a tease. I doubt you've ever looked at any woman that way. A gentleman wouldn't."

Grinning, Stephen jabbed his fork into a piece of ham, and just before he popped it in his mouth, he glanced up at her and warned, "I've never claimed to be a gentleman."

Laura's face reddened all the more. Squinting her eyes at him, she silently contradicted his case.

"Well, how could I be when I have an older brother like Reid?" His brown eyes twinkled. "I'm not even really sure about Father. Have I ever told you the *real* story behind his marriage proposal to Mother?"

"Stephen!" Charlotte exclaimed. "You might be full grown, but I still know how to make you behave." She reached over and made a grab for his earlobe, but he quickly ducked back out of harm's way, warm laughter spilling from both mother and son. "Don't ever listen to a word he says, Laura," Charlotte advised. "I don't think he knows how to be honest."

"Don't worry," Laura promised. "I figured that out a long time ago. And so has every young eligible girl for miles around. That's why he's still single. Every time he proposes, they don't know if they should believe him."

Reid had only been half listening to the conversation at the table, but Laura's last comment insisted he add his own opinion as to why Stephen hadn't married by now. "If you'd like the truth, Laura," he said, taking this as his chance to embarrass his brother for a change, "Stephen hasn't asked the girl of his dreams to marry him because you're already engaged to me. Isn't that right, little brother?"

No one seemed to notice how Stephen's smile wasn't as cheery as it had been. "That's right, Reid. I always have been and always will be in love with your fiancée."

"Then maybe *you* should marry her," Lawrence

Hamilton's deep voice boomed from the end of the table. "It doesn't appear that Reid ever will. Then at least *one* of you would father a few grandchildren for me before I'm too old to enjoy them." His brown eyes zeroed in on Reid. "Or dead out of sheer frustration."

Before any of them could say a word to calm him down, Lawrence wadded up his napkin, threw it down on the table, and came to his feet in an agitated rush. "If you'll excuse me, I think it's time I retired. For some reason I find this debate has taxed my nerves." He presented his older son with one last peevish glower, then left the room in a huff.

Reid could sense his mother's need to comfort him, to say just the right words that would excuse his father's conduct and subtly rebuke Reid's stubbornness for not complying to his father's wishes. It always went that way after the subject of marriage came up. And Reid probably had it coming. He just wasn't in the mood for it right then. He pushed back his chair, laid his napkin aside, and politely begged his leave. But rather than wait for permission, he exited the dining room in nearly the same manner as his father had done.

The evenings in late October could and often did turn chilly, despite the hot sun that beat down during the day with a relentless determination to melt everything it touched. Since Bess possessed only one extra blanket, which meant Bevan had the choice of lying on it rather than on the dirt floor or covering herself up with it, Bess decided to start a fire. It wasn't long at all before the tiny cabin warmed against the chill, and both girls felt the exhaustion of their day.

Bess elected to go to bed. Bevan lit the lantern and set it on the table where she had laid the paper, quill, and ink she had taken from the desk in Mr. Hamilton's bedroom, along with the necessary coin she would need to see her letter sent on its way. Bess had told her that she couldn't promise Eustace, the black slave entrusted to go into town for supplies once a week, would agree to give Bevan's letter to Mr. Hargrove at the general store or that Mr. Hargrove would put it on the next ship to England, only that she'd ask. It had been all the encouragement Bevan had needed, and once their duties for the night had been completed, she had hurried back to the cabin for the privacy she needed.

Several minutes passed while she stared at the blank piece of paper, not knowing where to begin and how much she should write in a letter. There had been many occasions over the past weeks when she had thought about her family and more specifically her father, and she had forced herself not to hold much hope of him still being alive. If Rynearson had lied about his nephew, then he had probably lied about freeing her father from prison. And he was sure to have decided against it after what she'd done to him. That thought brought the vision of Lady Rynearson to mind and she swallowed the tears burning her throat as she once again imagined what the woman's husband might have done to her after he guessed what had really happened while he was away. Bevan had failed the woman miserably and without David there to protect Lady Rynearson . . .

Bevan cringed at the thought of how cruel that man could be, and a pained expression troubled her brow. None of what she wrote in her letter would make any sense to her brothers if she didn't start at the beginning and that meant repeating what Uriah Faber had written in his journal. The memory of the horrible events she had read about on those pages frightened her all the way down to her toes, and she once again thanked God her name hadn't joined the others.

Perhaps I should only tell them where I am, that I'm all right and not ta worry, Bevan mused. *They can't do much without the journal anyway, and there's no sense in upsettin' them too soon. The rest will have ta wait until I get home.*

Having made up her mind, she leaned over the parchment and scribbled down her salutation to all three brothers. But before she had written another word, the angry voices of two men arguing just outside the cabin stirred her curiosity and awakened Bess at the same time.

"Whad is it?" the girl asked as she left the cot and followed Bevan to the window.

"I don't know," she whispered. "Sounds like one of them isn't too pleased with the other."

"Can yo' hear whad dey is sayin'?"

"Not really," Bevan confessed. "I can't even see who they are. Or *where* they are."

"Over dere!" Bess pointed to the dark figures she saw standing near Emmett Connors's cabin. "Oh lawdsy, Miss Irish. It's Massuh Reid and Massuh Connors."

Bevan had already recognized Reid's tall build and that *he* was the one who was angrier. He held a bowl in one hand and several times thrust it under the overseer's nose. Either the contents offended the man or he resented being treated in such a manner, for each time Reid threatened him, Connors jerked back and

328

snarled something Bevan couldn't distinguish.

"Massuh Reid sho' is hot," Bess whispered worriedly. "Ah never see'd him like dat 'fore. Ah wonder whad Massuh Connors did ta make him so mad."

"I have a feelin' we're about to find out, Bess," Bevan warned excitedly, when she saw Reid turn on his heel and head in their direction. Grabbing the girl's arm, she pulled her away from the window.

"Miss Irish?" Bess nervously asked. "Did yo' do somethin' yo' shouldn'ta?"

Guiding her roommate back to the cot, Bevan gently but hurriedly shoved her back down as she replied, "Around here, Bess, that could be just about anythin'. Cover up and pretend ya're asleep. If he's angry with me, there's no need for ya ta get involved."

"But—"

"Just do as I say. I can handle meself with him."

The frightened girl had barely pulled the thin blanket up over her when a hard knock shook the door an instant before the metal latch rattled and a rush of cool air came into the room behind Reid. Firelight bathed his tall physique and glowed in his dark eyes, making him look even more menacing than before. Bess couldn't stop the shudder that shook her tiny body or force herself to close her eyes. Master Reid seldom lost his temper with any of them, and even if his wrath was directed at something Irish had done, Bess still experienced a fear that his rage might spill over onto her.

"Bess," he said sternly, and she wasted no time in leaving the cot to stand next to her friend.

"Yassuh?"

"Take this back to the kitchen and tell Cleo to throw

it out," he instructed, holding out the bowl. "From now on the servants on this plantation will be eating decent food. Cleo knows it and so does Mr. Connors."

"Yassuh," Bess mumbled, her eyes lowered as she hurried across the narrow room to retrieve the dish. Her hand shook as she took the bowl from him, and afraid she might drop it and further enrage him, she clutched it to her chest and fled the cabin.

"I can't honestly say why," Reid announced as he caught the edge of the door and swung it shut, his dark glower centered on the beautiful chestnut-haired woman across from him, "but I get the feeling you were behind that. How did you know I'd be served that swill Connors calls food?"

Bevan shrugged a delicate shoulder, a devilish satisfaction lighting up her green eyes. "The luck of the Irish, I guess."

He stared at her a moment. "Hmmm," he murmured. "Your effort would have been for nothing, if I had refused dinner, which I very nearly did. Next time you have something to tell me, don't be quite so dramatic."

He absently studied the interior of the room, and frowned once he discovered how barren the place was. He'd never been inside one of the cabins after they'd been built, but he had expected more than this. His scowl deepened when he noticed only one small cot and the blanket spread out on the dirt floor, which obviously meant one of the two girls intended to sleep there. The explanation, he assumed Connors would give him, would be simply that he hadn't gotten around to supplying the extra bed or, more likely, Connors saw no need since the girls were nothing but slaves, not guests, as he had remarked earlier about their food.

Reid hated to admit his father might be right, but from the look of things, he'd neglected his responsibilities here at home or he would have known about such details. Well, that was about to change.

His attention fell on the table and the quill, ink, and parchment he saw lying there. He doubted any of his people knew how to read and write, which left the simple conclusion that Irish was the one who planned to use them. Glancing briefly at her, he stepped forward and spun the paper around to read what was written there without having to pick it up.

"Dear Kelly, Ryan, and Shea," he quoted, while silently admiring the penmanship of the author. He looked up. "Writing home?" he questioned sardonically. "For help?"

His presence in the small room seemed to overpower her. It became increasingly more difficult to breathe and she suddenly doubted her earlier claim to Bess that she could handle herself with Reid. Remembering how she had decided to hate him, she hardened her nerve and proudly raised her chin. "Are ya sayin' I'll be needin' it?"

"That depends," he replied, casually pulling out the chair and sitting down.

"On what?"

He flicked a crumb off the table and settled challenging dark eyes on her. "On what you hope to accomplish."

His threat didn't bother her. "If ya're implyin' that maybe I'd like ta kill ya, ya're right. But I won't need any help. In fact, I'd perfer doin' it all by meself."

Reid found her declaration amusing. "Would you?" he asked, his mouth twitching into a crooked smile.

"And just how would you go about it?"

Bevan's pert nose raised a notch. "While ya're sleepin'," she suggested. "Or maybe I'll just slip a little poison in your food. Ya wouldn't see it comin' that way, and once ya knew, it'd be too late." She glared at him for a second, then added, "But I really shouldn't be selfish, I suppose I should wait for me brothers. They deserve ta watch."

"Kelly, Ryan, and"—he glanced at her letter—"and Shea?"

She inhaled a quick breath to snap back a reply, realized he was pretending he didn't know who her brothers were, and exhaled angrily through clenched teeth. "I'm well aware of the fact that this is *your* cabin I'm in, on *your* property, that I'm eatin' *your* food and wearin' clothes *you* paid for, and that if ya wanted to, ya could have me thrown in jail for any reason ya could make up, *but . . ."* She sucked in another deep breath to help keep a tight rein on her anger, and finished, "I'm not afraid ta tell ya that I think ya should leave. We certainly don't want your *fiancée* ta get the wrong idea."

Reid knew Laura was aware of why he was there. She had been the one to suggest he talk with the girl, and therefore wouldn't think a thing of it.

"Why?" he asked, resting back in the chair, one arm laid casually on the table top. "Why do you really want me to leave?" He raised an eyebrow at her, but when she wouldn't answer, he added, "Laura has nothing to do with it. She knows I'm here."

"Does she?" Bevan sneered. "And what excuse did ya give her?"

Firelight caressed her silky skin and seemed to set

her auburn locks on fire, a sight that warmed him to the core and raised a few questions of his own. He could never remember having reacted to Laura's beauty in such a way, and Laura was indeed beautiful. He'd never been tempted to trace his fingers along the curve of her cheek or to press his mouth to hers as he felt drawn to do with this girl, and the discovery both surprised and troubled him. He felt a strong attraction to this young woman, which should have seemed natural, yet it troubled him. It wasn't that he'd never been aroused by the sight of a beautiful woman, only that the yearnings deep inside him were different now. It wasn't lust he felt. It was a need to comfort her, to love her, to reaffirm an earlier oath. . . .

That shocking revelation tingled the tips of every nerve in his body and awakened the vague image of a young man with chestnut hair and green eyes. But just as quickly as it had come to him, it vanished, leaving him more confused than ever, and he began to wonder about the real reason why he couldn't remember. Was his mind trying to protect him? From what? Looking at Irish again, her last question stirred in his mind.

"Excuse?" he repeated. "Would I need an excuse to talk with you?"

For a second Bevan sensed he asked in earnest. She had seen the puzzled expression come over his face a moment ago and she could almost hear the wonderment in his words. Yet his question contradicted his honesty. How could he *not* need an excuse for visiting her at this late hour, unchaperoned and behind a closed door? Laura might be understanding, but she was still a woman with woman's feelings. If he had really told Laura every detail of their affair, Laura would have to be a saint to allow him even an instant alone with her.

But of course! Bevan mused, her eyes narrowing. *He hasn't really told Laura everything. He only wanted me ta think he had so that I'd assume there was no sense in tryin' ta come between them.*

She folded her arms in front of her and strolled to the table. "Ya never told her, did ya?" she smirked. "About us. You and me. All the promises ya made. All the lies ya told me."

"Irish," he began, one hand raised in surrender as he awkwardly pushed up on his feet.

"Irish?" she mocked, her hands moving to her hips, arms akimbo. "Oh please, me love. Laura's not around ta hear. Call me Bevan."

"Bevan?" The name meant nothing to him, but the sweet smell of hay stirred his senses again.

"Bevan O'Rourke," she played along. "I know we haven't seen each other in several weeks, but I honestly didn't think ya'd forget me name. I haven't forgotten yours, *Graham.*" The teasing edge to her recital had vanished and the last was spit with ridicule and loathing. "Ya must have had a good laugh over that one, Reid Hamilton, makin' fools of me and me brothers. And us so willin' ta believe *anythin'* ya told us." Her chin trembled. "Ya're a bastard, ya are. A coldhearted, connivin' scoundrel. 'Tis a shame ya didn't really die the way all of us thought ya had. Was that a part of your plan? Ta win our trust and respect and then disappear without a word of explanation?" Tears glistened in her eyes. "Damn ya. Damn ya ta hell, Reid Hamilton."

The rage, the pain he had caused her, and the disgrace of having fallen for his charm shook her tiny frame. Unable to hold back her emotions, she silently cursed the sob that escaped her lips before she could hide it behind her fingertips. Whirling away from him, she went to the door and swung it wide as she presented him with a courageous profile.

"Get out!" she ordered, tears streaming down her face. "Get out before I cheat me brothers of the honor and kill ya meself."

Reid had never felt so helpless, so confused in his whole life. How could he right a wrong he wasn't aware of doing? And how could he possibly make her believe him? Telling her now that he couldn't remember anything about what happened between them would sound like an outright lie.

Exhaling an angry, frustrated sigh, he turned and took two steps closer to her. "Bevan," he began, though he wasn't sure what he would say next. "Bevan, I—"

"No!" she screamed at him. "Don't say a word. Don't say ya're sorry, that ya didn't mean ta hurt me. Don't lie ta me anymore." In a rage, she wiped the moisture from her cheeks and added, "Just do me one favor. Find the first ship ya can that will take me back home. Let me leave with some dignity. Let me walk away with the memory that ya were able to do one kind thin' for me." Green eyes filled with anguish lifted to look at him. "Give me somethin' good ta remember, somethin' else ta think about rather than imaginin' ya makin' love ta your wife." Her will to remain strong and determined, to not let him know he had beaten her, crumbled. "Oh God, Reid," she wept, her knees weak and the pain in her chest almost more than she could endure. "I loved ya more than anythin' else in me life."

Her confession couldn't have stunned him more if

she had told him he was truly the illegitimate son of King George and she, his twin sister. He couldn't move or think or speak a word. He just stood there, too paralyzed to blink or draw a breath. Then, slowly, that immense yearning he'd had earlier began to grow inside him.

Before either of them realized what he was going to do, he closed the distance between them in two long strides, kicked the door shut with the heel of his boot, took her in his arms, and kissed her savagely.

The feel of her supple curves pressed against him, the fragrance of her hair, the warmth of her lips touching his banished any doubts he might have had. This was where she belonged, locked in his embrace. He had a *right* to hold her. The fire she ignited in him had always been there, but no other woman had ever found the spark to set it ablaze. Its flames consumed him, seared his soul, and ravished his heart. A black void had smothered his memories of the time they shared, but the burning desire that raged through him now promised it had not been a fantasy he had only hoped was real. Bevan O'Rourke was his past, the key to his lost days, and with her help, he *would* remember.

The heat of his body molded to hers, his arms holding her close, and the urgency with which he kissed her chased away the ache that had ruled her existence. The scent of him filled her nostrils and stirred the passion she had thought was gone forever. It mocked her need to hate him and muddled her reasoning. She could think of nothing else in that moment other than the sweet warmth of his embrace, the way his lips moved hungrily over hers and his breath fell hot against her cheek while his tongue probed the depth of her mouth and traced the sharp edges of her teeth, how his hands caressed the curve of her spine, buttocks, and waist before one came up to claim the back of her head while the other gently entrapped her breast. His thumb stroked its taut peak through the thin fabric of her dress and sent warm shivers to her toes. It aroused a different kind of ache low in her belly and set her flesh on fire. It stirred the memories of those glorious moments they had shared before her world had come crashing down on her, before his lies overruled her love and turned it against him. It awakened her to reality.

"Nooo!" she wailed, tearing her mouth from his and shoving him away. Breathless, her chest heaving, she staggered back a step and glared at him with a look that could have daunted the bravest of men. "I'll not fall for your lies again, Reid Hamilton. I'll not let ya use me ta sate your lust, then turn your back on me as if ya don't know who I am. There'll be no more promises, no whispered vows. I'll not be your mistress while your wife waits for ya in your bed." A mixture of pride, rage, and heartache forced her to raise her hand and point at the door. "Get out!"

Regretting his impulsiveness of a moment ago, Reid exhaled a quiet, troubled sigh and turned for the door. With his hand on the knob, he paused and glanced over his shoulder at her, frowning suddenly when the image of three men appeared haloed around her. The tallest had dark hair and brown eyes. Next to him stood a young man with chestnut hair and emerald eyes the shade of Bevan's. But the third, the one with brown hair and green eyes, tugged heavily on Reid's memory an instant before the mirage vanished and a rush of cold air enveloped him. He blinked and a flash of stone, metal bars, and long muskets passed his vision and was gone. The smell of hay, a long-eared donkey, and a two-wheeled cart floated around in his brain, close enough for him to reach out and touch but too far to grasp. Raising his right hand, he studied the palm, sensing more than seeing the rake he had held at one time and the blisters his labor had caused. He could see a thatch-roofed cottage, a fireplace, stone fences, sheep, and finally a blackened sky tormented by an oncoming gale. He could smell the salt air and feel the rain beating against his face. He could hear a man's screams, then nothing at all . . . as if the pale light of a candle had been extinguished before he could completely focus his eyes on his surroundings. Darkness took its place and he plummeted back into the absence of time. Each fragment meant something and he was sure they were all connected in some way. He just couldn't place them in the right order. Nor had what he remembered thus far explained how he had met Bevan O'Rourke or why he had gone to the prison where Gordon and Eric had found him.

Gordon, he mused hopefully. *Maybe he can make some sense of it.* Lifting the latch he pulled the door open, then hesitated as he glanced back at the beautiful young Irish girl watching him with hatred gleaming in her eyes.

"I'll figure it all out, Bevan," he assured her, as if that were all it would take to win her forgiveness. "And when I have, I'll come on bended knee and ask that you hear me out." He curbed the desire to say more and forced himself to exit the cabin.

Chapter Eleven

Unbeknownst to Bevan, she had become a savior of sorts to the black community on the Hamilton plantation and a threat to the overseer. Because of her gallant rebellion against the food she had been served and because of Master Reid's visit to her cabin, several changes were made and everyone agreed they were because of her. Reducing the overcrowding in the slaves' living quarters took top priority, and where it was possible, additions were to be built on to the existing cabins. If an extra room or two wouldn't solve the problem, new lodgings were ordered built, and each cabin was to receive a wood floor and enough beds to accommodate the inhabitants. What really surprised everyone was how Master Reid had personally taken on the project. He had inspected each house, drawn up the individual plans, and supervised the delivery of needed supplies. And when it had come time for the actual construction to begin, he had shed his fancy clothes for homespun cotton, rolled up his sleeves, and helped carry lumber to its proper place. Talk among the older slaves had revealed how very much like his father Reid was, that before Lawrence Hamilton's health had prevented it, he too had often helped with the work. But that was before Emmett Connors had joined the staff.

"Miss Irish," Bess exclaimed, her brown eyes round and filled with excitement as the two girls watched the activity going on just outside their cabin, "Ah sho' was worried Massuh Reid would whip yo' dat night he come to de cabin. Ah never guessed he'd do dis fo' us. Whad yo' tell him, anyways?"

I told him I loved him, Bevan recalled silently, her brow knotted in an angry frown. *I let him know I still cared no matter what he'd done. I allowed him the pleasure of knowin' he'd won.* Furious with herself, she swung away from the window and went to kneel by the woodpile. "I found a place we can hide our things for a while, until after the floor's been laid at least. But we'll have to wait until later, when there aren't so many people around." She hurriedly shuffled the logs into a different pile, pushed the dirt aside, and added, "And me name's Bevan. Bevan O'Rourke, not Miss Irish . . . just plain Bevan."

Bess had heard the anger in her companion's voice. Although she couldn't imagine why, she felt it was directed at Master Reid. "Ah's glad to meet yo'," she softly replied as she came to kneel beside her and take the items Bevan held out to her. She wanted to ask why Bevan was upset with Master Reid, but past experience had taught her a hard lesson. Asking questions only got her in trouble. If she didn't want to get beaten, she had to keep quiet . . . about everything. Her new friend had been lucky. If Master Connors had been told to speak

340

to Bevan about her behavior rather than Master Reid taking care of it himself, things would have been different. Bevan would have been flogged. And her share of supper would have dropped in half.

Hoping Bevan might tell her on her own, Bess asked quietly, "Where yo' takin' dis stuff?"

"For now I'm goin' ta hide it under the blanket on me cot," Bevan replied as she quickly restacked the wood into its original pile. "Then, when I have a chance later, I'll take it ta that dead willow tree by the blacksmith's. I noticed yesterday that the trunk's hollowed out. Our things will be safe there for a while."

"And then whad yo' gonna do wid it?" Bess challenged worriedly. "We's can't hide it under the woodpile no mo'."

"Sure we can." Bevan grinned as she dusted off her hands and took the box and ledger from Bess. "I'll show ya a trick I use ta play on me brothers."

"Whad's dat?"

"Shea—he's me twin brother—he use ta like ta take me things, personal things like a shell or pretty stone I'd collected, and then he'd hide them from me just ta see how angry I'd get." She smiled at the memory and how Kelly and Ryan would pretend they didn't know he'd done it, while in fact they'd actually watched him. "So one day I decided ta put an end ta his pranks. There was a loose board in the floor of me room, and with a little work, I managed ta pull it up far enough ta slip all me treasures underneath it. Shea never figured out what I'd done with me things, and the same will work for us."

"Under de woodpile."

Bevan nodded with a wide grin parting her lips. "Aye. Under the woodpile."

"Yo' sho' is smart, Miss . . . er . . . Bevan," Bess corrected.

"Not really," Bevan disagreed. "It just comes natural after livin' with three brothers."

Bess started to tell her that she had three sisters and changed her mind. She had learned long ago not to get too friendly with someone because sooner or later that person would disappear. If she remained somewhat distant, then it didn't hurt so much when she lost a friend. Yet, Bess knew losing Bevan would hurt no matter how close they had or hadn't gotten. She already liked Bevan O'Rourke better than anyone else in her whole life, and she'd only just known her for a short time.

"Bevan," she said finally as she watched the girl cover up their possessions with the blanket and then plop the pillow on top to hide the lump it created. "Ah think Ah oughta warn yo' 'bout Massuh Connors."

Bevan hadn't actually met Emmett Connors yet, but she'd seen him several times, and she had already decided she didn't like him. "What about him?" she asked, facing her pretty friend.

"Ah hear'd talk. He's blamin' yo' fo' all his troubles, and dat mean he'll take it out on yo' anyway he can."

"Oh?" The idea didn't really frighten her. After all, what could he do to make her life any more miserable than it already was? Shoot her? He'd be doing her a favor.

"Ah just tells yo' so's yo'll watch out fo' him. He's a mean one, dat Massuh Connors, 'specially if'n yo' don't do whad he tells yo'. Ah seen him whip de hide right off a man's back one time fo' lookin' him in de eye."

Bevan's stomach curled. "I beg your pardon?"

342

"Yass'm. Dat's whad he did, all right. And Flo, she done talk back to him one time, so's de next day, he had Massuh Hamilton sell her man off. Told him some lie, I s'pose."

Bevan could feel the blood draining from her face. "Her man? Ya mean, her husband?"

Bess shrugged her narrow shoulders. "Ah guess yo' could call him dat. None of us'n is married de way de white folk is . . . not in no church, Ah mean, by a preacher man."

Bevan had to close her eyes to keep the room from spinning. When Bess started to relate another story, this time concerning a young girl of less than ten years, Bevan quickly raised a hand. "I understand, Bess. Please, say no more."

"Well, anyways, if'n yo' can, yo' best stay away from him. If'n yo' see him comin', go de other way."

"I'll do more than that," Bevan pledged. "I'll go straight to Master Reid and tell him—"

"No!" Bess gasped, grabbing her companion's hand as she raised a finger to her dark lips. "Yo' ain't never to tell nobody, 'specially Massuh Reid. If'n Massuh Connors ever found out, all of us'n would pay. Promise me, Bevan. Promise yo' won't tell Massuh Reid nothin'."

Bevan could hear the deep-rooted fear in the girl's voice. She wanted to comfort her, to promise her that as long as Bevan was alive, she'd see to it that no harm came to Bess. But just being alive wouldn't save Bess. Bevan was going home and that meant Bess would have to face Connors alone once Bevan was gone. "I can't promise ya that, Bess, not in all honesty. No one can see into the future. I *can* promise ya that if there's

343

another way ta protect ya other than goin' ta Master Reid, I'll use it. But I won't stand by either and let that wicked overseer beat someone because he didn't like the way he behaved. Ya'd be askin' too much of me."

"Ah understand," Bess quietly replied.

"And I won't cause more trouble for you and your people. I'll be goin' home soon, and it wouldn't be fair of me ta stir things up and then leave *you* to pay for it later."

"Home?" Tears instantly pooled in the corners of Bess's eyes. "Yo' ain't stayin'?"

Bevan hadn't meant to tell Bess that. She hadn't meant to let Bess like her either. But she had, and she regretted both. It hadn't taken Bevan long to realize the young girl needed a friend and that Bevan couldn't be that friend . . . not when it would last only a few weeks. It wouldn't be fair. But then nothing about Bess's situation was fair. Taking the girl's arm, Bevan drew her down on the cot beside her.

"I wasn't goin' ta tell ya this, but I guess I owe it ta ya," she began. "I'm not here by choice. I smuggled meself on board the *Lady Hawk* thinkin' it would take me home ta Ireland. I wound up here. I'm stayin' only long enough ta earn the money I'll need ta go home. Bess . . ." She paused, caught the girl's hands in hers, and offered, "If there's a way and Master Reid will allow it, I'd like for ya ta come with me. Me family lives on a small farm in Ireland, near Bray, and I'm sure they'd love ta have ya live with us."

Bess's chin sagged and a happiness warmed her brown eyes. "Yo' mean yo'd buy me?"

"Buy . . . ?" Bevan shook her head. "No . . . I mean, I would if that's the only way they'd let ya go, but ya

344

wouldn't be a slave. Ya'd be free . . . ta live with us, if ya wanted."

Bess's lower lip quivered. "Oh, Miss Bevan," she wept as she threw her arms around her. "Ah would! Ah surely would."

Infected by the girl's joy, Bevan laughed and hugged her close. "Don't go gettin' your hopes up too high, though," she warned, pushing Bess back to arm's length. "'Tis only a wish of mine. It might never come true, but I'll fight as hard as I can for it."

"Ah know," Bess assured her, sniffling. "Even if'n yo' fail, Ah'll always love yo' fo' thinkin' it. No one, 'ceptin' my mama, ever cared dat much 'bout me. Thank yo'."

Bess wrapped her arms around Bevan again and squeezed. But the smile that had lifted Bevan's spirits had disappeared and a worried frown took its place. She knew she'd never be able to buy Bess's freedom even if Reid was willing to sell her. It would take her *years* to earn enough and Bevan didn't want to stay there any longer than necessary. Her only other alternative would be to steal her.

"Something's bothering him," Stephen observed as he and Gordon Sanderson stood in the doorway of the warehouse watching his brother pound another nail into the skeletal framework of the new cabin he was building.

"Well, of course, there is," Gordon nervously agreed. "Wouldn't it bother you if you woke up one morning and discovered you couldn't remember why you'd been somewhere, what you'd done while you were there, and how much, if any, trouble you were in?"

Stephen shifted his weight onto his good leg, folded his arms over his chest, and leaned back against the door jamb, his gaze still riveted on Reid. "It's something else," he speculated. "Besides his memory loss."

Reid had asked Gordon not to tell any of his family about the conversation they'd had concerning Bevan. He wanted more time to think it through and just how he would go about breaking the news to his fiancée. Gordon had concurred since he didn't feel Laura should be subjected to such accusations if they weren't true. He would keep his promise, but Stephen had a way of tricking a man into saying something he wanted kept secret. But then, what precisely could Gordon tell him?

Bevan's name and her declaration of love hadn't meant any more to Gordon than it had Reid, but the fact that she had been with Reid long enough to fall in love with him made both of them nervous. Gordon had asked Reid why he didn't just tell her the truth, that the gunshot wound to his head had erased his memory of their time together, and would she please tell him everything that had happened, more pointedly why he had been at the prison in the first place. Reid had laughed sarcastically at Gordon's proposal, then suggested Gordon put himself in Bevan's place. Whatever Reid had done to her had made her angry enough to want to kill him. If Reid was to say he was sorry, that he couldn't remember any of the vows he had pledged or what had made her fall in love with him, she wouldn't believe him. Gordon had had to agree, but with nothing else left them, he felt it was a chance Reid had to take. Reid had reluctantly admitted Gordon was probably right, and he had confessed that that was what he'd more than likely wind up doing, but that he'd rather delay it awhile in the hope that being around Bevan might trigger something in his brain before he had to resort to such a drastic measure. However, if Stephen found out any of it, the choice wouldn't be Reid's to make.

"I think you're reading something into it that isn't there," Gordon replied, hoping Stephen would agree and drop the subject.

Stephen grinned, his eyes still trained on his brother's every move. "No offense, old man, but I've known Reid a lot longer than you. Yes, he's frustrated and angry, but he's nervous too." The door to one of the cabins near where Reid worked opened just then, and the young woman known only as Irish stepped out into the sunlight. She was a very pretty girl, and if Stephen's heart hadn't already been stolen by another, he might have looked at her differently. However, his attraction toward her wasn't of any concern. His brother's was. And the look on Reid's face right then, while he paused in his work to watch her walk toward the main house, certainly indicated more than just a mild interest. Stephen's smile widened. "Yes, sir, something else has my big brother doing things he doesn't ordinarily do." He straightened, wiggled his eyebrows at Gordon, and limped away.

"Irish? Is that you?"

Bevan came to a reluctant stop in the hallway just outside Lyndsy Marie's bedroom, silently cursing her failure to escape unnoticed. She realized the young woman was probably bored out of her wits having to stay in bed all day with no one around to keep her company, but Bevan really didn't want the job. She had been blessed with Laura's departure for home, despite the fact that she lived on the adjoining property and could drop in to visit any time she wanted, which only left Lyndsy Marie to avoid. She liked both women but just looking at them reminded her of Reid, and she had enough of him working so close to her cabin all the time.

"Aye, Miss Lyndsy Marie. 'Tis Irish ya heard," she replied wrinkling up her face as if she'd just been served that horrible stew again. "May I get ya somethin'?" she asked out of politeness, but she was hoping the answer would be no and that she'd be allowed to slip away with no more conversation than they'd already had.

"I was wondering if you'd do me a favor," the young woman called back.

Bevan's shoulders dropped. "A favor?"

"Yes. I was hoping you'd fix my hair the way you wear yours."

Instinctively, Bevan touched the thick curls piled high on her head and out of curiosity she moved to the bedroom door and pushed it open all the way. "Me hair?" she repeated, studying Lyndsy Marie's coiffure and thinking there was nothing wrong with it.

A bright smile warmed the woman's face. "I get so tired of wearing it the same way all the time and it gets so many tangles in it if I let it just hang loose. I like what you've done with yours. Do you think you could do that with mine?"

All Bevan had done was pull it back off her face and

tie it with a string on the top of her head. She had thought about braiding the long strands to keep the curls from tickling her neck and cheeks whenever she leaned forward to do something, but she hadn't had the time. In her opinion, it had no style. It just hung there. But if Lyndsy Marie liked it, Bevan would try to do the same with hers. She laid aside the neatly folded clean sheets she had taken from the line and went to the dresser for the comb and brush she saw lying there.

"I'll need a ribbon," she commented.

"Top drawer," Lyndsy Marie instructed. "Extra hairpins are in the gold box on top."

Bevan shook her head. "Just a ribbon." With supplies in hand, she approached the bed where Lyndsy Marie sat propped up against three fluffy pillows, the coverlet folded across her lap and her robe draped across the footboard. "Would ya be more comfortable there? Or can ya sit in a chair for a spell?"

"Whatever's easiest for you."

"A chair." She laid the hairbrush, comb, and ribbon on the night stand, moved the desk chair near the window, and aided her companion off the bed. "How long before the wee one's due?" Bevan asked as she helped Lyndsy Marie to sit down.

"Wee one? I think I'm having a horse," came the reply, accompanied with a groan. "But as far as I can figure, I'm late already."

Even though Bevan had never had any children of her own to know what it was like being pregnant, she could sympathize with her just by seeing how uncomfortable she was. "Once ya hold your babe in your arms, ya'll forget all the rest," she promised with a smile while she took the pins from Lyndsy Marie's dark hair.

"Probably. At least that's what Mother keeps telling me."

They became quiet for a few minutes while Bevan brushed out the long locks of raven black hair and Lyndsy Marie contemplated how she would go about asking the young Irish girl the questions Stephen wanted her to ask. Her brother had come to her room a short while ago with the notion that Reid knew more about Irish than he was letting on he did. She hadn't understood why it made a difference one way or the other, and Stephen had made her promise not to say a word to anyone if he told her what that difference was. Everyone in the family, except for perhaps their father, knew Reid resisted marrying Laura simply because he didn't love her the way a man who was considering such a commitment should love a woman, and that he didn't want to enter into a union that might end up hurting both him and Laura. It was Stephen's guess that Reid had a fondness for the Irish girl who had come to live with them whether Reid knew it or not. What Stephen couldn't surmise was how deep a fondness Reid had for her or if she felt the same toward Reid.

"Does it matter?" Lyndsy Marie had argued. "He's engaged to Laura. He *must* marry her."

"Even if it means he'd be unhappy?" Stephen had asked.

"Well, what about Laura? Should he sacrifice her happiness for his? Think of the shame she'd have to carry if he called it off simply because of his selfishness. It just isn't done. Marriage isn't based on love."

"Oh?" Stephen had challenged. "Why did you and

Henry get married?"

He had smiled softly at her when her face flushed a scarlet hue, knowing he had made his point with her. She and her husband had married for no other reason besides love. Stephen himself remained unwed because he wanted the same thing. Their brother's marriage had been arranged long before either of them were even born, without any consideration to Reid's *or* Laura's feelings on the matter. As far as Stephen was concerned, both of them had a right to make that decision on their own. And Stephen had gotten the feeling that *that* was what was truly bothering Reid. Irish, the beautiful chestnut-haired girl whose presence had disrupted everyone's lives, had made him aware of the fact that he should be allowed to make choices in his life. Whether she was a part of Reid's future, Stephen had no way of knowing for sure. But that was the reason he asked Lyndsy Marie to talk with her.

"What's your real name, Irish?" she bravely asked, wishing she could see the girl's face for her reaction, since Stephen was certain to ask what it had been.

"What makes ya think it isn't?" she countered.

"Just a guess, I suppose, because I've never met anyone with a name like that that it *wasn't* a nickname." Lyndsy Marie didn't like playing word games. She always felt being honest with someone was much more sincere than tricking a person. But Stephen had warned her that Irish might refuse to say anything at all if she asked her straight out. She frowned uneasily when she heard the girl's soft laughter.

"And how many people from Ireland have ya met?"

Lyndsy Marie hated to lie, too. "A few," she replied, biting her lower lip.

351

"And every one of them was nicknamed Irish?" Bevan laughed again, certain her companion was merely trying to hide her curiosity without being blunt. "Me name's Bevan," she finally admitted, once she had decided there was really no harm in letting her know. "Bevan O'Rourke."

"Bevan," Lyndsy Marie chanted as she twisted around in the chair to look at her. "Why, that's a *beautiful* name. Why didn't you want anyone to know what it was? You're not in some sort of trouble, are you? You're not running from someone? I mean, if you are, you don't have to be afraid of us. We'll help you." The concern on her face instantly changed to a grimace of pain. "Oh dear," she gasped, clutching her full belly. "Oh dear." Tears welled up in her eyes and she reached for Bevan's hand. "Bevan . . . I . . . think . . ." She whimpered a forlorn little sob, a delicate plea for help, and started to rise with Bevan's aid when a rush of warm water soaked the skirts of her nightgown and puddled on the floor at her feet. "Oh, my God!"

"Don't be scared," Bevan soothed her, slipping her arm under Lyndsy Marie's to pull her up. "'Tis the way it starts. Let's get ya back in bed."

"You won't leave me, will you, Bevan?" she half cried, half begged.

"Of course not. But ya've got ta lie down. Ya don't want your baby fallin' on the floor, do ya?"

Lyndsy Marie tried to laugh but the contraction which gripped her abdomen made her gasp instead. "It hurts, Bevan."

"I know," she replied, practically carrying the woman to her bed. "And it will get worse before it gets better. But I guarantee it'll be worth it." She removed all but one pillow from behind the girl's head, tossed off the coverlet, and drew up the sheet the way she remembered watching her mother do it when Kerry played midwife to a neighbor of theirs a few years back. "Now I want ya ta stay right there and don't try ta get up. I've—"

"No, Bevan, don't leave me! You—"

"I have ta tell someone ya're havin' your baby," she said, smiling sympathetically. "We'll be needin' a few things. I'm only goin' out inta the hall. Ya'll be able ta see me." She raised her brows at her and gently removed the fingers squeezing her arm. "All right?"

Lyndsy Marie's dark curls bounced with the nod of her head.

"Good," Bevan replied, taking a step backward before she spun on her heels and raced out of the room. At the banister overlooking the foyer, she gripped the railing, leaned, and shouted, "Vesta! Vesta, Miss Lyndsy Marie's child is coming! I'll be needin' your help. Hurry!"

The huge manor exploded with excitement. A flurry of servants carrying hot water, clean rags and towels, and anything else they thought might be helpful filed into the room on the heels of Lyndsy Marie's mother. Stephen and Reid appeared in the doorway but Charlotte quickly ushered them away, telling them that their sister's bedroom was no place for them right then. When they heard her scream in agony, they both decided their mother was right and hurried back down the staircase. Near the bottom they met Lawrence on his way up, and without breaking stride they turned him around, grabbed his arms—one son on each side— and escorted him to the parlor, where Reid suggested

353

they have a stiff glass of sherry while they waited for the birth of a new generation of Hamiltons. One drink became two, two turned to three, and before long all three men were pacing the floor when it seemed Lyndsy Marie's wails of pain relentlessly echoed down the staircase, filled the foyer, and bounced off the walls in the parlor all around them.

The eldest of the three Hamilton men had been through that same kind of experience before, when his wife gave birth to their children, but the memory wasn't fresh enough to give him any reassurance that his daughter would be all right. Stephen was reminded of the pain he'd suffered when he smashed his knee and how it seemed nothing anyone could do for him had helped relieve his agony, and he found himself wishing he could take away his sister's suffering and put it on himself. Reid, too, was remembering how his younger brother had lain in bed writhing in pain. This was different, however. This hadn't been his fault. Yet he still had trouble dealing with it, simply because there was nothing he could do to help speed up the birth of Lyndsy Marie's baby.

The only comfort he found, oddly enough, was that he had seen Bevan at his sister's side, holding her hand, cooing softly to her, and stroking her hair. He would have liked being there with Lyn, doing all the things Bevan was doing for her, but he realized too that his presence would only embarrass his sister. He had to be satisfied with the idea that Bevan was an extension of himself, and he wondered at such a thought. Why had that concept made him feel good? Why did it seem natural? And why Bevan? Why not Vesta or his mother or any of the other women crowded around the bed?

Why did the sight of Bevan warm him all the way through to his bones? Why did he wake up every morning thinking of her and plotting out ways to be near her?

A flood of different questions whirled around in his brain, and with glass in hand, he idly strolled to the window to look out at the tall masts of the *Lady Hawk* anchored in the bay, a heaviness pulling on his heart. *Dear God,* he thought, his dark brows drawn low over his eyes, *is it possible I loved the Irish wench? That isn't something a man would forget. Perhaps I unintentionally led her to believe I did . . . by something I said or the way I behaved.* Scowling into his glass, he raised it to his lips and swallowed the last of his sherry, grimacing at the hot sensation he felt in his mouth and down his throat. Bevan didn't strike him as the kind of woman who would let herself be fooled by a man's smile or kind words. Surely she hadn't fallen in love with him for such a simple reason. There had to be more.

Closing his eyes, he raised his chin and let his head fall back as he drew in a deep breath of the cool air pouring in through the opened window. He wanted to remember . . . he truly did. But deep down inside he feared knowing what had passed between them. If he had done more than smile at her, if he had indeed fallen in love with her and had said so, then he must have told her about Laura. He'd never lied to anyone in his whole life . . . not about something as important as being engaged.

"I haven't forgotten your name, *Graham.*"

Bevan's angry words exploded in his mind and jerked him upright. Graham? Who was Graham? What had she meant? Was there a chance she had mistaken him for someone else? *That* would certainly explain a few things—such as the possibility she had fallen in love with a man named Graham, a man who looked a lot like Reid. She'd even said they hadn't seen each other in several weeks. Maybe she had forgotten what he looked like, and . . .

And maybe if you have another drink, this whole nightmare will vanish, he mused disgustedly. *You're really pushing it, Reid, to think there's another man walking around somewhere who looks and talks and acts just like you. Stephen's my blood brother, for God's sake, and he's never been mistaken for me. You're in this up to your neck, ol' boy, and only you can get yourself out.* Turning sharply with the intention of refilling his glass, he nearly crashed into his brother standing quietly behind him.

"Good God, Stephen," he barked. "Why don't you give a fellow a little warning instead of sneaking up behind him like that? You're lucky I didn't knock you down." He brushed past him and went to the buffet.

"Sorry," Stephen apologized, a light smile curling his mouth. "I guess you didn't hear me when I spoke your name . . . four times." He shifted his gaze when Reid jerked around to glare at him. If his brother saw the humor in his eyes, it would only make Reid that much more angry. "I asked what had you so quiet," he said, clumsily settling himself down into a chair. "You seemed to be in another world."

Uncomfortable, Reid replied, "I was thinking about our sister."

Stephen smoothed a wrinkle from the knee of his breeches. "Oh," he responded quietly, though doubt was apparent in his tone of voice.

Reid started to challenge him, but knew that would be a mistake. Clamping his mouth shut instead, he returned to the window, where he resumed studying the ship in the distance as though he feared pirates would attack and take the *Lady Hawk* if he weren't watching.

"You've been thinking about her a lot lately, haven't you?" Stephen continued, finishing off his drink and setting the glass on the table beside him.

"About who?" Reid questioned, his words sharp.

"Lyndsy Marie," Stephen replied with a vague smile he quickly masked when Reid turned to frown at him.

"What are you talking about?"

"You said you were quiet because you were thinking about our sister. So I'm assuming she's the reason you've been withdrawn these last few days." He shrugged, closed his eyes, and laid his head back against the chair. "I could be wrong, I suppose."

Reid missed the trap his brother had set for him. "You usually are," he jeered, looking back outside again.

Opening one eye, Stephen peeked over at Reid. "Then you've been withdrawn for other reasons. Gordon said it was because you're frustrated over having lost your memory." He grinned openly when he saw how Reid's back stiffened. "But you know what I think?" he dared, lifting his head. "I think Irish's presence has you worried. I think you know more about her than you're telling. Who is she really, and why does she have you jumping around like your breeches are on fire?" His smile remained even after Reid turned on him with a look that would terrify an ordinary man.

A long moment passed in which the brothers stared at each other—one in anger, the other in bold persistence. Just when it seemed neither of them would back down, Reid's gaze shifted to their father, who had been too caught up in his own thoughts to hear his sons' exchange, then back at Stephen. Gulping down his sherry, he approached Stephen, briskly set his glass next to his brother's, and growled his excuse that he needed to get back to work.

I'm sure you do, Stephen mused lightheartedly as he watched Reid make a hurried exit. *Anything to keep from answering my question.*

Darkness accompanied Bevan on her walk from the manor. Stretching the tired muscles in her neck, she glanced up at the black sky overhead and hazarded a guess by the position of the full moon glowing warmly off to her right that it was well past midnight. Lyndsy Marie had been very lucky, though Bevan doubted she would see it that way. Her beautiful baby girl had come screaming into the world a little more than twelve hours after the first seizure of pain had begun. For most women the agony of delivering their firstborn usualy lasted a full day and night, sometimes longer. And oftentimes that feat could be difficult. The birth of Lyndsy Marie's daughter had been neither, and despite Bevan's insistence that her presence had very little to do with any of the process, Lyndsy Marie argued that she couldn't have done it without her.

A bright, happy smile crossed Bevan's face as she envisioned the pretty cherub face, tuft of black hair, dark eyes, and precious button nose of the baby she had been allowed to hold in her arms while the bed linens and Lyndsy Marie's gown were changed. The baby's crying had stopped almost immediately once she had been bathed and wrapped in warm clothes then given to her mother, and a silence had fallen upon the circle of women standing around the bed, each experiencing the glow of motherhood no man would ever feel or understand.

"Whad yo' gonna name her, Miz Lyndsy Marie?" Vesta had asked, and Bevan could still feel the thrill of the young woman's answer.

"I'm going to name her after a new friend of mine," she replied, smiling up at Bevan. "Someone I've just met but someone I like very much. I hope my daughter will honor your name, Bevan."

Joyful tears had moistened Bevan's eyes and more had tightened her throat. "'Tis I who am honored, Miss Lyndsy Marie," she had said. "And 'tis me wish that the two of ya live long and happy lives."

The group had departed after that, and although Bevan knew mother and daughter needed their rest, she would have liked staying just a little while longer. She wanted to sit beside the bed and watch the baby sleep. But the presence of Lyndsy Marie's mother had changed her mind. Bevan had been fortunate earlier in not having to answer any questions, and she knew Mrs. Hamilton would have a few of her own to ask if she and Bevan were left alone together, especially after Bevan had seen the interested look on the woman's lined face each time Bevan glanced up and found her staring. Bevan had already said more than she'd intended, and short of being rude to the lady of the manor, Bevan knew she would not escape so easily next time. As inconspicuously as she could manage, she had bid Lyndsy Marie good night and had left the room before Charlotte Hamilton could stop her.

Bevan could hardly remember another time in her life when she had felt more humbled by another's open display of affection. It was wonderful. But at the same time it saddened her. She had inadvertently established ties to the Hamilton family and to America that she wished she hadn't made. She would be going home soon and it was her wish to leave it all behind her . . . just as she would leave her memories of Reid behind her. Lyndsy Marie had made that impossible. Every time someone called Bevan's name she would think of a baby with black hair and dark eyes, and that would remind her of Lyndsy Marie. Then she'd remember the plantation in North Carolina, Bess and the cabin they shared, the sweet lady named Laura who had been the first to befriend her, and then, of course, she'd think of Reid.

Damn ya, she fumed as she hurried her step down the path in back of the warehouse. *I wish the earth would open up and swallow ya, Reid Hamilton. Only that would be too easy on ya. Ya deserve somethin' a bit more cruel. What ya don't deserve is a sister like Lyndsy Marie and a fine lass like Laura willin' ta marry ya.* A devilish, vengeful grin spoiled the angry line of her mouth as she conjured up the image of the ugliest, meanest woman she could imagine. If sorcery really existed, she'd find herself a witch and pay her to use her black magic on him. He'd wake up one morning in bed next to his bride. Only it wouldn't be Laura he'd find there. No, she'd be a woman twice his weight, who never bathed or combed her hair, and liked wearing the same dress day after day until it rotted and fell off her bulky frame. She'd have a wart on her chin, two missing teeth, and an aroma that preceded her wherever she went. Her voice would be high-pitched and earsplitting, and her favorite pastime would be lounging in bed . . . with Reid underneath her.

"Ah, wouldn't it be grand?" she giggled, cutting across the yard to the front door of her cabin. "And I'd have ya stranded on a small, deserted island so ya couldn't hide and ya couldn't get away. Ya'd be there ta serve her every beck and call, me arrogant, selfish lout. Then ya'd see what it's like ta be used."

She had just reached out for the doorknob when a muffled noise from inside the cabin stopped her. She was reasonably certain Bess was in there, since most everyone on the plantation had gone to bed hours earlier with the exception of those who had tended Lyndsy Marie. Chores would still have to be done no matter who was having a baby, and since work began at sunrise, the staff usually retired shortly after dinner. So why was Bess still awake? Or was it Bess?

Suddenly alarmed, Bevan quietly moved away from the door. No light shone from the window, and except for the noise, it appeared nothing was out of the ordinary. Then she heard a soft moan, or a cry perhaps, and she was drawn to look inside. With her back against the wall made of rough logs, she stepped sideways, leaned, and peered in through the window. Dark shadows hid nearly everything within their grasp with the exclusion of Bess's cot on the far wall where moonlight flooded in and bathed the couple lying there. Bevan knew instantly what was going on and she quickly ducked back out of sight, her face hot with embarrassment. Bess had never mentioned having a lover and Bevan couldn't understand why. Surely Bess didn't think Bevan would disapprove. How could she? From all Bevan had seen thus far, the slaves had a right to grab what little happiness they could . . . anytime they found it.

Silently thanking whatever it was that had made her hesitate instead of bursting in on Bess and her man, Bevan tiptoed away from the cabin to wait in the shadows of the huge oak a few yards away. She had only taken half a dozen steps when the door of the small abode opened behind her, and without thinking, she turned around. A soft, understanding smile had tilted the corners of her mouth upward and she was hoping Bess's young man would know from the look on her face that she was pleased her friend had a beau. Then her gaze fell on the tall, stocky build of Emmett Connors. The smile vanished instantly and a confused frown knotted her brow. For a second she wondered if she had really seen the overseer and Bess lying on the cot or if, perhaps, the woman wasn't Bess. Then something the young black girl had told her earlier registered in her brain.

"Massuh Connors got me dis here cabin."

Bevan hadn't thought a thing of it at the time. Now she understood completely. Especially now that she witnessed the man fastening his breeches as he stepped out into the moonlight, unaware of her presence. He'd gotten Bess a cabin of her own so that he could lie with her anytime he wanted without having to chase away the others who shared it with her!

Bevan's stomach twisted into a knot and she could feel the bile beginning to rise. Fearing she would get sick, she covered her mouth with her hand and started to turn away when Emmett Connors looked up and saw her.

"Well, well, well," he sneered, smoothing back his ruffled hair with one hand. "If it ain't Miss Irish." He jerked his head in the direction of the manor. "Been up at the main house pretending you're something you ain't? Or did Mr. Reid send for you because he needed a little lovin'? He sure don't get it from that lily white woman of his."

Bevan's nausea disappeared with the insults he flung. Her spine stiffened, her green eyes darkened, and her chin jutted out defiantly as she lowered her hand and glared back at him. "If ya're referrin' ta Miss Laura," she spat, "the reason your twisted little mind thinks that way is because she's a lady. I'm sure someone of your background wouldn't recognize one if she came up and slapped your face. Which is what ya deserve for talkin' like that."

"Ho-oh, you think so, huh?" he baited. "Well, if that's true, I don't have to worry about you slapping my face, do I?" His narrow-set brown eyes looked her up and down. "You sure ain't no lady."

The muscles in her right arm and hand flexed with the overwhelming urge to pick up something and smash him over the head with it. When she fled Lord Rynearson's house those many weeks ago, she never dreamed she'd meet a man who felt the same contempt for women as he had shown. Standing face to face with Emmett Connors proved how very possible it really was, and she fleetingly wondered if the two men might be related. She also assumed talking with him was senseless. He obviously didn't have the intelligence to carry on a respectable conversation. Gritting her teeth, she dropped her gaze away from him and started for the door.

"What's the matter, *Miss Irish?*" he jeered, jumping in her way. "Ain't you got no answer for that one?"

"Not one ya'd understand," she rallied hatefully.

"Oh?" he snarled, taking a step closer.

Bevan quickly and wisely retreated.

"Well, I think it's time you were told how an indentured servant is expected to behave, and what the punishment will be if you don't." Moonlight trickled down through the leafy overhang above them and fell against his face, clearly showing his rage and the danger in which Bevan had foolishly placed herself by reacting too quickly. "There's only one difference between you and Bess, and that's the color of your skin. You ain't gonna be treated no better. You ain't gonna get special privileges or any less work to do. You ain't to talk back, and when I tell you something, you say 'Yes, sir.' You ain't to interrupt me or look me in the eye."

Instinctively, Bevan dropped her gaze. The hatred in his voice and the expression on his face warned her that she had already pushed him too far.

"You do one thing that displeases me and that includes trying to complain to Mr. Reid about *anything,* and I'll personally tie you to a tree and flog the life out of you." He shot out a hand, cruelly caught her chin, and jerked her head up. "You got that, *Miss Irish?* Not a word to any of those up there in the main house . . . not about the food you're served, the place where you live, or who I like to bed. Understand?"

Bevan weakly nodded her head.

"What? I can't hear you."

"Yes, sir," she replied, truly frightened of him.

"Good," he growled, his hand slipping around to the back of her neck. "Now get to bed." Without warning he whirled, pulled her with him, then gave her a hard shove toward the cabin. She nearly fell, caught her balance, and awkwardly grabbed the doorknob to steady herself. Not bothering to look back at him, she lifted the latch and hurried inside.

Fear shook her whole body, and before her knees gave out, Bevan sank to the floor. Bess had tried to warn her about Emmett Connors but Bevan hadn't paid much attention. From now on she'd do exactly as Bess had suggested—when she saw him coming, she'd go the other way. It didn't mean, however, that "those in the main house" wouldn't learn of Connors's brutality. Perhaps not directly, but somehow Bevan would see to it that the Hamiltons found out what kind of man their overseer really was.

...u have an idea I can't shoulder my burden alone."

"Oh! And what kind of business is that?"

Small brown eyes peered up at him over a bundle...

Chapter Twelve

Verona, a bustling little town five miles in from the shoreline of New River Inlet, North Carolina, played host to so many visitors each time a frigate docked close by that ordinarily one more new face would have hardly been noticed. Such was not the case this particular morning. The odd little man, who tried very hard not to draw attention to himself while he asked the innkeeper for a room, received not only curious stares but whispered criticism as well.

"How long will you be staying, sir?" the innkeeper asked as he handed over a key and made a mental note that the stranger had no luggage of any kind. He'd oftentimes had customers who rented a room and didn't carry a bag, and he'd thought little of it. But something about this man warned the owner to keep an eye on him . . . and to ask to be paid in advance. He realized he probably wasn't being fair, but times were hard and he wasn't in the mood or had the financial stability to do charity work.

"Not long, I hope," the stranger replied. "It depends

on how quickly I can conclude my business here."

"Oh? And what kind of business is that?"

Small brown eyes peered up at him over a birdlike nose. "The personal kind," he answered, the implication quite clear that he had said all he intended to say.

"Well, I wish you success," the innkeeper replied when nothing else seemed appropriate. "Breakfast is served at seven if you'd care to eat in the commons."

"I wouldn't," the other responded as he turned and headed for the stairs, aware of how everyone in the place was staring at him. He'd gotten used to being gawked at over the years and how to deal with it. He didn't like it, but he knew he couldn't do a thing to change how people viewed him. He wished he could get everyone to see him for what he really was—the man inside the offensive exterior—to learn he had a kind heart and gentle soul and to understand that because of the way he was treated, he had to pretend to be otherwise.

At the top of the stairs, he paused, tempted to turn back around to face those watching him and return look for look. Yet, he realized he had already allowed too many to notice him, and his mission here had to be kept secret. No one was to know why he had come to America, who it was he followed, and what he intended to do once he found her. Wishing it could be different, he lowered his head and continued down the hall to his room.

Bevan had avoided Lyndsy Marie's room as much as possible for the past two days. Not only did she not want to face Laura, who had returned to the manor the instant word of the new baby had reached her, but every time Bevan turned around, it seemed she spotted Emmett Connors watching her. Although she had nothing to say to any of the Hamiltons, she feared the overseer thought otherwise, and rather than put herself in any kind of danger, she stayed away.

She also worried she might see Reid and Laura together. As much as she liked Laura, it pained her to watch Laura with him, the way she smiled lovingly at him, laughed at what he said, or innocently slid her arm in his as they walked along. It reminded her all too clearly of how she had felt about him at one time. She had considered asking Bess if there might be a different job for her to do, one that would keep her away from the house, but she knew making such a request would only raise Bess's curiosity, and Bevan didn't want to have to tell her a lie. Thus, she cautiously moved through the house, listening and watching for any sign of the family and Laura before she entered one of the bedchambers to do her work.

The morning had started out cool, but now that the sun was directly above her and beating down relentlessly on her head and shoulders, Bevan found herself pausing in her work every few minutes to wipe the perspiration from her brow and the back of her neck. The climate in the Colonies had been a surprise to her. She had assumed the nights would be chilly and the days warm . . . if the sun shone. She had never expected it to be so hot and certainly not so late in the year.

The bright sunshine made her squint, and combined with the steam rising from the washtub, she had a headache that pounded in her temples with the same steady rhythm as her heart. She'd been scrubbing dirty linens all morning and she longed for a break from the drudgery of her work and the chance to sit down and rest in the shade of the willow. But each time she considered doing just that, she'd look up, spot Reid—shirtsleeves rolled up and hammer in hand as he helped build a second new cabin—and stubbornly refused to let anyone think she couldn't work as hard or as long as he.

"Why don't ya take your fiancée on a picnic?" she mumbled, angrily rubbing a handful of linen against the washboard. "Ya don't act like a planter should, ya know."

"And just how is a planter supposed to behave?" asked a voice from behind her.

Startled, Bevan jerked upright, cracked her knee on the tub, and muffled her cry of pain as she spun around to see to whom she should apologize. The second her eyes met Stephen's, she felt like groaning for a very different reason. She smiled lamely instead.

"I don't believe you and I have ever actually been introduced," he continued, a warm smile brightening up his brown eyes. "But I certainly know who you are. You've made quite an impact on my entire family."

He stood only a few feet away from her, and even though Bevan had seen him several times before, it had been from a distance, which hadn't afforded her the opportunity to discover how much he resembled his brother . . . except for the eyes. Suddenly worried Connors might see them together and get the wrong idea, she glanced nervously toward the long row of cabins, half expecting to find him watching her.

Stephen took the brief moment she innocently gave

him to study the young woman's profile. There didn't appear to be a single flaw in the finely sculptured lines of her face. Her skin was smooth and creamy despite her sunburned nose. Thick, auburn curls fell softly down the back of her neck, and a slender body with just the right number of curves complemented the plain cotton dress she wore. It wasn't difficult for Stephen to understand what it was about her that had attracted his brother's attention, and according to their sister, this woman had a gentle, giving spirit. Noticing a trickle of perspiration running down the side of her face and how hot he was getting standing there in the sun, he remembered why he had volunteered to come for her.

"Lyndsy Marie's asking for you," he announced, mildly puzzled by the apprehensive look he saw on her face when she glanced back at him. "She says you haven't stopped by her room to see the baby."

"I . . . I've had work ta do," Bevan replied, hoping that would be enough of an excuse.

"Well, I'm here to give you permission to take a break," he proclaimed, stepping forward to catch her elbow and guide her toward the house. "Besides, you look like you could use it . . . and perhaps something cool to drink?"

Bevan wanted to object. She wanted to tell him that Connors might be watching and that someone would probably pay for her socializing with the family. But his insistent grip on her arm and the assumption that he would question her refusal stilled the desire and brought a troubled frown to her brow. In silence, she allowed him to escort her through the house, up the long staircase, and into his sister's room.

"Bevan!" Lyndsy Marie exclaimed happily upon

seeing her. "I'm so glad you're here." She motioned Bevan to the bed, where she sat propped up against a mound of pillows with her baby cradled in her arms. "Everyone tells me I'm crazy, but look!" She pulled the lace-trimmed blanket off her daughter's head. "Doesn't that look like red hair to you?"

A flood of warm happiness burst inside Bevan, and although the single curl tied with a pink ribbon on top of the baby's head looked more black than auburn to Bevan, she smiled joyfully. Lyndsy Marie had—in a subtle, innocent way—paid Bevan a great compliment. A little embarrassed and truly not wanting to hurt the woman's feelings, she shrugged and glanced beseechingly at Stephen.

"Well, I suppose . . . it might . . . well," she stuttered when he offered no help. She appraised the lock of hair again. "I guess it's really too soon ta tell, Miss Lyndsy Marie. It might change colors as she grows older. And 'tis me own opinion that she'll be happier if it isn't red."

"Why would you say that?" Lyndsy Marie inquired, her expression showing honest disappointment. "Your hair is beautiful."

Bevan laughed, humbled by the girl's honesty. "It has a way of gettin' me in trouble."

"Whatever do you mean?"

"I think I know," Stephen cut in. "Redheads are usually blamed for having bad tempers. Am I right?"

Bevan nodded. "And sometimes we're accused of bein' a leprechaun's mischief maker." She grinned and looked away dreamily. "At least that's what me brothers always claimed. They said that was the reason we never found our pot of gold, and I never tried to make them think otherwise. In fact, I—" She suddenly

371

realized what she had said and to whom, and her lighthearted mood turned heavy. Glancing first at Lyndsy Marie, then Stephen, she turned to leave. "I've got ta get back ta me work now."

"Poppycock," Lyndsy Marie exclaimed. "There's no work around this house that can't wait a few minutes. Come. Sit beside me and tell me more about your family." She patted the mattress and asked, "How many brothers do you have, Bevan?"

Bevan hesitated, knowing no way out, then reluctantly returned to the bed and sat down on the edge. "Three."

"Three?" Lyndsy Marie groaned. "And I thought I was cursed having two. And I suppose you're the youngest . . . just like me?"

Bevan nodded.

"And the oldest tries to run your life," Lyndsy Marie guessed. "Reid has always tried to run mine. He's half the reason I got married . . . just to get away from him."

"Don't believe her for a minute," Stephen warned playfully. "She married Henry because he was the first man to ask."

"Stephen!" Lyndsy Marie gasped. "You make it sound like I had no suitors at all other than Henry. I had plenty, but they all reminded me of you and Reid. That's why I turned them away. I didn't want to spend the rest of my life married to a man who treated me like his sister." She smiled triumphantly at having bested her brother, but the victory was short-lived.

"I guess you could say the same for Laura," Stephen piped in, silently thanking Lyndsy Marie for giving him the opening he needed.

The only reason he had brought Bevan to his sister's room was to talk about Reid where his sister would hear every word. Since Lyndsy Marie hadn't had the courage or the cunning to obtain the answers he wanted, Stephen knew it was up to him, and he didn't intend to let her out of his sight until he had them. Crossing to the dresser where Vesta had set a tray with lemonade, he poured a glassful, approached Bevan with it, then pulled out the desk chair to sit on while he watched her drink, deliberately ignoring Lyndsy Marie's heated stare.

"Reid loves Laura, but in the same way he cares about his sister," he continued, clumsily stretching out his crippled leg in front of him and pretending not to notice how Lyndsy Marie covertly shook her head. "They're supposed to get married but I doubt they ever will."

Bevan hoped neither of the siblings would see how uncomfortable Stephen's topic of conversation made her. She wanted to hear more but she was afraid she'd give herself away if she looked either of them in the eye. In an effort to hide her emotions, she set her glass on the night stand and asked Lyndsy Marie if she could hold the baby.

"You know why I think that is?" Stephen went on, refusing to be discouraged by the girl's seeming lack of interest.

"Oh, Stephen," his sister broke in, desperate to change the subject. "No one cares. And *I* think you're wrong anyway. They'll get married. Reid just needs time."

"How much time?" he countered. "They're not getting any younger. What's he waiting for? His memory to come back?"

A frown skirted across Bevan's brow and disappeared. "Maybe."

"Why?" Stephen persisted. "What difference does that make? The only thing he can't remember is what happened to him while he was in Ireland. It has nothing to do with Laura."

Feeling the need to defend her older brother, though she didn't know why, Lyndsy Marie rallied. "How do you know? Maybe something happened to him while he was there that he feels he must clear up before he's free to marry."

"If he can't remember, how does he know that?"

Lyndsy Marie stiffened, aghast. "Are you implying he made it all up. About not being able to remember, I mean? Good heavens, Stephen. He only missed getting killed by a few inches. The doctor said he was lucky only to have lost his memory."

"I know that. And I believe him. I'm sure he can't remember . . . at least not all of it, just bits and pieces." He purposely turned his full attention on Bevan. "And I feel Bevan's presence has helped stimulate his memory."

Bevan's cheeks burned instantly. "Me?" she echoed, her heart beating a little faster. She'd heard their dialogue, questioned the possibility some of it might be true, and doubted the rest. What a perfect explanation for Reid to pretend he didn't know who she was.

Her reaction was just what Stephen had expected. She did know something. He could see it in the flash of rage which darkened her pretty green eyes. "You're from Ireland, aren't you?"

"Aye," she answered testily as she handed the baby

back to her mother and stood. "So are a lot of other people, ya know. If ya're sayin' I'm the reason he's startin' ta remember"—she hissed the words—"then ya're absolutely right. But it isn't for the reason ya're thinkin'. He's feelin' guilty, as well he should, I might add, and ya'd be doin' me a service if ya let him go on feelin' that way . . . at least until I'm on me way home again."

"On your way home?" Lyndsy Marie whined as she watched Bevan walk for the door. "You just got here. You can't go back to Ireland. I won't let you. Little Bevan *needs* you. *I* need you."

"It wasn't me intention ta come here in the first place, Miss Lyndsy Marie," Bevan openly admitted as she paused in the doorway and looked back. "Had we not been days out ta sea when I found out, I would have jumped overboard and swam back ta shore. Now I must make do with what's happened. But only until your brother finds a ship willin' ta take me home." She could see her tirade had hurt the young woman. "It has nothin' ta do with you," she said a bit more softly. "Ya're a fine young lady and I'll always remember ya as one of me truest friends. But I have nothin' ta hold me here. I want ta go home . . . ta me family." The image of her father, Kelly, Ryan, and Shea flashed before her eyes, and with a muffled sob, she turned and hurriedly left the room.

"Damn you, Stephen John," Lyndsy Marie snapped, her own eyes glistening with unshed tears of rage and sorrow. "See what you've done?"

"What *I've* done?" he protested, struggling to get up. "My dear sister, *I* haven't done anything. Weren't you listening? Reid's behind her outburst, only he doesn't know it." He frowned pensively as he considered the thought. "Or does he?" he murmured, a vague smile slowly pulling at the corners of his mouth.

By the end of the second week of Bevan's stay on the Hamilton plantation, work on the slaves' living quarters was completed. It was a day Bevan wanted to celebrate, since it meant Reid would no longer have a reason for being near her cabin. Yet it also meant Connors would have free rein with the slaves again, since Reid wouldn't be around to see firsthand what was happening and Bevan's promise to Bess would keep her from reporting any incidents she felt were unjust. His absence also raised the clear possibility of the danger she was in. With each day that passed, it became more evident that Connors's interest in her was more than just watchful. The gleam in his eye had turned from pure hatred to a mixture of loathing and animal lust, and she feared her time was nearing when she would have to make a decision.

She and Bess had never discussed that night she found the overseer in the girl's bed or what he had threatened. Bevan knew her friend hadn't been a willing partner and talking about it would only embarrass her. What neither of them knew, however, was the revenge Bevan was planning for Emmett Connors. All she needed was the means and he'd be looking for new employment before he could figure out what had happened.

That instrument came sooner than she had expected and to such an extreme she regretted not having done something about Connors earlier. Her work that day had kept her away from the cabin until well after dark. Reid had complained to Vesta that the sheets on his bed lacked the fresh crispness they usually had, and without asking Bevan first, the housekeeper had stripped the bed, replaced the linens with clean ones, and sent instructions along with the dirty laundry for Bevan to wash them before she retired for the day. Her ploy had gone awry, for instead of causing Reid the annoyance, it was heaped on her, since she had already dumped out the wash water and extinguished the fire. It meant starting all over again as well as eating a cold supper.

By the time she headed for her cabin, darkness had fallen and the smell of the campfire where their dinner was cooked no longer filled the air. It didn't surprise Bevan, since she knew she'd be late coming home, but the unusual stillness that accompanied her passage pricked her nerves and made her wary. Something wasn't quite right, though she couldn't say exactly what it was. She considered blaming it on the fact that the children were nowhere around, but that was as it should be. Most of them were probably already in bed. Perhaps it was because no one was singing as was the custom of the black people right after dinner. But she wasn't *that* late getting home. Then maybe it was the absence of light in each and every cabin, and the appearance that *everyone* had gone to bed that seemed unnatural. Whatever it was, it made her hurry her step, for she suddenly feared being alone outside where she was unprotected.

Her own cabin was dark, and assuming Bess was asleep, Bevan entered quietly, using the muted moonlight falling into the room to see if a bowl had been left on the table for her. It had, and once she closed the door, she clumsily felt her way to it. Pulling out a chair, she sat down and began to eat, pleased with the taste of whatever it was she swallowed even though it was cold. The ache in her stomach soon ebbed, and once she'd had her fill, she left the table and crossed to the water bucket by the hearth to get a drink.

Crickets outside the window took up their chirping again and she could hear the rustle of leaves as a gentle breeze swayed the tall oaks standing guard over the premises. Shedding her dress, she shivered in the dark and wondered for the first time why Bess hadn't started a fire. Certain the place would become uncomfortably chilly before long, she returned to the hearth and knelt down before it to stack logs. Within minutes a small blaze warmed the air and cast the interior with a soft light. Rising, she glanced briefly at Bess, who lay facing the wall, deduced the girl was indeed asleep, and returned to her own cot.

But sleep wouldn't come right away, despite her aching muscles and weary temperament, and a few minutes later she was lying on her back staring up at the ceiling and the dancing shadows caused by the firelight. She usually refused to let herself think about Reid, but it was times like these when, no matter how hard she resisted, a sadness would creep over her and the image of him would fill her mind. She regretted her outburst with Stephen and Lyndsy Marie that day. She hadn't meant for anyone to know that she felt anything at all toward Reid, but his brother's wild notion about Reid having lost his memory because of the gunshot wound had simply been too much. She'd heard of people losing their memories but they were *old* people with too

378

much to remember. Reid wasn't old. He'd just used that as an excuse, a convenient alibi which left him free to resume his life with Laura and to ignore his ties to her. Well, if that was the way he wanted it, then so be it. She'd suffer a memory loss too. As soon as she left North Carolina, she would forget he even existed.

Determined to purge him from her throughts, she rolled onto her side and closed her eyes, hoping to fall asleep within a moment or two. She listened to the crickets, smelled the scent of the fire, and relaxed in the comfort of her new straw cot, allowing each sensation to lull her to sleep. However, before that could happen, a vague disheartening sound penetrated her private space and she sat up, a worried frown mocking her smooth brow.

"Bess?" she called out in a soft whisper. "Bess, are you cryin'?"

The girl didn't answer, but Bevan could see that Bess's shoulders were shaking. Slipping out of bed, she pulled the blanket around her and crossed to where Bess lay.

"What is it?" she asked, her voice tinged with anger. She was sure Emmett Connors had something to do with Bess's unhappiness.

"Nothin', miss," Bess muttered, refusing to turn her face toward Bevan.

Bevan sank to her knees and gently touched Bess's arm. "I'm your friend, Bess," she pledged. "I want ta comfort ya. And ta help, if I can. Tell me why ya're cryin'."

"It's too late," the girl wept. "Yo' can't do nothin' now. He's dead."

Bevan's entire body tingled with a cold fear. "Who's

dead, Bess?"

"Camille's boy."

The image of Godfrey, a willowy fourteen-year-old, came immediately to Bevan's mind. He had been a special young man, always smiling, and his big, round eyes had sparkled with happiness every time Bevan talked with him. His job had been to work in the fields, and although it was hard, laborious work, he'd done it without complaint, and his body had shown the results. He had been tall and well muscled and always so full of life. Now he was dead.

"What happened?" Bevan asked solemnly, holding back a tear.

"Ah don't know fo' sho'," Bess replied, her voice tight and strained with grief. "Ah mean Ah don't know whad he done to deserve a beatin'."

"A beatin'?" Bevan repeated, her sorrow vanishing and an all-too-familiar hatred rising up. Only one person on the Hamilton plantation ever thought he had the right to hit someone. "Are ya sayin' Connors whipped the lad ta death?" When Bess didn't answer, Bevan bolted to her feet. "And nobody tried ta stop him?"

Recognizing the sound of trouble in her friend's tone, Bess hurriedly sat up and grabbed Bevan's arm when Bevan started to whirl away. "*Ah* tried, Bevan. But he done hit me, too. His daddy tried but Massuh Connors, he clubbed Tyrone and cracked open his skull. He's lyin' near dead hisself. Please, Bevan, don't do nothin' to get yo'self hurt too. Ain't gonna do no good."

Bevan's stomach did a flip-flop at the sight of Bess's pretty face. Her lower lip was split and swollen and she could hardly open her left eye. Connors hadn't hit her once, but twice, and Bevan doubted he had used a bare fist.

"Does Master Reid know?" she asked, forcing out the words.

"No, and yo' ain't to tell him. Nobody is. Massuh Connors tells us not to say nothin' or he'll take it out on us."

Bevan didn't doubt the truth of his promise, but she also knew he'd have to be stopped before there weren't any slaves left to beat. She went to the water bucket, took down the towel from its peg, and soaked the cloth while she contemplated a method.

"How will he explain the lad's absence?" she asked, kneeling beside Bess again to administer aid to the girl's injuries.

"He'll tell Massus Reid dat Godfrey run off. He always does dat when he kelt one of us."

Bevan's stomach churned again. "There's been others?"

Bess nodded hesitantly.

"How many?"

"Ah don't know fo' sho'. Maybe dis many," she said, holding up one hand, the fingers and thumb parted.

Bevan shook her head. "Doesn't matter," she admitted angrily, forcing Bess to lie back down. "One is too many." She folded the damp towel and laid it over Bess's eye. "I want ya ta rest while I go see Cleo. Maybe she'll have somethin' we can use ta make the swellin' go down and somethin' ta make ya sleep. Will ya promise not ta move while I'm gone?"

"Yes'm," the girl replied. "But only if'n yo' promise me yo' won't say nothin' 'bout dis to any of de Hamiltons."

Bevan didn't respond right away. She was already debating the best and safest way to go about informing Reid of the cruelty his overseer inflicted upon helpless others. "I won't say a word," she finally answered. "I promise."

She left the cabin then, certain Bess would be all right for a while and that she'd do as Bevan had asked. But rather than heading for the kitchen, she turned and walked in the direction of the cabin where Godfrey had lived with his parents. She'd pay her respects first and then take care of Emmett Connors.

The entire Hamilton family adjourned to the veranda after dinner that night, including Lyndsy Marie, her baby, and Laura. The conversation around the table had been light and festive, and for the first time in a long while, Lawrence and his oldest son had been civil to each other. A soft evening breeze carried with it the sweet smells of early autumn, a slight chill, and a reminder that winter wasn't too far behind. Each member of the group either sipped his wine, rocked on the porch swing, or silently viewed the splendor of the dying sunset until the day's activities, or in Reid's case the paperwork he needed to finish, lured them back inside. Only Laura and Stephen remained and only then because of Reid's promise to return within a few minutes, at which time he would accompany Laura home to Cotton Hollow.

"You know," Stephen began, drawing in a deep breath of fresh night air as he and Laura stood side by side at the porch railing, "I think this time of year is my favorite. There always seems to be such a peacefulness about a fall evening."

"And it's a great way to catch a chill," Laura replied with a touch of sarcasm as she readjusted the shawl over her arms. "The days can be surprisingly hot and the nights too cool to stay outside for long."

A concerned frown knotted Stephen's brow as he faced her. "Are you cold? Would you rather go inside to the parlor?"

"No," she said, laughing. "I'm fine. I was just voicing an observation. I enjoy the bite of cool air on my cheeks now and then." The smile faded from her lips when Stephen turned back to study the last splash of color in the western sky above the tree tops. She had been hoping all night for a chance to speak with him alone. Draping the ends of her lace shawl around each other, she placed her hands on the railing and leaned forward slightly. "Stephen," she began in all seriousness, "may I tell you something that you'll swear you won't repeat?"

Alarmed and curious, he looked at her askance and replied, "You know you don't have to ask. I've never told anyone before what you and I discuss."

She smiled softly and said, "But this is different. It's personal and perhaps a little foolish, yet I feel it must be said."

Hearing the worry in her voice, he twisted and rested one hip on the railing, his bad leg stretched out behind her and innocently trapping her close. "Then say it, Laura. You know I'd never think you foolish. We've been friends too long for me to make light of something which bothers you."

She took a deep breath as if to find the courage to speak and exhaled in a rush. "It's about Reid."

"What about him?"

"I feel I'm losing him."

"Losing him? How do you mean?"

She laughed nervously, glanced at him from out of the corner of her eye, then stared off across the front lawn again, her chin raised high. "This is the foolish part. I feel I'm losing him to Bevan." She quickly clarified the statement. "I'm not saying there's anything going on between them. It's just a feeling I have. He hasn't been the same since he got home, and it's nothing I can put a finger on. I can't even tell you why I think Bevan is to blame—if that's the right word. I like Bevan. We all do. And she's never acted improperly toward Reid. In fact from what I've seen, she tries very hard to avoid him." She shrugged, a sign of helplessness. "I guess that's what has me concerned. They both seem to be avoiding each other, as if they're aware of what might happen should they find themselves alone together." She turned a pleading look on him. "Do you understand what I'm saying?"

Stephen fought hard not to reach out for her hand. She was so beautiful standing there with the last rays of daylight caressing her face and bathing her long, platinum hair. He honestly couldn't understand why his brother didn't love her the way he did. "Yes, Laura. More than you know."

"Am I wrong?"

A nervous half-smile wrinkled one side of his face. "You'd really have to ask Reid, I suppose. He's the only one who knows what's going on inside his head." He didn't want to admit he agreed with her or that he'd figured it out several days ago . . . especially after his conversation with Bevan. Nor did he want Laura to

384

think back later and decide he had any part in helping make up her mind. Whatever conclusion she drew had to be solely her own.

"But have you sensed it, too?" she persisted.

Uneasy, he started to respond then squirmed instead while he frantically searched his mind for a way to end the debate.

"You have, haven't you?" she sighed, judging by his behavior that the topic made him uncomfortable.

"I didn't say that," he defended.

"You didn't have to. I could see it on your face." She reached and gently stroked his cheek. "Don't let it bother you, Stephen. It isn't your fault." She sighed again and looked away. "It's no one's fault really. Reid and I just weren't meant for each other, that's all."

"That's not true." The idea that she might release his brother from their vow and then find someone else to marry scared him. With Reid, Stephen would at least have her as a sister-in-law.

"Of course it is. You know it and now so do I." She smiled sweetly at him. "If he looked at me the way you do, I might be inclined to feel differently. But he doesn't. There's no love for me in his eyes. I never get the feeling he's fighting to keep his hands off me. Why, he hasn't even kissed me, Stephen, not the way I imagine a man would who loved the woman he was to marry."

"But he *does* love you," he argued.

"As much and in the same way as he loves Lyndsy Marie. No, Stephen," she hurried on when he drew a breath to say something more on his brother's behalf. "Stop defending him. He's a grown man. You can't *make* him love me. You can't make anyone love someone just because it's the way it *should* be or because his father—my father—wants it." Her smile had a sadness around the edges. "I'd never be happy married to him knowing he didn't really love me and that *I* might be the reason he could never give himself, heart and soul, to someone else. I care too much for him to do that to him."

"Oh, Laura," he moaned forlornly. "You're not thinking about—"

"Yes, I am, Stephen," she replied without a hint of reluctance. "I've considered it quite a bit lately. In fact, I was even thinking about it *before* he left for England this last time. I know our fathers will be upset, but it can't be helped. They've surely come to realize that something was wrong between us."

Stephen's dark brows slanted downward, and rather than have her see how distressing her news was to him, he awkwardly pushed up on his feet and turned to glance absently out at the sunset. "So, what will your plans be . . . after," he asked, truly not wanting to know.

Laura tilted her head, wishing she could see his face more clearly. She desperately needed to see his reaction. "I'm not sure. But I'm hoping someone else will make his feelings known once he hears that I'm no longer engaged."

Without thinking, Stephen replied, "He'd be a fool if he didn't."

Unsure of his meaning, Laura gingerly reached up and touched his chin, turning his face to her. "You'd never be a fool, would you, Stephen?"

A silent understanding passed between them in that moment, but before Stephen could tell her that he'd been a fool for years by not speaking up, Reid made an untimely and unforgivable appearance on the veranda. Hoping Laura would know by the eager look on his face that he intended to pay her a visit bright and early in the morning, Stephen stood back and watched his brother lead her away. If he had truly grasped the meaning of her question, the two of them had a lot to discuss. Smiling happily, he leaned a shoulder against the railing post, devouring the sight of her until Reid had helped her into the carriage, closed the door behind them, and the rig pulled away.

Reid honestly couldn't say he was surprised by Laura's suggestion. He hadn't exactly been discreet in his feelings about marriage and subsequently how he felt about Laura. She had guaranteed him several times that their decision would not change how she thought of him, that until her last breath they would remain close friends, even if his father blamed *him* for the result. Yet, all in all, he still experienced a strange kind of emptiness inside him, one he couldn't comprehend as he sat back in the carriage seat staring out at the huge manor house looming up ahead of him in the distance. Perhaps it was because he'd been secure to some degree hiding behind the pretense of betrothal all these years. It meant he hadn't had to engage in the ritual of pursuing a mate just to please his father.

"Grrrugh," he brooded, slouching down even farther in the seat with his arms folded over his chest and his chin resting on his neck.

Laura had offered to confront her father alone with the announcement, which left Reid to deal with

Lawrence, a feat that most certainly would lead to a bitter argument. It had been the dream of the two men to see their plantation united as one through the marriage of their children. Now because of Reid, that dream would never be realized.

"You're selfish, Reid," he could hear his father rave. "You've never thought of anyone but yourself your entire life. I've worked hard to give you all the extras most men never have and you thank me by doing this, *defying* me. I gave you too much, that's what I did. You should have had to grow up being poor, the way I did. Then you'd be more appreciative."

Reid had listened to the same lecture countless times before whenever he'd gotten in trouble for something. The speech had really shamed Reid on the first occasion, since he'd only been seven years old at the time, and he'd believed every word of it. After that, it had become a game for him as he tried to silently recite the reprimand word for word before it left his father's mouth. As he grew older, he realized he wasn't a rebellious son the way his father wanted him to believe he was, only that the two of them had very strong, very different opinions and that his father had trouble accepting the possibility he might be wrong. Reid loved and respected his father and he was sure his father felt the same about him, but this time Reid might have pushed his father to the breaking point. Sighing heavily, he opened the carriage door and stepped down before the driver had reined it to a complete halt. He'd wait until after breakfast to broach the subject. Right now all he wanted was a good night's sleep, something he hadn't had since his return home.

Thoughts of Laura and how he hoped she'd find the

right man to love filled his head as he crossed the foyer, climbed the winding staircase, and traveled the hallway to his room. A quietness had enveloped the house, which told him he was the last to retire, and even though he yawned as he closed the door behind him and glanced at the lighted candle on the night stand— compliments of Jerome, his valet—Reid guessed he wouldn't fall asleep as quickly as he'd like. Of late it seemed his brain did its most vigorous work when his body was horizontal and he considered sitting up in the rocker if he thought it would make a difference.

"It won't," he muttered as he slid out of his jacket on his way to the armoire. "You could try to sleep standing up or hanging from your heels in the warehouse and nothing would help." A sarcastic smirk marred the handsome line of his mouth. "I could always drink myself unconscious. That might work." Doubting it, he hung up his coat and turned around to hold on to the bedpost for balance, while he kicked off his shoes. In that same moment, his gaze fell absently on the article lying on his bed. Unable to distinguish what it was, he abandoned the task of removing his other shoe and rounded the bed to examine the item close up.

"What the hell . . ." he grated out, snatching up the torn, bloodied remnants of the garment he had found.

Holding it up by the shoulder seams, he deduced by the size of the shirt and its quality that it belonged to one of the workers—a boy. But what was it doing on his bed? And why was the back of it in shreds, while the front showed no damage? Who had laid it there? And what did the bloodstains mean? The "who" came easily enough when he gave it a moment's thought. Hadn't Bevan gotten his attention one other time in practically

389

the same way when she managed to have her dinner served up on *his* table? A dark scowl crimped his brow as he turned back to the foot of his bed for his other shoe lying there on the floor. The swill his workers had been given was bad enough. *This* spoke of greater atrocities and he intended to get to the bottom of it.

Not bothering with his jacket, he headed for the door. He'd start by rousing Cleo from her bed. He might be blind to the goings-on concerning the blacks who lived on the plantation, but he'd caught on long ago that if one ever wanted to hear gossip, Cleo was the one to ask.

Bevan had learned from the cook that Miss Laura had stayed for dinner and then afterward Master Reid had taken her home. It hadn't given Bevan much time to sneak into his room since the round trip to Cotton Hollow would take less than half an hour and Cleo wasn't sure how long the couple had been gone. Bevan had risked discovery anyway simply because someone owed it to Godfrey.

Her mission had gone smoothly, and she had just left the house through the back door when she heard the carriage come down the lane. Hiding behind a huge willow, she waited to see what kind of reaction Reid would have and if he'd do exactly as she had expected he would. To her surprise, however, instead of marching directly to Connors's cabin, Reid stormed out the side door and hurried to Cleo's. She could see that he carried the bloodied shirt in his hand and she had thought he was smart enough to figure out that it belonged to one of the slaves. So why hadn't he confronted the overseer with it? The slaves were Connors's responsibility, not the cook's. Cleo wouldn't tell him anything. She'd be too scared.

"Damn," she muttered, thinking her efforts had all been for nothing. He'd listen to Cleo swear she didn't know who owned the shirt or how it had gotten in his room, and that as far as she was concerned everything was just dandy. He'd believe her—why would a nice lady like Cleo lie?—and then he'd go back to bed. "The fool," she fumed, turning away. Now she'd have to figure out some other way to let Reid know what was happening behind his back.

Chapter Thirteen

Reid didn't have to look in a mirror to know how drastically the expression in his eyes had changed. He had felt the color leave his face with Cleo's reluctant announcement that the shirt belonged to Godfrey and that he had been beaten to death. Once he had forced her to tell him who had laid the whip to the boy, his cheeks had flamed with unsuppressed rage. He hadn't bothered to ask what the boy had done simply because in his mind no crime fit such an extreme punishment, and certainly not the acts of a fourteen-year-old boy. Nor had he promised Cleo that he'd keep their conversation a secret to protect her. Once he found Emmett Connors, there would be no need for anyone on the plantation to fear retaliation from the man.

In long, angry strides, the shirt clutched tightly in his fist, Reid crossed the yard, walked past the warehouse, and followed the path dividing the two rows of cabins until it split and one veered off to the left, directing him to the place where he'd find the butcher of children. Reid had to admit he hadn't taken the time over the past few years to get to know the younger generation of workers and that he had only noticed Godfrey while Reid helped remodel the cabins. They hadn't talked all that much, but when they had, Reid had enjoyed every minute of it. The youngster had a fresh sense of humor and seemed eager to help Reid whenever he could. It just didn't make any sense for Connors to whip the boy, and certainly not long enough to kill him. The act spoke of a cold, cruel heart and a lack of respect for human life.

At the door of the overseer's cabin, Reid refused to give the man the decency of announcing his arrival by knocking. Instead, he seized the latch and rushed inside. A lighted candle on the table hinted that even though Connors was away at the moment, he intended to return soon, and Reid debated whether he should wait or go looking for him. He was about to leave and pay Bevan a visit since she seemed to know more about what went on than anyone else, when he espied Connors's whip rolled up and draped over the finial of a chair. A wave of nausea and disgust washed over him as he stared at it, and bitter rage loomed close once he had approached and held the braided leather in his hand. Dark stains of dried blood still clung to the tip, and Reid had to close his eyes and draw in a long, deep breath. The desire to kill the man with the same bloodied instrument he had used on the boy was beginning to overpower him.

Bevan had promised Camille and Tyrone that their son's death would not go unnoticed by those in the manor house. She had also sworn to them that

393

Connors would know who had gone against his orders, that if it meant the greatest of all sacrifices, she would gladly make it if it meant no one else would have to suffer. Now as she sat on the rotted tree stump in back of her cabin staring up at the moonlit night, she wondered if she had been too quick to make the oath. The Reid she had fallen in love with would have made the same promise and he wouldn't have stopped until he fulfilled it. He would have seen justice done. That had been the reason why she had taken the shirt and smuggled it into his room. They thought alike when it came to fair treatment. But this man was a different Reid from the one she had known, and from the looks of things, his idea of right and wrong was no longer the same as hers.

She thought of Stephen and wondered if he wouldn't judge the situation the same as his brother. Concluding that he probably would, she dismissed the notion of talking to him about Godfrey. Of course, there was always Lyndsy Marie, but it was obvious she had been a pampered young girl all her life. If Bevan told her such a horrifying story, she probably wouldn't believe it. Mr. and Mrs. Hamilton were out of the question. Why would they listen to anything she had to say? What was she to them? That left Laura.

"Ya're dreamin', Bevan," she muttered aloud. Laura would be the last person to interfere with how her fiancé's family ran their plantation. No, Reid had been her only hope. "So, ya little troublemaker," she whispered up at the stars, "'tis up ta *you* ta put a stop ta Emmett Connors."

An irritable frown drew her coppery brows together as she pondered the best method of disposing of the overseer. *I could club him over the head and drop his body down the well,* she thought, but the imagined results wrinkled her nose. *I could set his cabin on fire.* She shook her head. Too gruesome . . . although it was what he deserved. *If I could find a way ta get him ta hold still long enough, I'd whip him ta death, just as he did ta Godfrey.* That idea failed as those before it had, when she realized his screams would only remind her that, unlike him, she could not callously murder a person.

"I wish I could," she quietly hissed. "God, how I wish I could smash in your brains with a rock and then bury ya in the middle of a tobacco field." A devilishly wicked grin curled her mouth. "Or in the stable yard," she amended, envisioning the sight of horse after horse raising its tail high and depositing a fresh pile of manure on Connors's rotting carcass. "Oh, wouldn't that be a fittin' memorial?"

The cynical humor of the moment disappeared when a movement to her right caught her attention. Jerking her head around to look, she bolted to her feet and staggered back a step, wondering just how much, if any, of her inane chattering had been overheard.

"We have rules, Mick," Connors snarled, his head low as he approached her with slow, vengeful strides. "But you don't seem to care, do you? You think just 'cause you're Irish, you're better'n everybody else. Well, you ain't."

Remembering his earlier warnings, Bevan quickly lowered her eyes, but just enough to satisfy him while still being able to see how close he was getting.

"Where you been, Mick? Up at the house again? Did that pompous milksop invite you into his room? Or was it the other way around?" He continued to advance. "I'll wager it was. I've seen that look before. You females are all alike. You've been itching to wrap your boney little legs around him, haven't you? Well, it ain't gonna do you no good, bitch, 'cause if his seed takes, he'll just sell you off. That's what all those rich bastards do with their mistresses once they're too fat to ride."

Bevan wasn't sure if anger or fear weighed heavier on her shoulders. She wanted to lash out at him, but she knew he was capable of killing her without even blinking. She wisely chose to remain quiet as she covertly kept a safe distance between them.

"You'd do better with me," he alleged, his voice thick with lust. "I could get you anything you wanted, as long as you was nice to me. Ask Bess. Her work ain't hard. She had her own place to live before Hamilton said she had to share it with you. Well, I could do that for you, too. I could buy you things, pretty things . . . for your hair, your ears, and around your neck. Why, I might even take you places. *Stand still!*" he exploded once he realized he was no closer to her than when he first spotted her.

Bevan did as he ordered, but only to allow herself the time to figure out which way to run once he made his move.

"That's better," he sneered, taking another step. "You'll like what I can do for you. Why, I might even buy you from Hamilton and set you up in your own place in town. I've got money. I've got a lot of money. In fact, I'm thinking about buyin' a piece of land and becoming a planter myself. Then the high and mighty Hamiltons will have to treat me different. I'll be one of them then."

Bevan's laughter surprised not only Connors, but herself as well.

"What's so funny?" he demanded.

"Ya'd *never* compare to the Hamiltons," she blurted out, unable to hold back any longer. "It'd be like a glass of milk, you and the Hamiltons. Once it sat around long enough, the cream would rise ta the top, and I don't think I have ta tell ya which half would be you. Ya're a black-hearted degenerate with no soul or conscience. Ya take women against their will and ya kill defenseless children. Ya don't even deserve ta live on the same piece of land with people like the Hamiltons, and once they realize what happened to Godfrey, all the money in the world won't buy ya respectability. Ya're scum, Emmett Connors, the kind that floats across a stagnate pond."

His face had reddened with each insult she threw at him. The cords in his neck stood out. Fire raged in his eyes. Before Bevan could react and defend herself, he raised a fist, lunged, and smashed it against her cheek, hurling her to the ground. The cruel blow dazed her and left her feeling faint. Only the pain which exploded in her head kept her alert, but not enough to give her the strength to fight back. She winced at the agonizing grip on her wrist as Connors bent and hauled her to her feet, ready to deal a second blow. In a haze, she watched him raise his clenched hand, and she could almost feel the bone-crushing force before he hit her. Then suddenly, a strange, high-pitched whistling rent the air, and out of the darkness surrounding them, a black snakelike cord hissed and coiled itself with lightning speed around Connors's arm, jerking him away from her. Too weak to stand on her own, Bevan tumbled to the ground.

With a snap of his wrist, Reid unwound the whip from his victim's arm, then readied it to strike again. He hadn't heard the entire conversation between the two, but he'd heard enough to heighten his desire to kill the man. Emmett Connors was evil, and he had practiced his demented torture on women and children. That alone was bad enough. But he had chosen women and children living on the Hamilton plantation.

"I suggest, Mr. Connors," Reid ground out, his voice low and his manner dangerously close to exploding in a scalding rage, "that you leave this place as quickly as possible. If not, you'll be carried off . . . in a box."

"What?" Emmett howled as he rubbed his bruised wrist and cunningly stepped back beyond the range of the whip his employer worried in his right hand. "You're firing me because of her?" He jerked his head Bevan's way.

"Not because of her," Reid corrected, his tall, broad-shouldered frame stiff as he fought to control his wrath. "Because of what you did *to* her . . . what you *would* have done if I hadn't stopped you."

"I hit her," Connors argued. "So what? She disobeyed. It's my job to keep her in line."

"To what extent?" Reid challenged. "Death?"

"She's just a Mick, Mr. Hamilton," Connors rushed on. "One less won't make a difference." He could see by the way the man's nostrils flared all the more and how he gnashed his teeth that his defense had been the wrong thing to say. "I—I wouldn't have killed her. I—"

"You what?" Reid countered. "You would have raped her? Get off my land, Emmett Connors, and do it *now!*" Without any hesitation, he drew back the whip and snapped it forward with a deafening crack, cutting the air close to Connors's ear.

Fear overwhelmed the overseer. He had seen firsthand the effect of the whip, heard the desperate cries for mercy, smelled the blood. *He* had never shown compassion, and from the look in Reid Hamilton's eyes, he would receive none from him. Trembling, he stumbled back several steps, then turned and ran.

It took several seconds for the paralyzing rage to leave Reid's body. Cool night air touched his face and calmed his thumping heart. The chirping of crickets brought back reality. But it was the soft moan he heard coming from the dark shape huddled on the ground that snapped him out of the trancelike state he was in. Tossing aside the whip, he hurried to Bevan and knelt beside her.

"I think Vesta should have a look at that," he said, gingerly touching her cheek just below her bruised and already swollen eye.

"Thank ya, but no," Bevan managed to reply. Every ounce of her being wanted to remain strong and independent in front of this man, but the tears of pain and the fear which had consumed her body threatened to betray her. Shakily, she pushed up on her feet, fighting desperately against the wave of dizziness that blurred her vision. She sagged unwillingly against him.

"There'll be no arguing," he declared, bending slightly to swoop her up in his arms. "Because of my inadequacies, you had to risk your life to help others. I will not allow it to happen again."

*　　　*　　　*

Reid lost his place beside the bed where Bevan lay when it seemed the entire household crowded into the room a few moments later. Vesta had been summoned, but it was Charlotte Hamilton who administered aid to the young woman's injury. Lyndsy Marie was in tears and Stephen comforted her with a supportive arm around her waist and the promise Bevan would be all right. Lawrence, who unlike the others had taken time to get dressed, stood next to Reid, his mouth drawn in a tight line and his brown eyes dark with anger.

"You were too kind, Reid," his father growled. "You should have flogged the bastard before you let him go. A man like that doesn't deserve to get off that easy."

"Believe me, Father, I was sorely tempted," Reid admitted as he watched his mother place a cold compress on Bevan's cheek.

Now that it was over, he could recall the first emotion that had racked his body when he saw Connors lay a fist to Bevan. It hadn't been the usual sort of feeling a man has when he witnesses a woman being beaten. It had felt as though it had been a personal attack, as if Connors had hit *him* instead. *He* had felt her pain and the white hot rage which had seared his entire body had come from the sense that Connors was abusing someone very dear to him, that Reid had failed to protect the woman he loved. That revelation truly didn't surprise Reid. He'd been thinking those thoughts for several days now. He was sure that at one time he *had* loved this stubborn young Irish woman. What he couldn't deduce was whether or not something had happened to cool that emotion. Bevan had so much as said it had. She had told him that she *had* loved him . . . the past tense. Did it mean they both had fallen out of love? And why? What had caused it? If only he could remember . . .

"You know, young lady," he heard his father remark and he shook off his thoughts to listen. "If it hadn't been for your courage, it's no telling how long Connors would have continued on before one of us would have noticed." He glanced at his older son, then back at Bevan. "It would be very easy for me to blame Reid for all of this. But I can't. I'm just as guilty of neglecting my responsibilities as he is. When things run smoothly for years as they have around here, one tends to assume nothing will change. It took an outsider to prove how careless we'd gotten, and we're all in debt to you." He squared his shoulders and gave her a stern look. But the tenderness which glowed in his eyes hinted it was only a front. "To show my appreciation and to make up for the inexcusable manner in which you've been treated, I'm extending an invitation for you to remain, as our guest, in this house for as long as you wish to stay."

"Papa, that's wonderful," Lyndsy Marie sang, breaking loose of her brother's hold to sit on the edge of the bed opposite her mother. "Now you don't have to go home, Bevan."

"Home?" Charlotte repeated. "I wasn't aware she wanted to go home." Her gray eyes frowned at Bevan for a moment, then back at Lyndsy Marie, and finally over at her eldest son. "What nonsense is this, Reid? You said she was running away from something. Now she wants to return?" Her surprise melted into visible annoyance. "I think it's time we talked . . . *all* of us. I'm tired of pretending everything is just fine around here. Not only can I feel the tension, I *see* it. I want the truth, Reid, and I want it now."

Lawrence Hamilton had the reputation among his friends and business associates of being a strong leader, a man who made all the decisions, and who probably ran his personal life the same way. Only his immediate family knew it wasn't true. Charlotte, his petite, soft-spoken wife, was the one who really laid down the laws when it came to family matters, and Lawrence seldom, if ever, interfered. In the privacy of their own bedchambers, he would offer his opinion on how to discipline their children, but the final decision was always left up to Charlotte. Only once had he acted without consulting his wife and he was still paying for it. His announcement those many years ago that his firstborn son would marry his best friend's daughter in order to unite the two plantations had caused the one and only bitter argument between him and his wife. Charlotte had heatedly objected to the match solely on the point that Lawrence was assuming the couple would agree . . . and agree, they probably would. But out of loyalty and respect to their fathers and nothing more. Whether the two loved each other or not had little to do with it, and Charlotte had asked him to reconsider. She wanted her children to be happy and a forced marriage certainly wouldn't promise that. At the time Lawrence wouldn't admit she might be right, and out of stubborn pride, he'd refused to withdraw. Now, years later, he was seeing it for himself, although he would rather die than let her know. Thus, whenever Charlotte took command of a situation, he stepped back and let her have full rein.

"I'm afraid I don't know what you mean, Mother," Reid suggested, trying his level best to hide his uneasiness.

"Oh yes, you do," Lawrence cut in. "Mother and I have talked about it quite a bit lately. You haven't been the same since your return and it's obvious your behavior has something to do with Miss O'Rourke. Now, out with it, son. You know we don't keep secrets in this family."

Bevan couldn't recall ever having been made so uncomfortable in her life. She knew she was the root of this discussion, but she felt totally out of place. If the Hamiltons had family differences to discuss, they should do so without her there to hear them. Fighting off the thunderous pounding in her temples, she tried to rise and found herself pinned down against the pillows by Charlotte's firm and unyielding hand on her shoulder.

"This concerns you too, young lady. You might think I'm too old to remember, but I assure you I can still recognize love in a woman's eyes."

"Love?" Lyndsy Marie parrotted. "What are you saying?"

"I'm saying that while your brother was away, he and this sweet young girl met and fell in love." Her gaze captured Reid's. "Isn't that so?"

Reid could feel every pair of eyes in the room focused on him, and he chose not to take his own off his mother's insistent stare. He knew what he'd see in his father's expression and he didn't want to have to deal with it right then. Stephen's brown eyes would be sparkling and his mouth would twitch with his suppressed grin if Reid were to glance at him. Lyndsy Marie's look would be one of surprise and worry—she loved Laura and had always thought her brother and Laura should wed. An announcement to the contrary would shatter her hopes. His mother's gaze demanded a response and he knew he would not be excused until he had given her a satisfactory answer. But it was Bevan's eyes, those green, sensuous orbs that could shoot sparks of fire or chill him to the bone depending on her mood that he couldn't force himself to meet. She more than anyone else deserved to hear his answer. If only he could give her one. . . .

Finally, when the silence all around him seemed to be squeezing off his breath, he blinked and softly replied, "Yes, Mother, I'm sure we did."

The gentle lapping of the water against the shoreline, the creaking of the *Lady Hawk* as she rode the small wells hitting her bow, the frogs and an occasional hoot of an owl did little to sooth Reid's unrest or awaken the memories buried deep in his brain. He had hoped a walk to the pier would unlock the chains imprisoning his past and free the secrets that had crippled his emotions. He hated the feeling of helplessness which had crowded his days and nights and made a mockery of his very existence. He *wanted* to remember. He *had* to remember if he were to bring peace not only to himself, but to Laura, to his family, and most of all to Bevan O'Rourke.

"Bevan," he murmured with a heavy sigh as he half sat, half leaned against the mooring post, his arms folded over his chest and his gaze studying the ebony sky above him. If only she'd tell him the details of the time they had spent together, he might be able to piece the rest into place. But how could he ask her? She wouldn't believe he had really lost his memory. She'd assume it was a ploy to excuse himself from what they had shared. And he wouldn't blame her. What else was she to think when she learned that the man she had loved was already engaged to another?

The smell of freshly mowed hay filled his nostrils and he sucked in a quick breath, thinking to enjoy the sweet aroma. Yet all he smelled was the salt air and the fragrance of wild flowers. It took him a second to realize he had only imagined the essence, but once he had, he tried to concentrate on its meaning, especially since that scent had troubled him on several earlier occasions. It *had* to be connected with his stay in Ireland, his time with Bevan. But how?

The snapping of a twig and the crunch of dried leaves beneath someone's foot turned Reid's head around, and before he could recognize the shadowed figure of the person walking toward him, his father called out to him. Unwittingly, the muscles in Reid's body flexed as he expected yet another of his confrontations with the man.

"I thought I might find you here," Lawrence said, stepping onto the wooden pier. "Even as a boy you came to the docks to think when something bothered you." He paused a moment to smile at his son before he walked on past a ways and stopped. With his back to Reid, he stood with his feet apart, his spine straight and his arms folded behind him as he stared off across the inlet.

There was a surrendering, almost apologetic manner to his words and the way he had started out the conversation, and it triggered a subtle warning to Reid that *this* meeting between father and son would be different. Deciding not to cut in too soon, Reid settled back to listen.

"I should have taken the opportunity then, whenever I saw you down here, to follow you and ask if I could help sort out your problems. I realize now I was probably the reason you needed to be alone." His broad shoulders raised and lowered with the deep breath he took. "I wasn't a very good father, I'm afraid, but with your mother's help, I plan to change. I'll start by not asking you to forgive me, but to understand. I did what I thought was best. I made mistakes—we all do—and I'm hoping now to correct a few of them." He started to turn around, hesitated, then sighed instead.

"This thing with Laura," he began, walking to the next mooring post and assuming a position on it similar to his son's. "Your engagement, I mean." He studied his clasped hands a moment, then glanced up at Reid. "I never should have forced it on you . . . either of you. Your mother told me that the day I made the arrangement with Laura's father. It took me until tonight to understand why."

Reid could hardly believe what he was hearing. This had to be difficult for his father. He had never talked so openly before, and having to admit that he had made a few mistakes along the way was doubly hard for him. Hiding his surprise, Reid asked, "What happened tonight?"

"After you left, your mother got Miss O'Rourke to tell her about the two of you."

"What?" Reid exclaimed, his will to be patient evaporating. "How?"

"You know your mother," Lawrence remarked with a smile. "She can get *anyone* to talk if she sets her mind to it."

"So what did Bevan tell her?"

"It's quite a tragic story, I must say. And a bit of a shocker. It seems she and her brothers found you lying unconscious along the coast near where they lived, an apparent victim of a capsized ship that went down during a storm."

The vision of lightning, driving rain, and a wall of water flashed into Reid's head. He hung on to the image and forced himself to listen to the rest of what his father had to say.

"Since they were expecting to meet Lord Douglas Rynearson and his nephew that same night and at the same location, they assumed you were the nephew and that the uncle had drowned."

"His name was Graham," Reid supplied excitely, though he wasn't sure if he had merely drawn the conclusion or if he had remembered it.

Lawrence's brow furrowed. "Yes. How did you know?"

Reid shrugged. "Bevan mentioned the name. But to tell you the truth, it feels familiar. It also makes me a bit angry to hear the irony of it all. I was there because of Rynearson, and now, it seems, so were the O'Rourkes."

"I found that aspect a bit unnerving myself," Lawrence admitted.

Reid cocked a brow. "To say the least. So what else did she tell you?"

"Apparently, Lord Rynearson had promised to free Bevan's father from prison where he was awaiting execution, *if* she would marry the man's nephew in exchange."

A sudden anger creased Reid's brow. He shouldn't have been surprised to hear how arrogant Rynearson was. Reid knew that from his own personal experience with him. It just gnawed at him to think the bastard would take advantage of the O'Rourke's predicament. He forced back the desire to verbalize his feelings and concentrated on his father again.

"I guess only you can tell any of us why you let Miss O'Rourke and her brothers go on thinking you were Graham Rynearson, but you did. You also let them assume his uncle was dead. Again, it's up to you to fill in that missing piece. Whatever the reason, I trust it was a good one or you wouldn't have done it. I may not ever have told you this out loud, Reid, but you've got a very shrewd mind." Hr grinned and added, "You take after your father in that respect."

Reid couldn't stop the honest laughter that escaped his lips.

"Anyway, it seems you came up with the idea of breaking their father out of prison. I would assume because you didn't want Miss O'Rourke to marry the *real* Graham Rynearson." He squinted his eyes at his son and asked, "Is any of this touching the right nerve?"

Reid shook his head. "Not so far. But it certainly fills in a lot of blanks. Now I know why I was at the prison." He drew in a long, weary breath and stood. Exhaling, he raised his chin in the air and stared up at the black sky above him. "It also explains why Bevan hates me so."

"Hates you?" Lawrence repeated. "She doesn't hate you, Reid. She didn't exactly say she loved you, either," he added with a smile. "But I could certainly tell by the tone of her voice that she cares quite a deal. Or she did." Rising, he came to stand next to his son. "You have to see it from her side, my boy. She fell in love with a man who was keeping secrets; she saw that man get shot trying to save her father; she heard rumors from everyone who witnessed it that Graham had died; and then, lo and behold, when she arrives in America, she finds out that not only hadn't you died, but you had lied to her, you were engaged to be married, and you seemed not to remember anything about her. How else would she react?"

A crooked smile wrinkled Reid's cheek. "No differently, I suppose." Bending, he picked up a twig lying at his feet and idly broke it into little pieces. "Do you think I fell in love with her, too, Father?"

Realizing the agony his offspring was suffering, Lawrence reached up and laid his arm across Reid's shoulders. "What's not to love about her? She's beautiful, spirited, sensitive, and probably one of the most unselfish people God ever put on this earth. She was willing to sacrifice her happiness to save her father. Just now, she nearly gave up her life for a young boy she hardly even knew. How many other can you name like that? Not many, I would guess. Yes, Reid, you loved her. And you probably lied to her because of your commitment to Laura. I would say you had it in mind to come back home, admit everything to your fiancée *and* to your family, then sail back to Ireland for her once you were free to marry her."

Reid closed his eyes and moaned, "Then why can't I remember any of it? How can a man forget he loved someone?"

"Are you saying you have no feelings for her whatsoever?" his father posed.

The question prompted an assortment of sensations in Reid. Yes, he felt something for her. He just wasn't sure what it was. He respected her courage—what man wouldn't, when she had gone up against the likes of Emmett Connors? He admired her devotion to her family and her unselfishness in promising to marry a man she didn't even know just to save the life of her father. Her beauty stirred an impulse to stare; her spirit won his favor. And the time when he had kissed her, the passion he felt buring inside him had been unlike any he could ever remember experiencing. If she hadn't stopped him, he would have made love to her right there in the cabin. Or outside under the stars for everyone to see. But was that love? Or merely lust? Was that the foundation for a lasting relationship. What about the motivation behind the overpowering urge to kill Emmett Connors when Reid had arrived just in time to see him strike her? That hadn't been the simple act of a man coming to the rescue of a helpless woman. It had been more . . . much more.

"Stop torturing yourself, son," he heard his father say, and he glanced up to see the sympathetic smile on the man's face. "All the questions you're asking yourself right now will be answered. Maybe not tonight, but in time. Isn't that what the doctor told you? That the injury you suffered would have to heal completely before you'd be able to remember?"

Reid exhaled a tired sigh. "He also said I might never remember."

"Well, don't think about that," Lawrence ordered gently. "It won't do you any good anyway. Let it come naturally. Take it one day at a time. Why, I'm willing to bet that you'll wake up one morning and there'll be so many memories flooding your mind that you'll be too weak to get out of bed." Laughing, he gave Reid a rough pat on the back, adding, "And speaking of bed, don't you think it's time we got some rest? I don't know about you, but I'm not as young as I used to be. I need my sleep." He took a step, then asked, "Coming?"

Reid shook his head. "You go on. I'd like to stay here awhile longer."

"All right," Lawrence yielded. "But I don't want you beating yourself up because of something you can't control. You hear me?"

Reid's lips molded into a warm smile. "Yes, Father. I hear you."

"Well," Lawrence mocked, turning away. "That's a first. My son actually acknowledged that something his father had to say was worthy of his attention. What next? Will he break down and admit an old man isn't as stupid as he had always supposed?"

Laughter shook Reid's frame as he watched his father walk away and disappear into the shadows on his way back to the house. What Lawrence didn't know was that Reid had *always* listened to the man's advice. He might not have agreed with it, but he had always valued his father's opinion. Tonight it meant more to him than it ever had before. Tonight they had *talked* to each other. There hadn't been any harsh words, lectures, or fingers pointed accusingly. They had discussed an issue like two grown men, equals, and it made Reid feel good. They had finally broken down the wall that had kept them apart. And all because of Bevan.

The vision of her beautiful face, the color of her hair, the soft fragrance of her skin, and the lyrical way she talked infected his mind, and he smiled as he sat down on the mooring post again. Fate had brought them together and bad luck had torn them apart. The adventure had changed his life, and as a result, there was a large void that needed to be filled. He wished he could just go to her and ask her to be patient, that he was sure whatever he had told her there in the barn was the truth. He wanted to apologize for not being honest with her, for letting her think he was someone he wasn't when in fact he didn't know himself who he was. He wanted to convince her that he *had* loved her, that that much of it was true. But would she listen? Or would she run away again? A half-smile curved his mouth as he recalled how easily her anger had turned to lust that night he had followed her to the rotted remains of a cottage. She'd told him to go away, but when he touched her, she had eagerly accepted his advance. It had happened the same way when he found her in the henhouse and again when he had gone into the barn after her. He remembered how he had fought with himself right then to tell her the truth, to promise her that he would come back for her once he had settled whatever his mind had refused to allow him to remember. But the instant their lips had met, talking had been the last thing he had wanted to do.

The faraway look in his eye deepened when he was assailed with the sweet smell of hay again. They had made love right there in the barn . . . with the lop-eared donkey as a witness and her brothers asleep in the house. They hadn't spoken a word, made an oath, or pretended there would be plenty of tomorrows. She hadn't cried or begged or made him feel guilty. Perhaps that had been her plan, as leaving her had been the hardest thing he had had to do in his life. He had hoped she wouldn't come to the prison to watch, but it was what he had expected she would do. How devastating it must have been for her to see him get shot. Not only had it appeared she had lost the man she loved, but his attempt to save her father had failed as well.

Suddenly a flood of questions filled his head. He frowned and slowly came to his feet, not realizing that somewhere along the way the heavy shroud of repression had lifted or that he was walking away from the pier. Before he had stumbled into her life, Bevan had planned to marry Rynearson's nephew. Reid had let Bevan, Ryan, Kelly, and Shea believe Rynearson was dead because at the time he had no way of knowing it *wasn't* the truth. Then, after Reid disappeared, Rynearson and his nephew, the *real* Graham, had probably paid them a visit. That had to have been how she found out the truth about him. But did it also mean her father had been spared because she had married Graham Rynearson? What had she been doing in England? Why had she smuggled herself on board the *Lady Hawk*? From what had she been running away?

The need to know quickened his pace. Within seconds he was half walking, half running to the house. When he reached the veranda, he took the trio of steps in one leap, and raced to the front door. Bolting through it, he swung it shut behind him and rushed across the foyer, mounting the staircase two steps at a time. At the top he hurried down the hall and paused in front of the door to Bevan's room only long enough to seize the knob and fling the portal wide. He gave no thought to her privacy or that his family occupied the rooms a few doors down from hers. His need to hear her answers was simply more important than honoring formalities.

Moonlight tumbled into the room through a set of lace-covered French doors opposite him. The ashen stream fell across the floor and bathed the huge four-poster bed in a platinum light to his left, in which he could see a tiny shape snuggled beneath the heavy quilt. He started to call out to her, then hesitated, an odd pain gripping his heart. He had to know if she had married Rynearson's nephew, yet he feared her answer. If she had . . .

Suddenly, beautiful green eyes were looking up at him. His pulse thundered in his veins as he watched her sit up, the coverlet held against her bosom and the ruffled collar of her nightgown curled beneath her chin. Thick coppery hair cascaded in soft curls around her face and shoulders, and the image of the first time he had seen her exploded in his mind. He remembered awakening from a numbed sleep and the first vision he had seen was her lovely face as she bent close to tend his wound. He remembered the despair he'd felt once he'd realized he didn't know who he was, the fear that she and her brothers would kill him if he decided to be honest with them, and how he'd decided to keep quiet until he was sure of them—one way or the other. He had hardened her heart against him and he'd forced her to carry through with her agreement to wed. He deserved her scorn, her hatred.

Burdened with guilt and the agony of learning how foolish he had been, he released a trembling sigh and quietly closed the door. He owed it to her to explain why he had deceived her. All he could hope for now was that she'd honor him by hearing him out. Unwittingly he crossed to the French doors and stared out through the crisscross pattern of lace at the moonlit night.

"I'm sure an apology would sound hollow," he began in barely more than a whisper. "I know it would to me, if I were in your place. Nor can I expect you to believe a word I say, when it seems all I've ever done is lie to you. That I won't deny. What I will argue is the honesty of my feelings for you—how you perceived them, anyway, once you knew I wasn't who I led you to believe I was. I *did* love you, Bevan . . . from the first second I saw you. I also knew how unfair that would be to you until I had settled everything in my past. That's why I was keeping secrets, why I couldn't ask you to marry me right then. I had to be sure. But I wound up hurting everyone . . . you most of all." He took a deep breath and exhaled slowly. "I never meant to hurt you. I had every intention of coming back for you. I wanted you to share your life with me . . . as man and wife." He snorted derisively as he glanced over his shoulder at her, a strange smile parting his lips. "It's a little late now, wouldn't you say, for my memory to come back?"

She didn't move, but continued to stare at him, and he could almost feel the intensity behind the look. Knowing he had said all he could whether she believed him or not, he decided it was time for him to make a quiet exit . . . out of her room and out of her life. Pulling his gaze away from her, he moved for the door.

"Ya said ya *did* love me," she quoted, the comment stopping him after he had taken only a couple of steps. "Does that mean ya no longer do?"

Turning, he faced her squarely and replied, "No."

"How can ya be so sure? If ya just got your memory back, how can ya know 'tis love ya feel? Then as well as now?"

He stepped to the end of the bed and wrapped the fingers of his left hand around one of the finely carved posts. "It's quite simple, Bevan. Over the past weeks, I fell in love with you all over again. And now that I can remember our time together there on your farm—in the barn, the henhouse, the deserted cottage—I have something with which to compare my feelings. If I love you now, I loved you then."

A vague smile lifted the corners of her mouth and disappeared. "And ya think I should take ya at your word?"

He shook his dark head. "No. After what I've put you through, there's no reason why you should."

"Your father wouldn't agree," she replied, flipping off the quilt and swinging her bare feet to the floor.

"My father?" he questioned, his frown deepening when she stepped into the moonlight and he could see the ugly bruise near her eye. "What has he to do with it?"

She came to stand at the end of the bed, where she locked an arm around the tall post and stared back at him. "He told me how very much like himself ya are, that if someone is in trouble—even if it didn't concern ya—ya'd do all ya could ta help. 'Tis a fault, he said, but one he's proud of." She smiled and turned away to take up the vigil he had deserted at the French doors. "I think maybe he could still see the doubt in me eyes, because he said he hoped I'd believe *him* when he said ya honestly couldn't remember. Then he apologized for all the pain your foolishness caused and offered ta make up for it, if he could. He said he had a friend in your government he would contact about havin' me father released from prison—if by the grace of God he's still alive—and that as soon as it can be arranged, he'll be sendin' me home."

Her announcement made him thankful she had moved away from him as he was sure a mixture of relief, disappointment, and agony showed clearly on his face. She had unknowingly told him that she *hadn't* married Graham Rynearson or there would be no need to free her father. She had also told him that the hurt ran too deep for her to forgive him, and that because of his failure, Patrick O'Rourke had probably met his fate at the hands of the executioner.

"Do ya think that's for the best, Reid?" she posed after a moment of silence. "I mean me goin' home?" Before he could say anything, she faced him and asked, "Would it be what ya wanted?"

"No," he quickly responded. "It would be the last thing I'd want. But if you choose to return, I would understand." An emptiness assailed him and he felt as if his very life were draining away.

Bevan dropped her gaze away from him and turned back to look outside again. "I have ta go back ta Ireland," she said. "I've known no other place. 'Tis me home. I have to go back to me family." She fell quiet for a moment, then added sullenly, "Besides, I've no reason ta stay here."

Reid knew that if he didn't say something right then to change her mind, he'd lose her forever. "Yes, you have, Bevan." He pushed away from the bed and came to stand close behind her, wanting so desperately to wrap his arms around her and breathe in the sweet scent of her hair. "You're earned the love and respect of everyone here. We all want you to stay." He started to reach up and touch a silky lock of hair, then changed his mind. "I want you to stay, Bevan. I love you . . . more than anything else in my life. It was stupid of me to keep the truth from you all the while I was with you, but surely you must have known how much I cared. I nearly died for you, and if you leave, I'm sure this time I will." Her silence gave him the encouragement he needed to reach for her hand and pull her around to face him, forcing her to meet his eyes. "Let me love you, Bevan. Let me prove my faithfulness. Don't tear us apart because I thought with my heart instead of my head. Give me the chance to make it all up to you, to erase the bad memories with happy ones. Let me earn your trust."

Bevan had no reason not to believe him, but so much had happened between them that her mind was filled with doubt. More than that, she feared something else would happen to set them apart. Choked with emotion, she asked, "What about Laura? I don't think—"

"She released me from our pledge, Bevan . . . tonight . . . when I took her home. She said she knew long before I returned that I wasn't happy with our engagement, and that after meeting you, she knew *we* were meant to be together. Stephen knows it too. So does my mother." He smiled softly, remembering the conversation with his father a short while ago. "He might not have actually said it, but after talking with you and seeing how I behaved whenever you were around, Father has come to realize it, too." He took both her hands in his and held them against his chest. "Please, Bevan. Say you'll give me a chance. Just one week. At the end of that time, if you're still unsure, I'll have the *Lady Hawk* take you home."

Soft green eyes stared into his. "A week?" she asked. "Do ya think all ya'll need is a week?"

"I hope I've convinced you already, but if a week isn't

long enough, then I'll captain the *Lady Hawk* myself and have a full month more."

"And what if I'm still not certain? What will ya do then?" The edges of her mouth turned upward in a faint smile.

Hearing the laughter in her words, Reid sensed he had won. "Then I'll sell my ship and buy a piece of land next to your farm," he vowed playfully. "I'll put on my best suit of clothes, come to your house with flowers in my hand, and ask your brothers' permission to court you."

"For how long?" she teased, stepping close enough to feel the heat of his body against hers.

"For as long as it takes, Bevan O'Rourke," he promised, one hand reaching up to stroke the side of her face with the backs of his fingers. "The rest of my life, if need be, for without you, I would have no life at all."

"Ya have a fine way with words, Reid Hamilton," she breathed, rubbing her cheek against his hand. "How will I ever know ya speak the truth?"

"What would it take?" he asked, slipping his arm around her narrow waist and gently pulling her full against him.

"I'm not sure," she whispered, kissing his chin. "Perhaps a ring on me finger would help."

"Which finger?" he asked, lifting her right hand to his lips. "This one?" He brushed a kiss across her thumb. "Or this one?" He nibbled on her index finger. "What about this one?" He dotted his tongue along the next and Bevan giggled. "Would you like one for each finger? Or just one specifically?"

"Just one," she insisted, raising her left hand. "A

simple gold band that would tell the world ya made a pledge."

He caught her fingers and kissed them. "Until death do we part," he promised.

"Aye," she agreed. "And beyond." Pushing up on tiptoes, she slid her arms around his neck and pulled him down to meet her lips.

Their kiss exploded in a hot, savage declaration of undeniable passion. It spoke of forgiveness, trust, devotion, and the fury which had burned inside them both from the first moment they had met. It promised an eternity of absolute commitment to each other, and it erased any of Bevan's lingering doubt as the masculine scent of him filled her senses and sent her mind reeling. She returned his ardent embrace with a fierceness that seared her soul and left her weak and wanting more.

A warm, delicious shudder tumbled down her spine when his fingers moved along her neck to the pearl button on the back of her cotton gown and popped it free. Cool night air caressed the naked length of her as the garment slipped off her tiny frame and glided to the floor at her feet. She kicked the white cloth away as she worked the fastenings on his shirt loose and tugged the garment off the wide expanse of his shoulders and chest, kissing the iron thews with light, butterfly quickness while his hands moved along the curve of her back to her buttocks. Trailing a hot, sensuous path with her lips to the hollow at his throat, she could feel the rapid pulse beating there and sensed his impatience. Vowing not to let the moment end too soon, she used her tongue to follow the smooth length of his neck to his chin, where she nibbled lightly, then she brushed his opened mouth with hers before she kissed the tip of his nose, his cheek, and finally the lobe of one ear. She heard him moan as she traced the curl of his ear with her tongue and softly laid her breasts against his chest, the heat of his body scorching the taut peaks. She gasped when she felt him bend slightly then his strong arms captured her around the waist and in back of her knees to lift her up.

In eager expectation, Reid carried her to the bed and gently laid her down, his eyes dark with lust as he drank in the beauty of her nakedness, the creamy white curves on a mound of crisp linens and thick down, a pearl of perfection gleaming in the ashen light of the moon. Feeling his heart thundering against his chest and the raging desire pulsing through his veins, he twisted and sat down on the edge of the bed to remove his shoes and silk hose, his breath catching in his throat when she came up on her knees and pressed close against him. Her arms encircled him and the feel of her soft breasts rubbing invitingly along his back stirred his passion even higher until it became a sweet, hot ache in his loins. Every lost detail of their intimacy came flooding back as he recalled the ecstasy they had shared, and the thought that a single twist of fate had nearly stolen it from him chilled his heart for an instant.

Never again, he silently vowed, slipping his breeches off his hips.

Turning within her embrace, he caught her tightly and fell with her onto the thick, soft cushion of the bed, one hand moving along her outer thigh to her waist, then up to capture one breast, while his mouth fiercely claimed hers once more. He kissed her with all the passion of a man long denied the rapture this simple gesture could award him, and she responded in a manner that promised many more to come. Their tongues met and played, teased and aroused. Their flesh burned; their hearts beat wildly; and passion called for them to bring an end to their subtle torture. Rolling her beneath him, he parted her thighs with his knee as he braced himself above her and stared down into the sea green depths of her eyes.

"I love you, my Irish beauty," he whispered.

"Do ya?" she purred, entwining her fingers in the hair at his nape. "For how long, I wonder."

"Until you grow tired of me," he answered huskily.

The twinkle in her gaze disappeared. "Never," she replied, her parted lips awaiting his kiss as he gently eased his manhood, full and hard, deep inside her.

There came a warmth that singed every nerve, every fiber within them. It grew and spread until their blood coursed like fire through their veins. The heat of their passion carried them beyond the private solitude of their room to a sphere that filled them with hot desire and a desperate longing for more. With each sleek and powerful thrust of his hips, she arched her back and moved against him, matching his frenzied boldness with an impassioned eagerness of her own, until the height of their rapture was reached and a glorious explosion of blissful release sent them tumbling back to reality, breathless, chilled, contented.

Pulling her with him, Reid rolled onto his side, his arms locked around her and his lips tracing the delicate outline of her chin, lips, nose, cheeks, brow, then each closed eyelid. Again, the questions haunted him. How could he have ever forgotten this? How could the memory of his sweet Bevan have eluded him? Why had it taken him so long to remember? What was the purpose? To prove their undying love at all costs? It had nearly destroyed him.

"What are ya thinkin'?" her soft voice intruded.

He hugged her to him and rolled onto his back, cradling her against his chest while he gently fondled her breast and breathed in the scent of her hair and skin. "I was thinking how close I came to losing you."

His reply thrilled her. Bending her knee, she languidly rubbed her leg along his while she played with the dark matting of hair covering his rock-hard chest. "Would that have been so bad?"

"Bad?" he echoed disbelievingly. "I'd die without you."

A devilish grin curled her lips. "Not if ya hadn't remembered. Besides, ya would have found someone else ta love."

"Never!" he objected. "I never would have found someone who stirs the fire of passion in me the way you do."

The smile deepened and she hid it from him. "Is that all I do for ya? Stir your lust? Passion isn't all that makes a couple stay together, ya know."

"It isn't?" he teased, then winced when she plucked two hairs from his chest.

"No, it isn't," she scolded, sliding up on top of him with her arms folded and braced between them. "There's compassion and understanding, gentleness, sensitivity and unselfishness mixed in with passion and admiration. Are ya sayin' ya don't feel any of those for me?" When she saw the mischievous smirk to his mouth, she squinted her eyes at him and warned, "Be careful what ya say, Reid Hamilton, or your worst fears will come true."

He laughed, caught her face in his hands, and quickly kissed the tip of her nose. "I feel them all and more," he vowed. "But what about you? Can you say the same?"

A impish half-smile dimpled her cheek as she propped her chin in one hand. "I'd rather not answer that."

"What?" he exclaimed, catching her in his arms and rolling her beneath him. "And why not, may I ask?" He pressed her down in the soft cushion of feathers, tickling her sides unrelentingly until she had to plead her surrender to make him stop.

"I want ta keep ya guessin'," she teased. "That way if ya're not sure, ya'll have ta keep an eye on me . . . which means ya'd never let me out of your sight, and I wouldn't have ta worry about another woman catchin' your fancy."

"There's little worry of *that* ever happening," he promised. "There can't be another woman in the world to match you. I do agree, however, that I'd have to keep a close eye on you."

"Oh?" she rallied. "And why's that? Are ya sayin' ya think I'll be unfaithful?"

"No, not at all. You'll never have the time." The look in his eye suggested they would spend every available moment in bed, and he laughed when her mouth dropped open as if to say how presumptuous of him. Falling forward on his elbows, he touched his nose to hers and smiled lovingly into her eyes. "I'll have to keep a close eye on you just to ward off all the admirers thinking to steal a private moment with you."

"*All* me admirers?" she countered with a laugh. "Ya

make it sound like I had hundreds of them. Before *you* came along, the only men who looked at me were me brothers and only then because they wanted their supper or somethin' clean ta wear."

"I have a hard time believing that," he confessed, reaching for the quilt as he fell to her side and covered them up. He lay back on the pillows, drew her into the circle of his arms, and sighed contentedly. "It must be that all the men in Ireland are blind or fools. Which is it?"

"They're neither," she denied. "They're gentlemen."

"Ho-oh!" he exclaimed, laughing. "And you're saying I'm not?"

"Would a gentleman do what ya did?" she posed, grinning impishly.

"And what did I do?"

"Ya took advantage of me, that's what ya did." She rushed on before he could defend himself. "Here I was, a lonely young lass who had no idea what love was all about. Ya plied your sweet words, made promises ya couldn't keep, then wooed me right into your arms."

"Kicking and screaming," he mocked playfully.

Bevan laughed. "Well, maybe I didn't resist too hard."

"Not at all, you little minx," he corrected, pinching the end of her nose. The smile faded and his mood turned reflective. "I did make promises, though. At the time I thought . . . no, I *knew* I would keep them. I just didn't realize how difficult that would turn out to be."

"If ya had, would ya have behaved any differently?" she asked, snuggling deeper into the crook of his arm, her head resting on his chest while she absently listened to his steady heartbeat.

425

"I'd have only changed one aspect of it," he admitted. "I would have told you the truth the second I realized I was falling in love with you." He sighed, regretting his earlier failure to recognize the risks he was taking by lying to her. "If I live to be one hundred, it won't be long enough for me to ever come to terms with what I did to you . . . to your family." The thought of the O'Rourke clan reminded him of the real reason he had come to her room. "Bevan," he began, frowning, "what happened after I disappeared?" He could feel her tiny body stiffen, and he sensed her answer wouldn't be pleasant. Pushing up, he wrapped the quilt around them and settled her back against the headboard where he could study her face while she told him. "I need to know, Bevan, no matter how terrible it was."

The image of David came to mind first, and Bevan thought how curious that was. After all the things that had happened to her, her immediate reaction was to think of David and how he had died trying to help her. Tears pooled in her eyes, and she wondered if it wasn't because this was the first time she had felt safe enough to let go of her emotions. Smiling weakly at Reid, she put her arms around him and held on tight while she relived every detail of her adventure in verse.

It took every ounce of self-control Reid could find within himself not to voice his loathing for the man who had terrorized Bevan, her family, and everyone else Rynearson had touched along the way. Reid wasn't prone to violence, but he could remember his anger and how he had wished Rynearson had been standing in front of him when Gordon Sanderson told him how Rynearson had cheated them. In that instant he might have shown a different side to his character. Now he had more reason than ever to want to kill the man.

"The worst of it is that I fear he never carried through with his promise ta free my father," she added, her voice tight. "I want ta believe that he did . . . or that Mr. Magee found some other way to get him released. I just don't want ta think that he's—"

"Hush," Reid comforted. "Don't lose hope yet. The Society and your brothers are very resourceful. They'll have figured out something." He hugged her tight and kissed the top of her head. "What about the journal? Do you still have it?"

"Aye. Bess and I hid it under the floor boards in our cabin. I was planning to take it home with me and use it against Rynearson once I was sure he couldn't harm me father." Her lip trembled and she swallowed hard. "Reid?"

"Yes, Bevan."

"Deep in me heart I'm afraid it's too late."

"Don't think about it now," he insisted. "Think about how you're going to make Rynearson pay for everything he's ever done. Tell youself that as soon as the *Lady Hawk* is ready to sail, you and I and the journal will be going back to England. Between the three of us, we'll see the bastard hang."

Silence filled the room then as the couple clung tightly to each other and stared across the room at the silver light spilling in, their minds full of thoughts and their emotions churning in a mixture of happiness, grief, and worry.

Chapter Fourteen

Louis Palen took pride in how well he managed his tavern on the edge of town, and despite the fact that his business barely earned him enough to get by, he never let it show. The doors and window frames to the stone structure always had a fresh coat of paint, and he had replaced some of the damaged tiles on the roof not more than a month ago. The wood floor was waxed every Monday morning as were the table tops and bar. He never allowed any of the patrons to spit on the floor, and if a fight broke out, he ushered the quarreling roughnecks outside with a swing of the thick oak club he had chiseled to fit the grip of his hand. His patrons respected his wishes, and most feared his temper and the broken bones they would suffer if they ever connected with a single blow, either from his club or a meaty fist. Only one individual showed a careless lack of regard for the man's size and weight, and that person was Emmett Connors. Many had wondered how long it would be before the overseer from the Hamilton plantation tested Palen's tolerance, but when Connors burst through the door and sent it crashing against the wall, few disagreed there was a strong chance of it happening today.

"I suggest, Mr. Connors," Palen warned from behind the bar, his gray brows drawn tight over his eyes as he watched the man stalk across the room, "that you use a little wisdom when you come into my place, or you'll be picking your teeth up off the floor."

"Just pour me an ale and mind your own business," Emmett snarled as he headed for a far table.

"This is my business, and I decide who gets served and who gets thrown out," he advised. "If you want a drink, you'll act like a civilized human being or you can find someplace else to spend your money."

The challenge stopped Emmett midway across the room. He knew Palen meant what he said, but Emmett didn't scare easily, and since he suspected everyone in the place was hoping Palen would make good with his threat, Emmett decided it was up to him to disappoint them. Smiling contemptuously, he made a mocking bow and turned back for the door he'd left open.

"Yes, sir," he mocked, grabbing the brass knob and carefully swinging the portal shut. "Anything you say, sir." He glowered at Palen, then started back for the table. "Now may I have a mug of ale . . . please?"

Palen would have liked tossing the mean-tempered imbecile out on his ear just to prove he was a man of his word, and while he poured the mugful, he considered the idea a second time. His curiosity, however, forbid it. Emmett Connors only made an appearance in the tavern after dark, when his duties at the Hamilton plantation were over for the day. It wasn't quite noon yet, which hinted of trouble, and if Connors had done

429

something to upset Lawrence Hamilton, Palen wanted to hear about it.

"What are you doing in here so early, Connors?" he asked as he set the ale down on the table. "You get a day off for being such a kind and thoughtful man?"

Laughter broke out among the other customers and quickly faded when Connors swept them all with a heated glare. He'd spent the night with his favorite whore over at Miss Hilliard's, but once the sun had come up, she'd told him to leave. That combined with losing his job had put him in a foul mood. "Kindness ain't never got nobody anywhere, Palen," he growled before taking a long drink from the mug. "And Hamilton will soon figure that out for himself." He took a second swallow, slammed the mug down, and wiped his mouth with the back of his hand.

"Why's that?"

"He's givin' them blacks too much, that's why," he barked. "They don't need no new cabins. And the food they was gettin' was just fine. Everything was just fine 'til that Irish bitch came along."

Palen didn't notice the sudden interest one of the customers showed in their conversation. "What Irish bitch?"

"The one who smuggled herself on board the *Lady Hawk*. She ain't been nothin' but trouble since Hamilton put her in with Bess."

"Who's Bess? That little black girl you're always bragging about?"

"Yeah," Connors grumbled, slouching down in the chair.

Grinning, Palen started back for the bar. "You know what it sounds like to me? Sounds like you tried to crawl into bed with her and she told you to go straight to hell. Could explain why your hackles are up." He chuckled and added, "That or Hamilton finally got wise and fired you."

"And I'll tell you what I think, Palen," Connors seethed, his eyes narrowed as he glared at the barkeep. "I think you oughta keep your smart comments to yourself." His attention was drawn to the disfigured little man who rose from one of the tables near him and was hobbling to the door. "If you don't," he threatened, glaring at Palen again and jabbing a thumb at the stranger, "you'll be walkin' like him."

A few nervous chuckles followed Uriah Faber from the tavern.

Crouched low amid the shadows of a huge willow tree, Kelly, Ryan, and Shea studied the immense, two-story, multicolumned white mansion nestled among a forestry of green. Though none of them had said a word for the past half hour, each knew what the other was thinking. They had traveled a long way, endured many hardships, and had run terrible risks just to get here, and now that they were, they feared it might have all been in vain. The urchin at the dock back in England had said he had seen Bevan board the *Lady Hawk*, a merchant ship belonging to the Hamiltons of North Carolina. They had had to trust his word, since nothing else they had tried had given them any hope, and had hired on as deckhands to the first ship bound for the Colonies. The way had been rough for them, since none of the brothers had ever sailed before, and once the captain had learned they had lied about their "years of experience," they had nearly been thrown overboard in retaliation. As soon as the ship had docked in Williamsburg, Virginia, they had run off in the middle of the night and made their way to the Hamilton plantation—all on the slim hope they would find their sister once they arrived.

"Are ya sure there isn't a better way ta go about doin' this?" Kelly whispered as the three of them studied the activity going on at the house and near the dock.

"Like what?" Ryan snapped. "Don't ya remember Father talkin' about how the Colonists treat their people? Bevan might have gotten on the wrong ship, but it wouldn't have made a difference to Hamilton. He'll have made her work for him ta pay back her passage *and* ta earn enough ta buy her way back home again. He isn't goin' ta let her go just because we ask him." He frowned and thoughtfully surveyed the men at the wharf. "This is the *only* way we can take Bevan home." He turned to his younger brother. "Now ya know what ya're to do?"

Shea nodded. "I'm ta find where the slaves live and look for Bevan, while you and Kelly keep everyone busy. Once I find her, I'm ta tell her ta meet us here around midnight. That way she won't be missed until mornin'."

"Aye," Ryan replied, squeezing the boy's shoulder. "And what are ya to do if somethin' goes wrong?"

"I'm ta run as hard and as fast as I can, then meet ya back here after dark."

"Good," Ryan said. "Now wait until ya see us talkin' with the men at the pier before ya go. And good luck, Shea."

"The same ta ya, Ryan."

The brothers stared at each other for a moment, silently building up their courage, then Ryan and Kelly moved out from the shadow of the tree.

As hard as he tried, Reid couldn't keep his concentration centered on the ledger he was studying. Thoughts of Bevan and how they'd spent the night continued to distract him, and before he realized it, he was smiling. They had lain in each other's arms until the faint markings of dawn had played with the shadows and the worry that his family would find them had chased him from her room. Reid had left reluctantly and only because Bevan had insisted, saying that she thought too much of his family for them to find out in such an obvious manner that the two of them had settled their differences. He had agreed, but only after she had promised that they would announce their plans that evening at dinner.

"I could be wrong," interrupted a voice from the doorway of the study, "but you look as if you haven't had a minute of sleep, big brother."

Looking up, Reid saw the devilish smirk on Stephen's face as the young man leaned a shoulder against the door frame, his arms folded in front of him, and he decided not to comment.

"Yet, you seem rested," his brother continued playfully. "How can that be?" He pushed away from the door and limped farther into the room. "Might Miss O'Rourke have something to do with it?"

Reid fought back a grin. "I don't know, Stephen. You're the one doing the talking. You figure it out." He dropped his gaze and tried once more to concentrate on his work.

"Well," his brother went on, "I'd have to say yes."

"And why is that?" Reid challenged.

"Because I just spoke with her, and she had this funny look in her eye, a pleased kind of expression."

"Maybe she was just thrilled being in your presence," Reid mocked, reaching for a quill and piece of paper on which to make notes.

"Oh, I'm sure she was. But there was more to it than that." He waited for Reid to respond, and when he didn't, Stephen dared to imply, "You two weren't . . ." He waved a hand, suggesting the couple had been together all night.

Only Reid's eyes moved to look at him. "You have a dirty mind, Stephen," he charged before dipping the quill in the inkwell and jotting down several figures on the paper."

Stephen laughed good-naturedly. *"I* have a dirty mind? *You're* the one who misinterpreted my meaning. All I meant was—"

Reid shook his head. "Forget it," he said, falling back in his chair. "Arguing with you is senseless. No one ever wins. Just do Bevan a favor and keep your suspicions to yourself. All right?"

"Who would I tell?" Stephen teased as he perched a hip on the corner of the desk and leaned to examine the paper Reid was preparing. "What are you doing?"

The mood turned serious. "Checking out a hunch."

"On what?"

"On Emmett Connors." Reid shoved the ledger at his brother and pointed to one of the pages with the tip of his quill. "I think the bastard's been cheating us."

"How?"

"A little at a time. But over the years, it adds up."

Stephen was about to ask what had made Reid curious enough to investigate when Jeremy, their butler, called out to them from the doorway.

"Excuse me, sirs," he said, "but Captain Sanderson sent Mr. Dillion to tell you that there are some men down at the pier looking for work. He's wondering if you'd like to speak with them."

"I'll go," Stephen offered, rising. "You keep on that." He pointed at the ledger as he turned to leave. "I'd like nothing better than to have ol' Emmett pay his dues."

Bevan knew it couldn't be true, but the sun seemed brighter that morning, the sky bluer, the clouds bigger and whiter than ever before as she walked the distance from the mansion to the cabin she had shared with Bess. She hadn't slept a wink the night past and yet she wasn't tired, and she decided it had to have something to do with being in love.

Reid had told her to stay in bed all day and rest, that her injury could be more serious than it appeared. She had tried to convince him that she felt perfectly fine and that lounging around for more than an hour would drive her mad, but he wouldn't listen. He'd told her that now that they'd found each other again, he didn't want anything happening to her, and if it meant she had to be sentenced to her room, then that was how it would be. She had assumed he was serious until she saw the gleam in his eye and heard him admit that if he had any say in it, she would always be in bed . . . right where he could find her whenever he wished.

"Is that what ya really want?" she had asked him. "A

wife who is fat and lazy?"

"You'll never be fat," he had replied. "If anything, you'll be skinny from all that exercise."

Bevan giggled as she remembered how she had chased him out of her bed with the threat of telling her brothers—Kelly specifically—how he had taken advantage of her when she wasn't thinking clearly. He'd pretended to be worried, but she knew he wasn't really and that he had used it as an excuse to leave before anyone else in the house was up and about. Even though they had intended to announce their plans at dinner that night, they wanted to keep this special time together a secret. They had kissed passionately, whispered their eternal love, and had reluctantly parted.

She could still feel the warmth of his lips against hers as she cut across the yard to the front door of the cabin, and a smile curled her mouth as she recalled the pleasure she had taken in boldly watching him dress. She doubted she would ever grow tired of looking at him and marveled at the change in her feelings for him. She had gone from wanting to see him dead to praying they would live a hundred years together. But when her hand touched the doorknob, a chill embraced her. Life wasn't that simple. There would always be problems along the way. And the first one they had to solve was the matter of seeing Lord Douglas Rynearson brought before the magistrate in England.

Even though she knew the journal was perfectly safe under the floor boards in the cabin, she wanted Reid to have it. Twisting the knob, she went inside and briefly glanced around the room, as if she half expected to find Bess there instead of up at the main house doing her chores. Not bothering to shut the door behind her, she crossed to the woodpile, dropped to her knees, and moved the neatly stacked logs aside. Working a finger into the crack she had uncovered, she pried up first one board, then a second, and reached in to retrieve the book. Laying it down next to her, she replaced the boards, restacked the wood, and stood with the journal clutched tightly against her bosom. Reid had told her that he'd be working in the study most of the day, and that became her destination as she walked out of the cabin and quietly shut the door behind her. She would bother him only long enough for him to read the entries Uriah Faber had made, then ask that he lock up the book where it would be safe until they were ready to leave.

With her head down, she started back toward the mansion. She didn't see the dark shape of a man hidden behind the tree until a hand seemed to come from out of nowhere and cruelly grab her arm. In that same instant, the cold, hard muzzle of a gun was thrust in her neck below her left ear, promising death if she screamed. Seized with terror, her body began to shake, and she was unable to hold on to the journal. It slipped from her grasp and thudded on the ground at her feet. Then the evil laughter of the man filled her head, and the shock of his presence left her too numb to beg for her life.

"You really didn't think I'd just let you go, did you, Bevan?" Lord Rynearson challenged. "I went to a lot of trouble to have you. I've gone to a lot more trouble to have you again . . . you and that fool Uriah's diary." He kicked at the book. "Had I known about it, I would have disposed of it *and* him a long time ago, and I

437

wouldn't have had to chase after you." He let go of her arm and caught her around the waist, pulling her back against his hips and chest while he nuzzled his face in her hair. "I can give you everything you could ever want," he whispered huskily. "All the fine clothes and jewels, a big house, *everything!*" He rubbed his body against hers. "I can even make you my wife now . . . if that's what you'd like."

The bile began to rise in Bevan's throat. He didn't have to tell her Lady Rynearson was dead. She could feel it. He'd killed everyone who had stood in his way, and that had probably included her father. Hot tears stung her lids and she closed her eyes, willing herself to be strong. If she were to escape him, she had to keep a firm hold on her emotions. Rynearson was insane, and one wrong move or word on her part would sentence her to the same fate as all the other girls Rynearson had murdered over the past two years.

"Would you like that, Bevan?" he asked, his arm pressing up against her breasts. "Would you like being my wife?"

She tried to respond, but nothing would come out. She nodded instead.

"I thought you would. You're different from all the other girls I had. None of them wanted anything to do with me." He brushed his lips along her neck, unaware of how it made her cringe. "Oh, they liked the pretty diamonds I gave them to wear and the expensive clothes. But they didn't want me to touch them. *You* want me to touch you, don't you, Bevan?"

"Aye," she forced herself to say. "But not here." She swallowed hard and warned, "There's too many people around who might see us. We'll have ta go somewhere private. Let me get the journal, and then we'll leave."

"Yes, yes," he eagerly replied. "Get the book."

He let go of her, and Bevan thought to use the chance to run, counting on his lust for her to make him chase after her rather than use his pistol. But as she was about to bend down for the leather-bound book, an enraged howl filled the air and the flash of a man's body catapulted out from the shadow of the trees.

"Shea!" Bevan screamed the instant her brother threw himself at Rynearson, but the man was too quick for him. Rynearson spun, stepped back, and clubbed the barrel of his pistol alongside the boy's temple, plummeting Shea to the ground, unconscious. "No!" she wailed, falling to her knees beside him.

"I should have had them all killed," Rynearson snarled, leveling the gun on his prey. "I should have seen to it myself." He cocked the hammer and took aim. "I'll see to it now."

Thoughts of Bevan continued to run through Reid's head and ruin his concentration. Deciding his paperwork could wait until later, Reid closed the ledger, put the quill back in its well, and stood, stretching the muscles in his back as he headed for the door. He needed to talk with Gordon about his plans to sail back to England and how soon the *Lady Hawk* could be made ready. Relatively certain he would find the captain at the docks talking with Stephen and the men who had come looking for work, Reid left the house and walked in that direction.

A smile parted his lips as he followed the lane leading to the wharf, and the image of Bevan clouded his

439

vision. He could see her bright auburn hair, the emerald eyes filled with passion, and the soft line of her mouth and chin. He could smell the fragrance of her skin, hear her laughter, and taste the sweetness of their kiss. He could feel her slender body moving beneath him while they had made love only a few hours ago, and the thought that there would be many more nights like the one past filled him with joy. He loved Bevan more than anything else in his life, and now that they had declared their feelings for each other, nothing would stand in the way of their happiness.

Warm sunshine fell across his shoulders and the sweet smell of pine and fresh air filled his senses. He had always thought he would live out his days here on his father's plantation. Now he wasn't so sure. He planned to offer Bevan the choice, and if she preferred to settle in Ireland, he would understand and willingly go with her.

The sound of his brother's voice a short distance ahead of him drew his attention to the circle of men standing at the wharf. Stephen, Gordon, and Eric Dillion faced him, while two strangers stood with their backs to him. The moment his gaze fell upon the pair, a strange sensation washed over him, for even though he had yet to see their faces, there was something about the men that seemed familiar. In that moment, Stephen spotted him and waved him closer.

"Reid, I'd like to introduce you to the O'Grady brothers," he said, touching the arm of the tallest of the two and turning him around.

The instant their eyes met, Reid's mouth dropped open and no words would come out. Was he truly staring at Kelly O'Rourke? His gaze shifted to the man

440

at his side. And Ryan? Unwittingly, he glanced around looking for Shea. What were they doing there? And why had Stephen said their name was O'Grady? Were they in some kind of trouble? Had they come looking for him to help? He mentally shook off that notion. They couldn't have possibly known he lived here. They hadn't even known his real name. He swallowed his surprise, drew in a breath, and started to ask the first of a string of questions, when he saw how Kelly's face had reddened in anger and that he had doubled up his fist. Before Reid could second-guess him, he felt a staggering blow to his jaw that dropped him to the ground.

"Ya bastard!" the huge Irishman raved, struggling to get free of the many arms that had suddenly entrapped him. "Ya lyin', deceivin' bastard! I should have known ya were in on it. How much did Rynearson pay ya?"

Reid shook off the numbing pain and touched his fingertips to the blood at the corner of his mouth, wisely electing not to get up just yet. He knew Kelly had a right to think the worst of him. He'd be thinking the same way, too, if he were in the man's place. He only hoped he could convince him that it wasn't as it seemed before Kelly was able to break the hold Ryan, Gordon, and Eric had on him. Reid was sure Kelly would beat him to death if given half a chance.

"I know how it looks," he said, bending one knee and laying his arm across it after waving off his brother's offer to help him up. "But if you'll give me a chance to explain—"

"Why should I?" Kelly demanded. "So ya can make fools of us again?"

"Reid," Stephen cut in, "who are these men?"

"Bevan's brothers, Kelly and Ryan. I would imagine Shea is around here somewhere."

"Aye," Ryan sneered. "And we're hopin' we can say the same for Bevan."

Reid nodded toward the mansion. "She's in the house. She's fine. And if you'd rather she explained—"

The deafening crack of gunfire exploded all around them and cut short Reid's invitation to speak with their sister.

Terror darkened the shade of Bevan's eyes as she stared at the lifeless form of Lord Rynearson lying on the ground near her, then up at the little man who had killed him, while she cradled her unconscious brother in her arms. So much had happened in the last few minutes that her mind was awhirl. Was she next? Then her brother? And why had Uriah Faber stopped Rynearson from killing Shea? Didn't he know she had his journal, and that if it was given to the right people, Uriah would be found as guilty of murder as his employer? Shaking uncontrollably, she focused her eyes on the weapon in the man's hand.

"I should have done that a long time ago," he murmured, his attention centered on the bloodstain in the middle of Rynearson's back. "I never should have let him do the things he did." He raised the pistol, studied it for a brief moment, then tossed it to the ground. "I must have been mad to think I could protect Lady Rynearson from him." Tears filled his eyes and he began to tremble. Too weak to stand, he staggered to a rock and sat down.

"I loved her, you know," he said after a moment, and

Bevan decided not to say a word, but only to listen. "He used to beat her. He beat her so badly one time that she never fully recovered. That's when I suggested he take a mistress. I did it to make him forget about Lillian. And it worked. Except that he liked to beat his mistress too." He shook his head and stared down at his feet. "He beat all of his mistresses. He'd hit them until he killed them, and I had to dispose of the bodies. Then I'd find him another one. He would have killed you, too, if Lillian hadn't helped you get away." A tear rolled down his cheek and he roughly brushed it away.

"He was so angry when he found out. I didn't want to leave her alone with him, but he ordered me to get rid of Margaret's body." He glanced up at Bevan and explained, "Lillian's maid. You remember her, don't you?" He didn't wait for her answer. "Margaret tried to stop him from hitting Lillian, and when he shoved her aside, she fell and hit her head." His grief nearly got the better of him, and he quickly cleared his throat to stop the flood of tears. "While I was gone, he forced her to drink some poisoned tea. She was dead within a few minutes . . . before I could get back to stop him." He wiped his eyes again and smiled lamely. "That's when he told me that Lillian had given you the journal. I'm still not sure how I managed to escape him—he would have killed me too, if I hadn't—but I did, and that's when I decided how to get even, how to stop him from killing anybody else.

"I learned from a young boy at the docks that you'd gotten on Hamilton's ship. So I followed you here. I needed the journal, you see. It was my proof that Rynearson had killed those ten girls. I didn't know when I made the entries that the dates, times, and places would be so important, but they were." He glanced at the unmoving body again. "Or they could have been." He looked up at Bevan. "I guess I won't need it now, will I?"

The danger she had felt a moment ago vanished. Uriah hadn't come here to kill her. He was no threat to her . . . or to her brother. In fact, all she felt now was pity. "If ya had given the journal ta the authorities," she observed, "ya would have implicated yourself, ya know. Ya might not have murdered any of those girls, but ya helped cover up the crime. It would have been the same as slippin' the rope around your own neck."

Uriah smiled lopsidedly. "Yes, it probably would have. But I didn't care. Without Lillian, I had no reason to go on living. Besides, I owed it to her for letting her down."

Bevan could hear the pain in his voice, and she felt compelled to comfort him. "I realize I didn't have much of a chance ta get ta know Lady Rynearson, but in the few short minutes we talked, I learned what a kind and compassionate woman she was. She never would have blamed ya for bein' unable ta stop somethin' ya had no control over." She smiled softly at him. "If she were here right now, she'd tell ya that. And I'm sure she'd thank ya for carin' enough ta try."

Uriah raised his webbed hand and brushed away the moisture from his face. "Maybe," he replied, then came awkwardly to his feet when he heard the sound of racing footsteps coming their way. "I'd better be going."

"Where? Where will ya go?" she asked, certain it wasn't his wish to have to face whoever was about to join them, and why should he? Bevan could explain what had happened, who had killed Lord Rynearson and why. For all his part in the whole sordid affair, Uriah Faber had paid his dues the instant he'd pulled the trigger just now, and in Bevan's mind, nothing more should be asked of him.

"Don't know," he shrugged. "Somewhere." He turned to leave, paused and looked back at her. "You're the prettiest one he ever had. I'm glad nothing happened to you. Good-bye, Miss O'Rourke."

"Good-bye, Uriah Faber," she replied, watching his crippled form fade into the shadows.

Standing at the end of the veranda with Bevan tucked possessively under his arm, Reid watched in silent amusement while his father and Kelly tested their strength in an arm wrestling match. It only made sense to him that his family would like the O'Rourke brothers since they had already grown to love Bevan, but to see his father acting like a young, foolhardy boy made him realize that the only difference between him and his father was their age. In his heart and mind, he was still just as young as any of the men sitting around the table cheering him on.

Lawrence had shown a deeply sympathetic side once Ryan had told Bevan that their father was dead and that Rynearson had seen to it that a warrant for the brothers' arrests had been issued, forcing them to leave their homeland. Before anyone else could get to Bevan, Lawrence had enveloped the sobbing young woman in his arms to comfort her, a gesture rarely exhibited by the eldest Hamilton. It had amazed even Charlotte, though she had always known her husband wasn't as crusty as he'd wanted everyone to believe. Then he did something that truly surprised everyone. With Bevan still cradled in his protective hold, he had immediately insisted that the brothers stay on at the plantation and work for him, or if they wished, he'd use his influence to see that the false charges against them were dropped so that they could return home, if that was what they really wanted. When they hesitated, he had gone on to announce that he would give them a piece of land to farm . . . as payment for saving his son's life should they decide to stay in America. That had been more than a week ago, but Reid remembered thinking he had never been prouder of his father or more humbled by his open admission of love.

"Where's Stephen?" Bevan asked, breaking into his thoughts.

Giving her a squeeze, he kissed her temple and replied, "He's at Cotton Hollow." He laughed at a private thought, then added, "I would imagine he's quite nervous right now."

"About what?" she asked, enjoying the feel of his arms around her.

"He went there to ask Laura's father for permission to marry her. It seems the little beggar has been in love with her since the day she was born."

"And ya never knew?" Bevan remarked, surprised anyone could keep such a secret.

Reid laughed. "No, I never did. I guess that's because I was always too busy worrying about my own problems to notice that Stephen had a few of his own."

"Does your father know he's there and why?" she whispered, glancing back at the group of men seated around the wicker table.

"It was his idea Stephen ask. Father said he was through picking wives for his sons, and that if Stephen wanted her, he'd have to go ask all by himself." He smiled crookedly. "But don't let that sound like he was indifferent. I'm sure our father was holding his breath until he saw Stephen ride away."

"He cares a lot for Laura, doesn't he? Your father, I mean."

There was a funny edge to her question, as if there was more to it than just the words she had spoken, and he twisted her around to look him squarely in the eye. "Yes. He and her father have been friends for a long time. Does that bother you?"

She shrugged and looked away, but not before Reid noticed the slight coloring in her cheeks.

"Oh, Bevan, my love," he sang, hugging her close again. "I hope you're not thinking he harbors a resentment for you because she and I decided not to get married. I swear that's absolutely not true. In fact, he'd probably tell you how grateful he is."

"Grateful?" she echoed.

He smiled devilishly. "Uh-huh. You're the first woman to come along who ever made his older son think about settling down. He's been waiting for that for a long time."

His answer pleased her and erased the worry she felt. "*Are* ya ready ta settle down, Reid Hamilton?" she asked coquettishly.

"Of course. I mean, don't you think we should? Before the baby arrives?"

Her face flamed instantly. "What baby?" she demanded, breaking his hold on her and stepping back out of reach.

He gave her a silly look. "Well, my father wants grandchildren. He's said so many times. I just thought that perhaps we should be married first. But if you'd rather not . . ." He straightened sharply when she narrowed her eyes at him, wondering if maybe she had misunderstood that he was only playing with her.

"I think ya should try askin' me before ya make such an assumption, Mr. Hamilton," she berated, one hand resting on her hip. "I'm not one ta be taken for granted."

He was about to correct the error she had made when Lyndsy Marie came bursting out onto the veranda, a white lace veil draped across her arms. "Look Bevan," she called, smiling happily. "I found it. Just like I promised."

Reid's brow furrowed. "Found what, little sister?"

"Mama's wedding veil, you ninny. Bevan asked if she could wear it when the two of you get married."

Laughter tugged at Bevan's mouth and danced in her green eyes. Sensing the look Reid was giving her and that she was about to pay for the prank she had pulled, she spun on her heel and raced off the veranda before he could stop her.

"Good heavens," Lyndsy Marie exclaimed, jumping back out of the way when Reid nearly knocked her down in his haste to catch up to Bevan. "Did I say something I shouldn't have?"

Glancing up from the table, Ryan shifted his gaze from Lyndsy Marie to the couple dashing across the lawn and then back to the young woman again. "I doubt it, lass. Where we come from, 'tis a sign they care for each other." At Lyndsy Marie's bewildered look, Ryan grinned broadly and turned to watch Reid catch Bevan and swoop her up in his arms. Then Lyndsy Marie smiled, too, as she watched them, laughing and breathless, their eyes filled with love.